THE NEXT MRS. PARRISH

THE NEXT
MRS. PARRISH

Liv Constantine

QUERCUS

Published in the United States by Bantam Books, an imprint of Random House, a division of Penguin Random House LLC, New York.
First published in Great Britain in 2024 by

QUERCUS

Quercus Editions Ltd
Carmelite House
50 Victoria Embankment
London EC4Y 0DZ

An Hachette UK company

A CIP catalogue record for this book is available
from the British Library

HB ISBN 978 1 52944 008 9
TPB ISBN 978 1 52944 009 6
EBOOK ISBN 978 1 52944 011 9

1

Printed and bound in Great Britain by Clays Ltd, Elcograf S.p.A.

Papers used by Quercus are from well-managed forests and other responsible sources.

For Sean and Christopher

Love all, trust a few, do wrong to none.

—WILLIAM SHAKESPEARE,
All's Well That Ends Well, act 1, scene 1

THE NEXT MRS. PARRISH

AMBER

Amber Patterson Parrish hated visiting her husband at Camp Fed. Jackson had been living at the correctional facility for the past seven months. Fortunately for her, he didn't expect her to stay long, just long enough to give him the maximum allowable cash, thirty dollars, and time to bitch to her about the conditions he was forced to endure—the crap food, the flooding and ceiling leaks every time it rained, and the unending noise boomeranging off metal and concrete inside the grimy old building. Sometimes the visits went smoothly, other times the guards did something to screw with you.

Last week, she'd been sent home. Told that her outfit was too revealing. It was bullshit. She was proud of how great her toned abs and long legs looked in her Alex Perry jumpsuit, but what did the guards know about fashion? The only thing revealing about her outfit was what it brought out in *their* character. One of the other inmates' wives suggested Amber run over to Walmart and get a sweater to wear on top. Please. At least it had given her a chance to skip the visit that week. She despised sitting in the overcrowded room with the masses; unkempt, rude women who elbowed their way past her to grab seats first. The smells of cheap perfume and sweat that made her want to hold her breath. Everything about it was disgusting—the long rows of hard plastic chairs bolted together, the cold linoleum floor and stark white walls with prison regulations posted everywhere, the random pat searches that weren't at all random. She was pretty sure Jackson hated the visits as much as she did because he couldn't stand for Amber to witness him being vulnerable—wearing orange instead of his normal designer attire, at the mercy of the prison guards barking orders at him. He was no longer the all-powerful mogul, now just another inmate, no more special than anyone else. Thankfully it was only a forty-five-minute drive to Danbury, Connecticut, so she didn't have to waste her entire day.

Amber had worried at first that the scandal would make her persona non grata in Bishops Harbor, but apparently tax evasion was a crime that didn't garner much antipathy among the one-percenters. They were likely counting their blessings that they had avoided getting caught themselves. Besides, anyone who knew Jackson knew that he'd soon be back on top and didn't want to risk alienating him by shunning his wife. Thus, Amber was still able to enjoy her days at the country club, her weekly tennis matches, and a board position with the Bishops Harbor Historical Society.

Her days passed pleasantly enough, especially with no demanding husband at home to please. There were a few, the old guard, who turned up their noses at her, but then again, they'd rebuffed her from the beginning. She'd get them back when the time was right. The one fly in the ointment was that funds were running very low, and she'd had to let some of the household staff go. For the past month, she'd had to cook her own meals and drive herself everywhere. Plus, she hadn't bought a new outfit in over two months. If she didn't get an influx of cash soon, the nanny and housekeeper would have to be let go, she would have to forgo her salon visits and even let their club membership lapse. There were no secrets in Bishops Harbor. Word at the club would spread like wildfire. She wasn't about to let that happen.

Amber had a plan, though. She'd sell the boat. She knew the sixty-five-foot Hatteras was worth at least a million and a half, maybe more, so she'd put an ad in *Boat Trader* and on Boats.com. She already had three interested parties. Pretty soon their bank account would be overflowing once more, and she could go back to the life she'd become accustomed to.

Well, almost. Jackson would be home in a month, but she wasn't afraid of him anymore—not since she had laid the trap that gave her something to hold over his head. A few months after their marriage, when he'd found out that there was an outstanding warrant for her arrest in Missouri, he'd used that as leverage and became verbally abusive and debasing in the bedroom. She could have left him and owned up to what she'd been arrested for back home. She'd probably serve only a year or two for jury tampering, perjury, and bail jumping, but she'd sooner be dead than go back to the small-minded town she'd grown up in. She would not eat crow. It was far easier to put up with Jackson. His first wife had silently borne all his cruelty, but Amber was no Daphne.

She smiled, remembering the night she'd provoked him. It was the first time he hadn't been able to sustain an erection. She'd laughed and told him he was part of the Viagra crowd now, that maybe she should hire a new pool boy. He'd been furious. Furious enough to make the mistake of pushing her down on the bed and choking her, spewing obscenities. She'd recorded it all from the camera she'd hidden on the nightstand. That was the night she found equal footing. Jackson cared much more about his reputation than he did about having the upper hand. So, he'd wisely agreed to her terms: a marriage in name only, no more sex, no more demands. He'd have the arm candy he wanted, she the lifestyle, and their lives would go on. But that didn't mean she was looking forward to seeing him every day.

She sat in the drab waiting room now, impatient for them to bring Jackson in so she could get the visit over with. She looked up as the door opened and he walked in. She conceded that he looked none the worse for wear. In fact, he looked very fit, like he'd been working out. But then again, federal prison wasn't exactly Attica. He gave her a sardonic smile and when he sat down, she noticed that his thick dark hair was a little longer than he normally wore it.

She had to admit that even in his prison garb, Jackson looked more like a movie star playing a role than a real inmate.

"How's my devoted wife today?"

She returned a smile—her sweetest—and shrugged. "Missing you, of course. But only one more month, and you'll be home."

"I'm sure you're counting the days." He leaned forward and clasped his hands together. "On that note, I want you to throw a party for my release. It's important that we get in front of this. Let everyone know I'm back and ready to start something new. I've met an investment broker who has some great contacts. We're developing a new business plan."

Amber wondered what the banker was in for.

"Here's the guest list." He slid a piece of paper across the table.

Amber glanced at it. Was he serious?

"Jackson, there's only fifty thousand left in our accounts. That barely covers our monthly expenses. I told you I've already had to let Edgar and Margarita go. There's not enough to throw you an elaborate party. I'm having to cut corners all over the place. I'm tired of making sacrifices."

His eyes blazed. "Only fifty? There was close to half a million between both accounts when I came here. Where the hell did it go?"

"Come on. You can't have forgotten what things cost. It's been seven months; the money's running out." She leaned back and appraised him. "But I do have an idea. If we sell the boat, we can get at least a million and a half for it. Not to mention saving ten thousand a month in slip fees, electricity, maintenance, and insurance. Besides, it's seven years old. When you're back on top, you can buy a bigger one." And one that was named after her, and not his ex-wife and kids, she thought.

Jackson's face turned white. "Absolutely not!"

"Why not? It's not like anyone's using it. What's your attachment to a seven-year-old boat? We need the money."

He leaned in closer, giving her a piercing look. "Listen to me. Under no circumstances are you to sell the boat. Do you understand me? I promise you, there'll be plenty of money when I get out, but I need that boat."

"You must be dreaming. The company's gone; all that money went to pay back the IRS. The only assets we have are the house and that boat. Do you have a job waiting for you when you're released?"

"Look, I can't get into it here." He glanced up at the corner of the room where a camera was positioned, then back at her. "Just trust me on this. We'll be fine once I'm out. But *not* if you get rid of the boat."

Interesting, she thought. What did the boat have to do with it? "Okay, okay. I get it. It's your good luck charm. Fine. I won't sell it. But I certainly hope you're not lying to me. I've got my eye on the new Oscar de la Renta coming out in a few weeks."

He blew out a breath. "You'll have everything your greedy little heart desires. Just hold out for one more month. Got it?"

"If you say so. I'd better get going. Tennis at three." She smiled. "See you next week."

"Hold on. You said you'd bring pictures of my son with you."

They'd both agreed that their toddler, Jackson Junior, was better off staying at home with the nanny during these visits. She reached in her purse and pulled out an envelope. "Here you go. Some recent pictures of *our* son."

He took them from her, and she stood, eager to end the visit.

Once outside, she quickened her pace. She was going to see for herself what the hell he was hiding on that boat.

Amber pulled up to Mariners Point Marina, waiting as the camera recognized the RFID sticker on her car and the gates slowly opened. She parked, grabbed her tennis shoes from the passenger seat, and put them on. Next, she sent a quick text before getting out. *Hey, Jessica,* she wrote. *Something's come up. I won't be able to make our tennis game today. Apologies. I'll call you later. Tx.*

The day was sunny and warm. Amber took a deep breath of the bracing sea air as she walked to the slips, so refreshing after the stuffy visiting room at the prison. There was no way in hell she'd ever let them put her behind bars. She turned onto the third finger pier, where Amber had a few days ago directed the boat be moved to, after its being in dry dock during Jackson's incarceration. Walking past several power and sailboats, she approached the *Bellatada,* scowling at the name painted on the transom. Amber had been in such awe when she'd first stepped foot onto the sleek and elegant yacht, but she'd always hated that it was named for Jackson's daughters, Bella and Tallulah, and his ex-wife, Daphne. Especially as he liked to taunt Amber by reminding her that she had none of the bearing or elegance of the blond and beautiful Daphne. But today was not a time to bother herself with that.

She boarded the boat, moved belowdecks to the salon, and went straight to the safe in the main stateroom. Knowing the combination by heart, she spun the dial with anticipation. But once it was open, she deflated. Empty. It was unlikely that anything of value would be hidden in this part of the boat, but next she went through the salon, galley, and dinette anyway, moving cushions and feeling around underneath, opening drawers and cabinets, even checking the appliances. When she finished searching the main stateroom, she checked in each of the other three, feeling under mattresses, examining carpeting for any unusual bulges, rummaging through every piece of furniture. After two hours, she'd come up with nothing.

Amber returned to the deck and sighed as she sat on the captain's chair, fingering the steering wheel and pondering her next move. A thought occurred to her. She jumped up and pulled a toolbox from the cabinet under the wheel. Taking a screwdriver, she began working to unscrew the cap on the steering wheel, her excitement growing. Finally taking it off, she exhaled in disappointment.

Nothing hidden there. A search of the engine room and the fly-bridge produced no results either. The sun was beginning to set. All the frantic searching had been for naught. Amber was beyond frustrated. And furious. Something was stashed away on this boat—she was sure of it. She'd have to come back in the morning and look further, maybe cut open the cushions and check the headliner. Brimming with vexation, she needed to take it out on something.

Bellatada. That damn name caught the edges of Amber's vision. She looked over at the pole with the blue flag mounted on the transom where the name was imprinted. Her hands clenched into tight fists as a storm of fury and frustration exploded inside of her. She spun around and grabbed the first thing she saw, the long metal boat hook, and wrapping her fingers around it, marched to the stern and swung the metal rod against the flagpole. It struck with violent force. She hit it again and again, all the pent-up rage bursting out of her and onto the shaft. She grinned at the sound of wood cracking, and with all her might took one last titanic whack. Amber dropped the boat hook and with satisfaction watched the pole splinter and fall to the deck in pieces. Sweat poured down her face, stinging her eyes as she stared at the fragments. She frowned and, blinking several times, tried to focus. A long metal cylinder resembling a cigar tube, but thicker, lay among the splintered wood. She stooped down, unscrewed the cap, and pulled out a wad of silk cloth. There was still something in the tube, and turning it upside down, she carefully spilled the contents onto the deck. Hues of red and blue and yellow winked in the sun. She bent over for a closer look, a smile spreading across her face. Some kind of red and pink gems. And diamonds. Lots of them.

DAPHNE

When I was a little girl, I couldn't get enough of fairy tales. I especially loved the ones where the heroine escaped from the monster and went on to live happily ever after. But what I've come to learn is that sometimes there's no such thing as a happy ending. Yes, there's the blessed relief of freedom from tyranny and terror, but the scars live on. I still find myself reaching for the food journal Jackson made me keep, guilt consuming me when I eat anything not on his approved list. And then I remember, I don't have to keep track any longer. I see him in my dreams—or rather, my nightmares—varied scenarios in which I'm back with him, bewildered at why and how I find myself at his mercy, a prisoner in his carefully cultivated world. With the break of every dawn, I find release and breathe deeply air no longer tainted by his presence. There are times I have trouble trying to regain some of what he stole from me: trust in the goodness of others, the ability to let my guard down with new friends, belief in the veracity of my own judgment. I'm wary now. Careful in a way I never was before. But maybe that's a good thing.

California has been good for my daughters and me since we moved here a little over a year ago. Our home is peaceful. No angry arguments or yelling. People are friendly but not intrusive. A wave and a smile, a few polite words, and they let you go on with your day. My mother is in seventh heaven, thrilled to be a daily part of our lives, after being banished from it for so long. Jackson led her to believe that I didn't want her around too often, when the truth was, he delighted in keeping us apart. She takes the girls to school and all their activities and insists on cooking dinner for us every night. It feels good to be taken care of again, and so I let her. I continue my work for Julie's Smile, the foundation to raise money for cystic fibrosis that I'd started in memory of my sister, Julie, who died of the disease when she was sixteen. I've established a small headquarters here in Santa Cruz and continue to raise money for CF research. We don't do elaborate fundraisers like we used to in Bishops Harbor, but we generate support through social media and direct marketing campaigns. It's been a wonderful vehicle of healing for my mother too and a way for the two of us to feel we're still connected to my sister.

I've joined the neighborhood book club and it's so wonderful to make friends and be open with them. No more living in a silent hell and pretending it's paradise. We bond over our shared parenting struggles, philosophical views, and the occasional cute single dad spotted at the monthly PTA meeting. My life is serene and calm. I relish it.

"Since Tallulah's away, how about we cook the fillets you picked up the other day?" I suggest to my mother. Tallulah recently announced she was a vegetarian and can't abide even the smell of cooking meat.

"Great idea," she says, smiling.

We work together in the kitchen companionably, she seasoning the meat while I chop up veggies for a salad. I glance at my watch and see it's close to six. My friend Maggie will be dropping Bella home soon from her Girl Scout meeting.

My phone rings and I go to the counter to pick it up. I see the name of Tallulah's teacher on the screen and my stomach drops. She left two days ago for the eighth-grade field trip to D.C. I swipe left.

"Hello?"

"Mrs. Parrish?"

"Yes, is Tallulah okay?"

"Yes, she's fine. But we do have a problem."

My hand tightens around the phone. "What is it?"

"I'm afraid she snuck out of the hotel this morning and took a train to Connecticut."

"What do you mean? Is she——"

"We have her. Her friend, Molly, finally told us of her plans, and we were able to intercept her at the Bridgeport Train Station. Apparently, she was trying to get to her father. You'll need to make arrangements to have her flown back today. I'm afraid we can't risk her doing something like this again. We'll have her escorted to the plane, but you will have to purchase the ticket and give us the flight details."

My head is spinning. I can't believe this. How did she even get the train ticket? I wonder. Then I remember the credit card I gave her for emergencies. Anger and relief vie for dominance, but in the end, relief wins.

"Did her father know of her plans?" I ask.

"Apparently not. She said she was planning to take an Uber and surprise him."

"May I speak to her, please." I do my best to keep my voice even.

"She doesn't want to speak to you right now. I think it's best if you talk to her in person."

I skirt her questions about Jackson and custody.

I end the call and turn to my mother.

"What in the world was that all about?"

"Tallulah took a train to Connecticut," I say, and as I fill her in on the details, her face turns white.

"What was she thinking? She could have been kidnapped! She's out of control, Daphne."

As if I don't know that. At first, both Tallulah and Bella seemed to be thriving. They assimilated into their new school seamlessly, made new friends, threw themselves into activities. At home Tallulah's book of the moment was never far from her, but she'd become

THE NEXT MRS. PARRISH 13

a bit more outgoing. Bella seemed to reflect the California sun, with her bubbly personality and dazzling blond curls. In some ways she reminded me of Jackson—the good parts, her eyes the same blue as his and her take-charge personality rather unlike mine. Things were changing, however. They missed their father. And even though he was never violent or physically hurt them, I knew his psychological reign of terror would intensify and cripple them if he were in their lives. Bella struggled with reading, which embarrassed and infuriated him; in turn he would berate her when she stumbled over words. I can still hear him calling her stupid or ugly in those moments; I only hope her improved ability and newfound love of reading have blunted those memories. It still fills me with shame when I think of his cruel treatment. With Tallulah, he was kinder, more patient, and the two bonded over their shared love of literature. She was a daddy's girl from the start and despite her witnessing Jackson's darker moments, she seems to have banished them from her mind and remembers only the happy times.

"She told me before she left that she hates me for keeping her from Jackson. She doesn't understand that I'm only trying to protect her and Bella. I never imagined she'd do something like this," I say.

My mother purses her lips. "She's thirteen. Old enough to understand. You can't keep the truth from her forever. He tried to ruin our relationship, lying to me all those years and telling me you didn't want me to visit. He kept you a prisoner and isolated you from everyone. He's dangerous. The girls need to know . . ."

I put a hand up. I can't listen to another tirade about Jackson. Anytime one of the girls brings him up, she's ready to boil over and speak unkindly about him until I stop her with a look. She doesn't seem to get that her constant chatter about how awful he is only makes it harder to put the past behind me. "Not yet. If I tell Tallulah the things he did to me, how he essentially held me hostage all those years, I'll wipe out every good memory she has of us as a family. She's already depressed. That's not going to help her. And

Bella is only eleven. If I tell Tallulah everything, she'll tell her sister." When we left Connecticut, all I could think about was getting away from Jackson and starting over. Getting him to terminate his parental rights gave me the illusion that we were all free. I should have realized that no court document could sever the ties that bind him to our children.

She throws her hands up. "Well, you've got to do something. Next time you might not be so lucky."

Last night didn't go well. Tallulah wouldn't even look at me when I picked her up and despite my best efforts at getting her to talk, she crossed her arms and kept her lips tightly sealed. Only when I threatened to take her phone away did she admit that Jackson had no idea of her plan. I haven't spoken to Jackson since I left Bishops Harbor. This morning Tallulah wouldn't go to school and told me that if I didn't let her see her father, she'd run away and I'd never find her. I intend to verify that she's telling the truth, but I need to speak with my therapist before I open up the can of worms that will be getting in touch with Jackson.

I arrive at Dr. Marshall's office ten minutes early for our session and take a seat in the waiting room. I scroll through my phone distractedly, then grab a *People* magazine from the table and flip through it. Sighing, I put it back down and stand, pacing. Finally, the door to her office opens and she calls me in.

"How are things today, Daphne?" The petite older woman wrinkles her brow with concern as I take a seat. The three of us have been seeing her since we first moved to California.

I shake my head. "Not good. Tallulah still isn't speaking to me, except to refuse to go to school and to threaten to leave again. I don't know what to do."

She sighs. "You know that normally I'd never suggest you regain contact with your abuser. But this is a complicated situation. This could have ended very badly. Did Jackson have any idea of her plan?"

I shake my head. "She says no. I know I need to call him, but I dread it."

"This is obviously a very serious situation. You're very lucky that nothing happened to her, but as we discussed, Tallulah's depression is getting worse. Are you absolutely sure you're unwilling to tell her the truth about their father? What he did?"

My impatience surges; we've been over this many times before. Won't anyone let this rest? "I tried to tell the girls, to explain why I stayed all those years. Not everything, of course. I softened things, didn't tell them that he made me out to be crazy by having me committed. But the girls didn't take it well. It was obvious to me they didn't want to hear it. Despite how Jackson treated me, he was a good father to them. Most of the time, anyway."

I don't tell her about the way he mercilessly pushed Bella when she struggled to read, or how he refused to consider that she had a learning disability. "I'm not sure they could bear hearing the full truth. They might not even believe it. It could damage my relationship with them. I can't let that happen."

She gives me a look I can't interpret, purses her lips, and finally speaks. "I understand, but in that case, you need to get in touch with Jackson and tell him what's going on. Things have escalated. Tallulah has become reckless. What if she decides to hitchhike across the country? You can't risk her running away. Maybe he can arrange to come and visit, supervised of course, and we can all meet together to try to figure out a way for him to be in their lives in a safe way."

Safe is not a word I would ever associate with Jackson. I don't want him here, contaminating our lives. I can't abide the thought of him in my house, seeing where we live, knowing the intimate details of our lives.

"I'm not even sure if he's been released from prison yet. Plus, I don't know if he can leave the state."

"Why did Tallulah try to go see him if he's still in prison?"

I blow out a breath. "I never told her he was in prison."

"Well, what if you took the girls there?"

My stomach tightens. *There.* The place I fought so hard to escape.

"I can't go back."

"Well, if Jackson can't come here, I don't see any other options. Are you willing to risk her running off again? Or even hurting herself?"

"No, of course not. Do you think she'd actually . . ." I can't complete the sentence, I'm so horrified by the thought. "There must be another way." Alarm twists my stomach.

She cocks her head, her face full of understanding. "I don't see how if Jackson can't come here."

I sigh and think for a moment. "Maybe we could go next month when the girls are out of school. Rent something for the summer. But I need support. Can you recommend someone for us to see in Connecticut?"

"Yes, of course." She gives me a sympathetic look. "I realize this is the last thing you want to do. But legally he has no right to the children, so he has to play by your rules."

I scoff. "Jackson doesn't play by anyone else's rules." Then I shrug. "Maybe these months in prison have mellowed him." But I don't believe that for a minute.

Dr. Marshall leans back in her chair, tapping her pen on a pad. "Both girls are curious about their little brother, Jackson Junior. What are your thoughts about allowing them to meet him?"

It's a question I've wrestled with since he was born. He's innocent in all this, only two years old. I know how precious siblings are; I still miss my sister after all these years. If Tallulah and Bella have the chance to have a relationship with a brother, I don't want to stand in the way.

"The problem is Amber. She and I are not exactly on good terms. I absolutely don't want her having anything to do with my girls. She's devious and scheming, a liar who plays mind games and will stop at nothing to get her own way. I won't have them subjected to her manipulation. But she'll never let her son be a part of our lives unless we include her."

"Well, perhaps Jackson can persuade her to allow him to bring little Jackson with him."

"There's no way—"

She puts up her hand. "You know what, one step at a time. Let me find you a therapist to work with. Give him or her all the background, and you can navigate these issues then. And of course, you can talk to me any time while you're away. The main thing is to help Tallulah and Bella come to terms with living apart from their father."

I know she's right, but a sense of dread fills me, nonetheless. "Okay. I'll get in touch with him as soon as I can."

"Have you filled the prescription Dr. Parker sent to the pharmacy?"

I shake my head. "I don't need anything."

"Just fill it and take it with you. If you get too anxious, the Klonopin can help."

I nod. "All right, I will."

On the drive back home, I rehearse what I'll say to Jackson, how to appeal to his better self on behalf of Tallulah. I would go to hell and back for my children, but with Jackson involved, there may not be a way back. He's a master manipulator, capable of assuming whatever persona is most advantageous to him at the time. He swept into my life like a hero, making me believe he was the answer to everything I needed. After we were married, Jackson's behavior seemed controlling at times, but I rationalized it away, thinking I was perhaps being too sensitive. It wasn't until after Tallulah was born that he showed his true colors, knowing my love for her was my Achilles' heel. He would go from being loving and attentive to cold and critical in the blink of an eye, and I never quite knew what provoked him. I tried my best to please him and to make it work but when he threatened the safety of our child, I took her and left. He was one step ahead of me, though, and after making me appear unstable and having me committed to a sanatorium for months, there was little I could do once I returned home, without losing my child. I shiver when I think back to the first night he became physically violent with me. Tallulah had been almost two years old. We'd gone out to dinner with clients and the waiter complimented me on my choice of an appetizer, saying it was his favorite. We must have exchanged only a few words, but Jackson barely spoke to me on the way home. I kept asking what was wrong, but he claimed nothing was. In the middle of the night, I felt like I was suffocating. I began coughing and suddenly realized he was holding a pillow over my head. I struggled against him, and he finally let go. My relief was short-lived. He flicked the lamp on, and I saw that he held a knife in his hands, its blade gleaming close to my face. He pushed it against my neck.

"Were you dreaming of the waiter, slut?"

"Jackson, please. Put the knife down!"

"You humiliated me. Flirting with him like I wasn't even there."

He nicked my neck, and I felt the burn. He put his finger on the blood, then smeared it on my cheek. To this day, I still wake up in the middle of the night, breathless, worried that there will be a knife at my throat or a gun at my head, until I remember that I'm free of him. And now I have to go back.

3

AMBER

Amber had no idea if Jackson had stolen the diamonds or had obtained them legitimately. One thing was certain, however. She had to be cautious about who she showed them to, and thanks to good old Bunny, Amber knew just who to call.

Bunny Nichols was a woman Amber had met when Amber had wormed her way onto Daphne's charity committee a few years back. The third wife of a repugnant eighty-five-year-old multimillionaire, Bunny was the embodiment of every cliché about the trophy wife. Despite her ditzy vibe, she was actually quite cunning. She had turned Amber on to Stefan Becker, a jeweler with impeccable discretion, who was not only willing to help turn gems into cash but was also a master craftsman, an artist really, in making flawless replicas of the jewels being sold. The ever-resourceful Bunny had found Becker when her husband, March, slashed her budget after discovering she'd been cheating. It was ironic, really, since Amber was the one who'd sent March the compromising pictures of Bunny and her lover way back when Amber had first befriended Daphne and needed Bunny out of the way so she could take her place as cochairman on Daphne's charity gala committee. Of course, no one found out. Amber had availed herself of Becker's services a few months back when their bank account had begun to dwindle. She'd sold her Blue Nile tennis bracelet and the ruby and diamond ring Jackson had given her for their one-year anniversary—as if that were a milestone she wanted to celebrate—but the money was running out. She'd worn the fake the last time she visited Jackson in prison, and he'd been none the wiser. It gave her a little thrill to fool him.

The two thirty-foot streetlights with their diamond motif at the crosswalk of Fifth Avenue and Forty-seventh Street never failed to amuse Amber as she entered New York's Diamond District—a mere city block through which 90 percent of diamonds entering the United States passed. She walked a short distance on Forty-seventh Street and entered the thirty-four-story Gem Tower.

"ID, please," a uniformed man at the reception counter barked.

Amber handed him her driver's license, placed her index finger on the automated fingerprint identification system, and then proceeded through the scanner and onto the elevator. It seemed only seconds before the elevator reached the twenty-eighth floor and the doors silently opened. She unconsciously clutched her handbag more tightly, strode to the suite, and rang the bell. There was a buzz as the door opened and then quickly shut behind her. She now stood in a small space between two locked doors—the so-called mantrap. She heard another buzz and when the door in front of her opened, Amber entered a tranquil space. A striking young woman with coal black hair and skin so white that it looked almost translucent greeted her. The sleek black turtleneck dress she wore highlighted the elegance of her tall slender frame.

"Good afternoon, Mrs. Parrish. If you'll follow me, Mr. Becker is expecting you." Amber's eyes focused on the bright red lipstick as she spoke, so startling against the woman's pale skin.

"Thank you."

"Ah, Mrs. Parrish." Stefan Becker extended his hand to Amber when they reached his office. "So nice to see you again."

"And you," she replied, shaking his hand.

"Please have a seat." He placed a hand on one of the gray

leather chairs in front of his desk. "Would you care for something to drink?"

"No, I'm fine, thank you," Amber said, sitting down.

Becker went to his desk and sat, and Amber saw him give a slight nod to the young woman who then left the room and closed the door. She wondered if something was going on between them. There was no wedding ring on Becker's tanned finger, and even though he was probably a good fifteen years older than Miss Red Lips and had streaks of silver through his hair, he was extremely attractive in a buttoned-up sort of way.

Becker fingered the gold cuff link on his sleeve and leaned slightly forward. "You said on the phone that you had some stones you wished to have appraised and possibly sell."

"Yes." Amber withdrew a small drawstring pouch from her purse and handed it to Becker across the desk. She hadn't brought the whole cache, only one of the diamonds and one each of the pink and red stones she couldn't identify.

Becker opened the bag and carefully emptied the three stones onto a velvet-lined tray, picking up one after another with his tweezers and looking at them with his naked eyes. Then, picking up his loupe, he brought the first pink stone nearer, holding it with a diamond plunger and examining it more closely from all angles, then did the same with the red one. After a few minutes he looked up at her, frowning. "Where did you get these?"

"Why does that matter?"

He fixed her with an icy stare. "Do you know what this is?" he asked, holding up the red stone.

It was safer to say nothing, she realized, and she remained silent so that he would continue.

"This is a red diamond, one of the rarest and most valuable of all diamonds. Red diamonds come from the Argyle mine in Australia. The mine's been closed since 2020."

Amber felt her pulse quicken. "How much is it worth?" she asked breathlessly.

"A fancy red diamond can go for eighty thousand to one million dollars per carat. This stone is over one carat."

She moved to the edge of her seat, excitement coursing through her. "I have more stones. And what about the regular diamond? Is it valuable?"

Becker frowned again and cocked his head. "I have to ask again how they were acquired, Mrs. Parrish."

She pressed her lips together and decided to wing it. "They've been in my husband's family a long time. With my husband in prison, our financial situation has become precarious. He's asked me to sell the gems."

"And there is proof that these gems were lawfully procured?"

"I don't have any paperwork if that's what you mean, but as I said, they've been in the family forever."

Becker wrapped the stones in paper, handing them back to her and shaking his head. "I'm sorry, but without proof of their provenance, I can do nothing with these." He picked up a pen and began to write on a notepad.

"Wait—"

He put a hand up to stop her from speaking and slid a paper across the desk on which he'd written a name and phone number. "This man can help you. I'll let him know you'll be calling."

Amber grabbed the note, reading the name he'd written. She looked up from the paper, her eyes flashing. "Mr. Stones? Is this some kind of joke?"

"I assure you he is no joke." Becker rose from his chair and extended his hand once again. "I hope to do business with you another time."

Fat chance, Amber thought, ignoring the outstretched hand. She stuffed the note in her handbag and without a word marched from the room in fury.

She stood outside the building and leaned against the wall, trying to decide what to do next as traffic growled and people hurried past.

"Hey, lady. You buyin' or sellin'? What are you lookin' for?" a hawker yelled as he walked toward Amber.

She shook her head and waved him away. It was ridiculous to keep standing here. She had no choice, and pulling the piece of paper from her bag, she began walking as she tapped the number into her phone.

"Hello," a gruff voice said, answering on the second ring.

"Mr. Stones?"

"Who can I say is calling?"

Amber closed her eyes and inhaled. "Mrs. Amber Parrish."

"Hold on." The flat New York accent had an impatient edge.

She watched the traffic light change while she held, and when finally a deep voice said hello, it startled her. "Mr. Stones?"

"Yes."

"This is Amber Parrish. Stefan Becker gave me your name and number. He said you might be able to help me."

"Mr. Becker contacted me. If you'd like to discuss the items you have, come to my office."

Amber hesitated. She didn't know jack shit about this guy. "Well, what I'm wondering is if you can give me an appraisal and then sell some—"

"Mrs. Parrish," he interrupted her. "Any business you wish to conduct must be done in person. Do you understand?"

Amber was the last one to let impropriety stand in the way of what she wanted, but this seemed a little dangerous. "I understand. How soon can we meet?"

"Right away if you'd like. My office is just two buildings from Mr. Becker's," he said, and gave her the address.

The building wasn't as grand or as new as Stefan Becker's, and when Amber reached Mr. Stones's suite on the sixteenth floor, her eyes swept across the room. She was struck by its cold minimalist feel, the gray walls and carpet a backdrop to geometric furnishings that looked stiff and unyielding.

"You Amber Parrish?" an older man sitting at the desk asked.

"Yes, I'm here to see Mr. Stones."

"Mrs. Parrish, welcome." She turned toward the voice. He looked as if he'd been spawned from this very room, a six-foot figure dressed in a stark three-piece gray suit that was tailored to his exact measurements. A starched white shirt and gray silk tie, expertly knotted, completed the ensemble. His white-blond hair was closely cropped and his eyes, an icy blue, were without warmth. A slight aroma of fresh citrus met her as she approached him.

"Thank you for seeing me on such short notice," she said, ready to shake his hand, but Stones put no hand forward, instead giving a slight nod in acknowledgment.

"Certainly. Why don't we go into my office where we'll have privacy."

She followed him into a room that looked much the same as the outer one, and they sat opposite each other at a slim metal table.

"Mr. Stones. Is that your real name?" Amber said.

"The less you know about me, the better it is for both of us, Mrs. Parrish." He looked at her and smiled. "Now let's get down to business. I understand you have some gems you'd like me to look at."

Amber didn't like this guy. He was too full of himself, so superior and acting like he was in some kind of jewel heist movie. She said nothing as she took the folded paper from the pouch and placed it on the table, watching as he unwrapped the stones and with his tweezers picked up each one to examine through his eyeglass.

When he finished, he sat back in his chair and, rubbing his chin with an index finger, said. "The red diamond is superb. The pink too. And the white diamond is excellent quality—perfect color and clarity. As Stefan Becker told you, they are extremely valuable. And sellable. I will have no trouble moving these for you if you wish."

"How valuable? How much will I get?" Amber was already counting the zeros.

"That's an interesting question. The value varies, depending upon where you are in the chain."

She was really getting irritated now. "What does that mean, exactly?"

"To a buyer at full price, your one carat red diamond could easily fetch over two million dollars. The value for you would be 25 to 30 percent of its wholesale value, considerably less than two million. Somewhere between $500,000 and $600,000."

Amber shot up from her chair. "Excuse me? That's ridiculous. Who's making all that damn money? You? *I'm* the one with the diamonds."

"Quite true. But *I'm* the one with the connections. If you can prove where these diamonds were legitimately obtained, you are perfectly welcome to sell them directly."

She glared at him and sat down again, then reached into her handbag and took out her phone. "I have more. Three pink. One large blue, and several yellow and white. Here," she said thrusting the phone toward him. "Here are photos of the others. Can you up my percentage since there are so many?" If Amber hadn't been watching him carefully, she would have missed the quick flash of excitement cross his face when he looked at the first picture of the blue diamond.

He handed the phone back to her, his face expressionless once again. "We can certainly discuss that when I examine the other stones."

"How soon would I get paid? Do I have to wait until you sell them?" Amber needed that money in her hands and safely tucked away before Jackson was released. Her careful planning in landing Jackson as her husband and overthrowing Daphne as the reigning queen of Bishops Harbor wasn't going to be for nothing. All those months of pretending to be Daphne's friend, researching cystic fibrosis, working her ass off on Daphne's charity for her dead sister. It took a toll, having to act so sweet and obsequious, posing as a loyal friend who loved Daphne and her little brats. She thought back to all those boring evenings at Daphne's house, pretending to understand Daphne's grief over losing her sainted sister. The hours they spent talking about the illness that had claimed their sisters' lives, even though Amber's three sisters were very much alive and well— not that it would have bothered her much if one of them had died. After a while, Amber almost believed the lie herself.

And then her fawning over the powerful Jackson Parrish. Making him feel like he was a god. Reading the books he read, schooling herself in art and music masters so that she could hold her own with the most erudite. She'd worked her ass off at Parrish Industries, spending her off-hours learning the ins and outs of the business and becoming indispensable to Jackson, until one day he also started to notice how good her legs looked in short skirts. She'd stroked his ego and made herself into the perfect younger replacement for his wife. He'd fallen hard for Amber and given her everything she thought she wanted. But now she no longer held Jackson in her thrall, and she wasn't about to let him move back in and control the purse strings again. Amber was finally rich, the kind of rich she'd envied and coveted from the sidelines, but only as long as she was with Jackson, because all the money belonged to him. Amber had come from nothing, had clawed her way to the top, and now a golden opportunity had been dropped in her lap like a gift from the gods. Finally, the money would be all hers and hers alone. No way was she ever going back.

"No. As soon as I take possession, you will be paid. A wire transfer will be sent to your bank immediately. If you would like, I can take these three stones and wire the money to your account while you're here. Did you by any chance bring your bank information with you?"

She had opened an account in a Barbados bank, one recommended to her by a lawyer referred by her friend Remi Whitlock. He'd advised Amber to open the account in her son's name, and Amber, as his mother, would be custodian with power of attorney.

The lawyer took care of providing the bank with certified copies of Jackson Junior's birth certificate and the other required documents. For all intents and purposes, the money would be at her complete disposal, but there was less likelihood of too much scrutiny or too many questions asked if it looked as though it was just a mother putting money away for her son. The key, Amber was told, was that first step of opening the account and getting the money into the banking system. Once in, she could transfer money from there to anywhere in the world and to as many banks as she wished without any questions being asked.

She thought a moment. "I have the bank information for you, but I'd also like some of the money in cash. Can you do that today?"

"I can, but that would cost you a bit more."

She appraised him coolly, remembering the look of hunger in his eyes when he saw the photos of what was to come. Amber understood greed well. "I can understand how that might apply if I were selling one diamond, but let's be honest, Mr. Stones. You stand to make an extremely handsome profit once you've sold all I have. And since you take a larger share for those without provenance, in a way, my lack of proof of their origin works to your advantage. I believe you can well afford to give me cash for the three I've brought without any sort of markdown, don't you agree?" Amber's eyes locked with his.

He seemed to consider her for a second. "I think I'm able to give you some accommodation, Mrs. Parrish."

"Wonderful. In the meantime, I'll leave these with you and take the cash for them now."

"I'll calculate your earnings and have my assistant get your money ready." He put his hand out to Amber and they shook. "By the way," he said with a slight smile as they rose from their seats, "an interesting fact you might enjoy . . . a briefcase of two million dollars in $100 bills weighs twenty-two pounds. Fill it with euros in denominations of 500 and you can fit 8 million in that same briefcase. Unfortunately, the U.S. mint stopped issuing $500 bills in 1969."

Twenty minutes later, Amber left with a dark brown leather briefcase weighing fourteen and a half pounds. Next stop was the safe-deposit box she'd opened yesterday.

4

DAPHNE

By the time I get home, I've talked myself out of it. What was I thinking? Allowing Jackson back into our lives is not the answer. There has to be another way. Maybe I've been wrong in keeping the truth from my daughters. They're young, yes, but old enough to understand danger. As much as I've wanted to shield them from the naked truth about their father and all he's capable of, wouldn't it be better in the long run if they knew that I didn't make the decision to move them away lightly? I sigh as I pull into the drive, my heart heavy. The house is quiet when I enter, my mother at the kitchen table doing a crossword and Tallulah nowhere in sight. Bella is still at school.

"Has she come out of her room at all?" I ask as I walk into the kitchen.

"She let me make her some pancakes for breakfast."

"Did she say anything?"

"I tried to ask about it, but she got very angry and jumped up from the table. I apologized and told her I'd mind my own business. She sat down, ate her pancakes, and then went right back to her room."

I look over my shoulder, making sure Tallulah's not lurking in the hallway, and lower my voice, recapping my visit with the psychologist. "Tallulah's so angry at me for keeping her from Jackson. Dr. Marshall thinks it was too abrupt a rift." I hesitate, knowing the impact my next words are going to have. "She wants me to take the girls to see him this summer."

Her eyes are wide with disbelief. "You can't be seriously thinking of letting Jackson see them?"

"I don't know what else to do. What if she runs away? She could be trafficked, anything. I can't risk it."

She scoffs. "I'll tell you exactly what you do. You tell her the truth. What kind of man he really is. You keep that monster away from my granddaughters! Letting him back into their lives will not end well. Keeping him away is for their own good."

"Is it? I'm not so sure any longer. She's clearly in a lot of pain."

"Well, letting Jackson near her isn't going to make things any better."

"I have to do something. The therapist is very concerned and so am I." I stand. "I'm going to check on her."

I knock but Tallulah doesn't open the door. Pushing it open, I enter, and she gives me a rebellious look, one eye obscured by a lock of long brown hair. She's got headphones on and I can hear the rock music coming from them. Her pink Chuck Taylors are strewn on the floor next to her jean jacket and she's lying on her stomach, *The Hate U Give* propped on the pillow in front of her.

"I told you to leave me alone!" She turns back to her book.

"Please, sweetheart. I'm not mad at you. I just want to understand." I move closer to the bed and pull her headphones off and lay them on the bed.

"She's such a bitch!" she spits out.

"Who?" I ask, keeping my voice level.

"Mrs. Banner. She yelled at me in front of all my friends. Said I was a disgrace to the school. To the student council where I'm supposed to be a leader. Why can't she understand how hard it is? I was so close, just a few hours from our house. I couldn't let the chance go by. You moved us clear across the country to get away from him!" She turns now, her eyes mere slits, her nostrils flaring.

"Honey, you know that's not the whole story." It doesn't escape me that she still refers to the dwelling in Bishops Harbor as "our house." I sit down on the bed and take a deep breath, stalling for time and for inspiration. Her room is immaculate and tidy, with the exception of the jacket and shoes on the floor—the complete opposite of her sister's where chaos reigns. Tallulah's room is painted a tranquil sea blue and bookcases line every wall filled to the brim with the books she's devoured since we moved in. I think back to my room when I was her age, the posters of boys and bands taped to the wall, and marvel at how different hers is. She's always been my little adult, and I have to remind myself that despite her precociousness, she's still a child.

She pushes herself back against the headboard, putting more distance between us, and glares at me. "Just because he was a jerk to you doesn't give you the right to keep him from us. He was a good dad."

"When you're older you'll under—"

"Stop!" Her face is red. "Don't hand me that bullshit. It's just a convenient way for you to get what you want without having to explain anything. I'm not a baby. What is so terrible about him that you had to steal us away?"

This use of profanities is something new and it jars me. I can't tell her the terrible things he did to me. But I can tell her he's in prison, I decide.

"I know you think he's a good father. And maybe he was. But he's not a good man. He's in prison right now."

She laughs. "You think I don't know that? Wake up, Mom! It's the twenty-first century; there's a thing called the internet. He's there for tax evasion. Not exactly murder. So he hid some money from the government. Big deal. All the politicians are corrupt anyway. I want to see him."

Alarm pulses through me like an electric current. "How do you know that?"

She gives me a triumphant look. "I've spoken to him."

My mouth drops open. "You what? . . . How?" I can't imagine how she's managed this. Prisoners can't take incoming calls, and Jackson doesn't have any of our phone numbers.

"I called Amber. She conferenced us on her phone."

My face flushes hot. "Amber? Tallulah, really?"

"You left me no choice," she thunders. "At least she isn't trying to separate me from my father. She promised to take me to see him."

I stand up, needing to leave before I say something I'll regret. Amber is good at pretending to care, to be an ally. I think of how she made up a sister who died from cystic fibrosis in order to connect with me. All the stories she told me of the sister she had loved and lost and it was a complete and utter lie. And now she's talking to my daughter?

"We'll finish this later."

"Whatever," she shoots back.

My mother looks at me expectantly when I join her at the kitchen table. "She's spoken to Jackson," I tell her.

"Isn't that in violation of his restraining order?"

My patience snaps. "Mom, we've been over this before. There's no restraining order. He gave up his parental rights, but he hasn't broken any laws by speaking to her."

"How in the world did he get in touch with her?"

I shake my head. "Amber."

My mother rolls her eyes. "Of course. That woman would do anything to annoy you. What are you going to do?"

"I'm going to follow the advice of the therapist and go back." I put a hand up before she can object. "I'll set the ground rules, and he'll never be alone with them. Dr. Marshall is going to set us up with a therapist in Connecticut."

"I think it's a mistake."

She's made that crystal clear. "Maybe it is, but I have to do what I think is best for my daughters. I'm not going to have our relationship ruined because they think I'm unfairly keeping them from Jackson. At the end of summer, we'll be back here, and we'll have a whole year before we need to think about seeing him again."

She reaches out and puts a hand on mine. "I know it hurts you to see your girls upset, but, Daphne, you know how manipulative he is, and how controlling. I'm worried."

"Half his power came from his influence, and that's gone now. He's been shamed, imprisoned, and humbled. There's nothing he can do to me anymore, and I know he wouldn't hurt the girls."

"I can see you've made up your mind," she says quietly. "But if you insist on going, I'm coming with you."

"Absolutely not. You'd have to cancel your trip, and I'm not going to let you do that. You've been counting the days. You're going on that trip in two weeks."

"I can travel anytime. This is more important, Daphne."

My mother has been planning this vacation with her friends for the last two years—seven weeks in South America starting in Quito, Ecuador, and the Galápagos Islands and on to Peru and Bolivia. It's the trip of a lifetime for her and one she and my late father always dreamed about. "No, Mom. You've been looking forward to this for so long, and your friends will be hugely disappointed if you don't go. Not to mention that at this point it's nonrefundable. I can't let you do that."

She starts to object, but I stop her. "Look, Meredith is there. I'll be sure she's with me whenever Jackson's around. You need to go and not worry about me. I'm a big girl." The one good thing about going back to Bishops Harbor will be seeing my best friend, Meredith. She was the only genuine friend I made when I lived there. It was Meredith who first discovered that Amber was a fraud. And even though at the time I couldn't let Meredith know that I was investigating Amber and had to pretend to believe Amber's lies, she respected my choice. That's one of the qualities I love best about her—it's never about getting her way, or being right, but rather being supportive.

My mother shakes her head, but says no more, and I'm grateful that she's stopped trying to convince me otherwise. I look up when I hear footsteps and see Tallulah walking toward me.

"I'm sorry, Mom. I shouldn't have spoken to you like that. But you don't know how hard it is. It's like he's dead. I really miss him." A tear rolls down her cheek and my heart breaks. I open my arms, and she collapses against me.

"We'll go back for the summer. I'll make the arrangements."

She pulls back and looks at me. "Really? You mean it?"

I nod. "All I want is your happiness. We'll go back to Bishops Harbor for the summer. But you can't see him without me being there, and you'll just have to trust that I have my reasons. Everything I do is to protect you even if you don't believe that. Can you do that?"

A smile lights up her face, and she jumps up and down then hugs me again. "Yes, yes! Thank you, thank you!"

I close my eyes, hugging her tight, and hope with all my might that her gratitude doesn't one day turn into reproach.

5

DAISY ANN

Daisy Ann Briscoe, née Crawford, swam the last two laps of thirty in her backyard pool. It was four o'clock on Saturday afternoon in Dallas, and the temperature still hovered around the ninety-degree mark, with humidity at an unbearable 80 percent. She'd worked in her office for two hours this morning, then taken her sons, Tucker and Greyson, to their tennis lessons at the country club where she'd met her husband, Mason, for lunch. Afterward, they'd all come home and dispersed. As she climbed out of the pool and dried off, all she wanted was to take a cool shower, put on some comfy loungewear, and chill for the rest of the evening. Instead, they'd be leaving in an hour for her mother-in-law's seventy-fifth birthday bash.

As she went from the terrace into the conservatory, the drop in temperature made her shiver and pull her robe more tightly around her. She'd always hated air-conditioning, but without it, the hot muggy Texas climate could be insufferable. The Saltillo tile was warm on her bare feet, as she walked through the sunny room to the central hall and stairway. They'd lived in this modern home in Highland Park for over eleven years, from the time Daisy Ann was pregnant with Tucker, their first child. Mason, at six feet six and almost a head taller than Daisy Ann, had felt like the massive house was made for him, with its twelve-foot ceilings and tall wooden cantilevered front doors, and so she'd agreed to the purchase without looking further. Not that there was anything to complain about. The home was vast and spectacular, all stone and wood, with notable attention to detail throughout. It sat on almost an acre of property.

Daisy Ann, however, had grown up in quite different circumstances than her husband and was as far from a city girl as one could get. Her father's ranch in Denton County spanned over a hundred thousand acres and was over an hour away from Dallas. Her childhood had been full of adventure and exploration. She'd been a free spirit, an only child, with room to run and roam, to sit under a tree and dream undisturbed. She still missed the freedom of those endless vistas, the big sky, riding her horse like the wind. It was the place she loved most in the world, and her boys loved it too. The family spent lots of time at the ranch throughout the year. It delighted Daisy Ann to see Tucker and Greyson exploring her favorite old childhood haunts. How many nights had they all sat in a circle around a campfire under a sky full of stars, sipping hot chocolate with marshmallows and telling stories? She could still hear her father's deep belly laugh, the kind of laugh that was contagious. He would never see her boys grow into men, and they'd been robbed of a wise and bountiful grandfather. He'd been a healthy and vital sixty-five with so much to live for.

The house was quiet as she climbed the stairs, which meant that Mason was most likely in his office working and the boys in their bedrooms on their PlayStations. When she reached the landing, she went first to Tucker's bedroom. The door was open, and he was, as she suspected, on his computer. She glanced over at his bed, where two yellow labs were dozing, and smiled. Buck and Shot had been her father's dogs and while they had bonded with the entire family, the connection with Tucker was special. No matter how often Greyson tried to get them to sleep in his room, they always ended up back in here. "Hey, sugar. Time to get ready for Mimi's birthday party. We have to leave soon."

He swiveled the chair around to face her. "I'm already dressed," he said.

Eyeing her eleven-year-old son, she said, "You are *not* going to your grandmother's party in shorts and a T-shirt. Now change into long pants and a dress shirt." She could just picture Birdie's face if Tucker walked in dressed so casually.

"Aww, Mom. Why can't I go like this?"

Truthfully, she wondered that too, but her mother-in-law, Birdie, was old school. Old money, old manners, old Dallas. "Come on, Tuck. You know how Mimi is. Don't be difficult."

"Jeez. That's so stupid." He huffed and made a great show of getting up from his chair.

She chuckled to herself as she continued past Greyson's bedroom to her own. Without being told, her nine-year-old would already be in pressed khakis, a white button-down, and a plaid tie. He was a Briscoe through and through.

"Oh, you surprised me," she said as she entered the bedroom and saw Mason. "I thought you were still working."

"I probably should be, but I figured I'd better leave it before I got too involved. Don't want to be late for Mom's." Mason raised his eyebrows and made a mocking fearful face.

Daisy Ann laughed and went up on tiptoe to give him a kiss. "You're funny. I just got some lip from Tucker when I told him to change his clothes."

"He should count his blessings that you're his mama. I had to dress up all the time. I'm gonna jump in the shower. Want to join me?"

"Just how late do you want to be?"

Mason sighed and shook his head. "Right. Catch you tonight," he said, running a hand through his thick black hair and throwing a towel over his shoulder.

Blowing him a kiss, she relished the thought of making love with him later. She knew lots of couples cooled off after so many years together, but happily, that was not the case with her and Mason. After showering in her own bathroom, Daisy Ann went into the dressing room and pulled out a turquoise pantsuit, sleeveless and backless. It was flowy and summery, and the monochrome made her five-foot-eight frame appear even taller. The color had always been a great complement to her warm skin tones and white-blond hair. Scanning the shoe rack, she decided on her red Ferragamo sandals. Her mother's silver and turquoise drop earrings would be all the jewelry she'd need. Birdie would approve, Daisy Ann decided as she dressed. Although she and Mason often joked about his mother's eccentricities and her adherence to strict social protocol, Daisy Ann loved and respected her mother-in-law. Underneath Birdie's commanding and grand exterior was a warm and empathic woman who was able to make anyone feel comfortable. And despite the fact that she wanted things a certain way, she had a charisma that drew people to her. How often had Daisy Ann heard her say, *Charm is making the person you're talking to feel like the only person in the room.*

Daisy Ann put the finishing touches on her makeup and looked at her watch. Still plenty of time. Preston Hollow was a ten-to-fifteen-minute drive at most. As she descended the staircase, she was greeted with wolf whistles from Mason.

"Your mama looks amazing, doesn't she, boys?"

She adored him, had loved him since eighth grade when she was a boarder at Hockaday School and Mason a student at St. Mark's. They'd broken up briefly when they'd both gone off to college, but soon after graduation they got engaged. Daisy Ann had been twenty-three when they wed. Her beloved mother died just six months after she and Mason were married. And that's when Birdie stepped in to fill the void. Daisy Ann would be forever grateful for Birdie's love and strength during those dark days.

They had almost arrived at the house when she felt the vibration of her cell phone in her purse. She pulled it from her bag and glanced at the screen. A text. From Wade Ashford. She glanced over at Mason, then went back to her phone and swiped.

The account is running low again. You need to transfer more money. How long are you going to keep this up? It's time to make a new plan. She deleted the text and turned her phone off.

- 6 -

AMBER

Amber stretched and breathed in deeply, glancing at the clock on the nightstand. It was only six A.M., still early, but she had a lot to do before Jackson's release next month. She nudged the leg next to hers with her foot.

"Get up. I need you out of here."

The man mumbled something incoherent, then rolled over on top of her. "Morning. You don't really want me to leave just yet, do you?" He began to kiss her neck, slowly working his way down.

She was tempted to give in, but common sense prevailed, and she pushed him off her and got up. These past seven months with Jackson gone had allowed Amber to indulge herself and she'd taken full advantage. There was nothing quite like the feel of a twenty-one-year-old body. She loved being with men closer to her own age. Jackson was closing in on fifty, and let's face it, he had been a one-trick pony at best. She stood by the bed, naked, and waited until Marcus followed suit.

"The staff will be here at eight. Can't risk anyone seeing you." The truth was Amber had in her employ a live-in nanny for Jackson Junior who was well aware of the young studs parading through Amber's bedroom, but Marcus didn't need to know that.

He smirked and walked over to where she was standing. Amber's eyes rested a moment on his flat abs then took in the rest of him at full attention. Grabbing her, he pulled her close and she felt her resolve melt away. "Well, maybe just one more time . . ."

.　　　.　　　.

Once Marcus left, and after Amber showered and dressed, she peeked into Jackson Junior's room to find him still asleep. She lingered for a moment, watching him. He was such a beautiful child, and she enjoyed the compliments she got when they were out. But the temper tantrums and stubbornness made her want to scream. She knew it was normal for a two-year-old, but it didn't make it any easier to deal with. If she didn't have a nanny, she would completely lose her mind. She reached out and pushed a curl from his forehead. This is how she liked him, sweet and docile and sleeping.

She turned away and headed downstairs where she poured a cup of freshly brewed coffee, carrying it to the deck overlooking the Sound. It was a gorgeous May morning, and she inhaled the intoxicating salt air. She'd never tired of their Connecticut estate on the water, had fallen in love with the magnificent waterfront home the first time she'd seen it, when she was just a poor little helper bee groveling at Daphne's feet. Back then, she'd never been inside a house so grand, one in which dazzling views of the sea beckoned from wide windows and French doors. It never ceased to thrill her when she walked through its doors, knowing that it all belonged to her—and to Jackson as well, of course. It would all be changing now, however. She no longer needed Jackson or his money or his house, because now there was fourteen million dollars parked in an offshore account in her son's name. There was no reason to stay here with Jackson—theirs was a marriage in name only and he wouldn't miss her any more than she would miss him. When he came home from prison in June, he would find her gone. She was finally free to be herself, to take what she wanted when she wanted without kissing anyone's ass anymore. She'd never marry again, well, unless she met someone with billions, then maybe. But she definitely had enough money now to figure out how to parlay that into more. She was young and smart and with the right investments, she'd be sitting pretty for the rest of her life.

She rose from the lounge chair and went inside to her office. Well, she called it her office, but it was so much more than that. She unlocked the door and entered the space that was strictly her own. At once, the serene interior calmed her. She loved this room and all it contained. There was no clutter, nothing out of place. Every item had been carefully chosen by her, and it was the one room in the house where she felt most herself. Her books covered an entire wall from floor to ceiling. After years of having to borrow books from the library, the thrill of being able to buy any book she wanted never dulled for her. She made notes in their margins, underlined passages, inked her name inside each cover. They were her treasure . . . and her passport to the world.

The art in the room was simple and chosen for the artists, not the art itself. Women who were self-taught, like Élisabeth Louise Vigée Le Brun and Augusta Savage, who'd had to fight for recognition and admission to academies and art societies. They were a source of encouragement to Amber to keep striving despite setbacks and roadblocks. The entire room was a paean to talent, intellect, and determination.

Sitting at her desk, she breathed in the soothing scent of sandalwood and oud, smiling to herself. Who would have thought it would be so easy? Mr. Stones had been a bit of a challenge, but the rest had been smooth sailing. Her next step had been deciding where to go. Definitely out of the country, definitely Europe, but where? She finally decided that the best—and most fun—plan would be to figure that out once she'd traveled around the continent a bit, and so she'd booked a first-class ticket to Paris. She'd start there, visit a few luxury fashion houses, and dine on the Seine. One entire week would be dedicated to visiting the Louvre, and perhaps she would be there in time to see Delacroix's famous *Liberty Leading the People* before its removal for restoration. Just the thought of it made her shiver with delight. All her travel documents were in order, and the only thing left was composing a note she would leave for Jackson. She picked up the pen, thought for a minute, and then began to write the letter she would leave on their bed.

Jackson,

If you are reading this, you have already been told or gleaned the fact that I am gone. I'm sure you're as elated as I am that we are no longer together. Of course, your elation will be short-lived when you discover that your little horde of diamonds was used to finance my new life far away from you and Bishops Harbor. How kind and thoughtful of you to provide me with such a wonderful parting gift. In exchange for your generosity, I leave you little Jax.

I know your first instinct will be to go into search and destroy mode, but you would be wise to think twice about trying to find me. Don't forget that I know about the lies you told and who you paid to have Daphne committed all those years ago. It would be a shame if you forced me to come back and divulge that information. Unless, of course, you're missing life in prison.

So, that's it. Thanks again. You've been a real gem!

Amber

She slid the folded letter into an envelope, sealed it, and wrote Jackson's name on the front, then rose from her desk and left the room.

The nanny, Chloe, was sitting at the kitchen table feeding Jax, who was now awake and in his high chair.

"Good morning." Amber went to her son and kissed the top of his head. "How's my sweet boy this morning?"

He giggled, tapping the tray with the palm of his hand. "Mama."

She ruffled his hair and turned to Chloe. "I have a few errands to run this morning. I shouldn't be too long."

"Okay. I'll take Jax for a walk in a little while and then put him down for a nap later," Chloe said.

"Great." Amber nodded absently as she picked up her handbag

and went to the garage. Her flight was in just two days and there were a few last-minute things she still needed to take care of. Her first stop was the bank where she exchanged dollars for euros, enough to see her through the airports, ground transportation, and tips. Once in France, of course, she would open an account there and transfer some of the Barbados money. She'd made a reservation at an Accor hotel, an anonymous and ubiquitous low-budget chain where Jackson would never think to look for her. She didn't love the idea of staying there until she got her bearings, but she reminded herself that she had the rest of her life to live in luxury.

From the bank she went to the private vault company where she'd rented a safe-deposit box that was accessible 24/7. Her cash would be safe there until she needed to grab it. Best of all, no keys that she would have to hide, but instead, a code to unlock it. Last, the photography studio to pick up the professional portrait she'd had done of herself with Jax. This would be put in a special album for him along with a letter from Amber to her son explaining why she was forced to leave his father. Something for him to remember her by. She knew Jackson would trash it before Jax was old enough to see and understand it, but she'd make sure to take her own photos of the album and her letter against the day Jax came looking for her. Then she would show him the proof of how excruciatingly heartbreaking it had been to leave him behind. It didn't occur to her to think too hard about why, in actuality, it was rather easy to leave him. After all, your feelings were your feelings and there was nothing you could do about it. Why feel guilty? Amber had never understood the sentimentality of motherhood. The only reason she'd even had Jax was to snare Jackson. Sure, he was a cute baby and she cared about him. But to give up everything she'd worked so hard for to stick around to change diapers and wipe his nose? No thank you. That's what nannies were for. When he was older, and capable of intelligent conversation, then she'd reconnect. Maybe take him on some trips with her. But for now, it wouldn't really matter to him anyhow. Kids didn't even remember anything before the age of five.

By the time Amber had finished everything on her list it was two o'clock and she headed home, satisfied that everything was in place.

Amber didn't hear any annoying baby talk coming from the kitchen so Jax must still be napping. She climbed the stairs to the bedroom carrying all her packages. When she opened the door to the room, she gasped and took a step back. Jackson! Sitting on the bed, smiling, leaning against the headboard with his arms clasped behind his head. Her note was crumpled in a ball on the floor.

"Just read your little love letter. I'm so glad I was able to come say goodbye in person." His eyes narrowed, and his lips curled in a snarl.

"Jackson . . . ? How are you here?" She dropped the bags. Her panic was so acute that it was difficult for her to breathe.

"Early release for good behavior, my dear. But you don't seem very happy to see me."

"Of course I'm glad for you. I know you hated it there. So, you came from the prison straight to the house? The note was just a joke. I thought you'd find it amusing." She struggled to come up with something, anything, to make him believe her, but came up short.

Jackson flew up from the bed and stormed toward her until he was just inches from her face. "Do you think I'm fucking stupid? I saw the greedy look on your face that day you visited. You couldn't get out of there fast enough to get to that boat and see what was hiding there." Now his face was almost touching hers, one hand around her throat. "I found your travel documents. I guess the party I wanted is off the table. You planning a little trip?"

"Jackson, you're hurting me." She tugged at his wrist.

"You're going to hurt a lot more if you don't produce those diamonds right now," he hissed, his grip tightening.

When she started to choke, he finally let go. "Where are they?" he said.

"They're safe, okay?"

"Where the hell are they?"

"Where did you get them?" She was stalling for time.

"None of your damn business. They belong to me. Now tell me where they are."

"I sold them," she said.

"You what?" he screamed at her.

"I sold them to a broker in New York. I was paid well. Just a speck more than fourteen million. More than I'd anticipated. Apparently, there was a bidding war over the Fancy Intense blue diamond from South Africa. Extremely rare. But you probably knew that, yes?"

All the color drained from his face, and he said nothing, just staring at her, his eyes glassy. He dropped onto a chair, his left hand cradling his head. "You greedy bitch! You have no idea what you've done," he hissed.

When he finally looked up at her, Amber was shocked. She'd never seen fear etched so intensely across Jackson's face. "What do you mean?"

His expression changed to one of undisguised fury. "Never mind. Where's the money, Amber?"

"It's very safe and offshore. No one will find out about it."

He exhaled. "I want the account number. Now."

She tilted her head, suddenly feeling her courage return. "And why, exactly, would I give that to you? I can cut you in, though."

"What the hell do you mean you'll cut me in? Enough of this stupid game, Amber. The money belongs to me." Jackson's fists were balled so tight that his knuckles were white. She was amused at his struggle to remain calm.

"Oh, but that's where you're wrong. Finders keepers. Possession is . . . well, you know how the rest of it goes."

He sprang from the chair and lunged at her again, his eyes bulging and his hands once more around her neck. "I'll fucking kill you."

Amber began to cough, trying to get air as she pushed against him. She kneed him in the groin, and suddenly he let go.

She bent over, trying to catch her breath. When she was able to speak again, she glared at him. "If I die, those numbers die with me."

Jackson was delusional if he thought he'd ever get his hands on her money. He could examine every piece of paper in the house, search her phone, and explore her computer. The numbers existed only in her head. It was during the period when Amber had studied the works of ancient Greek playwrights and philosophers that she'd discovered Simonides, a Greek lyric poet born in 556 BC, who developed a memory technique that has come to be called the Method of Loci or the "Memory Palace," an effective method of information memorization and retention. You visualize a specific location in a physical space, like a house, and put a piece of information in each room. Then when you need to recall, you "walk" through the house and retrieve the information. She'd used this process often, and now, with the account and box numbers memorized, the "word house" would shield her money from Jackson's grasping hands.

Jackson gave her a scorching look. "This is not finished. And you're not going anywhere. I took your passport. And don't forget, one call to the Missouri police department and your ass will be arrested."

"You do that, and every lie you told about Daphne and every doctor and judge you paid off will be made public. Not to mention the little video I took that night you attacked me. You'll be back in prison so fast your head will spin." She returned his look with a defiant one. "Looks like we're at a stalemate."

It was time to change tactics. She softened her voice. "Okay, look. We're both reasonable people here. I'm sure we can plan to work this out in a way that's agreeable to both of us."

"What do you suggest?"

"Let's split the money and go our separate ways. Think of it as a severance package for me."

He was quiet for a long moment. "Here's the deal. You stay and throw me a welcome home party. I need to reestablish my presence here. I'll let you go but not yet. I'm sick of being married to you anyway. But . . . you're going to help me get Daphne back. It's time for her little idyll in California to come to an end."

Her mouth dropped open. "Daphne? What the hell are you talking about?"

He smiled. "Sit down. I'll fill you in."

7

AMBER

ackson's welcome home party was tonight. She should be strolling down the Champs-Élysées instead of stuck in Bishops Harbor, but until she played her part in Jackson's little scheme she was grounded with no passport. Amber soaked in the freestanding spa tub, anticipating with relish the looks of awe, and probably even disappointment, she would see on the faces of tonight's party guests. Every one of them would be happy to see her down and out, but none of them would ever entertain the thought of snubbing her or missing her party. Except for that bitch Meredith Stanton, that is. She remained true-blue to Daphne, and her iciness to Amber could have frozen the Sahara. As president of the Historical Society, and one of Bishops Harbor's most vaunted society bitches, Meredith practically had a stroke when Amber was nominated to the board, something that made Amber smile every time she thought about it. The woman might have oozed class and old money, but she was stuck in the last century with her Gerard Darel corduroys, Strathberry purses, and ubiquitous string of pearls.

She lifted a slender leg from the water and wiggled her toes. She was on top of the world, her bank account was fat, and she and Jackson were ready to move forward with their new agreement and plans. Suddenly the bathroom door opened and Jax came in, all noise and clatter.

"Mommy, Mommy," he squealed, running to the bathtub and plunging his small hands into the water.

Amber plopped her leg down with a splash and looked past him to Chloe, their nanny. "How many times do I have to tell you that I'm not to be disturbed while I'm in the bath?"

"I'm sorry. He was asking for you and I thought you might like to see him before the party. Since, you know, you'll be very busy once you've finished bathing."

Amber exhaled. "Fine. He can stay for a few minutes. But after that, as you said, I'll be very busy." She touched her son's cheek. He really was a pretty child, but how could he not be with Jackson and her as parents? She loved it when people admired Jax and told her how beautiful he was. It had been a while since Amber had seen a photograph of her other son, but she would bet anything he wasn't anywhere near as good-looking as Jax. Too bad. And too bad for him too that he was being raised by another woman. Oh well, it didn't matter. Jax was all hers, for now anyway. She smiled and gave his ear a gentle pinch. "How is Mama's little cutie pie. Have you been a good boy today?"

He giggled and did the part-talking, part-gibberish thing that was so tiresome. She'd enjoy him much more if he could actually speak in full intelligible sentences, but she supposed it would be at least another year before that happened and she would be gone by then. One thing she had done was to hire a French nanny for him just like the one Bella and Tallulah had had. Amber wasn't about to let those girls be the only Parrish children who could speak French. Amber herself had been taking lessons for the past year.

She let him continue playing in the water, at one point handing him the sea wool sponge to squeeze and dip and squeeze again, over and over. After fifteen minutes of this she reached out, tousling his hair, and said, "Okay, little one. It's time for you to go with Chloe," and nodded to the nanny.

After they'd gone, Amber stepped out of the tub, wrapping herself in a Turkish cotton towel. For tonight she'd chosen a very short, wildly colored paisley Versace, with slender straps that formed a V and a drape that fell gracefully across one hip. It was the perfect summer dress, sexy and refined at the same time. She smoothed a velvety lotion over her body until her skin glistened, moving on to her hair and makeup. When she finally slipped the dress over her shoulders, the feel of it against her naked body was delicious; no bra, no underwear, just the fine fabric caressing her skin. Standing in front of the mirror, she winked at her stunning reflection. Minimal makeup, hair pulled back in a glossy bun, toned and tanned arms and legs. Apart from her diamond engagement and wedding rings, the only jewelry she wore were enormous Roberto Coin gold hoop earrings. All eyes would be on her.

Amber had given the caterers detailed instructions and as she walked outside to the terrace and swimming pool, she saw with approval that all her directions had been followed to the letter. Multi-colored Hoi An silk lanterns hung from tree branches throughout the garden and lawn, and floating candle wish-lanterns skimmed across the surface of the pool water. Cloth-covered tables and chairs were placed on the terrace, which was illuminated with hundreds of flickering tea lights. The effect was otherworldly. At one end of the terrace a bar was set up, and Jackson stood there now, one elbow leaning casually on it, a drink in his hand.

"You're looking rather mouthwatering tonight," he said without expression as she approached.

Amber looked past him at the bartender who'd been in her bed earlier that morning. Her gaze rested on him for a split second and then she turned and smiled at Jackson. "All for my dear husband who is finally home."

Jackson let out a humorless laugh. "Right." He gulped down the remainder of his drink and put the empty glass on the bar. "Fill 'er up, buddy," he said, without looking at the bartender. "I see our first guests are arriving." He nodded toward the sliding glass wall that made the interior of the house flow to the outside terrace. "Shall we act the loving couple and greet them together?" He grabbed his refill with one hand and put his other arm around Amber's waist as they walked in step to welcome the first arrivals, Bob and Helene Lloyd.

"Amber, don't you look lovely. And, Jackson, it must feel wonderful to be home," Helene said.

"Thank you," Jackson said, and extended his hand. "Good to see you both."

"You too. Welcome back," Bob said, as they shook hands.

After a few minutes of small talk, Amber grew bored. "Will you excuse me, please, while I go check on something with the caterer?" she said with an apologetic smile, leaving Jackson with the Lloyds as she moved away from the trio.

Amber hadn't missed the strained smile and once-over from Helene. Along with Meredith Stanton and her husband, Randolph, Lloyd and Helene were at the pinnacle of Bishops Harbor's social pecking order and winning them over had been a coup for Amber. It had taken time and ingenuity, but that was something Amber had in spades. Helene was the chairperson for the garden club's annual Kentucky Derby party. Amber had been a lowly committee member, relegated to set up and clean up. An hour before the party, she had disabled the Wi-Fi with the handy device she'd bought on Amazon. She thought Helene was going to have a stroke. How were they going to watch the race? Amber let her run around in a tizzy for a good fifteen minutes before she offered to run home and get an HDMI cable. Helene had looked at her with a puzzled and annoyed expression.

"What good is that going to do? No one can figure out why the Wi-Fi is down. This is a disaster."

Amber calmly explained. "I can stream the race on my phone using data and connect my phone to the television, which is already connected to the large screen."

"You know how to do that?"

Amber smiled at her. "Yes, I've run a few events myself." She couldn't help adding, "One must always be prepared for every contingency." After that Helene magically remembered her name and

ceased publicly snubbing her. Of course, the friendship was super-
ficial at best, but having Helene as a bosom buddy was of no interest to Amber. She was interested only in being seen with her. And
the thorn in Meredith's side was an added bonus.

Amber strolled through the crowd greeting guests and stopping
briefly to speak with the caterer when she spotted Remi Whitlock
talking with a group of people. Remi's husband, Norris, was in
Paris on business tonight. Amber picked up her pace and walked
over to her.

"Remi, I'm so glad to see you. I thought you would be in Paris
with Norris," Amber said, giving her a quick hug.

"I'm leaving next week."

"You changed your plans to be here tonight?"

"But of course. Norris could not change his plans, unfortunately,
but I wouldn't have missed Jackson's homecoming," Remi said.

"He's happy to be home."

"And you, *mon petit oiseau,* look quite *magnifique.* You are happy
too, I see." Remi's eyes twinkled with merriment.

"*Mais naturellement.*" Amber smiled.

Remi Whitlock, the woman who'd referred Amber to her lawyer, was the epitome of unstudied elegance and chic. From the moment Amber met her, she'd been a bit in awe of Remi's relaxed
self-assurance and her captivating charm. It wasn't even that she
was beautiful, because she wasn't, but she had a certain allure that
was intriguing, and her French accent only added to it. Remi was
enormously wealthy with dwellings in Paris, New York, London,
and Saint Bart's, in addition to her Bishops Harbor home. The
woman was self-made, although the details of how she'd amassed
such a fortune were hazy. There was talk of art deals and a goods
broker in Belgium, but Amber never probed too closely. She sensed
an element of danger, and her instincts told her she'd be better off
not knowing too much about Remi's past.

She was the closest thing Amber had to a friend, but Amber
didn't really need friends and never had. She'd never understood

how her sisters could spend hours on the phone with their besties, spilling all their secrets.

Amber had never felt judged by the Frenchwoman, unlike the vibe she got from most other women in Bishops Harbor. A painter of fine arts, Remi appreciated Amber's interest in and knowledge of art, and together they made frequent trips to the Met, MoMA, and other New York museums and galleries. Being with Remi had improved Amber's French to the point where she could now proudly scan *Le Monde* and discuss news stories with Remi fluently. The funny thing was that from the beginning Amber recognized a look in Remi's eyes that said, *I see what you are, and I find you interesting.* There was something Amber respected in that. And if the relationship between the two women wasn't exactly what Amber would call a friendship, it filled something inside of Amber that she couldn't quite name.

Tonight, Remi wore a simple white sheath that looked as if it had been custom made for her, and her chestnut hair, parted in the middle, was pulled into a loose bun at the nape of her graceful neck. But it was the exquisite necklace around that neck that grabbed Amber's attention. Row after row of delicate gold leaves shimmered against Remi's skin, like foliage tumbling from an aspen tree. Amber loved the striking originality of it.

"Remi, your necklace is stunning. I've never seen anything like it."

"Isn't it wonderful? A White Orchid design. They have quite marvelous things."

"White Orchid. Who carries the line?" Amber filed away the name in her head.

"No one. One buys directly."

"You're being very mysterious, Remi. Now tell me how I can see their designs."

"You are in luck, my dear. There is a trunk show in New York on the eleventh. Very exclusive invitation list, but if you'd like, you can come with me."

"Oh, yes, I would love that. The eleventh. It's a date." As they parted, Amber smiled to herself, anticipating the event. She would reward herself with a scrumptious little present. After all, she was a multimillionaire now.

Over the next half hour, the outdoors was buzzing with chatter, loud laughter, the clinking of glasses. After she'd made her rounds, Amber stood back, away from the crowd, and watched. She observed these people who would never be real friends to her, the women comparing and appraising one another, their bodies put through rigorous workouts, polished and buffed, never an ounce of fat. It was hard work to stay ahead of the game, but it was worth every hour of sweat at the gym, every skipped meal. Amber, however, would always be more than a pretty, but vacuous, face. An unfortunate incident in Texas had taught her that good looks and cunning were not enough. The key to this world was knowledge, the more the better. Amber never stopped studying, from fine literature and history to financial markets and investing. The subjects were diverse, often difficult, and she dug into each one with purpose and commitment. She would never let herself be taken off guard again.

She took a sip of her sparkling water, her eyes following Jackson who moved from group to group. She had to admit that he looked great, and judging by the looks he was getting, most of the women here agreed with her. If they only knew what a shit he was. Not that it was a problem for her any longer. She smiled, picturing all those lovely little gems that had magically filled her bank account with millions. Except, of course, for the three she'd kept for emergencies.

"Amber!" Bunny's loud voice made Amber turn. She came rushing over, her husband trailing behind her. "You look amazing," Bunny said.

"Thanks. Good to see you both," Amber said.

"That dress. Fabulous," Bunny went on. "Doesn't she look fabulous, March?" Her collagen-infused lips, a bright velvet red, parted in a wide grin.

"Yes indeed. Nice party, Amber," March said.

March was aging, Amber thought, and standing next to his much younger wife made it that much more apparent, the hot pink dress hugging her sculpted body making him look old and frail next to her. She supposed there was something to be said for men who stuck with their original spouses and aged together with them. Poor March looked like his succession of young wives had taken its toll.

"Oh pooh." Bunny held up her glass and looked at March. "I'm all empty. Honey, would you be a dear and get me a little drink?"

The moment he walked away, she took Amber's arm in hers. "I've been wanting to talk to you all day," she said breathlessly.

"What is it?"

"Well, I was at the club yesterday and I ran into Lesley Fielding. I'd just finished a game of tennis and she was playing doubles on the court next to me. She's a good friend of Melinda Monahan's. I was going to head right to the locker room, but then I decided to wait until—"

Amber suppressed the urge to roll her eyes. "Get to the point, Bunny."

"Right. The Monahans are in Europe for the summer and they're renting out their fabulous house on the Sound. You know the one."

"So what?"

"So, a friend of Meredith's is renting it for the entire summer. It's someone from California. And the way Lesley spoke, it sounded like it's a woman. Without a husband. And with children." Bunny stopped speaking and gave Amber a long look. "I think it's Daphne."

"Daphne? Why on earth would she rent a house in Bishops Harbor?" Amber feigned ignorance.

Bunny shrugged. "I don't know. Maybe you should ask Jackson."

Amber simply nodded. She was well aware of Daphne's return to Bishops Harbor. Sweet Daphne was going to be very sorry that she'd decided to come back. But Amber couldn't have cared less about what awaited Daphne. Once Amber helped Jackson execute his plan against Daphne, Amber would be long gone.

8

DAISY ANN

aisy Ann checked her watch and saw that they were ten minutes early as their car passed through the open gates and around the circular driveway to her in-laws' home. A valet stood waiting to take their keys and park the Suburban while another one opened her door.

"Thank you," she said to him and stepped out of the vehicle.

She looked up at the enormous house as she, Mason, and the boys walked up the steps to the columned portico and front doors. The Briscoes' home was twice as large and twice as formal as Mason's and hers. It boasted three stories of cream-colored walls, furniture, and terrazzo tile, and Daisy Ann had often wondered how Birdie had raised three rambunctious boys in the elegant and pristine surroundings. She had to admit, though, that her own sons always loved coming here. With its game room, screening room, outdoor playhouse *and* treehouse, and plenty of toys and games to keep them busy, Tucker and Greyson were in heaven, and Birdie was guaranteed that children would spend little time on silk-covered furnishings. The boys each had their own bedroom for when they visited, which was not a problem in a house with nine of them to go around. The property was situated on three acres that accommodated tennis courts and the oversize in-ground pool and cabanas.

"Ah, my sweethearts," Birdie said, giving each of them a hug and kiss.

When Birdie leaned close to her, Daisy Ann breathed in the heady scent of her mother-in-law's signature perfume, Grand Soir. Birdie's blond hair was teased and set to a perfect bob—she had it done at the "beauty shop" twice a week. Her makeup was understated and perfectly applied and on her lips her signature Dior Rouge. Her slim figure, kept that way by a strict diet protocol from which she rarely wavered, was clad in a multicolored pastel Chanel halter dress of flowing silk. In fact, Birdie wore almost nothing but Chanel and had for as long as Daisy Ann had known her.

"You're the first ones here." Birdie took Daisy Ann's hand. "You look just beautiful," she said, and turned to Tucker and Greyson. "And you boys look mighty handsome." Her brow furrowed, and she took one of Tucker's hands in her own.

"Tucker, honey, your nails! They need a good scrubbing. Go into the kitchen and find Freida. She'll help you."

He groaned. "Aw, come on, Mimi, I wanna go see the carnival rides you got."

She gave him a stern look. "Now mind your manners, there's plenty of time for that. "You know what they say, cleanliness is next to godliness. Now scoot."

He gave Daisy Ann a beseeching look, but even though she found Birdie over the top at times, she shook her head and said, "Mind your mimi and do what she told you."

Greyson held his hands up for inspection. "How are my hands, Mimi?"

Birdie smiled. "Like a real gentleman's."

He beamed and gave his brother a slight snicker.

Mason took his mother in his arms, kissing her. "Happy birthday, Mother."

"Thank you, dear." Birdie smiled and patted his cheek, then fluffed her hair on the side he'd pressed against. "Now come, all of you, and see what my fabulous caterer has done."

It was the perfect house for entertaining, with lots of intimate seating areas and large rooms that flowed easily into one another.

Tonight, the entire first floor was decorated with white and gold balloons, hundreds of gold candles flickering luminously, and opulent bunches of gold and white flowers. A large, curved projection screen played a loop of photographs of Birdie with family and friends through the years.

Birdie Briscoe was something of an icon in Dallas society. Her family went way back. Her great-great-grandfather had arrived in Texas in the early 1800s and begun buying up land—she still had the original Spanish land grant from 1825. By the time Birdie came along, the family had already made millions from the extensive stands of timber that grew on the vast amount of acreage. Her husband, Chandler, Mason's father, had family roots that were not quite as deep as Birdie's. Chandler's great-grandfather founded the land development firm of Briscoe, Dixon, and Hart, and all the ensuing progeny had worked for the firm. Until Mason that is. He became a lawyer and left the company.

Generational Texas wealth and blood ran through Birdie's veins, and she had the added bonus of regal bearing and beauty. She loved telling the story of how Carrie Neiman, the cofounder of Neiman Marcus, had traveled to New York with Birdie's mother in 1921 to help her choose a wedding gown, and Birdie herself was a loyal Neiman customer. Daisy Ann had never seen her mother-in-law— nor had anyone, actually—dressed in any way but impeccably, whether it was a Saturday barbecue or a formal evening event. She looked nowhere near her seventy-five years, an accomplishment due not to surgeries or fillers, but to her enviable genes. She was strong-willed, with exacting standards of what good behavior demanded of her and others, and she was used to getting her way.

"Is that my wayward son I hear?" Chandler Briscoe's voice boomed through the hallway as he came bounding down the stairs. Daisy Ann didn't miss the pained look on Mason's face at his father's choice of words. A straw Stetson in one hand, he put his other around Daisy Ann's shoulder and gave it a tight squeeze. "Howdy, honey." He then extended a hand for Mason to shake. Anyone see-

ing the two men together would know immediately that they were
father and son. In fact, Mason was the son who most resembled his
father, with the same green eyes and tall full-bodied frame. And
although Chandler's hair was now a dazzling white, it was every bit
as thick and wavy as his son's.

"Hi, Daddy," Mason said. "Looks like it's gonna be a great party."

"Yes, they've done a fantastic job. Everything looks gorgeous,"
Daisy Ann agreed.

Chandler laughed. "I can't take credit. Your mother did it all."

Daisy Ann knew what that actually meant was that Birdie had
directed the party planner. This shindig had been in the works for
months now.

"I hear voices. Sounds like the party's getting started." Birdie's
dark blue eyes flashed with excitement. "Why don't y'all get a drink
while I go greet my guests."

"Mama, can we go see the rides now?" Tucker asked. Birdie had
told them about the children's funfair rides she'd ordered for all the
kids weeks ago.

"Sure. You guys go ahead and have fun."

They were off and running before Daisy Ann finished the sentence. She laughed and took Mason's hand. "Let's get a drink." Together they walked outside where several bars were set up under a
clear top tent that covered a huge expanse of lawn. A string quartet
played relaxing classical music during the cocktail hour. Chandler's
birthday surprise, however, was that Willie Nelson would be head-
lining later tonight—not the country band the planner had told
Birdie would be performing. Daisy Ann was as excited as a school-
girl when she'd found out.

She and Mason walked over to one of the bars where he ordered
his usual—a whiskey neat. Daisy Ann accepted a drink from one of
the roving waiters and took a sip. "Mmm. Sure you don't want to
change your mind? This margarita is perfect."

"I'm good," he said as they started to walk toward the center of
the tent to mingle, passing tiered tables laden with trays of food, a

sampling of which included smoked salmon, shrimp, rare roast beef, and delectable-looking nibbles. The choices went on and on. Champagne flowed, and plump ruby red strawberries and other fruits were mounded around a large assortment of cheeses. The most spectacular table was the one upon which sat the birthday cakes. Not one, but ten cakes, all spectacularly decorated and mouth-wateringly exquisite. Daisy Ann could just imagine what the kids' food tent contained. "Mother's in her element tonight. Center of attention and charming hostess with the mostest."

Daisy Ann thought the description was apt for a woman who could seem vain and arrogant but could also charm the birds out of the trees. As a mother-in-law, she could be tough at times and supportive at others, and in the beginning, Daisy Ann often felt like she was on a bucking bronco. When she and Mason got engaged, Birdie had gone into high gear, forcefully voicing her opinions on how everything, from the announcement and engagement party to the wedding itself and all things in between, should play out. Daisy Ann was ready to explode and had gone to her mother. She remembered the conversation as if it were yesterday.

"Mama, I can't take it anymore. She's driving me batty. I want to tell her to keep her big mouth shut and screw off." She was almost shouting.

"Daisy Ann. Language!" Marylou Ann, Daisy Ann's mother, had tried to defuse her daughter's anger. "She's excited, that's all. She just wants to feel a part of things. You should be glad that she's happy about the engagement."

"Of course she's happy. Why wouldn't she be?" But Daisy Ann knew that her mother was referring to Birdie's old family name and money, and although the Crawfords were every bit as rich as the Briscoes, they were profoundly nouveau.

"Yes, yes. I agree. I'm only telling you to be thankful that everyone is pleased because that's not always the case. And maybe you should try and be a little patient with Birdie. After all, she only has sons. She's not used to having a daughter."

"I *have* been patient. I'm sick of it. I want her to butt out and let us plan things our way."

Her mother gave her a look that she'd come to know would be followed by words of wisdom. "This is your wedding, my darling girl, and I understand that you're picturing exactly how you want it to be. It's also just one day in your life. A day that will be so busy and hectic and thrilling that much of it will be a big blur to you afterward. Your mother-in-law, however, will be part of your life for years to come. The last thing you want is to get this relationship off on the wrong foot. You will regret it for the rest of your life." Her mother had taken her daughter's hand and said, "I know you. You're not unkind. You know how to compromise. And I trust you to handle this with grace and thoughtfulness so that everyone is happy in the end."

It had been good advice, advice Daisy Ann had taken to heart. And when six months later Daisy Ann's mother died, Birdie was there for her. It was then that she saw the other side to this imperious woman—the side that could be tender and compassionate, and she became Daisy Ann's rock in those heartbroken months that followed.

She took another sip of her drink and saw that the house and grounds were filling with people and the party was now fully under way. Birdie's social circles were wide and diverse, and the guests ranged in age from their twenties all the way up to their eighties and nineties. If it was true that a party could be judged not by who's there, but who's not there, then Birdie's parties were always a resounding success. Anyone who was anyone was there. It was a sparkling array of designer fashion, both subtle and glittering, lavish jewels worth a fortune, elegant high heels, and even one woman in a pair of luxurious Philipp Plein boots despite the summer heat. Chandler had shown Daisy Ann the birthday gift he'd bought for Birdie—a three-strand oval diamond necklace for which he paid $176,000.

"Is that the governor over there?" Daisy Ann whispered to Mason. She couldn't tell with the cowboy hat and sunglasses he was wearing.

"Looks like it. Let's walk over."

Daisy Ann saw that the governor was talking to Wade Ashford. Damn. She hadn't realized that Wade would be here tonight. He was supposed to have been out of town. It was going to take a bit of fancy footwork to avoid him tonight, but there was no way she was going to let him corner her with her family around.

"I'll let you go and say hello, I'm going to check on the boys."

As she made her way out of the tent and down the path to the rides, she stopped several times to say hello to arriving guests.

"Running out on the party so soon?"

Daisy Ann spun around and forced herself to smile at her sister-in-law. Rose Sheridan Briscoe stared at Daisy Ann, a smirk on her pretty face. She was a southern belle through and through and butter wouldn't melt in her mouth, but she never missed the opportunity to get her digs in.

"I was just going to check on Greyson and Tucker," Daisy Ann said.

Rose tilted her head. "They're with their cousins and the younger folk down at the kids' corral. Birdie hired a band for the young set. They're havin' a good old time. So, no need for you to go running off, although why should it surprise me that you'd shirk your duties to this family."

Daisy Ann put her hands on her hips and felt the heat rise to her face. "Are you still going on about that? It was over a month ago. I had an important meeting I couldn't miss. How many times do you expect me to apologize?"

"Yes, we all know how much more important you are than the rest of us."

Daisy Ann wanted to slug her.

Rose shook her head and sighed dramatically. "I'm just sayin' . . . everyone else managed to be there for Birdie while Chandler was rushed into emergency surgery. Poor Mason kept looking at his phone, waiting for you to text him, I guess. But then again, Mason chose your family over his own anyhow. You are two peas in a pod."

Mason was the only one of the three sons who hadn't gone to work for Briscoe, Dixon, and Hart. The law had always called to him and after two years trying to fit in with his brothers, he'd quit and gone to law school, then taken a position at her father's oil company when he graduated. Her father, Jake, had come to love Mason like a son, and the two men became extremely close over the years. Mason was a lot like her father in many ways. Both of them strong and determined, hard workers with bold ideas, but never proud or arrogant. Her father had always said *Think big, but act with humility.* There was something exceptional about men who could be trailblazing leaders and still possess the common touch. No one was surprised when Mason, along with Daisy Ann, rose to the top hierarchy of the company, and he became its head after Jake's death.

The Briscoe family never failed to bring up what they considered Mason's misplaced loyalty, Chandler especially ribbing him about his "defection." Mason let it roll off his shoulders, but Daisy Ann knew that it bothered him. Being a Briscoe came with high expectations. This family insisted that everyone do everything together. Sunday dinners at Birdie and Chandler's no matter what, every holiday and birth, every birthday party and baptism, and on and on celebrated together. All the children and grandchildren spent a month in the summer at Birdie and Chandler's Jackson Hole compound. Daisy Ann's father had been a sport and gone along with it, became part of the clan, and the Briscoes had adored him, more than happy to include him in everything. She didn't know what would have happened if she'd had other siblings, or if her mother hadn't died. Once you married a Briscoe, they swallowed you up.

"Oh, for heaven's sake. I don't have time for this. Chandler had his appendix out, not heart surgery! It's not normal for a family to spend as much time together as this one. I'm sure the waiting room was filled to overflowing and annoying the hospital staff anyhow."

"Whatever you have to tell yourself. But maybe if you tried a little harder, you might actually enjoy being a part of this family."

"I do enjoy the family. Most of the members anyway." She gave Rose a pointed look.

"Well, I never . . ."

"That's the problem. You never know when to shut up." Daisy Ann stormed off, leaving Rose standing there. The woman was a pain in the ass and had been since the day she'd married Mason. Daisy Ann had tried to befriend her, had even asked her to be a bridesmaid in the wedding. Rose accepted but made a fuss about everything. The bridesmaid dress wasn't her color, she didn't like the flowers she had to hold, she wanted to walk with her husband, but he was the best man and there was no way Daisy Ann was making Rose her maid of honor. From the start, Rose had been threatened by Daisy Ann and was always kissing up to Birdie, *yes Birdie this* and *yes Birdie that.* Over the years Rose had grown even more jealous of Daisy Ann when she'd seen how close she was to Birdie despite speaking up when she didn't agree with something Birdie said or did. Daisy Ann had earned Birdie's grudging respect because she wasn't a mealymouthed scaredy-cat like Rose. And it burned Rose too that Mason was the apple of Birdie's eye. Her sister-in-law never tired of reminding her that it was her own husband, Royce, who was taking a load off Chandler by being his second-in-command. Daisy Ann hoped that Mason's middle brother, Franklin, would one day marry someone normal and then she'd have an ally against Rose, but thus far Franklin appeared to be a confirmed bachelor.

Still fuming, Daisy Ann rejoined the party and went looking for her husband. Grabbing another margarita from a passing waiter, she took a big sip. She was going to need a lot of tequila to get through the rest of the evening.

9

DAPHNE

My nerves are frayed as I wait for the Uber to pick us up from Westchester County Airport.

"Mom, how much longer?" Bella whines, stomping her sneaker-clad foot on the sidewalk.

I glance at my phone. "Just a couple more minutes."

"Why couldn't Dad pick us up?" Tallulah asks for the hundredth time. I'm already regretting my decision to come back. It's been only a couple of weeks since I made the call to Jackson to feel him out about our spending the summer here. He'd been released a few days before and I wasn't sure how he'd react. I was totally unprepared for how friendly he was, how un-Jackson-like his conciliatory tone and expressions of remorse. He apologized for everything, told me he was a changed man, and thanked me over and over for the chance to be back in the girls' lives. I didn't believe a word of it. But once I opened the door, there was no need for Tallulah and Bella to hide the fact that they were in contact with him. And so he knew exactly when we were arriving and had offered to pick us up. He was already encroaching on us in typical Jackson style, and I warned him that if he didn't let me set the pace, we'd be back on a plane to California, and he wouldn't see the girls until they were adults.

"Lu, let's not argue, please. We're going to get settled in, and you'll see your father tomorrow."

I receive a sullen look in response.

"I hope the house is nice," Bella says. "It's on the beach, right?"

"Yes, Meredith found us a great little cottage right on the beach near her summer house."

"I don't care where it is as long as it's close to Dad's house," Tallulah says.

I give her a tight smile and pick up the bags as a blue Volvo, our Uber, pulls up and we get in. While we drive, closing the distance between my old and my new life, I brace myself to prepare for the two to collide.

Meredith is waiting when we pull up, the door to the house wide open. She stretches out her arms to Bella and Tallulah and envelops each in a warm embrace. "I've missed you girls!"

Bella gives her a shy smile, and Tallulah looks at me as she answers. "We miss being here too. I'm happy to be back." With that she picks up her suitcase and stomps into the house.

I lock glances with Meredith who knows the whole story and she gives me a sympathetic eyebrow raise.

"Come on, I'll help you get settled." She picks up two suitcases and I grab two more, following behind her. We put the luggage down and Meredith gives us a quick tour.

The "cottage" is in actuality a five-bedroom Nantucket-style house on a point of land that feels safe and secluded. The interior is calm and tranquil, all blue and white, making the space cozy and inviting despite the size. An in-ground saltwater pool overlooks Long Island Sound.

"This is gorgeous, Mer, but we don't need something this big."

She waves a hand. "It's nice to have space. Besides, the Monahans are in Europe all summer and are thrilled to have someone looking after the place."

A sense of unease overtakes me, but I don't want to seem ungrateful. The house is not quite as grand as the one we lived in with Jackson, but it comes close. My girls have become content with much simpler surroundings, and I want to keep it that way. This doesn't feel like the most auspicious start to our summer.

I smile at Meredith. "Well, at least I know one of the neighbors is friendly."

We laugh as Bella and Tallulah come running downstairs in their bathing suits. "Can we go swimming?" Bella asks.

"Sure. Pool or beach?"

"Pool!" they both squeal.

"Do you want to catch up later, or do you want to come sit with me while I watch them?" I ask Meredith.

"I'll stay. Let me grab some waters from the fridge. I stocked everything for you this morning."

"Thank you. So thoughtful of you."

Meredith and I sit in the lounge chairs by the waterfall as Bella and Tallulah take turns going down the sliding board into the kidney-shaped pool.

Meredith's eyes crinkle as she smiles at me. "It's so good to have you here, Daph. I've missed you. It's not the same without you."

"I've missed you too. I wish I could steal you away to California with me."

"You love it there, don't you?"

"I do. It's been a sanctuary for all of us. Well, with the exception of Tallulah that is. Things were going so well at the beginning. The girls loved the school and the neighborhood, made lots of friends. Having my mom with us was and is a godsend. She's been absolutely wonderful." I feel the tears ready to spill over. "It's so comforting to have someone to help right the ship when I'm unsteady. I still can't shake the guilt I feel, how I allowed Jackson to keep her at arm's length for so many years." My mother isn't the only one I had to pretend with. Meredith had no idea that Jackson was abusive until after I had freed myself from him. There were so many times over the years that I longed to tell her the truth, but I hadn't dared. Meredith wasn't like the other women in my social circle. She was a genuine friend, one who cared nothing for outward appearances or social status. She was old money, raised to appreciate authenticity and loyalty. If I confided in her, I knew she would have done everything in her power to help me, but I couldn't risk losing my children. Jackson held that threat over my head every single day, reminding me that with one phone call he could use his sway to have me committed again for the psychosis he and the doctors had fabricated when Tallulah was just a baby.

When I finally told her the truth, after Jackson and I were getting divorced, Meredith wanted his head. She wanted to expose him, ruin his reputation in Bishops Harbor society. But I made her promise to keep quiet. In return for my silence, Jackson agreed to give me full custody of the girls. So Meredith never told a soul.

She puts her hand on my arm. "You were a victim, Daphne. In an abusive marriage. But you had the courage to free yourself and start over. That's something to be proud of, not feel guilty about."

"Intellectually, I know that. Believing it in my heart is another matter. I can't imagine how heartbroken I would feel if Tallulah or Bella cut me out of their lives the way Jackson made me do to my mother. It's another reason I think she was so dead set against my coming here. She's been a victim of Jackson too."

"It's behind you now. It's time to look ahead."

We're both quiet, deep in our own thoughts, until Meredith speaks. "Speaking of looking ahead, tell me a little about this man you've met. Sebastian, is it?"

I smile at the mention of his name. "Yes. He made an extremely generous donation to Julie's Smile. In fact, it was integral to my being able to buy the building where it's headquartered."

"Wow. How wonderful. What does he do?"

"International finance. He invests in other companies. He's very suave and at first, I was a little hesitant, but when I opened up about my history with Jackson, he was so supportive. Totally let me set the pace. He's been very patient."

"He sounds like a good man." She smiles at me and there's a twinkle in her eyes. "Is he someone you see yourself with long term?"

I sigh. "You know, Mer, I can't even think in those terms yet. We've talked about taking things to the next level. Neither my mother nor the girls have met him. It's too soon. But here's the thing. Meeting someone like him, seeing his compassion for those less fortunate, watching him give his help so freely and asking for nothing in return—well, it's reminded me that not all men have hidden agendas. He'd like things to get more serious. We were thinking of going away for a weekend together, but now, of course, I'm here. I'll see what happens when I'm back home."

"Sounds promising." Meredith sits up straight, clapping her hands together, and the gold bangles on her wrist make a jingling sound. "You know what we need?" she says with spirit. "One of our old-time beach nights. You and me, a bottle of red, and a full moon. We'll sit and talk till four in the morning like we used to and solve the whole world's problems."

I squeeze her hand. "Those were great times. You helped me keep my sanity."

"You're my best friend, Daph. Always will be."

I feel a lump in my throat and nod at her, unable to speak for a moment. Trying hard not to let myself be overcome with emotion. "So," I change course, "you'll have to catch me up on all the happenings here later on." I nod toward the girls.

She leans over and whispers. "I will. I have all the dirt on the little welcome home party thrown in the honor of a certain ex-con."

I start to chuckle, but the laugh turns to a gasp when I see a man walk up from the beach and open the gate to the pool. Jackson. He wasn't supposed to come here until tomorrow—I had clearly established my expectations, and he had given me his word to abide by them. But I know better than anyone, Jackson's word is worth about as much as an umbrella in a tornado.

10

DAISY ANN

As she waited for Wade Ashford to arrive, Daisy Ann absently fingered the necklace she wore. The design was her mother's, the first piece she'd fashioned and created over twenty-five years ago, after years of art and metal classes. The piece was a simple and elegant mixture of metals entwined and interwoven, and Daisy Ann, just ten years old at the time, had thought it one of the most beautiful necklaces she'd ever seen. Daisy Ann would sit on the bench in her mother's workroom, watching with fascination as her mother's hammer and tools manipulated metal to coil around precious and semiprecious stones or curl and bend to her blueprint. Sitting at her mother's side, she learned about the different metals like indium, rhenium, and ruthenium, a metal strong and beautiful like platinum, but at $72 an ounce, a much more affordable one than the $1,460 an ounce for platinum, the most expensive metal of all and more costly than gold. Marylou gifted many of the rings, bracelets, and necklaces she made to friends and family, but the collection still remained extensive upon her death.

On a pleasant Dallas evening a few years after her mother died, Daisy Ann, in a backless red gown and one of her mother's necklaces with a dazzling jade center, stood talking with a group of friends at the fundraising ball for the Dallas Museum of Art. As the group disbanded, she began making her way into one of the galleries when she felt a light tap on her shoulder and turned.

The tall man with a silver ponytail was debonair-looking and a stranger to her. "Pardon my forwardness," he said, bowing slightly. "My name is Rory Delacorte. I'm a silversmith. Your necklace is very beautiful. May I ask who designed it?"

Daisy Ann moved her hand to the necklace. "My mother."

His eyes widened in surprise. "Your mother is a jewelry designer? Are her pieces sold somewhere?"

It had all begun with that chance meeting. Together they created a website showcasing Marylou's creations, all of which sold out almost immediately. Daisy Ann hired Rory to begin fabricating more handmade jewelry from the many drawings her mother left and to head the operation they named White Orchid Designs, after her mother's favorite flower. At the beginning, Daisy Ann had continued to work with her father's oil company. But three years ago, when Jake died, Daisy Ann left her father's company, leaving her husband in charge, and dedicated herself to White Orchid. The company now included designers, a marketing team, and sales staff, and to Daisy Ann's delight, it continued to grow. Their business office was in a converted feed store in uptown Dallas, and Daisy Ann loved spending time there. For her, it was not only a labor of love but also a tribute to the mother she'd lost so early. There were times she felt as if Marylou's spirit was right alongside her as she worked.

Her assistant buzzed, and she picked up the phone.

"Yes?"

"Mr. Ashford's here."

"Thank you. Please send him in."

The door opened and Wade entered, his six-foot-four frame making her office suddenly seem smaller. He took his hat off, threw it on the love seat behind him, and took a seat in the chair in front of her desk.

"Well, Daisy Ann, you're harder to pin down than a feather in the wind."

She gave him her sweetest smile. "I'm here now, Wade. You know how busy things have been."

"I've been patient, but my investment in your company is not paying the dividends I expect."

They stared at each other for a moment, both silent, and she'd be damned if she'd look away first. Finally, he broke contact and then she spoke.

"I've told you before, this is temporary. We've had a tough eighteen months. So has everyone else. The pandemic took a bite out of our sales, but I'm confident we're going to make up for the shortfall in sales in no time. I wouldn't have made a personal loan to the company if I didn't believe that."

"That's all well and good, but materials have gone up, labor, et cetera. If we want to be profitable again, something's gotta give. No one is going to notice if you save some money by automating labor or using cheaper materials. People have no clue."

"You may have no clue. But our customers do, and I won't compromise on the quality of our goods just to save a buck."

He shook his head. "It's mighty fine to have your high standards, missy. But standards don't pay the bills. I want to see my investment yield returns again. I'm not much for charity, you know."

Now she was pissed. "Give it time. You know as well as I do that there are ups and downs in business. Don't you dare act like what you've done is charity. This has been a very profitable business until recently. You came to me, remember? Said you were looking to diversify. Your initial investment has already netted you four times what you put in. Now you're whining because one rough patch has stalled profits? Please. That's what you signed up for. It's all in our agreement."

"True. But I don't want this small leak in profits to become a flood." He shifted in the seat. "Now lookie here, Valene Mart made you a generous purchase offer, an offer you dismissed out of hand. You need to think on that again."

"Absolutely not," Daisy Ann said, slamming her fist on the desk. "They'll turn this company into a cheap imitation, taking our one-of-a-kind pieces and mass-producing them using inferior materials."

"They'll sell a helluva lot more pieces that way. And you'd be gettin' a portion of those profits."

"You know my position on this. This company is not just about money. And I don't appreciate all the texts and trying to corner me at family functions."

"Sorry. I'm used to doing business at any function."

She stood up. "Well, that's the difference between you and me. I like to keep my business separate from my family and I'd appreciate if you'd respect that from now on."

He rose and took his hat from the cushion and bowed to her while holding it out.

"Whatever you say, little lady. Understood. My apologies. Here's hoping we're back in the black soon."

After he left, Daisy Ann pulled up the latest QuickBooks summary on her computer. She hadn't been completely honest when she said the shortfall was almost made up for. Their material costs had almost doubled, and while sales were up, they were still far below where they'd been prepandemic. If things didn't improve soon, she'd have to put more money in, and that felt like a defeat to her. But the last thing she would do is sell to Valene Mart. That would feel like losing her mother all over again.

11

DAPHNE

ackson is all smiles as he walks toward me. I feel like my insides
have turned to ice. Meredith and I exchange a quick look and
we both stand, she slightly in front of me as if to guard me.
Before I can react, both girls are out of the pool and Tallulah is running toward him. Bella, however, hangs back.

"Daddy!" Tallulah squeals as she throws herself into his arms.
Tears are streaming down her face, and she holds him so tightly as
if she never wants to let go. Bella watches warily.

Jackson finally lets Tallulah go and looks at Bella. "Hi, sweetheart," he says, kneeling down.

"Hi, Daddy." She takes one step closer and then he pulls her
toward him, still holding on to Tallulah's hand, and the three of
them stay that way for what seems like an eternity. Tallulah's sobs
make her shoulders shake, and a dagger pierces my heart. After a
few minutes, I slowly walk toward them, and he finally releases the
girls and looks at me.

"Daphne. You're looking well."

I give him a tight smile, tempering my response as Tallulah and
Bella are also looking at me, while each holds one of Jackson's
hands. His polo shirt and shorts are wet, but he doesn't seem to care.

"We agreed that you'd come tomorrow." I know he's appeared
without warning to deliberately throw me off guard. I lived with
him too long and know his gambits only too well.

"I'm sorry but I couldn't wait. Knowing that my girls were just five minutes away made me feel like I would burst. I had to see them." He kneels down and puts a hand on each of their cheeks, studying them. "You've both grown up so much. It's been so long."

Meredith leans over and whispers to me. "Do you want me to stay?"

"Yes," I half whisper to her. I'm torn in half looking at the three of them. It breaks my heart to see how hard this separation has really been on them, especially Tallulah. I don't know how I deluded myself into thinking that simply moving away and starting a new life would fill the void that his absence left. All I could think about was how his inclusion in their lives could destroy them, but the truth is that banning him from their lives could also destroy them.

"So . . . um, do you want to come and sit down or—"

He peels off his shirt and I can see that prison hasn't softened him at all—he's still in great shape. "I think I'll take a swim with the girls if that's okay with you. You and I can catch up after?" He looks at Meredith, unsmiling. "Hello, Meredith."

She nods at him but says nothing.

Jackson empties his pockets of his keys and cell phone and puts them on the table.

"Last one in is a rotten egg!" He bounces on the diving board and executes a perfect dive into the pool.

Tallulah jumps in after him and Bella is the last to get in. Tallulah is having the time of her life, and Bella is finally warming up, joining in the fun and laughter. It scares me to see how quickly she's thawed. She's still fragile and it worries me to think that she might let herself become vulnerable to Jackson's cruelty again.

I breathe deeply, in and out as I've learned from my therapist, and do my best to hide the fact that all I want to do is grab my daughters and run.

·　　·　　·

Hours later, Meredith has left, and the girls are finally settled in their rooms, although between the time difference and their excitement I don't expect them to be asleep for hours. I don't invite Jackson into the house, telling him I think we should sit outside on the deck where our discussion won't be overheard.

Jackson sits across from me, the amber light from the outdoor lamps highlighting his features. He hasn't lost his good looks but does appear to have aged at least five years. I suppose prison does that to a person. He glances over at the book sitting on the table next to him. It's the latest Dean Koontz. He raises an eyebrow just a hair, but enough for me to know what he's thinking. I flash back to the weekly discussions we used to have about classical literature. I have nothing against the classics, but being forced to read *Don Quixote* and *Moby-Dick* in my spare time while raising young children was not my idea of relaxing. With Jackson's near constant surveillance, my every spare moment was orchestrated by him, and lightheartedness of any kind was definitely taboo.

I take a sip from my bottle of water, composing in my head how to begin this conversation. I decide honesty is the best approach.

"This is not a good start. You weren't supposed to come here until tomorrow. If you don't accept the boundaries I've set, this isn't going to work." Sitting across from him, it's hard for me to forget the tyrannical hold he had on me all those years, and I remind myself that he can no longer control me. I sit up a little straighter and stare at him.

He holds my gaze for a moment, then looks down at his hands. When he speaks, his tone is gentle. "I'm sorry. You're right. I was just so anxious to see the girls. You can't imagine how much I miss both of them." He shrugs. "I know I don't deserve a second chance with them, but I'm grateful that you've given it to me, no matter what the reason." He takes a deep breath, tents his hands, and continues. "Daphne, I'm so sorry. I can never apologize enough for everything I put you through. I know you're only here for the girls, and that's fine, but I hope that one day you'll be able to find it in your heart to forgive me."

I don't recognize this Jackson—this man before me who appears humbled and contrite. And I don't for one minute believe a word he says. I know all too well what a good actor he can be.

"You're right. I'm here for the girls. I'm not interested in re-hashing the past. I've put it behind me and that's where I intend to leave it. I want to be perfectly clear about that. It's time for you to go now."

He puts his hand up. "Of course, of course." I stand and he follows suit, and I lead him around front to where he's parked. He stops before getting in the car. "Daphne. I hope you know, prison changed me. I've learned to face my mistakes, to try to make amends for those I've hurt, but I can see I've already overstepped. Tell me how I can help."

"You can help by not showing up unannounced. If it happens again, I'll be forced to take the girls home and cut this visit short."

He shakes his head. "I'm sorry. I should've waited until tomorrow. It won't happen again. I'm glad you're here."

"I'm warning you, one misstep, and I'll tell them everything. I've shielded them from how bad things were with you out of concern for their mental well-being. But if you get out of line . . ."

"I won't. Just tell me what I need to do."

"We need to attend family therapy sessions together, and you can't do anything to undermine me. No matter what you say about changing, you will not have unsupervised visits with the girls." I watch his face carefully, looking for the telltale vein that always let me know when his temper was flaring. But there's no change of expression, no evidence of suppressed rage. The old Jackson would never have abided being spoken to this way. But now that he doesn't have the upper hand, he has to appear to be okay with it. It makes me want to see how far I can push him. "I imagine your calendar is fairly open right now. You've not secured employment yet, have you?"

He laughs, a genuine laugh, amusement suffusing his face. "Still the tactful Daphne. Jailbird's not exactly on any job requirement list right now. I'll be figuring out how to start over on my own again. I'm completely at your disposal for therapy appointments, supervised visits, whatever." He turns his hands palms up. "As I said. I'm just grateful for the chance to spend some time with our daughters. All on your terms."

"Okay, then. I'll text you the name of the therapist who's been recommended to me. I'd like for us to meet with her before you have another visit with the girls."

"Whatever you say." He opens his car door and gets in then calls out to me. "Oh, by the way, I'd really like little Jax to get to know his sisters this summer. Are you okay with that?"

I immediately think of Amber and what she'll say about this, but I don't mention her name. "Of course. I know they'd both like that very much."

He smiles at me. "Good night, Daph. See you soon."

I cringe at his use of my nickname. I don't answer, but simply turn and walk to the front door. I hear a noise and look up. Tallulah's at the upstairs window and I realize she's heard the entire exchange. She shakes her head, shooting me a dirty look, and slams the window shut.

12

AMBER

A mber stood at the front door waiting for Remi. The two of them planned to drive into New York, go to the jewelry presentation, and have dinner afterward. Amber had never attended a trunk show, so she had done a little reading about them beforehand. Apparently, the current trend was to do these events virtually, with goods offered and purchases completed online. The White Orchid Designs show, however, was strictly in person and was being held at the Baccarat Hotel to reveal new creations not yet for sale to the general public. The designers would be there to answer questions and, Amber assumed, proudly parade themselves before the adoring attendees.

When Remi's Chiron pulled up, Amber threw her shoulders back and, raising her head slightly, strode to the car.

"Hi. Thanks for driving," she said as she slid into the soft seat of the bright orange and black interior.

"Of course. I'm glad to have company." Remi put the car in gear, and they sped off. The combination of Bugatti and Remi's driving always gave Amber the feeling of being launched from a rocket.

As they sped along the Merritt, Remi ricocheted from lane to lane, passing anyone doing less than eighty. "How long have you been training for Le Mans?" Amber asked.

Remi's silvery laugh filled the small space. "I am impatient, no? Am I frightening you?"

"Not at all. Impatient people don't wait for things to happen. They make them happen."

Remi looked briefly at Amber and then back to the road ahead. "Hmm. That is quite a philosophy you have there."

"Well, obviously impatience must be undergirded with patience. If that makes sense."

Remi nodded and smiled, her eyes still locked on the road, and Amber admired her profile—the straight nose and high cheekbone. As always, Remi looked perfect. Around her neck she wore a pearl choker, a perfect complement to her white silk wrap dress. Amber had chosen to wear a simple black dress, sleeveless and fitted. At the last minute she'd taken off the diamond studs and replaced them with small gold earrings, then slipped on a wide gold bangle and her wedding rings. She'd admired herself in the mirror, feeling sophisticated and chic, but somehow Amber never felt she quite measured up to Remi's matchless style.

The hour-and-fifteen-minute drive from Bishops Harbor to Manhattan took Remi fifty-five minutes, and they pulled up to the Baccarat with time to spare. Amber saw the hotel valet's eyes widen as Remi got out of the car and handed him the keys along with several bills. "We shouldn't be more than two hours," she said to him.

The two women walked through the large, crowded lobby and took the elevator to the second-floor Petit Salon. A uniformed man stood at the entrance and looked at Remi's invitation, nodding and, with a smile, admitting them. It was not at all as Amber had pictured it. The suite looked like it was set up for an art exhibit, with sculpted stands of modern shapes and sizes spread around the space. On top of these obelisks sat one-of-a-kind pieces of jewelry, sparkling under the crisp white lights shining upon them. As they perused the displays, the room began to fill, and an undertow of excitement swelled.

Amber stopped to admire a silver necklace that was made up of a myriad of what appeared to be tiny branches woven intricately together. "Remi, look at this. Isn't it magnificent?"

"*Mais oui. Très charmant.*"

Amber stepped back and shook her head, awed by the artistry. "They're all so beautiful. I want everything."

"Have a glass of wine and then decide," Remi said, as a waiter approached.

Amber took a glass of red from the tray and sipped. She was not in any way a connoisseur, but she knew that what she was tasting was fine wine. As they continued wandering around the room, Amber saw at least five pieces that she'd love to own, but the one with the branches was the one she just had to have.

"I'm going to go take another look at the necklace with the little branches," she said to Remi.

Remi cocked her head to one side and looked past Amber. "I think Rory is going to say a few words. I've met him many times. A wonderful silversmith and artist. You'll enjoy hearing what he has to say."

A tall man with silver hair pulled back into a ponytail tapped against his wineglass and the crowd hushed and fixed their attention on him.

"Greetings to all of you and thank you so much for coming tonight. I'm Rory Delacorte, and this is one of my favorite evenings of the year when we have the chance to share our new design creations with you. Your opinions and impressions are invaluable to us, and, of course, so too are your purchases." At this there was a ripple of laughter, after which he talked for several more minutes about the crafting and handwork that went into the fabrication of the jewelry. Then he raised his glass to the crowd and said, "Thank you again. Take your time and look around. I am here to answer any questions. And I would love to hear your comments as well."

Amber observed the people present and for a split second the old feeling of not belonging swept over her. She straightened her shoulders and inhaled, shaking it off. She had as much right to be here as anyone else, she told herself. She was probably cleverer than half the people here, and she certainly had the money to buy whatever she wanted.

"Would you like to meet Rory?" Remi asked.

"I'd love to," Amber said, feeling confident and sure of herself once again.

"Come." She took Amber's hand and headed to him.

"Rory, I'd like you to meet a friend of mine. This is Amber Parrish. She's a great admirer of White Orchid's designs."

Amber extended her hand. "It's a pleasure to meet you, Mr. Delacorte."

"The pleasure is all mine. I'm glad you could come tonight. Is there a piece you particularly like?" he said.

"Yes, actually there is. It's the one over there." She pointed to the stand.

"Ah, yes. The twigs. You have a very good eye."

"Is it for sale?" Amber asked.

"Yes, of course. Everything here is." He looked past her and then back. "You're in luck. The owner and daughter of the designer of that particular piece is here."

Amber turned to see a stunning blonde walk toward them from across the room. As she got closer, Amber's pulse began to race, and she broke out in a sweat. It couldn't be. She turned toward Rory. "If you'll excuse me, I just remembered . . ."

He put a hand on her arm. "Wait, wait. You must meet Daisy Ann."

Amber took a swallow of her wine and exhaled.

"Daisy Ann, you have a new fan," Rory said, extending a hand to her.

Amber's back was still to her as she joined them.

"Oh, how nice," Daisy Ann said as she took her place next to him, but her voice turned hard the moment Amber pivoted to face her. "How did you get in here?"

Amber tried to speak, but no words would come. She looked helplessly at Remi and then Rory, both of whom were regarding Daisy Ann with puzzled expressions.

"She's my guest," Remi finally said.

"And she's interested in the twigs," Rory continued.

Daisy Ann's eyes were blazing. "You'll never own any White Orchid designs, you murderer!" Her voice cut through the room and there was dead silence. Everyone was staring at them.

Remi gasped, and Rory's brows knitted in a frown. "Daisy Ann, what's going on?"

Amber froze, her heart banging in her chest, as her eyes darted around the room, desperate for a way to disappear before things went any further.

A bitter laugh escaped Daisy Ann. "This, this . . . gold digger. She's the one who tricked my father into marrying her and then shot him point-blank. She got away with murder. I had to buy her off to get her to leave my house." She punctuated each sentence with a poke of her index finger to Amber's chest. "She's nothing but trash. A lowlife, lying, murdering piece of garbage."

Amber put her hand up. "Daisy Ann, you know that's not true. I was cleared. You have to stop . . ."

"Get out. I don't want to hear a single word from you. You're a lying bitch." She turned toward the room and pointed at Amber. "Don't trust this woman. She's a sociopath."

Completely overcome with embarrassment, Amber felt paralyzed as she looked at the sea of faces staring at her. The last time she had seen Daisy Ann had been after Jake Crawford's funeral when the family's snotty lawyer read Jake's will. Daisy Ann had taken great delight in delivering the news to Amber that she had inherited close to nothing. After all of Amber's research into Texas estate law, she had believed as Jake's wife she was entitled to half his assets as well as the family domicile. But apparently, before Amber came around, some other smart woman had made off with millions by marrying him on the rebound after his beloved wife died, and then divorcing him shortly afterward. Jake's precious daughter had convinced him to put everything in her name after that fiasco. All those months of planning, of turning herself into a woman who reminded him of his dead wife, sharing the bed of a man more than forty years her senior and all for nothing. She'd ended up leaving with a paltry hundred grand that was in Jake's name in a bank account instead of the millions she'd been due. And now she was faced with the same look of disgust from Daisy Ann, as if Amber were nothing more than a clump of dirt on her shoe. She grabbed Remi's arm, steering her away, and they made a fast retreat. Once in the elevator, Remi looked at her with what Amber could tell was suspicion.

"Amber, what was she talking about? Were you married to her father?"

Amber was fuming. Her past was always trying to catch up with her. Her marriage to Jake was over three years ago, and Daisy Ann had humiliated her back then, kicking her out of the house right after his funeral, treating her like she was some kind of scum. Her face was burning and the look of all those women just now, staring at her in horror, flashed before her. She could only hope that it wouldn't be all over Bishops Harbor by tomorrow. Just another reason for them to ostracize her. She'd worked hard at building a life, staking her claim in upscale society, even overcoming Jackson being sent to prison. And now that spoiled bitch might have destroyed it all in just seconds. Well, Amber wasn't a poor little nobody anymore. She had money. Plenty of it. And smarts. Daisy Ann thought she could keep Amber from owning one of her designs. No problem. She was going to figure out a way to own all of them and put that bitch in her place for good.

13

AMBER

As Amber hurried through the hotel lobby, it took every ounce of effort to hold back the hot tears of fury behind her eyes. It wasn't until she and Remi were safely in the car that she let them spill onto her cheeks. In her mind's eye she saw the hateful face of Daisy Ann, spewing those angry words, humiliating Amber in front of all those people, and then a succession of other faces. Daphne and all the women who looked down on Amber, who treated her like she was dirt. She wiped the tears from her face, taking deep breaths in and out to try to calm her racing heart.

Remi said nothing until they were well out of the city and on the Parkway. "What happened back there, Amber? Were you really married to her father?" Remi asked again.

"Yes. We were in love and so happy, but his daughter was always against us. She never accepted his remarriage." Amber stared out the passenger window, deliberately neglecting to disclose the fact that she and Jake had married without Daisy Ann's knowledge. In fact, it wasn't until after his death that Daisy Ann first learned of her father's marriage to Amber. She was never going to alert Daisy Ann to her presence in Jake's life until it was too late for her to prevent their marriage. Before meeting Jake, Amber had left home and landed in Nebraska, but she found herself in a dead-end town with a dead-end job. When her co-worker, Tanya, told her she was moving to Gunnison, Colorado, Amber did a little research, and what she learned altered her plans. She discovered that lots of rich

Texans spend their summers in Gunnison, Colorado. From a long list of wealthy men with summer homes in Gunnison, she carefully selected Jake, a lonely widower, and decided to move to Colorado with Tanya. He was the perfect choice. Widowed. Lots older, which meant less competition. Was good-looking enough, even though he was in his sixties. What made him more palatable was that he was smart. Intelligence could be as much of an aphrodisiac as looks, if not more so. Besides, she knew she'd be with him for only a short time. His true love had been his first wife, and from what Amber read, she was a real firecracker. Loved hunting, fishing, and all the macho habits Jake enjoyed. So, Amber did her homework, as she always did, and emulated his dead wife, dying her hair red just like Marylou's. She spent the winter learning how to tie flies and how to shoot a rifle, and by spring was taking fly-fishing lessons in readiness for Jake's arrival in June. To appeal to Jake's protective nature, she posed as a devoted daughter working to support her widowed mother, despite the fact that her father was still alive. She'd carried out her plan to the letter, marrying Jake in record time, but it all blew up after he died. How was she to know that all his assets were in his daughter's name and that she'd get nothing? That was one piece of information that was not available online. Amber had learned, though, and that's why before she lassoed Jackson, she'd made sure to get a job at his company and assess what was what.

There was a strained silence until Remi spoke again. "She said you shot him."

Amber's head snapped around to look at Remi. "We were hunting. It was a terrible accident. There was a thorough investigation that proved it was accidental. I was devastated. I was consumed by grief and then she accused me of murdering the man I loved and wanted to spend my life with. She was horrible to me. I'll never forgive her."

They drove the rest of the way in silence. On one hand, Amber was relieved not to be questioned further, but she was aware of a difference in Remi's demeanor. It seemed to Amber that Remi's

usual relaxed manner had turned to stiffness and a sort of watchful-
ness, as if Amber might be dangerous in some way.

Amber was still angry, but now her anger was turned inward.
She'd gotten complacent, let her guard down, and broken one of
her cardinal rules. She never should have attended an event without
doing her research and completely checking it out beforehand. If
she'd taken the time to look up White Orchid Designs, she would
have discovered that its owner was Daisy Ann Crawford Briscoe,
and she would have stayed away. She'd never divulged that brief
first marriage to Jackson or anyone else in Bishops Harbor. Tonight's
scene would be choice gossip all over town tomorrow. She needed to
be the one to tell Jackson, to give him her side of the story, before
he heard it from someone else. Life was a minefield and people
were always setting traps for you, out to get you, but this time Daisy
Ann was going to be the prey.

"Here we are," Remi said as she pulled up to the house, and
when their eyes met, Amber couldn't tell if there was sadness or
pity on Remi's face. Amber didn't bother reminding Remi that they
were supposed to have grabbed dinner together.

"Thank you. I'm sorry things got so ugly," Amber said as she
opened the car door.

Remi shrugged. "I'm sorry too. Take care, Amber."

She watched the sports car take off and wondered if this was the
end of her friendship, such as it was, with the woman she so admired. Remi was chic and sophisticated, with a mystique so different from the other women in Bishops Harbor. Remi's dinner parties
were legendary in the town, a sort of intellectual salon. Amber
knew that others were surprised that she had pierced Remi's inner
circle. Now Amber might be excluded. It wasn't fair. Heaving a
deep sigh, she climbed the steps to the front door and went inside.

The house was quiet, and she wondered if Jackson was in bed
already, but as she walked farther, she saw a light shining from be-
neath the closed door of his study. Steeling herself for what was to
come, she tapped lightly on the door.

"Come in."

Amber opened the door, took a step, and remained standing just inside the room. "Jax is asleep?" she asked.

Jackson closed his laptop and looked up at her. "He's been in bed since seven thirty. How was the show? Did you buy the place out?"

Amber shut the door behind her and went to sit in one of the chairs across from his desk. "I need to talk to you," she said.

He gave her a withering look. "Why? How much of my money did you spend?"

"You mean *our* money?"

Jackson's eyes flashed with anger, and for a moment Amber thought he might lunge across the desk at her. "No, I mean *my* money, Amber. Every penny of it is mine."

This conversation was going off in the wrong direction. "Fine. Let's not argue. I didn't buy anything. That's not what this is about."

"Just what is it about then?"

"There are some things you don't know about my past. Things I haven't told you."

Jackson's scornful laugh filled the room. "Why does it not surprise me that there is more to your sordid past than I already know. You're like the fucking gift that keeps on giving."

Amber clenched her teeth, determined to remain calm. She continued quietly, ignoring his dig. "After I left home, I—"

Jackson interrupted her. "You mean after you put that poor innocent schmuck in jail, abandoned your kid, and got a new identity? Is that what you mean?"

Amber sighed. Matthew Lockwood had deserved everything that happened to him. He'd been more than willing to screw Amber all summer long, and then when she'd gotten pregnant, he'd stood by and done nothing while his mother tried to make her have an abortion. What was she supposed to do, slink away while he went back to his rich girlfriend? Maybe he hadn't physically raped her, but he'd assaulted her dignity and tried to ruin her future. He'd still be rotting in that prison if Amber's own mother hadn't turned against her and told the authorities that Amber had lied about the rape. She would never forgive her mother for that betrayal. "Okay. I've done some things I'm not proud of, but you're not exactly a saint." Amber didn't give a crap about Matthew Lockwood or what she'd done, but she knew this conversation demanded a show of contrition on her part.

Jackson's eyes were trained on her.

"As I was saying, I moved to Colorado. I met someone—a widower, an older man—and we fell in love. His name was Jake Crawford. We got married." Amber stopped, looking at Jackson and deciding she needed to up the emotion. Her lower lip trembled, and tears filled her eyes, tears not of grief but of anger at the humiliation she'd suffered tonight. "He was killed in a hunting accident. It was horrible. I was devastated."

"Why are you telling me this now, Amber? What's prompted this sudden confession of yours."

"Jake's daughter never accepted our marriage. She hated me. Never gave me a chance. She was terrible to me at the funeral and afterward she kicked me out of her house."

"Why?"

"Why what?"

"Why did she kick you out?"

She shifted in her chair. "Daisy Ann—ridiculous name, isn't it—accused me of killing her father. Jake was rich. Very, very rich, and she made it her business to see that I got nothing from his massive estate. She got it all by saying I killed him."

Jackson frowned and shook his head. "Wait. I thought you said he was killed in a hunting accident."

"Yes. We went hunting together. I fired the shot, but it was an accident. I thought he was an elk moving."

A look of skepticism crossed Jackson's face. "Sounds pretty suspicious to me."

"No. It was a total accident. The police and the sheriff, and even the National Forest law enforcement thoroughly investigated and ruled it an accident, but she wouldn't accept that. I left there with nothing, abused and humiliated by that spoiled princess."

Jackson swiveled his chair, bringing it closer to the desk, and leaned forward. "Where is this all leading, Amber?"

"I saw her tonight. Daisy Ann. She owns the jewelry company that held the trunk show." Amber rose from her chair. "She screamed at me in front of everyone. Said I was trash and a gold digger and that I murdered her father. That no one should trust me. She humiliated me in front of all those people. It was horrendous. She's vile. I want to kill her." She was pacing now, her voice getting louder and more strident. "I want to amend our deal."

His eyes narrowed. "What do you mean?"

"Don't worry. I'll still help with your plans for Daphne, but you have to help me get even with Daisy Ann."

- 14 -

DAISY ANN

aisy Ann had been living with hate in her heart for the last three years. She had nursed it daily, and as it fed, it grew to such immense proportions that it had threatened to obliterate every other feeling inside of her. The hate had one focus: Amber Patterson. The woman who had tricked Daisy Ann's father, Jake Crawford, into marrying her, and then murdered him.

She still missed her father so much. They'd always been close but had grown even closer after her mother's death. He had been the steady influence in her life, the voice of reason when her temper got the best of her, the one who could always right her course. She'd been in her twenties and newly married when her mother, Marylou, had died. She and her father had grieved together, but while she had a new husband and a growing family to distract her, he had floundered. Then he'd met Susannah, a thirtysomething knockout and he fell fast and hard. Despite being suspicious of her intentions at first, Daisy Ann had hoped that she'd provide a respite from his loneliness. Even though Susannah was twenty years Jake's junior, she seemed to be genuinely in love with him. However, shortly after the marriage, her true colors emerged and she walked away with twenty million dollars in the divorce settlement. After his marriage had ended so swiftly and badly, Jake had sworn he'd never marry again. And he seemed happy in those interim years between Susannah and Amber. He worked hard, played hard, and was an involved grandfather to her children. After she'd given birth to her first son, she felt overwhelmed with a paralyzing fear that she was ill equipped, that she had no idea how to be a good mother. She longed for her own mother then, to dispense words of wisdom and comfort, but of course Marylou was gone by then. Daisy Ann would never forget that first night, lying in the hospital bed after Mason had left, staring at the ceiling, feeling so alone and desolate. It was after midnight when she heard footsteps entering the room and was shocked to see her father walk in and take a seat next to the bed.

"What in tarnation are you doing here at this hour?" she asked as she brushed a tear from her cheek.

He gave her his trademark grin. "I may have bribed the nurses to look the other way. I saw that look in your eye earlier. I know you're thrilled to be a mama, but I know my girl, and I'm betting you're lying here listing all the ways you're gonna mess this up."

She tried to smile, but the heaving sobs came instead, and he sat on the edge of the bed, holding her as her shoulders shook and her tears fell.

"Shh, shh now. It's gonna be fine. That little boy doesn't know it, but he just won the mama lottery. You are the kindest, most warm-hearted woman I know. And when he needs someone to fight for him, there's nobody better he could ever have in his corner."

"Thank you, Daddy. I just feel so overwhelmed. I want to do everything right. I miss Mama so much."

"I know you do, darlin'. But I'm here. As for doing everything right, you won't. But it'll be okay, because you'll do the most important thing right and that is love him with all you've got. And I promise you, I'll be right there beside you every step of the way." She felt herself well up at the memory. He was supposed to be here now.

Daisy Ann still couldn't understand what kind of witchcraft Amber had employed to ensnare him so easily. Her father had met Amber in the beginning of the summer. She'd been a waitress at the café in Gunnison where he went for breakfast every morning. After knowing her only a few short months, he had married her that September. Two weeks later he was dead. She'd never forget getting the phone call telling her that there'd been a hunting accident. And before that even had sunk in, that his wife had been the one to shoot him. His wife? He'd never even mentioned that he was seeing anyone to Daisy Ann. Amber casually announced she was Jake's new wife and then in the next breath, with no change in tone, told her that he was dead. When she flew to Colorado and met Amber, she'd known the minute she laid eyes on her that she was a stone-cold killer. The blankness in her stare, the rehearsed way she told Daisy Ann what had happened, all rang false. Her father had been hunting for over fifty years with no accidents; he wasn't some amateur. Daisy Ann knew he would have impressed upon Amber the importance of safety. The sheriff told her and Mason that it was officially an accident but she could see in his eyes that he didn't believe it either. There was just no proof. Amber's story was that she had stopped to go pee and Jake was ahead of her in the woods. She claimed she saw movement, thought he was an elk, and shot him in the back. It was ludicrous.

Daisy Ann had been determined to find out everything she could about the woman who'd breezed into her father's life and within a matter of months had become his wife and then shot him in the back in an alleged hunting accident. Daisy Ann's husband, Mason, had at first been supportive and sympathetic. He'd stepped in with the children to fill the gap, had listened to her go on for hours, updating him on every detail of her investigation into Amber. She'd hired a private detective shortly after Amber left Texas with her tail between her legs. Daisy Ann now had an extensive file showing all of Amber's moves from the moment she'd arrived in Gunnison, Colorado, where Daisy Ann's father owned a summer ranch. The detective had tracked her back to Eustis, Nebraska, where she'd been working as a waitress. No one there knew where she'd lived before Eustis, or much about her background, for that matter. She'd been in Gunnison only for a few months before she'd latched on to Daisy Ann's father. After his death, Amber had moved to Connecticut and gotten a job working at one of the local real estate offices.

The detective had sent Daisy Ann weekly reports, but there was never anything of significance. She had been confident that it would only be a matter of time before Amber set her sights on her next rich target. Daisy Ann would spend her whole week waiting for the email that would update her on Amber's moves, no matter how small. It took a toll. On her marriage and on her children. No matter how hard she tried to move on with her life, the unfinished business of proving Amber's guilt and making her pay, had driven her to the point of obsession. When finally, in desperation, Mason had threatened to leave her and take the children if she didn't stop, she'd reluctantly agreed. She'd let the detective go and forced herself to refrain from any more investigating. She resigned herself to the fact that she'd exhausted every avenue. She was never going to be able to prove Amber's guilt, and she had to stop letting the woman infect her life. She continued to pay the staff to look after the Colorado house, but she hadn't been back since she'd brought her father's body back to Dallas three years ago. Other than that, she'd done her best to resume her life and push everything to do with Amber to the back of her mind.

But now the hatred had returned with a more consuming zeal than ever. The moment she'd laid eyes on Amber, it all came rushing back. She hadn't even planned on attending the trunk show, but at the last minute she'd decided to make a weekend of it with some shopping and a show. When she returned home from New York after the show, the first thing Daisy Ann did was call the detective and put him back on the case. Just as she'd suspected, Amber had married for money again. She'd snagged millionaire Jackson Parrish who interestingly had just been released from prison for tax fraud among other financial crimes. They still lived in their estate by the sea and based on the lavish party she'd thrown for her husband's release, money didn't seem to be an issue. Seeing Amber thriving and living among the elite in her town made Daisy Ann's blood boil. A renewed sense of purpose filled her, and she was determined to find a way to make the woman pay. Her first stop would be Gunnison, Colorado, to personally interview everyone who had known Amber back then. Maybe the detective had missed something. She picked up the photograph on her dresser of Jake and her children at the Colorado house. "I'll bring her to justice, Daddy. I promise."

Mason walked into their bedroom, a frown on his face. "I can't believe you're going down this rabbit hole again. It almost broke our marriage up. Daisy Ann, I can't do this again."

She turned from the suitcase to look up at her husband. "She's up to her old tricks. Married rich and her poor husband just got out of prison. How much do you want to bet she's the one who engineered that? She's a cold, calculating gold digger, and I'm going to prove it. There could be a whole wake of dead husbands in her past. She doesn't deserve to be living in the lap of luxury in her cozy Connecticut town." She continued her packing.

Mason put a hand on her arm. "I know she's a horrible person. But she's already taken enough from you. Don't let her ruin your life. Our life. We've just gotten back to normal. The kids are happy. What good can come of your doing this?"

"Justice. Stopping her. That's what."

"What if it really was an accident? You can't be sure she did it on purpose. Maybe it was a terrible, tragic accident. You can't let it rule your life forever."

She didn't bother responding. They'd had this argument too many times. Her father had spent a lifetime hunting. There was no way that the bullet hole in his back had gotten there by accident. That bitch had shot him in cold blood; Daisy Ann knew it in her bones.

"Please, Mason. Nothing you say is going to dissuade me. I'll be back in a few days."

He shook his head and left the room, muttering under his breath.

. . .

As her private plane began making its descent into Gunnison, Daisy Ann felt a growing sense of apprehension. Looking out the window as they landed, she thought back to all the summers they'd spent at their Colorado ranch from the time she was a little girl. She'd always loved it here: six hundred and twenty-five acres of heaven in the Rocky Mountains.

The moment the door opened, and she started down the airstairs, she spotted Brian, her father's ranch hand, sprinting toward the plane.

"Hey, Daisy Ann. It's good to see you. I'll grab your bag," he said.

"Thanks, Brian." The sun was dazzling, the gorgeous sky clear and blue. But when Daisy Ann inhaled the thin dry air, it felt like her lungs couldn't quite get enough.

"I always forget how breathless I get when I first arrive," she said to Brian as he slid into the driver's seat beside her. He hadn't changed, she thought, maybe a few more laugh lines around his dark brown eyes, but the uniform was the same. Denim jeans, navy T-shirt, and a baseball cap with a picture of a largemouth bass on it.

He chuckled. "Yeah. Big change from Texas."

Brian pulled out of the small airport, and Daisy Ann was quiet as they drove past tidy houses, and through downtown. When they finally turned onto Ohio Creek Road, she rolled down her window and closed her eyes, breathing in the familiar fragrance of sage and pine as they drove for the next fifteen minutes.

"Here we are," Brian said. She sat up when he came to a stop in front of the house.

Daisy Ann swallowed and opened the car door, steeling herself as she looked up. It was odd how the house looked unchanged yet different at the same time. She walked up the steps of the wide veranda and stood in front of the massive double doors. As if sensing her hesitation, Brian waited silently next to her until she reached out her hand, curling her fingers around the long brass handle. Opening the door and entering the house, her mind exploded with memories. Mornings spent fishing in the creek with her father, she and her mother buying fresh fruits and vegetables and sampling homemade pastries at the farmers market on Saturdays, feeling so grown up when they went to Traci's studio together for mother-daughter massages. Standing on a kitchen chair while Brenda, their housekeeper, let her help with the cooking. Hiking Swampy Pass with her friends. And then that last terrible day when she came to claim her father's body and met Amber, the woman who killed him.

"Daisy Ann!" Brenda came rushing toward her. "So wonderful to see you. I've missed you. It's been too long." The older woman hugged Daisy Ann to her, patting her back.

Daisy Ann pulled away and took the woman's hand as she turned to Brian. "You can leave my bag here. I'll take it up later. Let's go sit at the kitchen table. I need to talk with both of you."

Seeing a look pass between Brian and Brenda, she realized they were afraid to hear what she had to say.

"I made some lemonade iced tea. Your favorite." Brenda hustled around the room, taking the pitcher from the fridge and pouring three glasses before sitting down.

"Thank you." Daisy Ann took a sip and put down the glass. She looked from one to the other. "First, I want to tell you how grateful I am to both of you. You've cared for my family and this ranch with love and dedication, and I can never thank you enough. I'm sorry I've been absent, but I just couldn't bear to be here after Daddy died."

Brenda reached out her hand and placed it on top of Daisy Ann's, patting it gently. "We understand, sweetheart. It's been hard for all of us. He was a great man. And your mama was a wonderful woman. How he got involved with that snake, I'll never know." She shook her head.

"Yes, well . . ." Daisy Ann exhaled. "I've made a decision about the house." She watched their faces drop. "It's been a really tough decision, but I've made up my mind."

Brian cast his eyes down at the table and absently ran his fingers around the rim of his glass. Brenda pressed her lips together, and Daisy Ann could tell she was trying not to cry. "I'm creating a life estate for you. The house will remain in my name, but you will both have the legal right to live in it for the rest of your lives. You two love this place as much as my father did. I know he would want you to continue living here. I can have the papers drawn up right away if you'll accept." She paused, seeing their astonished looks, and then hurried on. "The house is paid for, and I've set up an account to take care of taxes, maintenance, and general expenses, along with your continued salaries."

Brian spoke first. "I don't even know what to say. I mean, it's unbelievable. I figured you were going to tell us you were selling, but this, this is . . . Like I said, it's unbelievable."

Daisy Ann looked at Brenda, who had been with the Crawfords for almost twenty-eight years, from the time Daisy Ann was eight. She'd been like a second mother, a big sister, and a friend, all rolled into one. Tears were running down her cheeks. "This means so much, honey. But are you sure? I don't feel right accepting."

Daisy Ann shook her head. "I've never been more sure. You made this place into a cozy home for Daddy after Mama died. You worked day and night to help him get through. You're family."

The emotional toll of the morning had left Daisy Ann drained, and she'd taken a nap. When she came downstairs later, Brenda had a pot of chicken rice soup simmering on the stove.

"That smells wonderful," she said.

"You sit while I get you a bowl. I have some nice crusty bread heating too."

"Mmm. Will you have some with me?"

They ate in silence for a few minutes, and then Brenda spoke.

"I hope you'll still come and stay and bring the boys. They love it here too. They had such fun here with your daddy. And after all, the house is still yours and will belong to them one day."

An image formed in Daisy Ann's mind, her boys impatiently pulling on Jake's shirt, almost jumping out of their skin, hurrying him from his breakfast so they could go down to the lake and fish. "In time, Brenda. Maybe in time."

Brenda put her spoon down and pushed the bowl away. "Aren't there things you'd like to take from the house? I can help you pack them up."

"Not right now. I can't . . . I just can't go through his things. I don't even want to go into the bedroom where that horrible woman slept with him." She sighed. "Brenda, I saw her again. She's living in Connecticut. She landed on her feet. She came to my trunk show in New York."

Brenda's mouth fell open. "You're kidding!"

Daisy Ann filled her in.

Brenda shook her head back and forth. "That makes me sick. I knew that girl was trouble the first time I laid eyes on her. Told your father so, but she had him bewitched."

Daisy Ann shook her head. "I'll never understand how she got him to marry her so quickly. She convinced him to fire you, didn't she?"

Brenda nodded. "She didn't want anyone around to mess with her plans. She was clever and cunning. And mean. But with your dad, well, she was sweet as pie."

"Right. I sized her up from the first. She had to be cunning to fool Daddy. He was such a smart man. He could usually spot a phony miles away."

"He was lonely, Daisy Ann. He missed your mama, and he was getting old. When a man gets to be that age, he gets scared. It's too near the end to face it alone. Amber knew that, and she played on it. That red hair of hers was dyed. I know it. She tried to be a copy of your mama."

That part, Daisy Ann learned from the detective. He'd interviewed Tanya, the woman Amber had accompanied on the drive from Eustis to Gunnison. He'd tracked her down after interviewing Amber's employer at the café. She'd listed her prior employment at a restaurant in Crested Butte, and that's when he'd found Tanya. She'd told him that Amber used to be a blonde but had suddenly dyed her hair red before they left Nebraska. That was when Daisy Ann knew Amber had had a plan, long before she met Daisy Ann's father. And the reason why she'd left a more lucrative job at a trendy restaurant in Crested Butte, Colorado, an upscale ski town, to work at the café in Gunnison—the restaurant Jake was known to frequent daily when he was in town.

"She even came over here with your mama's peach cobbler. Made your daddy believe it was a coincidence that she made his favorite dessert; told him it was a family recipe of hers. But I saw the paper in her purse with the recipe from the Junior League of Dallas. She must have found it on the internet."

Daisy Ann's face grew hot. The idea of Amber using information about her dear mother made her want to spit nails. Was there no limit to how low she would stoop? "You never told me that. Did you see anything else interesting?"

"She had a folder in her bag. Motel receipt, some information on fly-fishing. She and your daddy were actually walking back from fishing so I didn't have time to look through everything. But I saw a phone number with the name of a guy next to it. I copied it and called the number after she left. The guy who answered was M something. Martin or Mitchell. When I asked if he knew an Amber Patterson, he said no. I figured it was a dead end."

"Do you still have his number?"

Brenda nodded. "I think so, somewhere. I'm sure I left the paper in one of my purses. I'll check."

"That would be great. It's like Amber had no life before a few years ago. We haven't been able to dig up anything on family or past jobs. Maybe this man can help."

"I'll see if I can find his number. But be careful. That woman is evil and who knows what kind of person this man is."

"Don't worry. This ain't my first rodeo. I can take care of myself. I've got some appointments in town; I'm going to take Daddy's truck for the day."

"I'll go get you the keys."

No matter what Mason said, Daisy Ann wasn't giving up this time. She wasn't going to rest until she found what she needed to make Amber pay.

- 15 -

DAPHNE

"Why do we have to go to therapy?" Tallulah whines, her arms crossed and her eyes shooting daggers at me. She stops in front of the door, blocking it. "I'm finally able to see Dad and you're making it all creepy by forcing us to talk to a stranger."

I don't want to be late and make a bad impression, but I take a deep breath and turn to her. "It's important that your dad understand the boundaries I've set. I'm only looking out for your welfare. You have to trust me on this."

"How is making me spill my guts to some shrink looking out for me? I just want to spend time with him. This is bullshit."

"That's enough. And watch your language. I'm not discussing this right now. We need to go."

"No."

"Young lady, you either get in that car right now or we'll cut this visit short and fly back to California."

Her eyes well up. "Why are you being such a bitch?"

Before the shock wears off and I can respond, Bella shouts at her.

"Don't talk to Mommy that way!"

"I know you're upset, Tallulah, but you cannot call me names. This is exactly why we need to go to therapy. Let's go."

She gives me a sullen look and steps aside. She doesn't speak to me the entire drive and Bella and I make casual conversation, trying to ignore the hostility oozing from Tallulah. We pull up to the office at the same time a black Mercedes S class drives in. I don't know how Jackson is able to afford a six-figure car after the IRS took all his funds, but then again, it's Jackson. Tallulah is out of the car and running toward him before I even put the car in park, and I sigh. I hope this therapist is as good as Dr. Marshall says.

"Good morning, Daphne, Bella." Jackson gives me his megawatt smile as he walks with his arm around Tallulah.

"Hi, Daddy," Bella answers but doesn't make a move toward him. I tighten my hold on her hand. I merely nod at him.

We're only in the waiting room a few minutes before the door opens and an attractive brunette in her forties beckons us inside. She extends a hand to me. "I'm Hannah, you must be Daphne. Unfortunately, Dr. Levander has been called out of town due to a death in the family. He's asked me to step in for him." I'm not only surprised at the first name, but also unsettled by not seeing the therapist Dr. Marshall recommended. I simply smile, however, and shake her hand. "Nice to meet you." After greetings have been shared all around, she looks at the girls.

"I'd like to have a few minutes with your parents. Do you mind waiting here?" She points to a bookcase. "There are books, as well as some iPads loaded with shows and movies."

"We have our own iPads, we'll be fine," Tallulah says, not bothering to look at her.

We follow her inside. The office is modern and stark, with a leather sofa and two chairs across from it. I take a chair, and Jackson the sofa.

Hannah adjusts her black-framed glasses and begins. "Thank you, Daphne, for allowing Dr. Marshall to fill Dr. Levander in on the work you've been doing with her. I'd like to commend both of you for putting your differences aside for the sake of your daughters. It's so important for parents to have a united front."

I scoff. "Let me be clear. There's no unity here. The only reason I've agreed to let Jackson have any role in my daughters' lives is out of concern for their emotional well-being. As Dr. Marshall has shared my file with you and if you've read it, you know I have every reason to never trust him again."

Hannah's expression gives nothing away, nor does Jackson's for that matter.

"I do understand, Daphne. I also know what Jackson has been through in the past year and with his permission, I've spoken to his parole officer who believes he's a changed man." She crosses her legs and leans forward. "I would be in the wrong profession if I didn't think people were capable of change."

I feel the heat rise to my face. "I'm not here to debate human nature. I need you to help me make Tallulah, our older daughter, understand that I'm putting rules in place for her own good. Jackson has no parental rights, but I'm willing to allow him time with the girls as long as I'm present when he sees them. She's already fighting me on this."

Jackson finally speaks. "Daphne, I promise to abide by the parameters you've set. I don't have any desire to confuse Tallulah or to cause strain to your relationship with her. I'm so grateful for the opportunity to see the girls that I have no intention of doing anything to jeopardize that. I hope you can believe me."

Hannah looks like a proud teacher, and I want to slap the smile off her face. I realize this is not going to be therapy but rather play-acting and I need to be as good as Jackson. I turn to him. "It's so good to hear that. I really appreciate your willingness to work with me. And I do know that you care as much about our children's happiness as I do. I hope you can understand that after everything you put me through—you know, the gaslighting, the sexual humiliation, starvation diets—that, um, it's going to take me a while. And Bella too—after all, you constantly made fun of her learning disability. But maybe now that she can read you won't tell her she looks ugly when she stutters over a word."

Hannah's smile is replaced by a look of horror, and that little vein in Jackson's forehead is pulsing.

I sit back and smile. "Shall we invite the children in?"

16

DAISY ANN

Daisy Ann had brought her Amber file with her to Gunnison and had arranged to meet with everyone listed in the detective's report. She'd spent the night at the house and Brenda prepared a breakfast of homemade waffles for her. Seeing Brenda again was comforting but staying in the house still didn't feel right. After breakfast she went to the café but didn't learn anything of value. Obviously, Amber had deliberately kept to herself, and other than commenting on how she sucked up to Jake, no one had anything new to offer. Next on her list was Tanya, the woman Amber had traveled with from Nebraska. She pulled in front of the row of townhouses and parked in front. The lawn was well maintained, and flower boxes in the windows showcased purple and yellow petunias. She took a deep breath as she walked to the front door, eager for answers, and rang the bell. A young woman holding a baby on one hip answered.

"Tanya?"

"Yes, ma'am. You must be Daisy Ann. Come on in."

She led Daisy Ann into the kitchen and pointed to a chair at the wooden table. "Please have a seat. I was just about to feed her." She put the baby in a highchair. "Can I get you something to drink?"

Daisy Ann shook her head. "No thanks."

Tanya pulled out a jar of baby food and began spooning it into her daughter's mouth. "So, what can I help you with? You said you were a friend of Amber's?"

Daisy Ann nodded. She had no idea what Tanya's feelings toward Amber were, so she'd decided to take a roundabout approach. "Yes, I'm trying to locate her. Did she keep in touch with you after she left?"

"No. After she moved out of my friend Greta's, where we were staying at the time, we really never heard from her. Greta was pissed. She claims Amber stole some of her clothes. I don't know if that's really true. But I never did understand why she left a good job at D'Jangos to work at the W. I mean no way did she make as much in tips."

"Did she say why she wanted to work there?"

Tanya shook her head. "No, she was kinda cagey about it." She shrugged. "She wasn't one for really confiding much."

"Did you ever see her after she got married?"

"I didn't even know she did get married until I saw that article about the shooting. Terrible thing. I did get in touch with her after to offer my condolences."

"Oh?"

"Yeah, she was pretty torn up about it. Said she couldn't stay here anymore."

"Did she explain how it happened or say anything about it?"

"No. She just kept saying it was a terrible accident. I don't understand how it happened. My husband works for Country Outfitters. At the time of the shooting, we were dating. Anyhow, he said he remembered her. She took shooting lessons from one of his co-workers. The guy said she was good. A deadeye. I was really surprised that she made such a mistake."

Daisy Ann felt her blood boiling. "That's strange. Can you give me the name of her instructor?"

"Sure. His name is Frank Winters."

Daisy Ann stood. "Thanks so much for taking the time to talk to me." She looked at the baby then back at Tanya. "Enjoy that sweet baby."

She drove around the block, parked, and made a call.

"Gunnison Country Outfitters."

"Yes, is Frank Winters available?"

"He's out on a pack trip with a group. He'll be back on Friday."

"Could you please leave a message for him? Ask him to call Daisy Ann Briscoe?" She spelled her name and left her mobile number. "It's important."

"Yes, ma'am. I'll give him the message."

Sighing, she put the truck in drive and headed back to the house. It had been a tough morning with all the talk about her father causing her to relive the whole nightmare again. It felt like all the energy had been sucked out of her, and every inch of her body ached with fatigue and grief. It was time to leave. There was nothing more for her here.

When her plane left Gunnison, Daisy Ann knew she'd never return to Colorado. The house had felt all wrong without her father's large presence, hollow and oddly unfamiliar, despite all the summers she'd spent there. Her mother had died more than thirteen years ago, but there were times it felt like yesterday—times when the grief came out of nowhere, sudden and staggering. Her mother and father were both gone now. She thought about the times she'd heard adults talk about feeling like orphans after the last parent died. It had sounded a little melodramatic to her, but now she understood. She was bidding a final goodbye to her childhood, to the mother and father who had loved her unconditionally—her connection to the past severed forever.

As an only child, Daisy Ann had been both daughter and son to her father. She was in the saddle before she could walk, and by the time she was fourteen, she could shoot a tin can off a fence post at thirty feet. Then there were all those times the three of them would go night fishing on Lake Fork to beat the Texas heat, patiently waiting for the bass to be lured by the noise and vibration of their top-water lures and spinnerbaits. But as much as Daisy Ann thoroughly embraced this Texas cheek and bravado, she was equally at ease with her femininity. It was freeing, actually, to be able to inhabit both worlds, and she was grateful to both her parents for giving her that freedom.

After landing back in Texas and being picked up by Derek, her driver, Daisy Ann was on her way home when her text tone sounded, and she swiped to read it. From Brenda.

I found the number of the man who knew Amber. Good luck.

Daisy Ann navigated to a reverse number site and punched in the number. The result came back immediately. Martin C. Age 28. Eustis, Nebraska. Bingo! She did a quick search on restaurants in the area, then dialed the number. After three rings, a male voice answered.

"Hello."

"Is this Martin?"

"Who's asking?

"My name is Marion Chambers," she began the spiel she'd memorized. "I represent an online shopping marketing agency and you're one of ten customers who have won one of our sweepstakes prizes. It's a five-hundred-dollar Visa gift card. I just need to have you sign for it. Could we meet?"

"Is this for real? Seriously?"

"Yes. It's our customer appreciation campaign."

"How did you get my name? I never signed up for any sweep-stakes."

"We entered the names of all our online shoppers, and you are one of the lucky winners."

"So where do I sign this paper? Do I need to come to your office or what?" He still didn't sound fully convinced.

"No, no. I'm one of the sales reps, and I'm constantly on the road, but I'll be in Eustis this Friday. Could you meet me at the Pool Hall? I can never get enough of their cheesy potatoes."

"I don't know. What company did you say you were with again?"

"Brand Marketing. We work with stores to increase traffic. I could mail the card to you if you prefer. I would just need your mailing address."

"Um . . . I guess I could just meet you."

"Great. Shall we say five thirty at the Pool Hall?"

"Fine."

She leaned back in the car and closed her eyes. A few minutes later, she felt a small bump and opened her eyes as Derek pulled up the driveway. She was tired but knew that Mason would want to talk about how her trip had gone. She ran her fingers through her hair, pulled a lip gloss from her purse, sweeping it quickly across her lips.

He was waiting at the door as her car pulled up and she got out.

"Hi, babe," he said, taking Daisy Ann in his arms. "I missed you. Our bed was colder than a banker's heart on foreclosure day."

She laughed and gave him a tight squeeze. "I missed you too, honey. But I'm afraid you're going to have to miss me for a little longer."

"Why, what's going on?"

"I'm leaving for Eustis, Nebraska, in the morning."

17

AMBER

Days after the trunk show Amber was still licking her wounds. The one thing she was grateful for was that word of her humiliation had not managed to reach Bishops Harbor. She'd written to Remi on one of her finest Benneton Graveur note cards, saying how sorry she was about what had happened and reiterating her innocence. No doubt a text would have been quicker and easier, but Amber had read enough to know that a handwritten note on fine stationery revealed a certain grace and refinement of the sender. She knew Remi had joined her husband, Norris, in Paris, so she wasn't too alarmed that she hadn't heard back from her yet.

She'd been putting off having a more in-depth conversation with Jackson about Daisy Ann until she'd done more research into White Orchid Designs. For Amber's purposes, the *About* page on the company website didn't offer much. There was a dramatic photograph of Daisy Ann wearing *the necklace* that was the inspiration behind White Orchid's founding; a necklace designed and hand-crafted by Daisy Ann's mother. One thing did stand out, however, and that was the fact that although the company was begun by Daisy Ann ten years ago, it hadn't become a full-time venture until just three years ago, following her father's death. Prior to that, it appeared to be more of a vanity project than a real business. Daisy Ann was quoted as saying: *My father always said that you must fall in love with your work to be successful and happy. He was passionate about what he did. After his death, I realized that what I loved was creating these beautiful pieces, and so I left the oil company and followed my passion, dedicating myself to White Orchid Designs full-time.* Amber stopped reading and sat back for a moment, digesting what she'd just taken in. So, Daisy Ann had worked for Jake's company all those years, when really what she'd wanted to do was run White Orchid. When Amber killed Jake, she had freed that entitled and spoiled prima donna and enabled her to quit her job and do what she loved. Daisy Ann should be grateful to Amber, and instead she'd treated her like rotting trash. It was time for Amber to get even with this condescending bitch once and for all. Devising a plan of action would now be her top priority. As Jake had always said, *Keep your saddle oiled, and your gun greased.*

She scrolled through more website hits until she came to an article in *Entrepreneur Magazine.* Amber's nose wrinkled in annoyance when she saw the photo of Daisy Ann looking gorgeous in a red double-breasted suit, her blond hair swept up in an elegant bun and a sampling of her jewelry designs spread out on a table in front of her. She scanned the article, then reread the last section of the interview.

"Ms. Briscoe, you've had several offers to buy your company. The latest from Valene Mart. Would you consider selling and making your beautiful designs accessible to a larger audience?"

"One of the things that makes White Orchid so special is that each design is unique. While of course I'd love to grow our customer base, I would never do so by allowing my designs to be duplicated and mass-produced."

Amber bookmarked the page, then went back to the search bar and entered Valene Mart. She'd never heard of it, but it was a large chain in the Southwest that sold everything from toasters to tires. She could see why Daisy Ann wouldn't want them to distribute her designs. She clicked on the jewelry tab and saw that the most expensive item was less than a hundred dollars. A far cry from the thousands Daisy Ann made on a single piece. Very interesting.

"Mommy, Mommy."

Amber looked up from her laptop to see her son running toward her with Jackson right behind him. They were both in T-shirts and bathing trunks. "Hi, sweetie. Are you and Daddy going swimming?"

He nodded, smiling, and Jackson said, "I'm going to Daphne's. It's time Jax met his sisters."

"Really? It would have been nice for you to tell me ahead of time. What if I had plans with him?"

"Get real, Amber. The most time you've ever spent with him was in the delivery room."

"That's not fair," she said, her voice shrill.

Jackson closed his eyes, shaking his head for a moment. "We're leaving." He took Jax's hand and something in that possessive gesture gave Amber second thoughts. A picture formed in her mind of a perfect little family—Jackson in the pool with their son, surrounded by blond, leggy Daphne and her two daughters. Amber was the one who'd gotten fatter and more swollen over nine interminable months, the one who had suffered through six hours of labor and then an excruciating delivery to give Jackson the son he so desperately sought. And afterward, all the dieting, Pilates, and fitness training to get back into shape. She wasn't about to let Jackson use her son as a pawn in his quest with Daphne. Jax was *her* pawn to use, dammit.

She slammed down the lid of the computer and jumped up from the chair. "Wait."

Jackson stopped, turning to look at her.

Even though she had a foot out the door already, it irked her to think of Daphne spending any time with Jax. He was hers after all. "Why does he have to meet them now? He's a toddler. Why can't it wait until he's older? It's not like they're all going to hang out together. He's just a baby."

"They are his *family*. Brothers and sisters grow up *together*. That's how they *bond*." Jackson's words came out slowly and precisely, as if he was talking to a child.

Amber glared at him, her jaw clenched. She felt like spitting. "Since when did you become so sentimental about family bonds?"

"You wouldn't understand."

"You're right, I don't."

"Everything with you is intrigue and scheming. You've never done anything with purely good or decent motives, so how could I expect you to get it?"

"Your motives are hardly decent, Jackson, so cut the morally superior act."

He gave her a withering look and left the room with Jax.

Amber's heart was beating so fast, she could feel a pounding in her ears. It was laughable, Jackson throwing around words like goodness and decency. He of all people should be the last one to accuse her of scheming. Especially with what he had planned for Daphne. Until Amber could make it clear that she was the one doing the leaving, she didn't want anyone to see Jackson spending too much time with Daphne. She wasn't about to let him make a fool of her. This was a small town, and she knew that everyone would love to see her ousted from the Parrish estate and Daphne returned to it. From the outside Daphne and Jackson had appeared to have the perfect marriage, and Amber was painted as the interloper. Yes, it was true that she'd seduced him and gotten pregnant while he was still married to Daphne, but so what? He was the one who'd been married, not her. She was sick and tired of taking the blame. No more. Amber was preparing for battle, and this was going to be a take-no-prisoners kind of war.

18

DAPHNE

Meredith and I sit on the beach watching the girls as they swim, and I chronicle for her Jackson's and my first session with the therapist. "I'm glad you had the guts to tell her how he treated poor Bella." Her eyes are blazing. "What did the therapist say after that?"

"She tried to regain her composure, but she couldn't wipe the horrified look off her face. At least it made her see Jackson in a different light."

"I'd say so. No one likes a bully, especially one who makes fun of his own child. He must have been royally pissed."

"He was. But he didn't let it show . . . too much. Just that little vein in his head dancing." Telling Meredith about it now, I feel the same delight at his shock and discomfort as I did when it happened.

"So, are you going to find someone new?"

I shake my head. "No, it's pointless. We're only here two months. He doesn't have any power over me any longer, so I'll just monitor his visits and we'll be back in California soon."

She raises an eyebrow. "It's just . . . I worry. Jackson's always got something up his sleeve. I don't want to see you get hurt again."

"It's different now. I see through him. I fell for his lies and deceit once, but he won't fool me again. And I think he knows it." I stop talking when I see Tallulah come out of the water.

She wanders up and plops down on the towel next to me. "I'm bored. Dad texted me to see if we want to go to the city tomorrow. Can we?"

I exchange a glance with Meredith then turn to Tallulah. "Honey, you know the rules. Dad can visit but I need to be there."

She rolls her eyes. "This is so lame. He's not going to kidnap us, come on, Mom. I want to spend time with my father."

I try to keep my voice even. "Those are the rules, Lu. There's nothing more to discuss."

"No, there *is* more to discuss." Her words are loud and angry, and I can see a storm brewing in her eyes. "You don't care how I feel or what I want. All you want is to hurt Dad. Haven't you hurt him enough already?" She jumps up and starts to walk away from me.

Meredith raises her eyebrows and looks at me with sympathy.

"Are you coming back in?" Bella calls from the water.

"No!" Tallulah shouts and keeps walking along the shoreline.

Bella hits the water with her fists. "Why'd you get out?"

"Because it sucks here." Tallulah sits down on the sand near the water's edge, her knees drawn up and her arms around her legs. Bella comes skipping out of the water and drops down next to her.

My phone buzzes and I look down, still off-balance after Tallulah's outburst. A text from Jackson.

Can I come by in a bit? I want to bring Jax to meet the girls. Please?

I want to pretend I don't see it, but I would only be putting off the inevitable. Looking at Meredith, I say, "Jackson wants to come over. Now. With his son."

Her mouth turns down at the edges and she shakes her head. "I can't be here. I have a dermatologist appointment in an hour. And anyway, it's pretty short notice, isn't it?"

"Yeah, it is. But it would probably be good for Tallulah. Don't worry, I'll be fine on my own. He would never do anything stupid in front of the kids. He's trying to be Mr. Nice Guy, remember?"

Meredith looks doubtful. "I guess."

I type back a response and stroll to where Tallulah and Bella sit. "Girls, your father's coming over and he's bringing your brother. Won't that be nice?"

"Yeah, great. Hanging out with a baby. Can't wait," Tallulah says then stands up and walks back to the house.

"I want to meet him," Bella says. She wraps the towel I've given her around her waist and leans against me. I put my arms around her, grateful that one of my daughters still seems to like me. "How old is he?"

"Two."

"I like babies. They're cute," Bella says. She frowns in concentration. "So, I guess I'm not the baby anymore. I'm a big sister now."

I suddenly think of Amber and know there's no way she's going to encourage a genuine relationship between my children and her son, but I simply nod. "Yes, sweetie. You are."

Twenty minutes later I hear the low purr of Jackson's Mercedes. Tallulah has been sulking all morning, but Bella is in a good mood and jumps up to open the door. Her father smiles at her, hugging her with one arm while holding Jackson Junior in the other.

I haven't seen Jackson's son since he was a tiny baby. He's now a toddler, and I can't help but smile when he studies me with big brown eyes. He's adorable, with chubby cheeks, brown curly hair, and lashes to die for. I tentatively approach, aware that toddlers are wary of strangers. Bella has no such restraint.

"Hi, Jackson! I'm your big sister."

The child struggles to get down, and Jackson sets him on the floor. Bella sits cross-legged while holding a teddy bear, and he toddles over to her. I watch, surprised as he takes it, then allows her to pull him onto her lap.

"He likes you. We call him Jax," Jackson tells her.

"He's a friendly little guy," I comment.

Jackson laughs. "He is. I was worried he wouldn't know me, but it's like I was never gone."

"Dad!" Tallulah comes running into the room and throws her arms around Jackson.

"Hi, sweetie. Come meet your brother," he says.

She deposits herself on the floor next to Bella and holds her arms out. Jax goes right to her. "Hi, Jackson."

"We call him Jax," Bella tells her.

Tallulah ignores her. "I'm your big sister."

"He already knows *I'm* his big sister," Bella says, her eyes flashing.

Jax's chubby little hands swat at Tallulah's face and she laughs. He squirms out of her arms and toddles away, then picks up speed as he runs toward the French doors leading to the pool. Jackson strides across the room and sweeps him up.

"Where do you think you're going, little man?" He laughs as he swings him in the air and the baby squeals with delight.

It's surreal, standing here watching it all. To the casual observer we look like a happy, normal family, with Jackson the fun-loving doting father.

"Why don't we take Jax and the girls down to the beach. I've set out chairs and an umbrella. There are tons of beach toys here, so I took a bunch of those down as well. Maybe Jax would enjoy playing in the sand."

Jackson smiles. "Great idea. Amber keeps a suit and sun hat in the diaper bag."

It's the first time her name's been mentioned, and at the sound of it I feel my stomach clench. I had hoped to never have to see that despicable woman again but that's an unrealistic expectation now.

At the beach, Tallulah and Bella immediately kneel on the sand with Jax, vying with each other to show him what every toy does. He picks up fistfuls of sand, laughing, his arms bouncing up and down as he opens his fingers and lets the granules drop. I'm surprised at how much they're enjoying him, and when I look over at

Jackson, I see a softness in his expression, and that surprises me too. His gaze moves from the children to me. "This is nice," he says.

"Yes, the girls are really taken with him."

"No, I mean this." He sweeps his arm out. "All of us together."

I shift uneasily in the chair and say nothing. Now I wish Meredith were here.

His eyes focus intently on mine. "Thank you for bringing the girls. You have no idea how much it means to me. I know it wasn't easy for you." He stops for a minute, and it looks as if he's trying to maintain his composure. "I had a lot of time to think while I was locked away. Time to think about what's important and what's not. Time to think about the past and the things I've done. I wasn't always good to you, Daphne, and I'm sorry."

I'm stunned by his confession. "I . . . I don't know what to say."

"You don't have to say anything. I just want you to know that I'm sorry."

We sit in silence while the girls entertain Jax, running back and forth with buckets of water and building a drizzle castle with him. As the sun begins to lower in the sky, Jackson rises and stoops over his son. "It's getting late, buddy. Time to go home," he says, and picks up Jax.

The child starts crying, kicking his legs as Jackson lifts him up. "No. No."

Bella jumps up and strokes his back. "It's okay, Jax. We'll play again tomorrow, okay?"

Jax cocks his head and looks at Bella, and for a moment I think he's going to start crying again. Instead, he laughs at her, and Jackson says, "Wave bye-bye to your sisters." He lifts one plump little arm and flaps his hand up and down.

"See you tomorrow then?" Jackson looks at me.

"We'll talk," I say, and he nods once, giving me an understanding half smile.

Later, after we've cleaned up, had dinner, and retired for the night, I lie awake and think about what Jackson said. What did he want me to say when he apologized? *Oh, that's all right. I forgive you for putting me in an asylum, for abusing me, for trying to make me out to be a bad mother.* My body aches with tension, like a cornered animal ready to pounce. Maybe he's sincere, but my antennae are on high alert and standing at attention.

19

DAISY ANN

Each time the door to the bar and grill opened Daisy Ann looked up expectantly, but Martin still hadn't shown. He was half an hour late, and she was getting worried. Maybe he'd figured out that the sweepstakes was a scam. The next time the door opened, though, a young guy wearing jeans and a leather jacket walked in. Thin brown hair hung limply at his collar, and part of a multicolored tattoo ran up the side of his neck. He stood there, looking around, and Daisy Ann realized it must be him. They made eye contact, and she waved him over. He walked toward her booth and stopped in front of her.

"Ms. Chambers?"

She nodded. "You must be Martin. Please, have a seat. Care for something to drink?"

He slid into the booth. "Nah, I can't stay long. What do I gotta sign?"

"First things first." She gave him a bright smile and pulled out an envelope. "There's five hundred dollars in this envelope." She opened the flap to let him see. "But I'm not exactly who I said I was."

His eyes narrowed. "What is this?"

"I'm not really from the marketing agency."

He started to get up. "I knew this was a load of crap. Look, lady, whoever you are, I don't need any trouble."

Daisy Ann put a hand up. "Now hold your horses. I'm not here to give you any trouble. You'll get your money. I need some information on a friend of yours, and I was afraid you might not show up if I told you the truth."

He hesitated a few seconds and then slowly slid back down, all the while eyeing the envelope.

"What friend?"

"My father was Jake Crawford. A woman named Amber Patterson murdered him. I'm trying to find out about her background, but I hit a dead end. I reckon you might know something about her." At the mention of Amber's name, Martin paled.

"I don't know any Amber."

"Now that's strange since a piece of paper with your name and number was found among her things." She leaned forward. "I'm willing to give you five hundred to tell me who she really is, and then you'll never hear from me again."

"How do I know you're not with law enforcement or something. Trying to trick me?"

"Have you done something illegal?" She shook her head. "Never mind. Heavens to Betsy, I'm not the police." She pulled some papers from her purse and pointed.

"That's the article about the so-called accident that killed my father. You see," she said, pointing to a photograph in the middle of the article, "that's Amber's picture. She shot my father in the back. Here's his obituary." She pointed again. "There's my name. I'm his daughter." Daisy Ann retrieved her license from her wallet and slid it across the table. "There's proof. I'm just a grieving daughter."

Martin took it all in and blew out a breath. "Shit. Yeah, I know her. She always was a piece of work. What do you want to know?"

"Her real name for starters. I know the real Amber Patterson's dead. My detective found that out."

He ran a hand through his hair. "On second thought, can I get a beer?"

Daisy Ann nodded and flagged down the waitress.

"Gimme a Stella," he said, then looked down at the table, shredding a napkin as he spoke. "Her real name is Lana Crump. We went to school together back in Blue Springs, Missouri. She helped me out when I got in trouble but made a point of reminding me that I owed her. Lana never does anything out of the goodness of her heart. So I had no choice but to return the favor and got her a new identity."

Daisy Ann was taking notes. "How'd you do that?"

He leaned in toward her, lowering his voice. "I work in vital records here. I could get in a lot of trouble if anyone found out . . ."

"Don't worry. I told you, all I want is information."

"I gave her a copy of a missing girl's birth certificate—Amber Patterson." He stopped when the waitress appeared with his beer, and after she set it down, he took a long swallow and began again. "Lana used it to get a new ID. I also hooked her up with a friend who got her a job. That's the last I saw of her. To be honest, she gives me the creeps."

"Why is that?"

He shrugged. "She was always clever, and she knew it. One step ahead of everyone else. But too big for her britches, you know? Felt like she deserved better. Her family was nice enough, but they didn't have a lot of money. Not the kind of money she wanted, anyway. Dad owned a dry cleaner. She had to work there on the weekends, and she hated it. I left right after high school, so I wasn't around anymore but I heard some stuff."

"What stuff?"

He raised an eyebrow. "She got knocked up by Matthew Lockwood and then accused him of rape. The Lockwoods have lots of money. Poor guy went to prison until Lana's own mother came forward and said she'd been lying. Lana was pissed off that Matthew wouldn't marry her. Then I heard he got stabbed while locked up and is in a wheelchair now." He shook his head. "I definitely wouldn't want to cross her. She called me and said she needed to leave town. That she needed a new identity. There was an outstanding warrant for her in Missouri for lying in court."

Daisy Ann was stunned although she didn't know why anything should shock her about this vile woman. "Did she have the child?"

"Yeah. Left him behind when she bolted. I guess Matthew has him."

"Do her parents still live there?"

"Far as I know."

She pushed the envelope toward him. "Thank you. I really appreciate your help. Can you write down the address of the Lockwoods as well as her parents?" She pushed the pad of paper toward him and handed him her pen.

He took the pen and looked up at her. "I don't know the Crumps' address, but their dry cleaners is downtown on Main Street. Five Star Cleaners."

"Okay. What about the Lockwoods?"

"That address I know by heart. Used to cut their grass." He wrote it down on the pad, then picked up the beer, and drained the bottle.

"Thank you. If I have any other questions, do you mind if I call you?"

He shook his head. "No problem. I'm real sorry about your dad," he said, rising.

Daisy Ann arrived in Blue Springs, Missouri, a day later. Her first stop was the Lockwood residence. She had decided it would be best to show up unannounced and take her chances. Besides which, they had an unlisted number. She pulled up the long driveway to the top of the hill where a white colonial with tall pillars and a generous front porch stood. Daisy Ann guessed it must have four or five bedrooms and be close to four thousand square feet. After driving by the house Amber (aka Lana) had grown up in—a small rancher in a modest neighborhood—she could understand why Amber would have been envious at the time. But it was rather average compared to the wealth Amber now enjoyed being married to Jackson Parrish.

She parked her rental car, walked up the steps to the front porch, and rang the bell. The door was opened by a uniformed woman.

"May I help you?"

Daisy Ann smiled at her. "I'm here to see Mrs. Lockwood."

The woman frowned. "Are you expected?"

Daisy Ann shook her head. "No. But please let her know we have a common enemy. Lana Crump."

"Wait here, please." She shut the door and Daisy Ann waited. Seconds later she was welcomed inside.

"Please come this way; Mrs. Lockwood is on the sunporch."

Daisy Ann followed behind the woman, through the marble-floored entryway, taking in the curved staircase lined with what looked like oil paintings of family members, past the kitchen, one rather in need of updates from its nineties look of white appliances and oak cabinets. They reached the sunporch, which ran the length of the house and faced a nicely landscaped yard that backed up to woods. Mrs. Lockwood sat at a round table in front of a large jigsaw puzzle, one piece in hand as she peered at the puzzle and then fit the part in. She was dressed in a blue knit pantsuit, her short gray hair done in that "once a week at the hairdresser" way, and was painfully thin, frail even. She looked up as Daisy Ann entered.

"Who are you and how do you know Lana?"

So much for social niceties, Daisy Ann thought, an exhortation of her mother-in-law's coming to mind, *Good manners are not to be taken on and off like pearls*. She extended a hand.

"Hello, ma'am. My name is Daisy Ann Briscoe, and Lana killed my father."

Mrs. Lockwood blanched, then pointed to a chair. "Please have a seat." She looked up. "Frannie, please bring some refreshments."

Daisy Ann took the chair across from the older woman. "I'm sorry if I shocked you, but I don't believe in beating around the bush."

"Neither do I, Ms. Briscoe, so what exactly does this have to do with me?"

"The murder of my father, nothing. But I know about Lana and your son and all that he's suffered because of her. She got away with it. And she got away with killing my father. That is what we have in common, Mrs. Lockwood." Daisy Ann locked eyes with the woman and saw only indifference there.

"What is it that you want from me?" Mrs. Lockwood asked.

"I suppose I'm looking for any information on Lana Crump that will help me prove my father's death was not an accident."

"I don't see how I can help you with that."

"Can you tell me anything about your interactions with the girl?"

"I can tell you that she's a grasping little guttersnipe who lured my son into a sexual relationship. She deliberately got pregnant so that he would marry her. Fortunately, he was too smart to tie himself to such a nasty piece of work, but he paid dearly for it. He is in a wheelchair for life because of her."

"If I can get enough evidence to have her charged, would you be willing to testify at a trial?"

"I'm sorry, but I can't help you. My son is married to a wonderful young woman. He has custody of the child Lana bore, a precious boy whom I dearly love. As much as I want her to pay for what she did to Matthew, I can't risk her coming back into our lives. I wouldn't put it past her to try and get custody of little Matty just for spite, and the crazy courts just might give it to her. They are too often overly sympathetic to the mother. In this case the mother is a monster. No. I won't let that happen. That girl is poison. I won't have her near my family." She rose from her chair. "I think you should leave now."

"But—"

"I have nothing more to say to you. Frannie will see you out."
And with that she left the room.

Daisy Ann's teeth were clenched so hard it felt like her jaw
might break. The woman was insufferable. She walked to the car
feeling deflated, but as she thought about it, she realized that any
testimony of Lockwood's would be unhelpful. It was in the past and
had no bearing on Jake's murder. The one interesting thing that
came out of the visit was the fact that Mrs. Lockwood had no interest in finding Lana/Amber and bringing her to justice. That was
good news for Daisy Ann. She wanted Amber all to herself.

20

DAPHNE

Things are going well with Jackson, but I keep waiting for the other shoe to drop. We've been here for three weeks and other than showing up early that first day, he has been respectful of my wishes. He even took the brunt of Tallulah's scorn when she asked if they could go over to his house, the house we all used to live in, and he told her it wasn't a good idea, that she might be upset to see the changes Amber had made. I was grateful. The last thing Tallulah needs is to see that her old room has been completely re-done and belongs to Jax. Especially as the girls are growing very fond of little Jax, as am I. Jackson brings him over every morning, and we've fallen into an easy routine where we spend a few hours on the beach and then have lunch by the pool. I'm not letting my guard down, naturally, because I know better than anyone what a good actor Jackson can be. But, for the sake of our children, I hold on to a small hope that maybe prison has really changed him.

"Let's get your sunscreen on and then we can go down to the beach," I call over to Bella.

Bella runs over and stands still while I lather her up. "How come Tallulah doesn't have to wear sunscreen?"

I smile. "She does, but she doesn't need Mommy's help except maybe on her back." Although to be honest, I suspect Tallulah is more concerned with her tan than with sun protection.

Bella shakes her head, her blond curls catching the sunlight. "She thinks she's so grown up. It gets on my nerves."

I laugh. "I hear you, kiddo."

"Daddy and Jax are coming, right?"

"Yep. They should be here any minute."

As if on cue, Jackson pulls up the drive in an SUV. "There they are now. Let's head outside." I open the door and let Bella out, then shut it behind me.

"What've you got there?" I ask Jackson who is pulling out a large board and two paddles from the back.

"I thought the girls would enjoy this. Have they gone paddle-boarding before?"

I shake my head. "I think maybe Tallulah has, not sure."

"It's a lot of fun. Do you mind grabbing Jax so I can bring the board down?"

"Sure," I say and open the back door. Jax smiles at me, and I give him a kiss on his chubby cheek. "Hi, sweetie." I unbuckle him and pick him up. I'd forgotten how sweet babies are, how good it feels to hold one in your arms.

"Oh, I picked up some drinks. Two iced coffees for you and me, both with Bailey's creamer—I know how you like that—and lemonade for the kids. Take either one." He puts the board and paddles under one arm and grabs the drinks with his other hand.

"Thank you. That was nice." Carrying Jax, I walk down to our setup on the beach. Tallulah looks up from her book and stands up when she sees Jackson approaching.

"Hi, Dad."

He sets the paddleboard down on the beach. "I picked up a double board. I thought you and Bella would have fun taking it out."

"Cool, thanks. I've done it a few times."

"Can we go now?" Bella asks.

Jackson looks at me. "Are you okay with it? I'll go in the water, and they can stay close to the swim buoys."

I nod. "Sure, I'll watch the baby." I put Jax down in the enclosure under the umbrella with a shovel and various sand toys. He plops down happily and begins to play.

"Great."

The three of them run off and I'm filled with a strange sense of longing and melancholy. Things with Jackson and me had started with such promise all those years ago. If only he had been the man he'd pretended to be, we could have been so happy. In retrospect, maybe I should have noticed the red flags, what I now know was love bombing. I think of the gifts he showered me with, how he hired a private plane to fly me to New Hampshire when my father had his heart attack. The way he would suggest what I wear when we went out, even down to the shoes, as if I were a doll he was dressing. At the time, I let his charm and my attraction to him drown out the voice of reason. It was all too good to be true. If only it hadn't been a masquerade, we'd still be a family. My daughters wouldn't have had their world ripped apart, could have grown up in the warmth and security of our home instead of pining for a father three thousand miles away.

I've had my fill of caffeine for the day, so I pick up one of the lemonades instead and lean back in the chair watching as Jackson helps the girls onto the board and they begin to paddle horizontally to the shore. It's the most relaxed I've been in a long time. Bella struggles to stand up and get her balance, toppling into the water after a few seconds. I start to get out of my chair but sit back down when Jackson's right there to help her back up. Besides, they're only waist deep in the water. Chiding myself, I take a deep breath and finish my drink, then put the empty cup in the beach bag.

Pulling a sippy cup of water from the cooler, I hand it to Jax, and he takes it and drinks. It's hot today and despite his being under the umbrella I don't want him to get overheated. He's such a happy little boy, and I wonder what kind of mother Amber is. Even though she doesn't strike me as the maternal type, her son's happiness must mean she's good to him. Or at least I hope so. But I do find it curious that Amber doesn't seem to be objecting to Jax's daily visits with us. The sun is making me drowsy, and I'd like nothing more than to close my eyes and take a nap. I have to keep an eye on the baby, so I lean forward, trying to summon some energy, but the pull of sleep is irresistible, and I lean back in the chair. Maybe I'll just close my eyes for a minute.

Rough hands are pulling on me and I try to open my eyes, but it's like they're sewn shut. I hear voices yelling, chaos all around me. Finally, I come to and there's a police officer standing in front of me.

"Ma'am, are you okay?"

I look around. Jax is gone from the enclosure. But then I see Amber holding him. And the girls, Bella crying, Tallulah looking angry, standing with Jackson and Amber a few feet away. My eyes keep trying to close.

"What's happening?" I can barely get the words out and I sound different to my ears.

Amber's face is red. "I'll tell you what's happening. You got high again, and your kids almost drowned. The tide took them way out and a lifeguard had to get them. And you left my baby all alone."

"That's not . . . No!" I struggle to stay awake but feel myself falling back into the abyss. From what seems like a great distance, I hear their voices. Snatches of conversation.

"Officer . . . not first time. . . . problem with alcohol . . . swore she was clean."

I open my eyes again, and Jackson is standing over me. "Did you mix your antianxiety meds with alcohol again?"

"What? What are you . . ."

The officer gives me a look I don't like. "We need to call DCF. The children will have to come with me."

It takes everything I have to snap out of this feeling of sinking.

"Can I come with them?" Jackson asks.

The officer shakes his head. "I'm sorry but until the Department of Children and Families clears you, they'll have to stay in my custody. You can meet us at the station if you like." He turns to me. "Ma'am, maybe you should get medical attention. It can be dangerous to mix alcohol and drugs."

Alcohol and drugs? What is he talking about? I try to stand and fall back into the chair. I call over to the girls, "Sweeties, I'm sorry. I don't know what happened." I still speak as though I have marbles in my mouth. Am I having a stroke?

Jackson stands in front of them, shielding them from me. "You need to get to the hospital. I'll go to the station and wait for DCF." He turns to the officer. "Can you arrange for someone to take her to Norwalk Hospital. I can call her friend Meredith Stanton and have her meet them there."

"Yes, I'll call someone."

I don't want to go to the hospital, but I can hardly speak. "The girls?"

"Don't worry, I'll take care of everything." Then he smiles at me. It's the same smile he gave me when he had me committed twelve years ago. I try to think but my brain isn't working right, and it's like I'm stuck in quicksand. My eyes close again and everything goes black.

21

AMBER

Amber left Jackson at the police station where he was waiting to meet with someone from the Department of Children and Families to see about bringing the girls home with him. Jax's constant babbling was on her last nerve and the first thing she did was call for Chloe to take him. She hated noise, and now she'd have two *more* noisy children running about. At least Chloe would do most of the heavy lifting if that came to pass. And anyway, Amber would be gone in a few days. She'd have to make the best of it while she was still here. Tallulah wouldn't be a problem—she and Amber had formed a tenuous bond over the girl's desperation to be in touch with Jackson. It would be fun to lord that over Daphne and even help to sabotage Tallulah's relationship with her mother before Amber left. It had always irked Amber how loyal those little brats were to Daphne. Unfortunately, Bella was most likely a lost cause, but then again, Jackson had told Amber how taken she was with little Jax. She could use that to her advantage. The more she thought about it, she could probably turn them both against their sainted mother. Especially now that it appeared as though Daphne had gotten drunk *and* high and put her own children's lives at risk.

The plan had come fully together a few days ago. Jackson had spotted the Klonopin in Daphne's medicine cabinet during one of his many visits to her beach house. Nosy as he is, he counted them and saw only one had been taken. That didn't surprise Amber— Daphne had always been such a boring straight arrow. The combination of pills and Beluga vodka, which Jackson said was so pure and smooth that it tasted like water, did the trick. Once she drank the drink he'd laced, it was less than half an hour before she was passed out. In the meantime, Jackson had let the girls take the paddleboard out past the swim buoys and toward the public beach. He'd timed it so that the tide was coming in and the water would be deep where they were. Amber, parked a short distance away, ran down to the beach as soon as she got Jackson's text, and she sat on the sand with Jax. Jackson stood out of sight of the lifeguard watching Tallulah and Bella paddleboarding. The day was windy, and when it became obvious that the girls were tiring and having a hard time getting in, Jackson ran to the lifeguard and yelled for help. Once they were safely onshore, Jackson told the lifeguard that their mother was supposed to have been watching them. Amber was the one who called the police. Not only had Daphne let her own daughters almost drown, she told them, but the woman had left Jax unattended on a blanket next to her. Amber used her best sobbing voice to explain that when she arrived, poor baby Jax was almost in the water. Amber had played her part beautifully and Jackson had given her back her passport. But before she started a new life abroad, she had some scores to settle. If she didn't, Amber would spend the rest of her life looking over her shoulder, wondering who was out there trying to destroy her. By the time she was through, Daisy Ann would rue the day she ever declared war on Amber. She would be sorry she hadn't left the past in the past.

Jackson was keeping his end of the bargain to help her get back at Daisy Ann, and his financial expertise had come in handy as they formulated the next plan together. After some extensive research into Daisy Ann's company, Amber had discovered that even though it was privately held, stock had been issued. The Texas Secretary of State website listed only two current stockholders, Daisy Ann Briscoe, who held 70 percent, and Wade Ashford, who held 30 percent. Why did that name sound familiar? When she typed it into Google images, a man in his late sixties with a ten-gallon hat and a round craggy face populated the screen. She remembered now. He had been a friend of Daisy Ann's father, Jake. Amber had actually met him at the café in Gunnison when he'd come to Colorado to meet with Jake on business. This was before she and Jake were a couple—when she was still a waitress there. But after they were married, Jake confided to Amber that he no longer had respect for the man. When she'd pressed him for a reason, he wouldn't say—Jake was not a gossip. But curiosity got the better of her when she overheard Jake terminate his business with Ashford. She'd wondered why. Wade was as rich as Jake, and the two of them had planned to buy a development together. So, Amber tearfully confessed that when Wade had been in town, he'd hit on her quite aggressively and she'd had to fight him off. It was a total fabrication, of course, but it enraged Jake and he then told her the reason for his antipathy. And what a reason it was. And now little Daisy Ann was in business with the man. She supposed Jake had died before he was able to warn Daisy Ann about him. Amber was going to do some digging and if she was right in what she suspected, Wade would be her first line of attack in getting back at Daisy Ann.

As for the disintegration of their marriage, Jackson had agreed to tell everyone it was her idea. That she wanted to move on. He would get his half of the diamond money as soon as they completed her plan of revenge against Daisy Ann. Jackson didn't know about the three diamonds she'd kept in reserve for herself. They would bring another six million, according to Mr. Stones's assessment. Jackson and Amber were meeting with the lawyer to set up the shell company that would act as Amber's front. Once that was taken care of, she'd follow through with the second part of the plan and go to where her immediate future beckoned. Dallas.

Hours later, Jackson arrived at home with the girls in tow. At Amber's instruction, the cook had prepared a feast of fried chicken, mac and cheese, milkshakes, and double fudge brownies. Tallulah and Bella were quiet as they followed Jackson into the house. Amber pasted a sad expression on her face and embraced Tallulah, then a stiff Bella.

"My dears, what a traumatic day this has been. You must be starving. I've cooked up all your favorites." She texted the nanny to let her know the girls had arrived, and moments later Chloe arrived with Jax in tow.

Jackson gently pushed them toward her. "Go on, girls; Chloe will get you settled. I need to talk to Amber for a minute."

He and Amber went into his study.

"Where's Daphne?" Amber asked as he closed the door behind them.

"At the hospital. She was so out of it that they wanted to check her out. I made sure I didn't give her anything lethal but of course I couldn't tell them that. I was granted emergency custody of the girls until DCF's investigation is completed."

"I'm surprised you were able to bring the girls back so quickly."

"It helps when your lawyer is golf buddies with a judge. I'll have them for at least thirty days, maybe longer. Depends on how long their investigation into Daphne takes."

"How do you think the girls are doing?"

He shrugged. "They'll be okay. They were surprised and shocked, but I explained that their mother had done this before. That sometimes when she gets overstressed this is what happens. They're obviously going to want her to come here. Which is exactly how I'll get her to come."

"Okay, well, I assume it won't hurt your temporary custody if I'm out of here in the next few weeks?"

He shook his head. "No, and your being here is not exactly conducive to my campaign to get Daphne back."

Amber laughed. "You really think she's going to come back to you after what you've done?"

Jackson walked over to the bar cart and poured himself a bourbon. He gave Amber a sardonic look. "I know this is hard for you to understand, but in some women, the maternal instinct is strong. Primal. Daphne will do whatever she needs to make sure the girls are happy and safe."

Amber felt a spark of jealousy despite the fact that she wasn't in love with Jackson. What was so special about Daphne that he would go to such lengths to get her back, while he didn't give a shit about Amber leaving? "Answer me something."

"Shoot."

"Why do you want her back so badly? She doesn't love you; in fact, she hates you. She's just a suburban mom. Don't you find her boring?"

He gave her a disparaging look. "Daphne is my finest creation. I molded her into a polished, elegant woman of refinement— qualities you only pretend to have. And I want that back in my life. With more of my masterful honing, she'll be even more perfect than before. And for your information, I happen to find her anything but boring."

Amber felt the fury build up and before she could stop herself, she slapped him across the face. Hard. She braced herself for his reaction, but he merely began to laugh.

"See what I mean. You just proved my point. You're nothing but an alley cat disguised as a purebred."

22

DAPHNE

When I awaken and open my eyes, it takes me a minute to figure out where I am. A figure moves to my left, and suddenly I see Meredith's worried face as she stands next to my bed looking down at me. But it's not my bed. As my eyes dart around the room, I take in the IV tube running from the crook of my arm to a bag of fluids and the gown I'm wearing. I'm in the hospital.

"You're awake. How do you feel? Are you okay?" she asks.

"Why—What happened?" I shake my head as if to clear it. The fog slowly lifts and then I begin to remember. The beach. The girls. Taken away by the police. I spring up, needing to get to them, when a wave of dizziness makes me fall back again.

Meredith rests a hand on my shoulder. "Hey, take it easy."

I look at her and she must see the confusion on my face. "Jackson called me and told me they were bringing you here. Daph, you overdosed." Her eyebrows knit together in concern. "I didn't know you were taking antianxiety meds. They had to treat you with something to counteract the pills. You also had alcohol in your blood."

"No, no." I shake my head. "I didn't take anything, and I would never drink while watching the kids. You know that. My therapist prescribed the pills for anxiety, and the last time I took one, it threw me for a loop. I was totally out of it. Tallulah almost called 911 when she couldn't wake me up. I don't even know why I brought the damn pills with me. Jackson must have found them. He had to have done this to me."

"What do you mean? How?"

And then it hits me. The lemonade. He had to have drugged it. I bet he put Klonopin in the drinks. That bastard, he must have spiked all of them. "He's lying. He did it. I know he did it." I tell Meredith about the drinks he brought.

"Unreal! That son of a bitch could have killed you! What the hell is he up to?"

I go cold. The children. "Where are the girls?"

Meredith's hand flies to her mouth. "With Jackson. A judge issued him an emergency custody order. He did this to get the kids from you." She goes to her purse and pulls out her cell phone. "You need a lawyer. I'm calling Dean right now."

Hours later I'm finally discharged from the hospital and sitting in the reception room outside the office of Dean Manchester, Esquire. Meredith has already apprised him of my situation, and he's pulling in the top family law attorney from the firm to help with the case. I've been calling Tallulah's cell phone over and over, and it rolls right to voicemail every time. Now I wish I hadn't been so adamant about making Bella wait another year to get a cell phone. I keep flashing to the anger on Tallulah's face at the beach. I spring up from the leather couch and begin to pace again.

Meredith watches me walk back and forth and finally says, "Daph, sit." She pats the cushion.

"I can't stand it. I'm so worried. Do you think the girls are okay?"

Meredith nods. "I'm sure they're fine. No matter what, Jackson loves them. He's not going to hurt them."

"But he's going to do whatever he can to damage my relationship with them. This is his revenge for keeping them from him. If you'd seen the way Tallulah looked at me." I try to take a deep breath, but I feel like I'm suffocating. "What if she believes I did this on purpose? All his talk about changing. Being sorry for how he treated me. What a load of crap. I should have listened to my mother and stayed far away."

Meredith puts her arm around me. "I know this is hard, sweetie. But you need to calm down. We're going to get this sorted out. I promise."

The door opens and Dean steps out. I've met him socially but have never seen him in a professional setting. This silver-haired man in a tailored suit and starched shirt looks high-powered and formidable, unlike the casual and charming guy I've seen on the tennis court.

"Hello, Meredith, Daphne," he says with a warm smile. "Please, come in."

He shuts the door behind us, and Meredith and I each take a chair across from the large crescent-shaped desk. Plush carpet, wall-to-wall bookcases, and subdued lighting give the room a hushed and protective feel, as if whatever business you conduct here will be effectual.

"Would either of you care for something to drink?"

We both shake our heads.

"Very well." He focuses his attention on me when he speaks. "Daphne, I'm very sorry that you find yourself in these circumstances. Meredith has given me some background, but I'd like to hear what happened in your words."

I take a deep breath, gathering my thoughts. "After my divorce, I moved to California with my daughters. The marriage was not a good one—Jackson was abusive, and I was able to get him to terminate his parental rights."

He cocks an eyebrow. "Really? How did you manage that?"

"Without getting into a lot of detail, I knew something incriminating about his new wife and threatened to expose her if he didn't terminate his rights. I know it sounds bad, but trust me, the last thing my girls needed was his influence in their lives."

THE NEXT MRS. PARRISH 141

He says nothing. Waiting for me to continue.

"The only reason I came back to Bishops Harbor is because my oldest, Tallulah, has been very depressed." I fill him in on what happened on her field trip. "My therapist thought it necessary for me to allow her and her sister to establish some sort of relationship with their father." I bring him up to speed on how things have been going and Jackson's charade of having changed. "The last thing I remember is drinking the lemonade he brought and then being awakened by the police."

He nods. "Of course I know of your husband's problems with the government. I'm actually very surprised, given the circumstances, that he was able to get an emergency order of custody. The courts don't look kindly upon parents who voluntarily forfeit their rights, and the fact that he's got a prison record also makes his suitability questionable."

I know the reason before he even articulates it. I give him a wry look. "I'm guessing the judge is a friend of his."

"It appears so." He sighs. "I don't know if you're aware of this, but Mr. Parrish has informed DCF that you suffered from postpartum psychosis and were a danger to your first child when she was a baby. They'll be interviewing the doctors who treated you when you were admitted to the hospital there as well as the psychiatrist you were ordered to see following your release."

"But all of that's a lie. Jackson set me up then too." I protest.

"I believe you, I do. But you have to understand how it's going to appear to the social workers. Blaming your ex-husband for both events. It makes you look bad."

Frustration overtakes me, and I want to grab the glass globe on his desk and smash it to smithereens. "So what am I supposed to do?"

"We're going to have to come up with a strategy for when you're interviewed by DCF. I need to give that some more thought and will be consulting with one of my associates whose specialty is family law. I'll be with you during the interview with DCF, and please, no matter what, do not speak to anyone about this without my being present."

"All right, I understand. But how long will all of this take? I need to see my girls."

"As soon as they file the order of temporary custody, the OTC, we will appeal it. They have to set the hearing within thirty days of the appeal. We'll use that time to gather evidence of your suitability and get your character witness testimonies."

"So in thirty days then, I should be able to get them back?"

He tilts his head. "It's not quite that simple. It's within thirty days from the *filing* of the OTC. Jackson has the girls under an emergency order. The court still has to file the paperwork, which could take a bit longer. We'll push as much as we can."

"Can you speak to my therapist? She can attest to my sanity and to what's happened in the past with Jackson. Surely if she speaks to the social workers that will help."

"Give me her information. That will definitely help."

Meredith leans forward. "Dean, we're worried about Jackson having the girls. Is there any way we can get custody transferred to Daphne's mother? We could get her here on the next plane and she could stay with me."

I nod. "She's in Peru right now. I don't even know how long it would take for her to arrange to get back here." I hate the thought of ruining her trip, but it doesn't seem like I have any choice. "Hopefully she has cell service on the boat."

Dean raises his eyebrows. "I'm not sure that will work. Jackson has given a statement that she has dementia. It's quite possible that she'd have to undergo psychological testing before they'd release the girls to her."

"That's ridiculous!" I say. "Why would they believe that?"

"Apparently your daughter, Tallulah, corroborated that. I can only assume it's because she wants to stay with him. If he gets his parental rights reinstated, he would take precedence over a grand-parent anyway."

My mouth drops open. I can't believe Tallulah would agree to such a heinous lie. I shake my head. "I'm not going to drag my mother into the middle of this if it's not even going to do any good."

"I'm not at all confident that it would be an easy thing to have custody transferred in light of your daughter backing up Jackson's assertion," he says.

I can't think of a response, and I stare at him mutely.

Dean stands up, and the meeting comes to an end. "We have to assume that he's going to continue to play dirty. I have folks doing some digging. Try to keep your head while I put together a game plan."

"I don't know how I'm supposed to go on like everything's okay. My older daughter won't answer my phone calls, and I have no idea how Bella, my youngest, is coping. This is unbearable."

Meredith reaches over and squeezes my hand. Dean gives me a kind look. "I'm going to move as quickly as I can. But you don't want to do anything that could hurt your chances in the long run."

My blood runs cold. All I've been thinking about is clearing up this misunderstanding and taking the girls back to California. I hadn't considered the possibility that Jackson might actually be playing for keeps. "Are you saying I could lose custody?"

He puts a hand up. "Let's not even go there."

"But it's possible?"

He gives me a somber look. "Anything's possible."

23

DAISY ANN

aisy Ann wasn't sure what to expect when she pulled up to the front of Amber/Lana's childhood home. She'd phoned after leaving the Lockwood residence and recited to Lana's mother the story she'd concocted—that her name was Annie and she and Lana had shared an apartment in Atlanta, and she was trying to get in touch with Lana to return her portion of the security deposit. Daisy Ann knew that Florence hadn't spoken to her daughter since she'd left some years ago, but there was always the possibility that Amber might get in touch with her mother again. That's why she'd given Florence a false name—she didn't want to risk Amber finding out that she'd been here. The woman had been so eager for information about her daughter that she invited Daisy Ann to come right over. Turning off the engine, Daisy Ann sat for a minute, rehearsing what she wanted to say. She was intent on finding out as much as she could about Amber, or Lana. Sometimes the most seemingly insignificant information could be the key to unraveling a puzzle. And Amber was certainly a puzzle, a most vexing one at that.

As she got out of the car, she noticed the small but neatly manicured front lawn and the weedless garden bed filled with beautiful yellow coneflowers. She rang the bell, and moments later the door was opened by a woman who looked to be in her fifties. She smiled at Daisy Ann and extended her hand. Daisy Ann searched her face for any resemblance to Amber, but aside from the high cheekbones there was little else. The woman wearing a halter apron over her flowery dress was slight, with short graying hair and a face that looked weary, as if she carried the weight of the world on her shoulders. Daisy Ann felt a shiver of anticipation go through her. After all this time, she was closing in on Amber.

"You must be Annie. I'm Florence Crump. Please come in."

"Thank you. It's nice to meet you, Mrs. Crump," she said carefully, not completely confident that she could disguise her Texas accent, but she figured Florence wouldn't know the difference between a Texas and Georgia accent.

"Oh, please call me Florence," she said.

She followed Florence down a narrow hallway to the kitchen, where a plate of chocolate chip cookies sat on a round table covered in a bright yellow and blue cloth. It was obvious the cookies had just come from the oven, judging by the mouthwatering aroma in the air.

"Please sit down. Would you care for coffee or tea?"

"Oh, if you've already made it, coffee would be great. Just black. Thank you, ma'am." Daisy Ann looked around while Florence got the coffee. The room was immaculate, the linoleum floor waxed to a high gloss, and the laminated countertop almost entirely clutter-free, with the exception of a silver toaster and an olive-green set of canisters. Starched white curtains hung at the window above the sink, and small pots of primroses lined the sill. This was a woman who took great pride in her home.

Florence set the mug on the table and sat. "I hope some of your good manners rubbed off on Lana while she roomed with you."

Daisy Ann smiled. "That's nice of you to say. I always found Lana to be polite, though."

"You said you were roommates in Atlanta? So, she's been in Georgia all this time? How long did you live together? When was the last time you saw her?"

Daisy Ann knew this part could be a bit tricky. "We shared the apartment for a year. She left when the year was up, but I stayed on another year. Now I have the security deposit back and I want to give Lana her half, but unfortunately, the phone number she left for me is no longer in service, and I have no way to get in touch with her. Do you have any idea where she might have gone?"

Color rose in Florence's cheeks. "It's a sad state of affairs when a mother has no idea where her child is, but Lana always was . . . different. She disappeared one morning almost four years ago and at first, we worried that something had happened to her. She's made some enemies." She shook her head. "Then I found that all my emergency cash was gone, and I realized she'd left on her own."

Daisy Ann assumed the enemies she was talking about were the Lockwoods, but she pretended to know nothing about Lana's criminal activities. "Enemies?"

Florence nodded. "I feel bad talking about her, but the truth is the truth. She got involved with a young boy, got pregnant, and then accused him of rape. We believed her. Supported her and then to find out . . . well, she'd made it up when he wouldn't marry her. Her son was two and a half when she told me the truth. Poor Matthew, the young man she lied about, went to prison and was there all that time for a crime he didn't commit. I had to do something."

Daisy Ann feigned surprise. "That's terrible. Are you sure she made it up?"

"I'm sure. She bragged about it to her sister Penny, and Penny told me. When I confronted Lana, she said he deserved it for treating her like she was nothing. Well, as you can imagine, I wasn't very popular with her when I told the authorities. I didn't realize they'd arrest her for perjury. We posted her bail, but then she left. Left her only son, little Matty, and never looked back."

Not her only son anymore, Daisy Ann thought. "Gosh. I can't believe she'd leave her child. That must have been so hard for her."

Florence lowered her eyes. "I don't think it was. Her sisters and I paid more attention to Matty than she did. She couldn't be bothered with him half the time."

"Does he live with you?"

"No. With his dad and stepmom. Eugenia Lockwood never had much use for us, but after what Lana did, she hated us and did everything in her power to make sure we couldn't have anything to do with Matty. She's not a nice woman. She tried getting Lana's parental rights terminated, which would have ended ours as well. Luckily the judge wouldn't go for it. We get to see Matty once a month on the last Sunday." She sighed. "It's not enough, but what can we do?"

"My gosh, I'm so sorry."

"I'll show you a picture," Florence said. She quickly left the kitchen and came back with a framed photograph. "Here he is. Such a doll."

An adorable dark-haired little boy in a school uniform stared back at her. Daisy Ann couldn't imagine how a mother could abandon her child. But then again, this was Amber they were talking about. "I'm so sorry," she repeated. "That must be hard for you."

"It is, but one day he'll be old enough to decide for himself and we'll be here waiting for him. I'm blessed that my other daughters have given me grandchildren and we're all close. It makes me sad, though, that Matty hardly knows his cousins."

"What a shame," Daisy Ann said.

"Lana never was much for family, you know? She used to say she didn't understand how she ended up in this family, that there must have been some mistake. Like she didn't belong with us. Always wanted more. Nothing we did was ever good enough. I think she was kind of ashamed of us. But we're honest, hardworking folk, and I pray that one day Lana will see that. I mean, if I could find her, maybe if she came back, she could get partial custody. I'd be happy to help her with him."

"Wouldn't she go to jail for running from a warrant?"

Florence sighed. "Yes, probably for a few years, but she's young. I'd watch him in the meantime. If I could afford it, I'd hire somebody to try and find her, but we're hardly making ends meet as it is. And her sisters want nothing to do with her. She was always awful to them. Anyway, it's obvious she doesn't want to be found by us."

She wiped a tear from her eye. "I know she's done bad things, but she's still my child. I can't help but wonder what I did wrong."

Daisy Ann felt a deep sympathy for this kindhearted woman, who was so warm and lovely, and wanted to do something for her. She reached into her purse and pulled out an envelope, handing it to Florence. "It's the security deposit money I told you about. Two thousand dollars. I went to the bank and got cash. I remember Lana telling me that when we moved out and she got the security deposit back, she was going to send it to you to repay you for the money she took when she left."

"Thank you. So kind of you to bring it to me."

"And as far as wondering what you did wrong, you can't blame yourself. I really believe we're all born with our personalities intact."

"That's what my husband says. We both scratch our heads wondering how in the world she can do the things she does. She was such a darling little girl. Everyone would stop and say how pretty she was. Smart as a whip too and daring. Nothing scared her. Except tunnels. She's got a touch of claustrophobia."

Daisy Ann wondered how Amber would fare in a small prison cell.

24

DAPHNE

t's been three days since Jackson took the girls to his house and I still haven't been able to speak to them. I was tempted to drive over there, but Dean, my attorney, strenuously advised against it. Meredith, bless her, hasn't left my side and her company is the only thing keeping me from completely losing my mind.

"Can you drive over there, Mer? You're not restricted from seeing them."

"I'm happy to, but I'm not sure what good it will do. Maybe it's best if we wait to see what Dean advises."

My phone rings, and I jump up. I look at the screen and my heart skips a beat. "It's Jackson," I say to Meredith. Grabbing it, I answer.

"Jackson?"

"It's me, Mommy."

My legs almost buckle, and I fall back on the sofa. "Bella. Honey, are you okay?"

"I miss you, Mommy. Why did you leave us?"

"I didn't leave you, sweetie. It's . . . it's a misunderstanding. I'm trying to get it fixed so I can come get you."

"Amber said you don't love us anymore."

A rage unlike any I've ever known envelops me. I take a deep breath, forcing back the scream in the back of my throat. "Of course I love you. I don't know why she would tell you that. I love you more than anything."

"Mommy, please come get us."

She begins to cry, and my heart shatters into a million pieces. I grip the phone tighter, my head spinning, trying to think of what I could possibly say to make her feel better.

"Daphne?"

Jackson's voice cuts through me.

"What is wrong with you? How could you do this?" I'm screaming now, and Meredith runs over and puts a hand on my arm.

"Calm down," she whispers.

"You miserable son of a bitch. You drugged me and stole my children."

"I'd advise you to calm down if you ever want to see Tallulah and Bella again."

"You won't get away with this."

He laughs. "I already have. I miss my family. But it's not complete. I want you back."

His words rock me. "You're out of your mind. I'll never come back to you. How could you possibly think I'd ever come back after you pull something like this?"

"Drastic times require drastic measures." His voice softens, it's the tone he uses when he's pouring the honey on. "Daphne, my love, you'll come to see in time that what I did, I did for the best of our family. Amber's leaving tomorrow. We're divorcing. I've already cleared it with DCF, since you were negligent not abusive, as long as you're not left alone with the children, they have no issue with your being here. I want us to work toward becoming a family again."

I'm so stunned I can't speak. He's certifiable. If he was insane before, he's now completely and utterly delusional. "Tell DCF the truth and then maybe we can have a chance. But not this way." I'm lying, of course, but maybe he'll buy it. I'll do whatever I have to in order to get my children back.

He chuckles. "Nice try, Daph. You know I can't do that. Number one—I'd get in a lot of trouble. And number two—you'd just take the girls and leave without giving me a chance to prove what a good husband I can be. I wasn't lying. I have changed. I should never have cheated on you. Never let you get away. You're my one true love, and I'll do anything to prove myself to you again."

Despite my better judgment, I try to reason with him. "Jackson, don't you see how wrong this is? You're telling me you love me. That I can trust you again, yet you've made me out to be a drunk and a drug addict in front of our children. In front of the community. I'm being investigated as an unfit mother! How can you expect me to believe you've changed and that we have a future when you've done something so despicable?"

"I'm sorry that it had to be this way, but tell me honestly, would you have ever given me a chance otherwise? This was the only way. I know it seems harsh and unfair, but you'll be cleared and by then you'll be in love with me again and all will be well."

That he actually believes I could ever love him again completely astounds me. "I need time to think," I say, stalling for time.

"Don't take too long; otherwise, I may decide that the girls are better off without you. After all, what is there to think about? Either you want to be with them or you don't."

25

AMBER

t was Amber's last day in Bishops Harbor. If she could have accomplished a revenge plan completely alone, she would have done so, but unfortunately, since she needed Jackson's financial expertise, that meant she'd have to share the diamond money with him if she wanted his help. She would still end up with enough money to take care of herself for life, and Jackson didn't know about the gems she still had hidden. Those would be 100 percent hers. Besides, being too greedy could get you in trouble. As her father was fond of saying: *Pigs get fed, hogs get slaughtered.* Of course, that was the only smart thing she ever heard him say. She and Jackson had finalized their business arrangement yesterday and formed an LLC in which they were equal partners. They named it Delancey-Flynn. Amber liked the sound of it. A former prison friend of Jackson's, Hugo Bennett, would be their front man. He was charming, British, and apparently a consummate con man. If all went as she hoped, the LLC would soon own a part of Daisy Ann's business. It was a long shot and hinged on two things: her hunch about Daisy Ann's partner, Wade Ashford, being correct and Valene Mart's interest in buying out the company. Amber had no doubt that Wade was crooked; Jake had admitted that much. What she didn't yet know was if she'd be able to get the leverage she needed to make him dance to her tune. After her meeting tomorrow she'd know for sure. Then she'd move on to the second part of their plan. She wasn't too concerned. If this plan didn't work out, she'd come up

with another way to make Daisy Ann pay. Amber was good at revenge. There was always a way.

She walked outside to the deck overlooking Long Island Sound
and breathed deeply. She would miss this view, but when she finished what she set out to do, she would have a new view, one that
belonged to her and her alone, far away from this small town and
its small-minded people. She wasn't the same stars-in-her-eyes,
naive young woman she'd been when she'd first stepped foot in this
house. Back then, she'd thought living here with the charismatic
and powerful Jackson Parrish was the ultimate prize. Now she
knew that true success and power came from being independent.
From having the money and influence to do whatever you wanted,
wherever you wanted, and answering to no one. Thanks to those
beautiful little rocks, that's exactly what she now had. A thrill of
anticipation ran through her at what lay ahead, when the buzz of
conversation made her turn around to see Chloe and the girls walking toward her.

"The girls would like to take a swim. Is that okay with you?"

"Is Jax still napping?"

"*Oui, madame.*"

"Fine. Just make sure you take his monitor with you. I've got a
busy afternoon."

"When is my mom coming over?" Bella asked, moving in front
of Amber, her little hands on her hips.

"Chloe, take Tallulah outside. Bella will be out shortly."

"Let's go sit down for a minute," she told the child. Bella followed her over to the sofa and sat.

"She's coming soon. But I want to prepare you."

Bella looked at her suspiciously.

"Your mom didn't really want to come. She said she was having
so much fun with her friends drinking and . . . stuff. But your dad
told her how much you miss her. She said she didn't care, but he
finally talked her into it. So don't be surprised if she doesn't stay
long. She doesn't really love you that much."

Bella stared at her a long moment. "You're a liar! My mom loves me very much."

Amber shrugged. "Really? Is that why she almost let you drown? If your dad and I hadn't come along, you might be dead right now. But it's not really her fault. She has an addiction. She cares more about feeling good. That's why she drank all that whiskey and took those pills. I feel sorry for her, but still, I'd watch my back around her if I were you."

Bella's lower lip trembled, and tears sprang to her eyes. "I hate you!" She jumped from the sofa and ran outside. Amber laughed. She'd planted a seed. No matter how much Bella wanted to believe Amber's words to be untrue, she wouldn't be able to forget them, and a small part of her would always wonder. She'd probably talk to Tallulah, who would confirm Amber's assertion. Amber had had a long talk with Tallulah last night, explaining that Daphne had had substance issues in the past. Poor Tallulah looked heartbroken when Amber told her that her mother had been forced to spend months in a sanatorium because she'd almost hurt Tallulah as a baby. Amber might be gone soon, but the damage she'd done to the mother-daughter relationship was her parting gift to Daphne—a gift that would haunt them all long after Amber's departure.

Before leaving the next morning, Amber went into Jax's room. He was awake, staring up at the mobile over his head. She walked over to the crib and picked him up. He rested his head on her shoulder.

"Mama."

For a brief moment, she felt regret. Could she really leave another child? She hadn't given her other son much thought, even though he'd been Jax's age when she'd left him. She'd grown fond of Jax. The way he looked at her so adoringly, the way he lit up when she entered a room. But if she took him, then Jackson wouldn't help her with the plan against Daisy Ann. And then where would she be? No, it was better this way. Besides, if she ended up missing him too badly, she could always come back and get him. She gave him a kiss on the cheek and put him back in his crib. He began to fuss and she quickly left the room and went downstairs to the car waiting to take her to the airport.

When Amber arrived at Dallas Fort Worth International the driver she'd prearranged was waiting with a sign bearing her name. She walked over to him.

"Grab my luggage. It's with the porter over there." She pointed. "I'm going to the ladies' room, then I'll meet you outside."

When she exited the airport, she was assaulted by the humidity. She'd forgotten how damn muggy Texas was. The last time she'd been here was for Jake's funeral over three years ago. Instead of being comforted as his widow, she'd been met with scorn and suspicion, not only by his daughter but also by all their snobby friends. Not one person offered Amber any condolences; instead, they'd all appraised her with hostility and suspicion. She had made Jake a happy man in the few months before she shot him. He'd admitted to her that he had all but given up on love, that he thought he was past that stage of his life. She'd brought romance and hot sex and adoration to a man who was past his prime. She'd saved him from a future of decline and, most likely, illness. Wasn't it better that he died before he became too old to enjoy his hobbies? And he'd died doing something he loved best: hunting. She'd made sure the shot would make his end swift. The whole experience in Dallas afterward had been unbearable. She'd been forced to slink out of town, her belongings in trash bags, after Daisy Ann had pettily confiscated the Bottega luggage Amber had purchased, not realizing the AmEx she'd used belonged not to Jake but to his daughter. Well, she was back, and this time, she'd be the one with the upper hand. She slipped into the black SUV and breathed a sigh of relief to feel the cool air.

"Here's our first stop." Amber handed the driver a piece of paper with an address, leaned back, and closed her eyes.

"Should take us 'bout half an hour to get there, ma'am. Hope you had a good flight. You here on business or pleasure?"

"I'm not the chatting type. Just drive." Why did service people think it was charming to talk to their customers? It was irritating as hell.

"Yes, ma'am."

She dozed until the car came to a stop in front of a gray-and-white craftsman-style home on a small lot.

"I'll be a little while. Just sit tight until I'm back."

He nodded. He was learning, Amber thought.

She walked up the steps to the wide front porch where a wicker table and potted plant stood between two rocking chairs. She mentally prepared herself to play the concerned do-gooder. If she didn't have an outstanding warrant back home hanging over her head, she'd head straight to Hollywood, because she was an excellent actor. Whatever role she took on, she wore like a second skin. It was so easy to become whatever someone needed her to be. It was exhilarating, this ability to make others see her in whatever light she chose. It made her feel powerful. Amber rang the bell and waited, feeling like she was going to wilt in this heat. She was about to ring it again when she heard heels clicking and the door opened. An attractive brunette, a little heavy on the makeup, wearing designer jeans and cowboy boots stood there.

"Amber?"

Amber smiled. "Yes. You must be Nancy."

"Come on in."

Amber followed her into the open interior with its shiny wood floors, built-in bookcases, and cozy window seats. The scent of a vanilla candle filled the air. The living room, dining room, and kitchen were one big space, and they sat at the dining room table where a dish of homemade muffins, plates, and cloth napkins were already placed.

"Would you like some iced tea?"

Amber nodded. "Love some, thanks."

Nancy filled a glass for each of them and brought them to the table.

"You said on the phone that Jake told you about my husband?" Nancy said.

Amber recalled her conversation with Jake and how he'd been so disgusted to learn that Wade Ashford had stolen a patent from Nancy's husband, Shane Ellis. "Yes. I'm so sorry that Jake wasn't able to help you. Honestly, I was so devastated after his accident that I completely forgot that you had called him for help. It wasn't until a friend of mine mentioned Wade's name as a potential investor in her business that it all came rushing back."

Nancy gave her a sad look. "I'm so sorry about your husband. It was just terrible. I read about it in the papers. Jake Crawford was a well-loved man here in Dallas."

Amber pretended to wipe a tear from her eye. "It was just horrible. I'll never be able to forgive myself. He wasn't supposed to be in front of me. I don't know why he ran ahead, and then he didn't have a safety vest on . . ." She put her head in her hands, her shoulders shaking.

Nancy put a hand on Amber's back. "There, there, honey. It's okay. You don't have to talk about it. I know what it's like to lose your husband in an accident."

Amber looked up. "Look at us, two sad widows." She sighed and played dumb. "Well, anyhow, I thought I would try to help you on behalf of Jake. I remember him telling me that Wade did something shady to your husband. But I can't recall the exact details."

Nancy nodded. "That loathsome man stole my husband's invention. It's his fault Shane's dead. He may as well have killed him with his own hands."

Amber could see the anger in the woman's eyes. Her whole demeanor changed as she started talking about what happened.

"Shane was always tinkering with things. Fancied himself an inventor of sorts. Had turned our garage into a workshop. Coming up with ideas for this and that. None of it really took off. He was project manager for one of Wade's construction companies. Shane saw a good friend get injured when a nail from a nail gun malfunction penetrated his protective goggles. So he started working on improving them. Took him five years but he finally perfected the design. Problem was, we didn't have the money for prototypes and distribution. So he went to Wade to see if he would invest."

"When was this?"

"Six years ago. Shane came home one day all excited. He said Wade loved the design and wanted to go in on it with him. Fifty-fifty partners. Wade would put up all the money. Have the goggles manufactured, help with advertising and sales. Sounded great. He told Shane not to share the design with anyone, that someone could steal it. He said he'd do all the legal things too. Get the patent."

Amber knew where this was going.

"Wade is the one who applied for the patent?"

Nancy nodded. "Yeah. Only he put it in his own name, didn't add Shane. 'Course we didn't find that out for a while. It seemed like all was going great. They started producing them, sales were through the roof. And then he gave Shane a check for a hundred thousand dollars and said he didn't need him no more."

"That's horrible. What did Shane do?"

"There was nothing Shane could do. We went to lawyers; he filed an ethics complaint, but nothing worked. He'd given Wade all the original documents and drawings. Wade Ashford made millions."

Amber was stunned. How could Shane have been so stupid not to keep proof of his ownership? "Are you sure he didn't keep anything? Early designs? Emails to Wade? Nothing?"

Nancy shook her head. "If he did, he didn't tell me."

Amber took a tiny sip of tea, thinking. "You said he died in an accident. What happened?"

"The day Wade showed his true colors, Shane called me. He was inconsolable. He said he was going to stop for a drink and then come right home, but he never got here. I'd gotten a text from him saying he was coming home, but then he was killed in an accident on the way—crashed into a telephone pole." She wiped a tear from her cheek. "If that criminal hadn't screwed him over, he'd still be alive."

Amber digested this information, her mind racing. "I assume the accident was investigated. There's no chance that . . ."

Nancy shook her head. "Yes, of course. But I've always wondered if there's any way Wade had something to do with it. I can't prove anything. This whole thing has just eaten me alive. I was four months pregnant at the time. I miscarried." Nancy pressed her lips together and Amber could see she was trying to hold it together. "I've lost everything," she finally said.

"I'm so sorry," Amber said and then had a thought. "Maybe Shane *did* have a copy. If Wade was responsible in some way for the accident, it would mean Shane might have had proof that Wade didn't want to come to light. Did you go through all his things from his office?"

"Yeah, but Wade owns the construction company he worked for, so even if there was anything, he would have taken it."

"What about a home office? His computer?"

Nancy gave Amber an annoyed look. "I know you wanna help. But of course I went through everything. I'm telling you, there's nothing anywhere." Her hand went to the necklace she was wearing—a gold dragon encrusted with blue-and-red stones—and she rubbed the pendant between her fingers. Amber had noticed her doing it earlier, like a nervous tick or something.

"That's a beautiful necklace." In truth, it was kind of odd looking and something about it made Amber curious.

"Oh, thanks. It's not real. Shane gave me plenty of real jewelry. But this was the last gift he gave me."

"That's sweet. Was it a birthday gift?"

Nancy shook her head. "No, in fact, he kind of made a joke of it. Said it caught his eye and he hoped I wouldn't think it was cheap, said he had a feeling it was a good luck charm. And then one day when I was taking it off it came apart." She lifted it over her head and pulled a tiny bar on the side. "It's a flash drive. He put a picture of the two of us on it. I was hoping it might have information on it, you know, some kind of file pertaining to the patent or something, but there's nothing. Just the photograph."

A lightbulb went off in Amber's mind. "Could I see it?"

"Um, okay, sure." Nancy handed it to Amber.

"Do you mind if I take a look on your computer?"

"I guess not. I'll grab my laptop."

She was back in a minute with it. When she turned it on and slid the flash drive in, it was just as Nancy said, a picture popped up of Nancy and Shane.

"Can I try something?" Amber asked.

Nancy slid the laptop over to her. Amber used a shortcut to open the flash drive's folder. No files showed up. But Amber knew a thing or two about computers. During her tenure working for Jackson's assistant at Parrish Industries, she'd learned plenty about how to corrupt, hide, and password protect files when she was gaslighting his assistant in order to replace her. She went to the view tab and poked around in advanced settings before checking for hidden files, folders, and drives. That's when the screen populated.

"What is that?" Nancy pointed to a file labeled Development.

"I have a feeling it's the ticket to taking down Wade Ashford."

26

DAPHNE

"Under no circumstances should you agree to move back into that house." Howard Grimms, Dean's family law colleague, sits across from me at a glass table in his office. He's taken over my case, but Dean will stay on the team at Meredith's request.

"How can I not? If I don't, Bella will think I don't care about her. Jackson's not going to let me talk to her, and besides, she's too young to understand all the complexities of this situation. And I'm already guilty in Tallulah's mind. Every day that goes by more damage is being done to my relationship with them."

He shakes his head. "Look, I get it. But don't you see that by moving back in with him you're negating your claims that your husband was abusive and that he engineered what happened all those years ago when you were committed? How are we going to convince Family Court that he's the unfit parent, not you, if you move back into the house? And he's still married. That's not going to look good."

I sigh, not wanting to admit he's right, even though I know he is. "Have you made any headway with DCF? Where are they with the investigation?"

He purses his lips. "They've barely started. They're overworked and understaffed. Since the girls are in a stable environment, they see no need to expedite things."

My heart is pounding so hard I put a hand to my chest trying to slow it. "So you expect me to just sit back and wait while they take forever to do their jobs? I can't do that!"

"You have to think of the long—"

I spring up from my chair, pacing now. "If you say the long game, I'll scream. This is not a game. This is my life. My children's lives. You don't know what Jackson is like. The gaslighting. The psychological games. I will not subject my children to that. I have to move back in and protect them."

He throws his hands up. "It's your decision. I think it's unwise, and I'm strenuously advising against it. You'd be at his mercy. He can spin this any way he wants, and you could end up in worse shape."

"You think my chances are better if I refuse him and hope that the investigation bears out the truth, that I'm a good mother and they have no reason to keep me from the girls?"

He nods. "Exactly. By acquiescing to him now, in the long run you may lose big-time. I can't imagine how difficult this is for you, but isn't it better for your kids to be sad for a couple of months and then back with you for good, rather than risk losing them?"

Dean gives me a sympathetic look. "I have to agree with Howard. I think you need to ride this out."

I sit back down. "Realistically, when can I expect to be cleared?"

"It could take sixty days or even longer. I've got the affidavit from your therapist, and I've sent that over to them. We're working on getting character references from all the names you and Meredith gave us. I'll stay on their backs and try to get this cleared up sooner. That will help."

"I appreciate that. Okay. I'll call Jackson and tell him that I can't move in. I just hope by the time this is over my daughters don't hate me."

Both Dean and Howard stand, a signal that the meeting is over. I gather my things and walk to the door. "Please, do your best to make this go away sooner rather than later. I don't know how long I can go on like this."

Howard nods. "I promise."

Meredith is waiting for me at the beach house. She's made lunch and set a beautiful table, but I have no appetite. We sit down, and I take a sip of iced tea.

"How'd it go?"

I fill her in, and she listens, rapt.

"Oh, Daphne, I'm sorry you're going through this. It's unimaginable. I have to say, though, as much as I understand your needing to be with the girls, I have to agree with Dean and Howard. The thought of you living in that house again, being at his mercy, it terrifies me."

"I know. But I'm not the same person he married. I'm stronger now. If I didn't worry that my going there would affect my chances in the long run, I could do it for a month or so. I don't know, I guess I have to trust the lawyers. They're the experts."

Meredith shakes her head. "This is so unfair! That bastard is a criminal with a record and a judge believes him over you. I knew that Jackson had friends in high places, but I didn't realize he still had that much influence in this town." She takes a bite of her sandwich. "I'm surprised to hear that Amber's leaving. She has to be royally pissed that he wants you back."

"Apparently, she's ready to move on. She never loved him, and Jackson doesn't know how to love. We all know that."

There's a knock at the door and we both look at each other.

"Are you expecting someone?"

I shake my head and get up and go to the hallway. When I open the door, there's a man standing there.

"Daphne Parrish?"

"Yes?"

He hands something to me. "You've been served."

I look at him agape.

But he's already turned and walking away. I open the envelope and scan the document, and my body goes cold. Meredith comes into the hallway.

"Who was that?"

I turn to her, still numb with shock. "Jackson is suing me for custody."

27

AMBER

Amber sat waiting in the lobby, annoyed as the clock ticked past the appointment time with Wade Ashford. She'd called, posing as Delancey-Flynn's acquisitions VP, and introducing herself as Beatrice Bennett. Ashford had made her wait an entire week before he was willing to clear some time for her. That alone had put her in a bad mood, and now he was making her wait again. She'd make him regret treating her with such little respect. She'd convinced Nancy to let her take the thumb drive and print out the contents, promising her that she'd negotiate with Wade to get compensation for her. At first Nancy had wanted to take the proof of her husband's ownership straight to the authorities, but Amber warned her that she might never see the money if she had to wait for a full-scale investigation. That would give him time to hide the money or for the authorities to seize it. Amber had no idea if that was true, but she made Nancy believe that her best shot was letting Amber take the lead.

The surroundings were lavish, ridiculous, really, for an office building, with an ornate coffered ceiling at least thirty feet high, two enormous chandeliers, and gold leaf columns separating the balcony from the lower level. Gleaming tile floors and art deco chairs dotted the lobby. There was even a Steinway grand piano. *Nothing like flaunting your wealth,* she thought. At half past two, someone finally came out to fetch her.

"Mr. Ashford will see you now."

Amber waited for an apology for being kept waiting but none came. She picked up her black Tod's briefcase and followed the woman down the hall to a bank of elevators. They rode up the twenty floors in silence and she was taken to another lobby. She was about to complain about more waiting, but the woman knocked on a door, and Wade appeared. He looked much the same as she remembered, maybe a little paunchier around the middle. He smiled at Amber and held out a hand.

"You must be Beatrice Bennett. Nice to meet you. Please come in." It was clear that he didn't remember her. But then again, in his eyes she had just been a lowly waitress when she met him in Gunnison, there to do his bidding. She couldn't remember if he'd been at Jake's funeral; there had been so many people attending and the day was a blur in her mind now. She shook his hand and went inside.

"Please have a seat. Can I get you something to drink?"

She shook her head. "I'm fine." She glanced around the large office, which screamed man cave. On the wall behind his desk was a lion's head, its teeth bared and dangerous looking, and on his desk sat a framed photo of a grinning Wade holding a rifle and standing next to a dead rhino. This asshole was a big-game hunter. How repulsive. She flexed her fingers, wishing for a moment when she could pick up a rifle and shoot this cowardly prick who paid big money to kill animals bred for slaughter. He took a seat behind his mammoth desk, kicked his boot-clad feet up onto it, and leaned back in the chair. "So, little lady, what exactly can I do for you?"

She stared at him for a moment, then spoke. "You can start by addressing me as Mrs. Bennett."

His eyes narrowed and his smile disappeared. "Pardon me?"

She leaned forward in her chair. "I'm not your little lady. And I don't appreciate having been kept waiting a half hour for a meeting that took a week to schedule."

His face turned red. He swung his legs down from his desk and stood up. "Now just a cotton-pickin' minute."

"Don't get your knickers in a twist. You're going to want to hear what I have to say."

He took a seat again, still scowling. "I'm listening."

"It has to do with a patent on innovative protective goggles. For some reason, the patent is in your name only, but you didn't invent them, did you?"

Wade shot up from his chair again, his voice rising. "You need to leave."

She pulled out some papers from her briefcase and tossed them onto his desk.

"I think you might want to look at these."

He sat, grabbing the papers and scanning, his eye widening.

"Where'd you get these?" He looked up at her, his eyes squinting in anger.

"The more salient question is, do you think you're going to get away with screwing over Shane Ellis?"

"Just who the hell are you?"

"I'm a businesswoman with a proposition. Now before we go any further, I want you to know there are more copies of those documents. If anything were to happen to me, say an auto accident or some other misfortune, they will be made public, and your despicable actions made known to everyone."

"What do you want?"

"Information, for starters. You own thirty percent of the private stock in White Orchid Designs. Did a onetime investment get you those shares or are you still funneling money into Daisy Ann Briscoe's company?"

He looked at her like she had two heads. "I don't understand. What does White Orchid have to do with this patent business? I thought you were here to get money for Nancy Ellis."

"Who said I'm here to help Nancy? An opportunist like yourself should understand." She pointed at the documents on the desk. "This is my leverage. You don't need to worry about why I want what I want. And you'd better not let Mrs. Briscoe know anything about this meeting. My husband, Hugo, and I are interested in investing in her company."

He gave her a confused look. "First you come in here threatening me, and now you're asking about investing. What do you really want? How much for your silence?"

Amber shook her head. "I don't want your money. I want information. How much did Valene Mart offer to buy the company?"

"I'm really not comfortable disclosing . . ."

She stood up. "Fine. I'll just share what I know with the authorities."

"Okay, okay. Don't pitch a hissy fit! They offered her thirty-one million. Much more than the company's worth. That's how anxious they were. We would have made a pretty penny."

"She turned them down. Why?"

"They wanted to mass-produce White Orchid Designs. She could've made a fortune, but Daisy Ann about had a stroke when I suggested she consider it."

"I guess when you already have a fortune it's easy to be cavalier about saying no." It made Amber sick to think how spoiled and entitled the little princess was.

"It's not just that. White Orchid means a lot to her. The original designs were her mama's. This company's like another one of her babies. She'd rather see it close than have it taken over by some huge company that will turn her jewelry into cheap imitations."

That confirmed what Amber had read from the article from a year ago. Good. Daisy Ann still didn't want them to buy her precious company.

"Back to our business, Mr. Ashford. We're no Valene Mart. We want to elevate her designs. We have contacts in Europe. Upscale with a capital U," she said, reeling off the false story she and Jackson had come up with. "We want twenty-five percent, and we're willing to make a generous offer for her shares."

"I'll try, but I'm telling you, she won't want to give up that much. She's hell-bent on keeping voting control."

Amber was out of patience. "She owns seventy percent right now. She'll have forty-five, you'll have thirty, and Delancey-Flynn, the new investor, twenty-five. Then when it's done, you'll sell us your shares as well."

Amber could see the lightbulb moment in his eyes.

"So you want controlling interest," he said.

"Precisely."

"What is this really about? Who are you?"

"I told you. I'm a businesswoman. Now do we have a deal?"

"How do I know you won't keep holding those papers over my head. What's to keep you from continuing to blackmail me?"

"Well, I guess you're just going to have to take my word for it. I don't care about what you did to Shane. If he was stupid enough to let it happen, that's on him. Besides, I have a feeling that things don't go well for people who screw you over. I don't want any trouble from you. You do this for me, and those papers will disappear. You'll talk Briscoe into taking a meeting?"

He shook his head. "I don't think so. I don't know you from Adam. So you have some proof that Shane came up with the idea. All I have to say is that he sold it to me. After all, I did pay him."

"Well, maybe if his wife was dead too, that would work. But she's alive and willing to take you to court to prove that is not the case. You can either help me, or you can get yourself into a legal battle that will sully your reputation and hurt your bank account. So what do you say?"

He stared at her for a long moment before speaking. "Yes, ma'am," he answered, his voice laced with sarcasm. "But it's not gonna be easy."

Amber shrugged. "I imagine it will be easier than trying to explain why you stole someone else's idea and made millions. You have two weeks."

28

DAPHNE

call Jackson as soon as I've calmed down enough to think straight. He answers on the first ring.

"I assume you got the papers?" There's a hint of amusement in his voice, and I can picture the gloating smile on his face.

"What game are you playing at, Jackson? You claim to be a changed man, a family man, yet you're trying to take your children away from their mother?"

He tsks. "Really, Daphne. You're looking at this entirely the wrong way. I'm trying to give my children *both* their parents."

"How do you imagine that?"

"Clearly you need a little incentive to come back. Amber and I have separated. Once my divorce is final and you and I are married again, the custody suit will be moot. By this time next year, you'll be Mrs. Jackson Parrish again."

I feel like vomiting. "Is extortion really how you want to get me back? Where's your pride?"

But instead of getting angry, he softens his tone. It's the voice he uses to lull his adversaries into a false sense of security. "Thanks to you, I left my pride in prison. There's nothing more important to me than my family. I've always believed the ends justify the means, and I know you'll be happy once we're together again."

"Is this some kind of trick? You don't want to be together any more than I do. In fact, that's the last thing I want. We're adults. Can't we work this out without these pointless games?"

"Hmm. I'm afraid not, Daphne. You see, I really do want you back, and I'll do whatever I must to make that happen."

I'm quiet, struggling to find the words to say.

"I love you, Daphne. I always have, and I know that deep down, you love me too. But don't worry, I'll give you time once you move back. We'll take it slowly, just like when we first met. I won't rush you into my bedroom. It won't be long before we'll be one big happy family again. And you have to admit, you've grown fond of Jax. Won't it be nice to have a baby again?"

"What are you talking about? Jax has a mother."

"Amber's giving me full custody. He needs a mother. You. They all need their mother. I'm willing to suffer your anger for now, because I know you'll be grateful once you see how happy we can be."

It shouldn't surprise me that Amber is leaving another child behind, but I'm shocked, nonetheless. That woman must have ice in her veins. Poor little Jax. And poor Tallulah and Bella, caught in the middle of this. I suddenly need to hear their voices.

"Can I please talk to the girls?" I ask.

Surprisingly, he agrees quickly. "Sure. Hold on."

A few seconds later, Tallulah's voice comes over the line. "What?"

I've never heard her sound so flat, so devoid of any emotion, and I tighten my grip on the phone. "Lu, I miss you. Are you okay?"

"Why wouldn't I be? *Dad's* not a drug addict. We're doing just fine."

I clench my jaw. What has he been telling her? "Honey, I'm not a drug addict. I don't know what . . ."

"Save it, Mom. I know all about what happened when I was a baby. I can't believe all this time you've made Dad seem like the dangerous one, when it was you all along."

It feels as though my heart is being ripped from my chest. "He's lying to you. I would never put you in danger."

But she's gone and Jackson is back. "You've been filling her head with lies," I tell him.

"Now, Daphne, it's true that you were hospitalized when she was a baby. She's old enough to understand. No one is perfect. Come home. Amber is gone. We'll sit down and explain everything together. I'll help you to win Lu back."

His voice, patronizing and mocking, infuriates me, and it takes all my self-control not to tell him to go screw himself. But I know he's not going to back down. He's going to see this through to the end, no matter who gets hurt. Nothing will stop him. I swallow my rage and take deep breaths. "You win, Jackson. I'll be there tomorrow."

"Attagirl. I'll have the cook prepare something special for dinner."

I hope you choke on it, I think. "Tomorrow then." I end the call and leave my bedroom, returning to the kitchen where Meredith is waiting.

"Well?"

"He's got Tallulah convinced that I'm some kind of drug addict. She would barely talk to me. I have to go back."

"But, Daphne . . ."

"I have no choice. The longer he has them to himself, the more damage he'll do."

"We should call the lawyers."

I shake my head. "They're just going to tell me to wait. What's the point? Even if I do wait and the DCF investigation is dropped, I still have to fight him for custody. And you can bet he'll use every dirty trick in the book to win. I can't wait any longer. I have to protect my daughters."

"So what's your plan? Just go back and live with him forever?"

I shake my head. "Of course not. I'll figure something out. But for now, I have to make him think he's won."

Meredith gives me a long look that says she thinks he *has* won. "Daph, what about sex? Does he expect you to sleep with him?"

I make a face. "Gentleman that he is, he's said I can have my own room until I'm ready to welcome him back into my bed. Like that's ever going to happen."

Meredith arches her eyebrows. "Don't be naive. That won't last long."

I nod. "Yeah, I know. One step at a time. I can't worry about that now. I need to get to my girls. The rest will fall into place."

She gives me a worried look. "Why don't you let me see if Randolph can speak to a different judge? It's a shame that he doesn't know the one who's assigned to your case. Maybe he can persuade the judge to find in your favor earlier."

"I appreciate it, Mer, but the last thing I need is to be accused of trying to bribe a judge or something. I have a bad feeling that could come back to haunt me. I'll be okay."

"I hope you know what you're doing. And of course, I'm here for whatever you need."

I squeeze her hand. "Thanks. I'm counting on it."

29

AMBER

A mber left Wade Ashford's office satisfied with how the meeting had gone. She had every expectation that he would follow through as she'd instructed. But the best part was the new information she'd gotten about Valene Mart. It seemed they were still interested in buying, which she would verify; if true, it meant Amber could safely use the diamond money to buy White Orchid stock with the assurance that she'd get her money back pretty quickly. And even better was the fact that Amber would make a nice profit on her investment with what Valene Mart would be willing to pay to buy the stock from her. That made sharing the money with Jackson more palatable. Once that was finished, she would leave Dallas for greener and more interesting pastures. She was sick and tired of others trying to make her feel less than. All her life, she'd been looked down upon. And then when she'd finally thought she'd secured her position in high society, Jackson had been arrested and she'd been the subject of gossip and ridicule once again. Now she had her own money, but it wasn't enough. She wasn't going to just run away and hide. This was a matter of pride, of reclaiming her dignity. Daisy Ann had humiliated her in front of all those people. Rich, influential people whose approval Amber had worked so hard to gain. The burning need to take Daisy Ann down, to prove that she could best her, to take away the one thing Daisy Ann prized in her heart—

her mother's legacy—was all-consuming. She wouldn't rest until she had her retribution.

She sighed in contentment and leaned against the headrest of the back seat. The driver had wisely continued to refrain from speaking unless spoken to, so this afternoon she would call the car agency and request his services for the duration of her stay in Dallas. Now, as the SUV slowed and turned into Turtle Creek and the entrance to Rosewood Mansion, Amber peered out her window, smiling as the hotel came into view. She'd been staying here for a week now and loved every minute of it.

Sunlight sparkled on the peachy pink stucco of the elegant building with its Palladian windows and canopied entrance. She'd read that it once had been a private estate built to copy early Italian renaissance style, and Amber nodded in approval. A valet wearing a plaid suede jacket and cap approached the car and opened her door. Before exiting she tapped on the front seat. "I won't need you until tomorrow. Pick me up at nine," she said to the driver in dismissal.

"Yes, ma'am" was all he said.

Amber walked briskly to the entrance and through the French doors to an airy reception area that resembled a rotunda. The domed ceiling must have been thirty feet high, she thought, and it was magnificently decorated with ornamental plasterwork that cascaded down the walls of the tall ceiling.

Once in her suite, she threw her handbag on the sofa and sat, tapping Jackson's contact on her phone. It rang twice before he picked up.

"How did it go?" he asked.

"What, no hello? How are you?" she taunted, lifting her legs and pushing a high heel off each tired foot with the other.

"Oh, sorry. How are you, Amber? How is the weather, and how is your hotel room? How about we cut the shit and get to the point? How did the fucking meeting go?"

She smiled. It was such fun to get him riled up, especially when she was sixteen hundred miles away and out of reach. "Well, first of all, Wade Ashford is a pseudomacho misogynist piece of shit."

There was laughter on the other end of the line. "I'm sure you put him in his place. What about the shares?"

Amber recounted their conversation to Jackson. "If your paroled prison friend Hugo, who can't leave the state, does his job, we'll be able to convince Daisy Ann to sell. We need to dangle the idea that some of the royals will be wearing her designs. All she cares about is cachet. That's why she turned down all that money from Valene Mart. She's a rich bitch who doesn't need any more money. But prestige, that's her hot button. If we play this right, we'll come out of it with a tidy profit to share."

"You're confident Ashford will be able to get her to take the meeting?"

"He'll figure it out and make it happen to save his own ass. He's a weasel. And weasels are predators. Do you know that weasels do a little war dance when they've cornered their prey? I can just see that son of a bitch Ashford waving his damn shotgun and doing a war dance in his high-heeled cowboy boots."

There was silence on Jackson's end.

"Wade's going to come through, Jackson. I have no doubt."

"Okay. Everything's ready. I've taken care of every detail, and our company looks completely legitimate to anyone checking it out. The website's up, all the documents have been filed. It certainly passed Wade Ashford's scrutiny. Wade will be hearing from Hugo next week, but Hugo will be conveniently out of the country, so my attorney, Leonard Simms, will take the meeting in person and Hugo will be on Zoom. All this will go like clockwork, and as long as Daphne is here and you hold up your end, I'm with you. Once we've sold to Valene Mart and the transactions are completed, we'll split the money and dissolve the LLC," Jackson said.

"I've given Ashford two weeks. In the meantime, I'll have a little look around town and get myself set up here. And remember, don't try any funny business with the money; otherwise, I'll change my mind and fight you for custody of Jax. The courts still favor the mother, you know."

"Don't worry. As you'll see when you get the paperwork, the money can't be transferred without both our signatures and unique log-ons. That should give you some peace of mind."

"And how are things going with the lovely Daphne? Is she falling in love with you all over again?" Her voice dripped with sarcasm.

"Kind of you to ask about Daphne. I thought maybe you'd ask about your son. How foolish of me."

"Go to hell, Jackson," she said, and disconnected.

There was no one better than Jackson at stoking her fury. Amber turned off the phone so that she wouldn't be disturbed by him or anyone else. What was it about men that they needed to control everything? Jackson and his manipulations. Jake Crawford hiding his money from her. Wade Ashford killing big game so that he could hang their heads on his walls and show what a he-man he was. Show-offs, all of them, constantly having to prove what big balls they had, how smart and powerful they were. Well, she would show them. Amber was going to outsmart them all.

She rose from the sofa and padded barefoot to the bathroom off the bedroom. The sizable room contained a large walk-in shower and freestanding soaking tub. Amber turned on the water and picked up a crystal jar, pouring exotic-smelling bath salts from it into the tub. While it filled, she undressed, donning the complimentary white waffle robe, and looked around the suite in satisfaction. The rooms were large and gracefully furnished, the colors soft and muted, emitting a feeling of calm and sophistication. When she'd booked the three-thousand-dollar-a-night suite, an amount that was mere peanuts to her now, Amber had felt a flutter of delight in her stomach. As she studied the art on the walls and ran her hand across the fine bed linens, a powerful sense of autonomy swept over her. Yes, she'd been in more sumptuous surroundings before, had lived and stayed in more magnificent spaces, but none of those places had been hers alone. And even though she was only renting this suite, it was *her* money that had secured it. *All hers.* There was no one she had to please or answer to or pretend to love. She flopped onto the bed and stretched, laughing out loud.

- 30 -

DAISY ANN

Daisy Ann had flown back to Texas last night, and it was after midnight when she finally crawled into bed next to a sleeping Mason. She'd been relieved that he hadn't waited up—she'd been too tired to continue their argument about her renewed investigation into Amber. When she woke up, his side of the bed was empty, and she could hear the shower going. Yawning, she got out of bed and slipped on a robe. Coffee. She desperately needed coffee. On her way downstairs, she peeked into each of the boys' bedrooms and, as she suspected, they were both still fast asleep. Both dogs jumped from Tucker's bed and slipped past her through the open door.

"I guess you're ready for breakfast," she said, as they padded down the hallway. After feeding them, she made a pot of coffee and sat down at the breakfast bar with her phone. Still no voicemail or text message from Frank Winters, the man who'd taught Amber how to shoot back in Gunnison. Despite not having learned anything that proved Amber's guilt, she had learned plenty about her character or lack thereof. She was now more determined than ever to bring Amber to justice. Amber had murdered Jake in cold blood, and Daisy Ann wasn't going to rest until she had what she needed to make her pay. What was she missing? The answer had to be back in Colorado.

"Hey." Mason walked over to the counter and poured them each a cup of coffee, then came and sat next to Daisy Ann.

"Morning," she said, not missing the fact that he hadn't leaned in to kiss her. "You're still mad?" she asked.

He sighed. "I'm not mad, I'm worried. I don't want to see you get lost chasing this down again. It almost broke us before."

She reached out and squeezed his hand. "I know. And I won't let that happen again. I promise. It's just . . . seeing her that night in her designer duds, looking all smug and arrogant, it was like no time had gone by at all. She's a grifter. I know it, and everyone I talked to confirmed it. Amber's not even her real name. It's Lana Crump. And there's a warrant out for her arrest back in Blue Springs, Missouri."

"A warrant? What for?"

"Accused some poor boy of rape, and he went to prison. She was lying because he wouldn't marry her after she got pregnant." She filled him in on the details she'd learned from Mrs. Crump. "Her own mother turned her in. That's when she stole money from her parents and left her son with them. What kind of person does that?"

Mason's brows shot up. "That's unbelievable! Well, there you go. You can call the authorities, and they'll arrest her."

"And then what? She gets a year or two for perjury and skipping bail? No. The woman's a total sociopath, and I'm going to prove that she murdered my father. She had to slip up somehow. There has to be a witness somewhere or something the police missed. I'm going to have to go back to Gunnison again. Possibly back to Nebraska too. This Matthew, the one she sent to prison, might be able to shed some more light on things for me."

Mason's face turned red. "Have you forgotten that we have two children who need your attention? Between this thing with Amber and all your hours working, you're never here. Not to mention, me. I'd like to have my wife back. You can't keep running all over the place playing detective."

"Mason, what would you do? If someone killed one of your parents, would you just forget about it? You loved Daddy too. Come on.

I tried to move on. It's fate, her coming back into my life. A reminder that I should have never let this go."

His tone softened. "Honey, I'm sorry. I know how hard this is for you, but you've exhausted every avenue. I don't want you to make yourself sick over this." He raised his brows. "There's something else I wanted to talk to you about. Wade called me."

She felt the heat rise to her face. What the hell was Wade calling Mason for? It was her business not Mason's. "What did he want?"

"He told me you put another three million into Orchid."

"It's my money, Mason, and it's none of your business."

"Back up now. What affects you is definitely my business. The stress of a struggling business on top of everything else is too much."

She was going to give Wade hell for dragging Mason into this. "It's not struggling. We're having to recover from lost sales during the pandemic and rising materials costs, but we'll be back in the black soon. People are out and about again."

"I'm just saying, maybe you take a break for a while. Slow things down."

"Do I tell you how to run your business? I have people depending on their jobs. I'm not going to start firing folks to save a buck."

Mason shrugged. "I get that, but if the business doesn't support itself . . . And you know what your daddy always said. Only a fool invests their own money into a business."

"Don't you dare quote my daddy to me! My daddy also cared about the folks who worked for him. Loyalty. That's what he taught me. And, not that I owe you any explanations, but I've given the company a business loan. It'll pay me back with interest. Now that's the last I want to hear about it."

He shook his head and stood up. "Fine. I have to get to work, anyhow. The boys have been looking forward to staying home from camp today to spend some time with you. You're still taking them to the Frontiers of Flight Museum, right?"

Shit. She'd forgotten. She was supposed to meet with Wade today. She'd have to cancel him. "Yeah, of course. Looking forward to it."

"Good." He drained his mug and set it down, looking at her as if he was trying to decide to speak. "You know, I can see you're under way too much pressure right now. This Amber thing has become an obsession—"

She started to object, but he kept on talking.

"You need to focus on our family. You missed Tucker's tennis match while you were gone, and he was pretty upset. I think your priorities are out of order."

"Easy now! I've been to more of his games than you can shake a stick at. How many have you gone to? Not many, I can tell you that." Her voice rose. "I can't debate with you right now. I need to get the boys up. Get breakfast for them and get on the road. Get! Go on, get out of here."

Buck ran over to Daisy Ann and put a paw on her leg, looking up with big brown eyes. He was a sensitive pooch and hated hearing raised voices. She reached down and stroked his head absentmindedly while still glaring at Mason.

Mason shook his head and marched off.

After he left, Daisy Ann sent a quick text to Wade letting him know she had to reschedule. Her thoughts full of Amber, she went upstairs to get dressed and wake the boys.

She'd had a great time with the boys at the museum, but her exhaustion was catching up to her. It was close to four and she hadn't given any thought to dinner. Rosalie was off today, and even though Daisy Ann knew she'd only have to say the word and Zena, her full-time house manager, would rustle something up, she said nothing. Zena had enough to do with the accounts and managing the rest of the staff. Oh well, pizza was always a favorite with the boys, and Mason wouldn't be home until after dinner, so it was perfect. Her

phone rang and she looked at the screen. Wade. Again. She'd ignored all five of his calls when she'd been at the museum. She poked
the green answer icon and spoke.

"Where in the hell do you get off talking to Mason about my
business?"

"Well, hello to you too. Sorry, Daisy Ann, but I'm just looking
out for you. I only did what your daddy would've done."

"You're not my daddy, and I'll thank you to remember that."

"Fine. Fine. But now that we're on the subject, I really think we
ought to see what these potential investors have to say."

Her business was the last thing on her mind right now. Although
she'd never admit it to him, Mason was right, her vendetta against
Amber was becoming all-consuming again. "I haven't given it
much thought, Wade. Can't it wait a little longer?"

"Not too much. They could lose interest. They have some great
ideas for expansion. I think it could be a mighty fine deal. It could
mean lots more business and could pay you back at the same time.
Guy named Hugo Bennett, with Delancey-Flynn, wants to meet."

"You've vetted them?"

"Naturally."

"I'm not sure, but I guess a meeting can't hurt. Set it up."

"It may have to be virtual. He's traveling in Europe right now."

"That's fine, just schedule it."

"Will do."

The sound of a car driving up surprised her, and she walked to
the living room and looked out the window. She sighed in exaspera-
tion when she saw the white Mercedes sedan. What was Birdie
doing here? Taking a deep breath, Daisy Ann walked to the front
door and opened it, pasting a smile on her face as her mother-in-law
walked toward her.

"What a nice surprise."

Birdie gave her a peck on the cheek. "My apologies, dear, you
know I'd normally never drop by unannounced, but Mason asked
me to come."

Daisy Ann felt her stomach clench. "You're welcome anytime, please come in."

She started to take a few steps across the hall and Daisy Ann made a point of looking at her shoes.

Birdie stopped and sighed. "I forgot. Your generation is so germophobic." She slipped off her Emmy London pumps and placed them on the custom shoe cabinet Mason had built for the hallway.

"Thank you," Daisy Ann said.

Suddenly, Buck and Shot dashed into the entry hall, tails wagging, and ran up to Birdie. Before she could stop him, Shot jumped up, both paws on Birdie's chest.

"Shot, down," Daisy Ann commanded, but he ignored her.

Birdie laughed and ruffled his head. "All right, boy, down now." The dog immediately sat.

"I'm glad he listens to someone," Daisy Ann said, rolling her eyes.

"You have to be stern, darlin'. They have to know you mean business."

The women made their way into the kitchen.

"Can I get you some coffee or tea?"

"No, thank you. I'm not staying long. I'm sure you'll be having supper soon." Birdie sniffed the air. "Although I don't smell anything cooking."

Daisy Ann thought back to when Birdie had come to stay for a week after Tucker was born. The first thing she did every morning was plan the menu for that evening. Daisy Ann was more of a fly-by-the-seat-of-her-pants gal, and fortunately in recent years Rosalie was here five days a week and did all the cooking.

"Dinner plans got away from me, so I'm ordering pizza."

Birdie pursed her lips. "It's a good habit to decide the day before what you'll be having for dinner. Good planning is the key to running an efficient household."

That and a huge household staff, Daisy Ann wanted to say. "I'll keep that in mind," she said, fighting to keep the sarcasm from her voice. She ran a hand through her hair and sighed. "It's been a day," she said, leading Birdie to the living room where they sat together.

Birdie folded her hands in her lap. "Well, that's what I'm here to talk to you about. Mason told me that you've been traipsing all over the country trying to get evidence against that horrid woman."

Daisy Ann took a deep breath, telling herself to stay calm. Why did everyone have to stick their nose in her business? It was maddening. "Did he tell you that she came to my trunk show in New York?"

Birdie nodded. "Yes. I can't imagine how awful that must have been. But, Daisy Ann, honey, you've already looked into this, and it was fruitless. What makes you think you'll find anything now, other than heartache?"

"I've found out her real name and her background. Brenda remembered something that put me in touch with a man who gave her a new identity. Don't you see, I've actually been able to find out a lot." She filled Birdie in on everyone she'd spoken with.

"I understand you've confirmed this woman is a liar and a fraud. I agree with Mason; turn her in and let the authorities deal with her and then move on. None of this will amount to a hill of beans in regard to your poor daddy's murder."

"You don't know that." Daisy Ann's voice rose despite her attempts to stay calm. "Who knows what else I might find? I'm waiting to hear back from the man who taught her to shoot. He may know something . . ."

Birdie put a hand up. "Enough. You're getting all riled up. None of this will bring your daddy back, and he wouldn't want you to be consumed by this. You have a family depending on you. It's time to put this to rest once and for all."

Daisy Ann stood up. "Birdie, I love you, but respectfully, you have no right telling me what to do. My daddy should still be alive. He should be watching his grandchildren grow up. He should be coming to Sunday supper. He should be hunting and fishing and doing all the things he loved. And I will never stop until I make her pay for taking him from me." Hot tears rolled down her cheeks. "Besides, what if she does this to her next husband? I have a duty to stop her. Now, if you don't mind, I need to go and see about ordering that pizza."

After Birdie left, her phone rang and she saw Frank Winters's name on the screen. *Finally*, she thought. After they exchanged pleasantries, she explained the reason for her call.

"My father was Jake Crawford. You may remember, he was killed in a hunting accident?"

"Of course. Everyone knew Mr. Crawford. Terrible tragedy."

"I wanted to find out some information on Amber, his wife." She stumbled on the word. "I understand she took shooting lessons from you."

"Yes, ma'am. She was a novice, but it didn't take her too long to get comfortable with a gun."

"Did she say why she wanted to learn?"

"Just that she might want to start hunting."

"Hmm. I think she was hunting for fortune. I believe she shot my father on purpose." Daisy Ann felt the heat spread across her face as the old fury overcame her. Frank didn't respond immediately but cleared his throat then spoke.

"I'm not saying I'm the best judge of character, but she was a cold one. Very determined, very single-minded. By the time her lessons were finished, she was a good shot. I'll admit, when I heard about what happened it didn't ring true. I was very clear with her about safety protocol. She knew better than to shoot with her husband being out in front of her."

"I just wish there was some way to prove it," Daisy Ann said.

"Well, did the authorities check to see if there were any trail cams in the area?"

"Eventually they did. At the time I was too upset and didn't think to tell them, but later, I called and reminded them about the cams. Daddy was always furious about the poachers, and I know he had plenty of cameras set up. I went to the police station myself and spent hours looking through them all. Nothing."

"That's the only thing I can think of. I'm mighty sorry."

When the call ended, Daisy Ann sat thinking about her next move, trying to decide whether or not to use what she'd learned about Amber's arrest warrant and have her picked up for her crimes back in Missouri and be done with it all. It wasn't the same as a murder charge but at least it would disrupt her cushy life in Bishops Harbor. She went to her office for some peace and quiet to try to sort things out.

31

DAPHNE

My urgent need to see my daughters is the only thing tempering my complete and utter terror about walking back into the home I once shared with Jackson. I pull up to the house, or more accurately, the thirty-room estate, and I remember the awe I felt the first time I saw it all those years ago when I was still in my twenties and not used to that kind of wealth. I'd actually been a bit turned off by the excess, thinking at the time of how much good it could have done for the families I met with at the charity where I was working. I suppose it didn't take me long to acclimate to Jackson's world of wealth and privilege even though it was never the world I sought. And of course, in the beginning he was wonderful.

I park my car and sit for a moment, taking it all in. The grounds are pristine, of course, the hydrangeas in full bloom, the wisteria winding its way up columns to the trellis, and the house itself immaculate and without blemish. I start to get out of the car, but dizziness overcomes me, and I lean back against the headrest, breathing deeply, telling myself it will be all right. Since I've left I often dream that I'm back here living with Jackson, and I'm always horrified and confused. In the dream I don't understand how it happened, why I came back. And now the nightmare has become a reality. Just like before, he's using my children to imprison me. But I'm not the same Daphne as before. And no matter what, I won't be here for long. I'll find a way out for me and the girls. But in the meantime, I'm forced to play this charade where I've come back to be a family with a man who has no idea what the word truly means. I open the door and step out of the car. Grabbing my suitcase and handbag I put one foot in front of the other and walk toward the front door.

I knock and a trim man with closely cropped gray hair appears. He's formally dressed in a dark suit, white shirt, and tie.

"Hello, ma'am. Mr. Parrish is expecting you. I'm Edgar, the house manager." He gives me a slight bow.

He's got a very proper British accent, and I wonder if this is one of Amber's pretensions or if Jackson has hired him expressly for my presence here. As he picks up my suitcase, I follow him from the foyer to Jackson's study. We stand together in silence while he knocks on the door.

"Yes?" Jackson's voice comes through.

"Mrs. Parrish has arrived, sir."

"Send her in."

He opens the door and I walk in, seeing nothing has changed. I take a seat in one of the leather chairs in front of Jackson's desk.

"Your house manager? Am I to be treated like a guest?"

Jackson smiles. "Of course not. This is your home now. I'll introduce you to the entire staff later and they'll be told to take orders from you."

I want to tell him that my interest is not in the staff. "Where are the girls?"

"Chloe—that's the nanny—took them to the movies. I wanted some time alone with you before you saw them."

I start to protest but stop myself. "To discuss ground rules, I presume."

He gives me an approving look. "Yes. Exactly. I've told the girls that you and I are working on reconciliation. Tallulah is over the moon, but Bella is more reticent. I don't know what you've told her, but I expect you to get on the same page as me. I won't have you trying to turn either of them against me."

"Oh, you mean, like you've done with Tallulah who thinks I'm a drug addict now?"

He has the grace to look sheepish. "I'm sorry about that, but as I told you, I didn't know any other way to bring our reunion to pass. We'll sit down with them together and tell them that you have an anxiety disorder because of your sister's illness and early death."

I cannot believe he is bringing up Julie. "I won't blame my sister's cystic fibrosis for giving me some fake anxiety disorder. How dare you even—"

"Daphne, calm down. I'm flexible. We don't have to use Julie. I'm just saying we need to explain what happened when Tallulah was a baby and explain that what happened recently is related but that you're better now. Everything's going to be fine."

"And if I don't go along?"

"Please don't force me to play hardball. I really want things to be different this time. But I can't have you telling the girls that I manufactured what happened at the beach. They'll hate me, and I won't allow that. They're too young to understand that I was justified in doing so."

Can he actually believe his own words? Trying to reason with him is pointless.

He cocks his head and gives me a lopsided smile. "Do you ever think about us, Daphne? About the first time we kissed? The first time we made love?"

The feeling of nausea overwhelms me again. The thought of being intimate with this man sickens me. "No, Jackson, I don't," I manage to say.

"You wouldn't tell me if you did, would you? After all, I'm still married. I wouldn't expect you to admit that. That's one of the things I love about you. You have principles. You're a lady, not a cheap pretender like my soon-to-be ex-wife." He pushes against the back of the reclining desk chair and regards me once again. "Amber was a huge mistake. I've missed you, and I'm going to make it up to you. You'll see."

I want to spit at him. My head feels like it's going to explode, and I keep thinking, *How on earth did I wind up here again?* When I say nothing, Jackson gets up from his chair.

"Enough talk about the past. We'll look only to the future. Now, let me show you to your room."

We walk up the stairs side by side and pass the familiar art on the walls. Amber has changed very little from all I've seen thus far. When we reach the landing, Jackson turns right, away from the main bedroom we used to share, and to the guest rooms wing. My relief is palpable. He stops at the far end of the hall. He's clever and has put me as far away from his room as possible in order to lull me into a false sense of safety. He hands me a key. "I don't want you to be afraid. You're free to lock your door at all times if you wish."

I take the key and nod, but I'm not stupid enough to think he doesn't have a duplicate. I follow him into the room, the largest of all the guest rooms and the one in which my mother stayed on the rare occasions Jackson permitted her to visit. It has a lovely view with French doors leading to a small balcony facing the Sound. My suitcase is open and sitting on a luggage stand, the work of Edgar no doubt, and despite the beauty of the bedroom, I feel as if I'm in prison.

"I know you like this room. After our bedroom, it's the best one in the house," he says, moving closer to me, but at the mention of "our bedroom" my skin crawls.

"Thank you. I'd like to unpack and lie down for a bit until the girls get back."

He smiles and comes so close our bodies are almost touching. "Of course. You rest. I'll be thinking of you lying upstairs, so close to me again." I can feel his breath against my cheek as he leans in. "You were always the one, Daphne. You always will be." His lips touch my ear, and I feel a quick flash of pain as his teeth come down on my earlobe. He moves slightly and looks me in the eyes. "You always liked it spicy, didn't you?" He laughs. "You get some rest now," he says, and leaves.

The warnings of Meredith and my mother come back to me. I told them I could handle this, that I am not the same woman who was married to Jackson. I told myself the same thing. Was I fooling myself? Did the years away from him dull my recollections because I wanted to forget what a monster he was? I know one thing. I cannot underestimate him. I must have my wits about me at all times.

32

AMBER

Amber stepped out of the shower refreshed and ready to face the day. She dressed in the outfit she'd laid out last night—a cream silk boatneck top, black linen pants, and white calfskin sandals—tucking in the shirt and wrapping a wide Valentino belt around her waist. Giving herself a thumbs-up at her reflection in the floor-to-ceiling mirrors, she sat on the bed, picked up the hotel phone, and scheduled a massage for five thirty.

The car was waiting when she walked outside, and the moment the driver saw her, he scrambled to get the door for her.

"Thank you," she said.

She was pleased when he got back into the driver's seat and sat mute, waiting for direction from her. No inane chatter this time. "We have several stops this morning. Here they are." Amber handed him a piece of paper with four addresses.

"Yes, ma'am." He pulled onto Turtle Creek Boulevard and drove.

He was young, probably in his late twenties, Amber figured, as she studied his profile, and for a moment felt something close to empathy. The people he drove around were most likely well-heeled, maybe some even famous, and she wondered if that got to him, seeing the way the 1 percent lived.

"What's your name?" she asked.

It took him a moment and then he looked in the rearview mirror. "Bobby."

"Okay, Bobby, when we get to the school, I don't want you to park. Just drive around it very slowly so that I can take it all in."

"Right."

They drove another fifteen minutes and as they approached the property, Bobby slowed down to a crawl. Amber put down her window and observed. The Hockaday School campus was huge, more like the size of a small community college, with manicured lawns, tennis courts, and gleaming buildings. So this is where the rich bitch had gone to school. Exclusive and privileged. Amber imagined what it must be like inside. She'd seen pictures online of the buildings, the grounds, and students in uniform playing lacrosse. In photographs, they all looked happy and carefree, confident and sure of themselves, like a rare and protected species, a world apart from other mere mortals. They had parents who gave them every advantage, took them to visit colleges, and advised them on all the career opportunities before them. Amber would bet their summer vacations and school-year breaks were spent traveling to wonderful places, being exposed to other countries and cultures.

So different from Amber's blue-collar parents and public-school experience—one brick building on four acres at most. She balled her hands into fists, her resentment mounting. It was so unfair that an accident of birth could either make or break your life. Throughout high school, all Amber ever thought about was the day she would finally graduate and be able to leave that second-rate school and town and family. She'd always known she didn't belong there, that she should have been born to rich parents like Daisy Ann had.

Daisy Ann's husband had gone to St. Mark's, a private boys' school nearby. How practical of the landed families to ensure that their sons and daughters would mix near each other. Like breeding fine Angus cattle.

"I'm finished here." She put her window up and looked away. "Let's go on to Highland Park."

She bit the inside of her mouth and drummed her fingers on the leather seat when the car turned onto Daisy Ann's street. She'd looked up the house online, of course, but nothing beat an in-person look.

"Don't stop, just slow down a little as we pass," she said as they approached the stone gates leading to the house. A picture may be worth a thousand words, but it didn't hold a candle to seeing something with your own eyes. Amber had stayed in the Crawford mansion when they'd buried Jake, the mansion Daisy Ann had been born in and lived in until she went off to college. Now, not only did Daisy Ann live in *this* gorgeous stone manor with her husband and sons, but she also still owned her father's home and the ranch in Colorado. Daisy Ann's life was perfect and always had been, yet she couldn't spare one ounce of kindness for Amber—kicking her out after Jake's death and then publicly humiliating her in New York. How exquisitely divine it was going to be to take this woman down.

"Okay. I've seen enough. I have a one o'clock appointment downtown. That should give us plenty of time," she said to Bobby.

During the drive, Amber went over in her mind what she wanted to say. Valene Mart had made an offer to buy out White Orchid once, and when she'd spoken briefly on the phone to their senior vice president of acquisitions, it sounded as if they were still more than eager to talk. She'd given her name as Beatrice Bennett again, acquisitions VP of Delancey-Flynn, the bogus private equity firm Jackson had set up.

They pulled up to the sleek contemporary building, and Amber felt that tingle of excitement she always got when she was about to go into acting mode. "Not sure how long I'll be," she said, opening the car door.

"I'll be here, ma'am," Bobby replied.

The offices were expansive, taking up the entire fifth floor of the large building, and she was escorted to a small conference room where a woman and two men rose as she entered.

The tall redheaded woman extended her hand. "Ms. Bennett, I'm Vivienne Wallace. We spoke on the phone. It's a pleasure to meet you."

"And you," Amber said, taking in the creamy complexion and beautifully well-cut dress she wore.

She swept an arm toward the men. "This is Todd Hill and Roderick Lincoln. The third," she added, "but he goes by Roddy. They're part of our acquisitions team."

Amber gave a nod and smiled at the men, both youngish and one of them drop-dead gorgeous. Roderick the third was obviously the son of Valene Mart CEO Roderick Lincoln, Jr. Todd was the hunk. Her eyes lingered a little longer on him and something passed between them.

"Please have a seat. May I get you something to drink?" Vivienne asked.

Amber sat, seeing that a bottled water had been placed at each seat. "I'm fine with water, thank you."

"Fine. Shall we get down to business then? You said on the phone that you are in talks with Daisy Ann Briscoe to acquire her stock in White Orchid Designs, is that correct?"

"Yes. As I told you, this is preliminary and it's also top secret. If she found out that we intend to sell to you, she'd never agree to the deal." Amber paused, looking at each of them in turn. "Mrs. Briscoe is seriously considering our offer to purchase twenty-five shares from her. We have another shareholder willing to sell us his thirty. What my company proposes is that we purchase the stock for resale to you. With fifty-five shares and a controlling position, you can take the company wherever you wish. What we need from you is the price per share you are prepared to pay."

"I can tell you what we offered before. It was an outright buyout and the price we offered is pretty much general knowledge," Vivienne said.

"What we'd pay per share of stock would depend on more current projections of profit and loss," Roddy chimed in officiously.

Amber looked over at "the third," who looked to her like the family genes had been diluted by the time they got to him. "That hardly seems relevant, given you're going to gobble the company up and mass-produce the designs. It's not as though you're going to continue running it as is."

"That's true but——"

She didn't have time to play games. She wanted a number and a commitment from them, she needed to know what her profit would be before using her hard-earned money to buy up Daisy Ann's stock.

"Roddy, is it okay if I call you that?" She didn't wait for his assent. "I have it on very good authority that you're jonesing for those designs. I've been to your stores. Your jewelry is shit. Those designs will elevate you way above your competition. Now, I'm going to go down to your lovely café and get me a Coke. When I get back, either y'all are in or y'all are out. I didn't just fall off the turnip truck. I have other prospects to see. I reckon your daddy won't be too happy if you let this opportunity slip through your fingers." *A few more weeks here and I might even have a southern accent*, Amber thought, as she sashayed out the door.

She came back twenty minutes later and left with a written commitment, good for ninety days, to purchase fifty-five shares of White Orchid stock at a price well above what she'd be paying for Daisy Ann's shares.

They rose and shook hands all around, but Amber held Hot Guy's hand a beat longer, then handed each of them one of her cards, making sure he was the one who got her scribbled note on the back.

"Okay, Bobby," Amber said as she slid into the back seat of the SUV. "Last stop is Highland Park Village. I'll be an hour or two, so why don't you go have something to eat? I'll text you when I'm ready to be picked up."

Before they reached the upscale center, Amber's phone pinged. A text from Hot Guy (aka Todd): *How about I save you a stool at Double D Bar. Say nine o'clock?* She grinned and texted back. *I'm there.*

She went first to Alexander McQueen and bought an off-the-shoulder slashed minidress in white, then strolled to Miron Crosby where she decided on a pair of midi cowboy boots in white python after trying on at least ten other pairs. Finally, just for the heck of it, Amber walked to the Cartier store and chose a Juste un Clou bracelet. Not that she needed any jewelry, but, hey, what did need have to do with it?

Amber looked at her watch. A quick text to Bobby and she should be back at Rosewood by five at the latest, just in time for her massage. Then a leisurely soak and a tiny bite of something before dressing. She shivered with delight as she pictured Todd sitting on the edge of her suite's king-size bed while she gave him a little show, naked except for her new white cowboy boots.

33

DAPHNE

When I open the closet to hang up my things, I'm shocked to see it already filled with designer outfits. I'm thrown back in time to our honeymoon when Jackson presented me with an array of dresses, shoes, and accessories. All at once my heart is racing, and the icy fingers of fear wrap themselves around me. I stand still and close my eyes, telling myself that I am no longer afraid of Jackson, that I am strong, that he has no power over me. While I'm here I'll have to be prepared for more memories of his control and abuse, like land mines ready to explode when I least expect it.

I grab the first hanger and look at the label on the red pantsuit—Dior, size four. I shake my head as I continue to the next items, Stella McCartney jumper, Tom Ford pants set, Armani blazer. All of them size four. There are shoes too, Blahniks, Gucci, Louboutin's. I don't dress like this anymore. I wear sandals and sneakers, not four-inch heels. I haven't bought anything designer since I left Connecticut. And I'm no size four any longer, nor do I wish to be. For years he made me keep a food journal to track every morsel that I ate. I had to weigh myself daily to make sure I didn't gain an ounce. According to Jackson, eight weeks was sufficient time to bounce back from pregnancy. After I had Bella, those last ten pounds were stubborn. She was a colicky baby, and I was sleep deprived. I didn't have the energy to drag myself to the gym. Exactly eight weeks to the day, he strode into the bedroom, a determined look on his face, holding a garment bag.

"We're going to the club tonight. I got you a new dress."

"Jackson, I'm wiped out. I just want to go to bed early."

He scoffed. "All you do is sleep. I'm sick of doing nothing. Go fix yourself up and get dressed."

He thrust the bag at me, and I unzipped it. A gorgeous red Versace, size four. I knew it wouldn't fit. I sighed. "Okay, I'll go shower, but this dress looks too small."

He moved closer, his face inches from mine. "Listen to me, you fat cow. You will wear this dress even if you have to put on three pairs of Spanx. Maybe it'll motivate you to lose the baby weight. You're disgusting."

I held back tears as I ran from the room and showered. I could barely zip the dress—it pinched my skin, emphasized my swollen belly—but somehow I got it on. I didn't know how I was going to get through the evening wearing it. When we got to the club, I saw he'd invited three other couples to join us. The fabric dug into me as I sat there trying not to breathe too deeply. I leaned forward to pick up my glass of water, and suddenly, I heard it, the sound of ripping. Mortified, I turned to Jackson and saw the amused smirk on his face.

"Daphne, I told you that you weren't ready for a size four." He shook his head. "Just accept you're a bigger girl now that you've popped out two kids."

Now I slam the closet door shut. Maybe these clothes belong to Amber. I wouldn't be surprised if she'd filled every closet in this house with her crap. I reopen the closet door, push everything to one side, and place the few things I've brought on the rod.

I march down the stairs and find Jackson still in his study. "You forgot to empty the closet in the room I'm staying in. Amber's things are in there."

He smiles at me. "I didn't forget. I bought those for you. A welcome home present."

"I can choose my own clothing, thank you very much."

He cocks an eyebrow. "I don't know if it's living in California that's to blame, but you have to admit, you've gotten a bit slovenly. Jeans and T-shirts get old after a while. And once I get my business going again, we'll need to entertain. You'll need to have appropriate attire."

Play along, play along, I tell myself. I won't do myself any favors by tipping my hand. "I guess you're right. But, Jackson, they're the wrong size. I'm not a four anymore."

He stands and appraises me, his eyes traveling from my head down to my feet. "Yes, I can see you've put on some weight. No matter, we'll take care of that. I noticed Bella's a bit chubby as well, so I've already instructed the cook to prepare keto meals."

"Please tell me you didn't say anything to her about her weight. That's how eating disorders can start."

He shrugs. "I may have mentioned that we eat healthy here. There's nothing wrong with that."

"Jackson—"

"Mommy!" Bella bursts into the room, her arms outstretched, and crashes into me. I wrap her in my arms, tears springing to my eyes as I hug her tight, not wanting to let go.

"Darling! I've missed you so much."

"Me too."

Tallulah is leaning against the doorjamb with her arms crossed in front of her. She is staring at me with undisguised hostility. I release Bella, walk over to her, and give her a hug. She accepts it stiffly, and I pull back. "It's so good to see you. I've been going crazy missing you both."

"Let's all go into the living room and have a talk," Jackson says.

The three of us follow along like good little soldiers. Bella reaches out for my hand, and I hold it as we go. Jackson takes a seat on one of the sofas, and Tallulah sits next to him. Bella and I sit across from them, still holding hands.

"I've already explained to the girls how sometimes you get sad and take too much medicine. They understand that it's not something you want to do, but you need our help."

I say nothing, waiting for him to go on.

"Now, DCF knows that you're here, but you're not allowed to be alone with the girls until the investigation is finished. Chloe and the rest of the staff are aware of that. But it's fine anyway because I plan to be here with you most of the time. We need family time, right?"

I take a deep breath, trying to figure out what to say. I need to set the record straight with Bella and Tallulah and let them know that I'm not going to go off the deep end and take drugs, like he's implying. "I'm not sad. I'm very happy to be with my girls. I promise that there's nothing for you to worry about. Just like you've never had to worry before. What happened at the beach was an accident."

Tallulah's eyes narrow. "What do you mean?"

"You know my therapist prescribed that medicine for me if I got anxious. The dosage information was wrong. I took two, like it said, but the directions should have said one. That's why I fell asleep." I look at Jackson and see a glint of admiration in his eyes. I've managed to redeem myself without making him the villain. "As far as what happened when you were a baby, Tallulah, I'm sure you've heard about postpartum depression. My hormones were all out of whack. But you were never in danger. I was paranoid. Thinking Daddy was out to hurt me, and I ran away with you. That's what happened. I would never hurt you. Either of you."

I immediately see the relief in Tallulah's eyes, and I'm heartened. She really does want to believe me, to be assured of my love for her. "So you didn't do anything bad to me?"

Jackson starts to talk, but I cut him off.

"Of course not. And your daddy loves you far too much to have ever let me come home if he thought I was a danger to you. I just needed for my hormones to balance and to realize that it was safe for me to come home to him."

Anger flashes across his face, and I'll probably pay for this later, but I don't care. I won't have my children afraid of me.

He clears his throat. "Okay, well, now that we've cleared that up, we need to remember that the social workers are still concerned about Mommy, and until they say she is all better, you can't be alone in the house with her or go anywhere alone with her. I'll be here most of the time, but if I do go out for anything, Edgar or Chloe or the cook will be here when I'm not. So that won't be an issue."

"That's dumb. Why are those social people being so mean?" Bella asks.

Jackson smiles at her. "They're just doing their job. All this will be behind us soon and then life will go back to normal. That reminds me, we need to get your applications in for school."

"We already have schools," Tallulah says. "Why can't you come to California with us? We like it there."

He seems to consider this. "Hmm, let me think about that."

Over my dead body.

34

DAISY ANN

aisy Ann ended her call and got out of the car. When she walked into the building and up to her office, Wade was already in there, perched on the edge of her desk, one leg swinging back and forth as he spoke to another man. As soon as he saw her walk in, he sprang up, and gave her an apologetic look. She felt her annoyance growing. She'd have to talk to her assistant about letting people into her office when she wasn't there.

"Daisy Ann, this is Leonard Simms," Wade said as the gentleman rose to face her.

She gave Wade a curt nod then turned to the man and held out a hand. His serious expression and old-fashioned wire-rimmed glasses gave him a humorless air. He wore a neatly pressed gray suit, and when he took her hand in his, she was startled by its extreme slenderness. His handshake, however, was firm and strong.

"Daisy Ann Briscoe."

"Nice to meet you, ma'am. I'm Mr. Bennett's attorney. As you know, he's out of the country on business and will be joining on Zoom."

"Yes. Let's go into the conference room, shall we? We're all set up for the call." Daisy Ann walked to the door without waiting for a response.

"Farah, please find out what these gentlemen would like to drink. I'll have my usual. Thanks."

The men followed her to the conference room, and she took a

seat at the head of the table. After her assistant had given everyone coffee, and Daisy Ann her chai latte, she set up the computer, retreated, and shut the door.

Daisy Ann clicked on the keyboard of the laptop and the image was projected onto the big screen on the wall. She opened up the Zoom room and within seconds, a man's face appeared. He was distinguished looking, dark hair graying at the temples, clean shaven, a George Clooney look-alike in a starched white shirt.

"Good morning, Mr. Bennett," Daisy Ann said.

"Please call me Hugo. Thank you for taking the meeting. I apologize that I can't be there in person. I'll be in Singapore a few more days, but I didn't want to miss this opportunity," he said in an upper-class British accent.

"I imagine you must be ready to retire soon. It's almost midnight there."

He laughed. "I don't sleep much these days. Too much going on. I'll get straight to it. I've been wanting to diversify my investments for some time. I understand you were hit hard by the pandemic as many businesses have been, but your P&L was outstanding prior to that. Even a few years later, we're all trying to catch up. Wade has shared some of your plans for expanding into private trunk shows and reaching some new markets, and I can help with that."

"How so?" Daisy Ann asked.

"I have extensive contacts in Europe, high-end jewelers who would love to carry custom pieces. Might even be able to get some royals wearing your designs."

Daisy Ann never thought that big. Her company was her homage to her mother, a way to honor the artistic integrity of her designs and to keep her memory alive. She smiled at the thought of what her mother would say if one of her pieces graced the neck of a princess or duchess. Even Birdie would be impressed.

"That sounds . . . intriguing."

"I've emailed over a list of who I'd start with. You can check it all out. I think you'll find we'd make great partners."

They spoke for a while longer, more tiptoeing around and getting to know each other chatter.

"Thank you, Hugo. I'll certainly consider your offer seriously. Give me a few days and I'll get back to you."

Daisy Ann stood. "Wade, will you see Mr. Simms out and then come back to my office?" She extended her hand again. "Nice to meet you. I'll be in touch."

When Wade returned, Daisy Ann was seated behind her desk.

"Well, what did you think?" he asked.

"I need to look everything over, send it to the lawyers, but I was impressed. It's a bonus that in addition to the money he's willing to invest, he can also help us expand. Europe. It would be kinda cool."

Wade nodded. "I think it's a no-brainer."

She arched an eyebrow. "Easy for you to say. I'm still hesitant to sell a full twenty-five percent. I don't like being left with less than a fifty percent say. Think they'd do it for nineteen shares?"

He shook his head. "That's an odd number. They want a quarter of the business. They were very clear on that. You'll still have the majority voting share. With your forty-five, and my thirty, they'll have the least say at twenty-five percent. Nothing to worry about."

"Counteroffer at nineteen. My daddy taught me to always keep at least fifty-one percent if at all possible."

Wade narrowed his eyes and started to say something then stopped. After a few more moments he spoke. "All right. But what if they say no? This is a huge opportunity. Imagine the kind of exposure they could give us. How thrilled would your mama be to have British royalty wearing one of her creations?"

She considered that for a moment. "I still say we try for nineteen. If they say no, negotiate. But see what you can do."

"I'll do my best. What's your real bottom line? If they're about to walk away, can I okay the twenty-five?"

She blew out her breath, quiet, thinking. Finally, she answered. "Yeah, but only as a last resort."

35

AMBER

Amber turned over in bed and slowly opened her eyes, quickly shrinking back. Todd's face was inches from hers, his eyes wide open and staring at her.

"What the hell? You scared me to death. Like some kind of crazy apparition." She was wide awake now.

"You're beautiful. I like looking at you when you sleep." He ran a finger along her cheek, but Amber pushed his hand away and leaped out of bed.

Did he think that tired cliché was romantic? Todd was a hunk and the sex had been great, but that didn't make up for the fact that he was boring and unoriginal. One night would have been adequate. She never should have let him hang around for a week but he was good in bed and a minor distraction. Now it was time to get rid of him.

"I'm going to take a shower," she said and headed to the bathroom.

"I'll come in with you."

She turned abruptly. "No. You won't. I have a busy day, Todd. No time for play. Why don't you let yourself out, and I'll call you later?" A lie. Amber had no intention of calling Todd ever again.

"Okay, babe. See you tonight."

In your dreams, she said to herself as she got into the shower and the hot water rained down on her. Was this how men felt when they finished using up what they wanted from a woman? she wondered.

Amber didn't have a high regard for men, but now, after Todd, she could in a way kind of understand their shitty behavior. There were people in this world who were born losers, who were just asking to be crapped on by the powerful, and for too long most of the powerful had been men. But that was changing. Now women were joining the ranks of power holders, and Amber was one of them. She didn't have to put up with any garbage, didn't have to stroke anyone's ego, didn't have to be with someone she didn't want. Amber got to call the shots. This is what it felt like to be a man, she thought, and it felt damn good.

Today was her big day, the day when all the planning and scheming would yield results, and so she'd carefully chosen what to wear. An apple-green Maison Common fringe tweed jacket and white wide-legged pants. Elegant and also feminine and summery. Minimal silver accessories to complement the silver buttons on the jacket.

Two days ago, Amber had wired funds from her offshore account to Delancey-Flynn, the LLC that would be purchasing Daisy Ann's stock. Now she was waiting for a call to tell her the sale was a fait accompli. At precisely nine thirty her phone rang. "Jackson," she said and sat at the suite's desk, opening her laptop.

"I'm emailing the paperwork to you. You'll need to sign the documents and return them to me. Once you've done that, the stock certificates will be issued and you will own twenty-five percent of White Orchid Designs," he said.

Amber could almost feel the blood coursing through her veins as her excitement grew. "Perfect. I'll sign and get them right back to you."

In a few seconds his email popped up. "Here we go," she said, downloading the attachment. She quickly read through and signed. "Coming back to you now," she said.

"Good. You're seeing Wade today, right?" Jackson asked.

"We're meeting at eleven. Everything's on track. I'll call you as soon as I'm finished there."

"Sounds good. Later," Jackson said and clicked off.

Bobby was waiting when Amber reached the lobby. She inhaled deeply, straightened her jacket, and strode to the car.

"Good morning, Bobby." She flashed her brightest smile at him, and when he looked a bit puzzled, she almost laughed out loud. Riding on cloud nine was pretty mind-blowing.

As the car neared the building, Amber unbuckled her seatbelt and leaned forward toward Bobby. "I shouldn't be too long. If you want to park or get a coffee, I can text you when I'm finished."

"Oh. That would be great. Thanks. I'll get your door." He hopped out of the car and ran to her side of the vehicle.

Amber felt ten feet tall as she walked from the lobby to the elevator and into Wade's office. He stood when she walked in, and the first thing she noticed was how much taller he appeared. She took in the checkered shirt and dark jeans and then looked down at his boots. Dark leather with fancy scrollwork and what looked like four-inch heels with lifts.

"Mornin' lit—, uh, Mrs. Bennett. Mighty fine day out there. Why don't you have yourself a seat and we'll get right down to business." Wade indicated the chair next to his desk.

Amber sat down as Wade rearranged some papers around his desk before taking a seat himself.

"I presume all is in order?" she said.

"Yes, ma'am. Your bank wired the money to my account this morning. I've signed the stock transfer documents, so all I need is your signature on these as well. Wanna make sure every *i* is dotted and every *t* is crossed." He handed her the papers, grinning, and Amber could swear his face looked just like a weasel's.

She scanned each line, taking her time, and then signed her name. "Here's your copy," she said, reaching across the desk. "Now, the stock certificates," she said.

"'Course. Just as soon as we have all this notarized." He pressed the intercom and in seconds a man entered the room, signed and stamped the documents, and withdrew. Wade smiled and passed an envelope to her. "Your stock certificates, ma'am."

Amber's heart did a little leap as she held 30 percent of Daisy Ann's company in her hands. With this morning's additional 25 percent, she was now the controlling stockholder of White Orchid Designs. She closed her eyes, savoring her moment. How many people had told her she wasn't good enough, had tried to stop her, had tried to keep her out. She'd outsmarted every damn one of them, from the Lockwood bitch to Jake Crawford and Daphne and Jackson and now Daisy Ann. Opening her eyes, she nodded once to Wade and stood. "Thank you. It's been a pleasure doing business with you. You may be assured that your secret is safe with me." It was safe with her, but not with Nancy. She would be giving her back the flash drive and advising her to go ahead with legal action. Mr. Big-Game Hunter would finally know what it felt like to be the trophy head.

"I hope so, Missus. I certainly hope so."

Jubilation might be an understatement for how Amber was feeling as she left the building and walked outside. Everyone had a price. For Jackson it was Daphne. For Wade, fear of exposure. But Daisy Ann's was the best as far as Amber was concerned. Jackson had told her how eager Daisy Ann had been on the Zoom call when Hugo Bennett mentioned the possibility of selling her pieces to royalty. It was funny. Amber supposed it was a universal impulse to keep trying to rise above yourself.

She'd forgotten to text Bobby, but he was waiting right where she'd left him, and he quickly scrambled to open her door.

"You know, Bobby," she said from the back seat, "I might have been a little hard on you at the beginning. You've been a great driver, and this is to show my appreciation." Amber handed him an envelope containing $500 in cash. With the windfall profit she'd be making, Amber could afford to be generous. And besides, it was her way of giving back to one of the drones who was invisible to the 1 percent. Just like Amber used to be.

As soon as Amber got back to the room, she phoned Jackson.

He answered on the second ring. "Hey. All finished?"

"Mission accomplished. I'm holding the shares in my hand right now. It's a beautiful sight."

"Have you set up the meeting with Valene Mart?"

"Yes, two weeks. You told me to wait until the stock is registered with the Texas Secretary of State so they can confirm our owner-ship. Wade said that could take up to ten business days."

After ending the call with Jackson, Amber peeled off her clothes and took a quick shower. This Dallas humidity was a son of a bitch. How did they stand it? She put on a cotton sundress and checked her phone messages, erasing all four of Todd's without listening to them. She planned to go downstairs and have a few drinks at the Mansion Bar tonight to celebrate. Who knew what she might run into? And tomorrow. What she had planned for tomorrow was going to make it a red-letter day for Amber. For Daisy Ann, not so much.

DAPHNE

Jackson's facade as a changed man cracks more and more every day. The first week he was unfailingly polite, albeit controlling and practically omniscient. The only time I have to myself is when I sleep. My joy at being reunited with my girls is the only thing mitigating the sheer agony of being with him day in and day out. We hardly ever leave the property as he insists that we need family time to bond and learn how to live together once again. Every meal is healthy, and perfectly proportioned by the cook, who apparently has a degree in nutrition. Snacks are off-limits except for some fruit in the afternoon. Mealtime discussions center around whatever educational documentary we've all watched together. There are some fun breaks, though: We swim in the pool, go kayaking, and play board games. Activities Jackson never had time for when we were actually a family. Little Jax has taken to Tallulah and Bella like he's known them all his life, and it makes me happy to witness the affection between them all. Chloe, the nanny, does most of the caretaking but I enjoy the time I have with Jax, and my heart breaks for this sweet child whose mother has abandoned him.

This second week Jackson's patience is wearing thin, as is the girls'. They miss scrolling through social media on their iPads (another thing he limits). They want to watch their favorite shows and read the books they choose, not be forced to watch documentaries and read the educational books Jackson thrusts upon them. He snapped at Bella for asking for seconds, then for looking at her iPad while we watched a show about the history of the snail. Yes, the history of the snail. Even Tallulah is getting tired of it. At first, she was so happy to have her father back that she bent over backward trying to please him. But now she's bored and frustrated. She is almost a teenager, after all, and Jackson has put the reins on too tight.

Every evening after the girls are in bed, it's our time alone. He spends this time trying to convince me that he's a good man. We drink wine, which is the only thing I look forward to, and we talk. And talk. He tells me things about his childhood that he never shared before. Things that I assume are supposed to make me more sympathetic toward him. Tonight, he veers down a different path. One that I've dreaded but have known was coming.

"Daphne, I've been patient. Given you your space, yet I don't feel you're making any effort to return my affections."

It's a beautiful night and we're sitting outside on the deck facing the water. I'm on a love seat and he's across from me in a chair. He gets up and sits next to me, so close that I can feel the hair on his arm as our flesh touches. He's wearing Creed, his signature cologne, and the smell throws me back in time. I take a deep breath, my heart racing, and try to calm myself. He puts a hand on my leg, and it takes everything I have not to push it off.

"Please tell me you feel it too," he says. "Our connection is still there."

"You have to understand, Jackson. I'm really trying but after everything that's happened, it's hard."

"Is there someone else?" His hand tightens on my thigh.

"What? No."

"Are you sure? I can't stand the thought of another man touching you. Tell me the truth. I need to know."

"Jackson, all I've been concerned about since our divorce is taking care of the girls. There's no one else."

"That's good. You're so pure. So good, Daphne." He moves his hand up and down my leg now. "All I can think about is being inside you again. Becoming one forever. I want to make love to you. I fantasize about it every night."

"Jackson, please. I'm not ready. You need—"

"I need *you*. That's what I need." He takes my hand and moves it to his groin. I can feel his erection. "See. That's what you do to me." His voice is gruff, and I'm afraid of what he'll do next. I scramble, trying to come up with something, anything to diffuse the situation. I feign outrage. I pull my hand away.

"You're still married, Jackson. You made your choice. You picked Amber over me and now you expect me to take you back with open arms? Do you know how much you hurt me?"

I don't know if he'll buy it. Before I left and moved to California, I admitted to tricking him into leaving me, but I'm betting that his ego will allow him to believe that I made that up to cover my hurt. He's quiet for a long time, then he speaks.

"I'm sorry. I know I hurt you. I get that you're still angry. But I don't love her. I never loved her. It was always you. You have to forgive me. We can be so happy. But you need to let me back in."

I brace myself for what I'm about to do, pretending I'm an actor in a film, and that this is not real. I lean in and kiss him. A deep kiss, full of passion and promise. Then I pull back. "It still hurts so much. I just need a little more time before I can trust you again."

He caresses my face, his eyes searching mine, and leans in for another kiss. After what seems an eternity, he releases me. "A little more time." He stands up. "Just a little." Without another word he goes into the house leaving me alone and shaken. When I hear his footsteps on the stairs, I get up and lean over the side of the deck and vomit.

Later that night, a little after two A.M., Tallulah wakes me. We rarely get time alone, as he insists the girls be in bed by ten and adhere to a strict lights-out policy. I don't turn the light on for fear of waking him just a few doors down.

"Mom, this isn't how I want to spend my summer vacation," she whispers.

"I know, honey. I tried to tell you."

"Talk to him. Get him to ease up."

"He's not going to listen to me."

"Why? I don't get it. You're getting back together so why would you do that if you're going to let him be a dictator?"

I hesitate. She still doesn't know that Jackson and Amber were the ones behind the incident at the beach that put me in this predicament. Jackson warned me that if I told them, he'd make sure I never saw them again. I know he's capable of that. In her mind, this reunion is genuine and for now I have to make sure she continues to believe that. No matter how much I want to tell her the truth, I can't risk it. Not yet anyway.

"We're all just feeling our way. Dad is trying to make up for all the time he missed with you, and he doesn't quite have the hang of parenting older kids. You know?"

"It's so stupid. I've kept my mouth shut, but I can't anymore."

"That's fine, honey. You should be honest with him. Tell him that you're not having fun. That you're not a baby. Maybe he'll lighten up."

"You think so?"

"Yes. Absolutely."

Tallulah goes back to her room, and I toss and turn the rest of the night, hoping the advice I gave her won't come back to bite me.

This morning we're all seated at the dining room table and Jackson's giving us the itinerary for the day as our breakfast is served—egg white omelets with spinach and mushrooms.

"Tallulah's told me that she's going a bit stir-crazy, and I apologize."

I look up at him in surprise, then at Tallulah who gives me a cat-that-swallowed-the-canary smile.

He continues. "I'll admit, I've been wanting to keep you all to myself after not seeing you for so long. But it's time to reassimilate into the world again." He laughs. It's the laugh reserved for clients, and it makes me cringe. As I study his face, still so handsome with his chiseled features, his cobalt blue eyes, I feel nothing but revulsion and wonder how I ever loved him. "I know you girls are bored sitting around here with us all day. I was thinking you would enjoy sailing camp at the club. You'll meet other kids your age, learn a great skill, maybe get invited to a party or two." At this he winks at Tallulah.

"That sounds awesome," Tallulah replies.

"I don't know," Bella says, her voice quiet. "Sailing sounds kind of scary."

"It's not scary at all," Jackson reassures her. "You'll take it very slow, and someone will be with you all the time. Promise. You can also both take tennis lessons. And . . . you'll have full access to the restaurant and snack bar."

At this Bella lights up. "Really?"

He nods. "Really. I know I need to give you both more freedom. We'll figure it out."

That must have been some talk Tallulah had with him. He seems to have sorted everything out.

He pulls something from his pocket. "One more thing. I've gotten us tickets to go see *Clue* this Saturday at Charterhouse Academy."

It's the school he wants the girls to attend in the fall. "How nice. Matinee or evening?" I ask.

"The two o'clock show and then we can have dinner afterward. How does that sound?"

Bella lights up. "Yay! That sounds fun."

Tallulah is not so enthusiastic. "I guess. Dad, tell Mom what else you agreed to."

"Ah yes. My darling daughter tells me I've been acting like a dinosaur in regard to the screens. No more limits on screen time. It is summer after all."

Who is this man and what has he done with Jackson? There's a spontaneous outcry of joy from both, then he puts a finger up.

"Except mealtimes, of course. Agreed?"

They murmur their assent. Tallulah looks triumphant, believing she's got the magic touch with her father. I know it's all just more smoke and mirrors. He'll be freaking out in no time when he sees them zoned out on their electronics for more than an hour. And when he gets the bill from the club filled with ice cream and junk, that will be the end of the freedom ride. But that doesn't matter, because after Saturday we'll be gone. Jackson doesn't know it yet, but he's just given me an escape hatch.

- 37 -

DAPHNE

Saturday has arrived, and everything is in place. Meredith will be waiting for us outside the school after the play starts. She's familiar with the layout, having sent her own children to Charterhouse. The play is in the auditorium on the first floor. Down two hallways is a faculty bathroom that has a window right next to the parking lot. The restroom will likely be locked, but Meredith is on the board of the school and has arranged to hide a key under a plant next to the door. It all sounds very cloak-and-dagger and a bit far-fetched, but maybe if I pretend I'm in a spy movie, I won't be so terrified. I'll have only a few minutes to convince the girls to leave with me, to make them understand it's for their own good, and I still haven't quite figured out what I'm going to say. Meredith is lending us a car that's registered to her daughter, which should give me enough time to get out of the state and catch a bus. There'll be plenty of cash in the car and we'll stay in small motels once we're far enough from Bishops Harbor to hide out safely. We worked it out over the phone a few nights ago when Jackson had gone out for a while, and I knew I wouldn't be overheard.

"Are you sure you don't mind getting involved? If I'm caught, you could get in trouble for helping me."

"It's ridiculous. They're your children," Meredith says.

"I know, Mer, but right now Jackson has temporary custody. He's got us on lockdown here, and things are getting bad."

"Let me call the lawyers and let them know. Maybe they . . ."

"No. I'm not doing anything to risk leaving the girls here without me. I only have to stay hidden until the hearing challenging the order of temporary custody. That gives me a few weeks to gather everything I need to prove Jackson set me up."

"But won't it hurt your chances at the hearing that you've violated the order and taken the girls?"

"Not when I explain why I had to do it. Dr. Marshall has offered to fly in and testify on my behalf. Her notes from the past year detailing all his abuse will stand up. I have to try, Mer. I can't stay there another day. I don't know what he might do next."

She exhales a loud breath. "Okay, I'll make the arrangements. Please be careful."

"I will."

Jackson is waiting for us in the car even though we don't have to leave for another ten minutes. Punctual to Jackson means early, and on time means late. I stop by Bella's room and sigh when I see she's still not dressed but is lying on the bed immersed in *The Clue of the Broken Locket.* Ever since I introduced her to Nancy Drew, she's become obsessed and reads at least a book a week. It makes me so happy to see her newfound love of reading, especially as she struggled to learn just a few years ago.

"Honey, come on. Dad's waiting for us."

She looks up. "It's time to go already?"

I hold out the jeans she's thrown on the bed. "Hurry, get dressed. I'll see you downstairs."

When I reach the hallway, Tallulah is running out the door and getting into the car. I take a deep breath, checking my watch every few seconds, my impatience growing. Finally, Bella comes down the stairs, gives me a bright smile, and we leave the house together. We pull off at exactly one thirty. My heart is racing as I contemplate my plan. At intermission, I have to get the girls to the ladies' room but not too soon. I have to make sure there's a long line so that it can appear as if I've just remembered the other bathroom. Then I'll lead them to it and get them to follow me outside.

When we get to the school, there's already a crowd gathered. As we're led into the lobby, I notice the snack bar.

"How about if I get everyone a drink?" I need to make sure that a bathroom break is warranted.

Jackson gives me a look. "Let's all go over together." He puts a hand on my back and steers me toward the concession stand. "Waters for everyone?" he asks.

"I want a candy bar," Bella says. Tallulah is quiet.

Jackson turns to her. "We just had lunch, and I'm taking you out for a special dinner after. I don't think you need to stuff your face with candy." He smiles in a vain effort to deflect his harsh words.

She frowns and looks at me. If I didn't know that we'd soon be free from his grip, I would make a case for her, but I don't want to rock the boat. "Daddy's right, sweetie. How about if you save that sweet tooth for dessert tonight?"

Jackson shoots me a look of annoyance, and I pretend not to notice. "Waters for all of us," I say in a bright voice.

We take our seats, and the play begins. I can hardly pay attention, but I force myself to laugh when I hear others laughing. Jackson leans close to me, and I cringe as his leg makes contact with mine and he exerts gentle pressure. Finally, it's intermission and the house lights go up.

"Bathroom break, girls?"

Tallulah shakes her head. "I'm fine."

"Go ahead, Lu. Once it's over I want to get right out of here," Jackson says.

For once I'm grateful for Jackson's bossiness.

She sighs. "Fine."

"You staying here?" I ask him.

"Yeah, don't want to lose our seats."

We walk among the crowd and toward the long line at the bathroom. "I know another one," I say to the girls. "Follow me."

We walk down the hallway and turn right out of sight of everyone. I try the door, and it's locked.

"Ugh, Mom! This is for teachers," Tallulah says.

Bella is jumping up and down. "I need to pee."

"Okay, hold on." I find the key under the plant and put it in the
lock.

"How did you . . ." Tallulah starts.

"Doesn't matter. Come on."

I lock the door behind us, and Bella goes into a stall.

I look at Tallulah. "I need you to listen to me. I did not take any
pills that day. Your father put them in the drink I had. You see how
controlling he's been. I have never lied to you, and you must believe
me now. We have to go. I'll explain more, but I'm begging you to
trust me on this."

Bella comes out of the stall, her eyes wide.

"What's happening?"

I open the window and point. "We need to go. I promise I'll explain everything. I hoist Bella onto the ledge by the window and
she crawls out. I turn and Tallulah is standing there, arms crossed,
her face etched with indecision. "Lu, come on. You know in your
heart what's right. Please."

Something in my voice must convince her because she follows
her sister without another word. I breathe a sigh of relief and climb
out next. I see the white Toyota 4Runner in the parking lot, and we
run toward the car. I unlock it, and the girls and I get in. I wipe the
perspiration from my lip as my heart races. I start the car and put it
into reverse. Before it can move, a black Mercedes SUV pulls in
behind me, blocking my exit. There are cars in front of and next to
me, so there's no escape. A shot of dread runs through me as I realize it's Jackson's. He leaps out of the car and bangs on my window.
I open the window and he leans in. He doesn't look angry or surprised. He looks smug.

He whispers so that the girls can't hear. "Come on, Daph. Next
time you make a plan, you might want to make sure it's not in front

of one of the outdoor cameras." He shakes his head. Then he looks at the girls. "I'm so glad I stopped you in time. Mom's having delusions again. We need to get her help. Come on."

The cameras. How stupid of me.

I get out of the car, numb, and follow him to his SUV. Another car pulls up, and I realize it's Chloe. Jackson turns to the girls.

"Chloe will take you home. I need to get Mom to the doctor."

"No, I wanna stay with Mom," Bella says.

Jackson crouches down so he's on her level. "We'll be home soon. I just need to talk to Mom alone first."

"Mom said you drugged her," Tallulah says, looking at him accusingly.

He tilts his head. "Your mom didn't even drink the coffee I brought her. She drank one of the lemonades I brought for you girls. Do you really think I would have drugged your drinks?"

Tallulah seems to consider this. He goes on.

"Honey, I know this is scary. But drug addicts blame others. It's not your mom's fault. She needs help."

"Jackson, come on, that's not . . ."

He gives me a look of steel. "If you continue in denial, I'm afraid this arrangement won't work."

My shoulders slump in defeat. "Girls, go ahead with Chloe. I'll be home later. It's okay."

They leave and I get into Jackson's car.

As we drive away, he reaches out and puts a hand on mine, squeezing it tightly. "I'm very disappointed, Daphne. I thought we were making such progress. I'm afraid you aren't well."

"Enough with the games, Jackson. You had all your bases covered with Amber showing up at the beach that day. But I'm going to call the authorities and expose her. Jax's mother is going to jail for her crimes back in Missouri. Maybe then she'll come clean."

He pulls the car over and shifts in his seat to look at me. "I wouldn't advise it. You do that, and I'll make sure that you never,

ever, see those girls again. I'll alert DCF that you attempted to kidnap them. Chloe is a witness. You might even go to jail."

"What do you want from me, Jackson? I don't love you. Do you really think you can force me to be a loving wife again?"

"You may need some pharmaceutical help. I'll be letting the DCF investigator know that you've had some delusions and they'll mandate therapy for you if you're to continue living in the same house as the girls. I'm confident with some therapy and some medication you'll be the loyal, docile Daphne that I love so much."

"I'm not going back to that quack that lied for you all those years ago."

He shakes his head. "Dr. Graham is retired. Last I heard the man had only a few months to live. We'll go back to the woman we had that one session with, Hannah, right? You've already made quite an impression on her. Of course, once she realizes all those awful things you said about me were just a product of your delusions, she'll be quite relieved to know that I'm actually a good guy. I think we will develop a nice rapport, don't you?"

Great, Hannah the obtuse, who Jackson will have eating out of his hands. I lean back and close my eyes. He may have won this round, but the fight's not over.

38

AMBER

A mber put the finishing touches on her makeup and appraised herself in the mirror. Daisy Ann would shit a brick when Amber waltzed into her showcase party tonight. This time she wouldn't be able to kick Amber out, and she couldn't wait to see the look on Daisy Ann's face when Amber dropped the bomb that she was now the majority owner of Daisy Ann's vanity company. It was unfortunate that Hugo, on parole like Jackson, wasn't allowed to leave Connecticut, otherwise she would have had him escort her tonight. That would have been a more subtle way for the truth to dawn on Daisy Ann. This was probably better anyway. Let her think she had the upper hand and then Amber would eviscerate her in front of everyone. She fingered the bold silver necklace, filigreed and hammered to exquisite perfection. It was the crown jewel of White Orchid's new Ottoman Empire Collection, and Wade had snuck it out this morning. The necklace dazzled against the stark plainness of Amber's black sheath. She couldn't wait to see the look on Daisy Ann's face when she saw it on Amber's perfect neck.

She texted Bobby to let him know she'd be down shortly and to make sure the car was a cool sixty-eight degrees. Taking a sip from the glass of Fleur de Miraval, she toasted herself in the mirror. "Onward and upward. Only the best from now on." The champagne was delicious, and she savored the taste, remembering when the best wine she could afford was under twenty dollars. She'd left that version of herself far behind and she had no intention of ever going back.

Bobby opened the door for her when she walked toward the white limousine she'd ordered for tonight. It was just a short drive to the Dallas Country Club, where, Wade had told her, they were expecting over two hundred guests this evening. He would be ducking out after Amber arrived to avoid a confrontation with Daisy Ann when she learned he'd betrayed her. He still thought he'd gotten away clean. Amber was waiting until she sold her shares to Valene Mart and made her exit from Texas before she gave the information back to Nancy and he discovered that Amber had screwed him over.

As the car pulled up to the front of the building, Amber sat a moment watching as women clad in their designer best walked through the doors.

"I'm ready."

Bobby walked around, opened her door, and extended a hand to help her out. Taking a deep breath, she stepped out of the limo, straightened her shoulders, and marched inside, delighting in the looks of interest and admiration she received. The room was crowded, and she didn't spot Daisy Ann right away. Tables were strategically placed with the jewelry displayed under glass and segregated by type. She walked over to scan the bracelets. A well-dressed older woman was standing nearby and chatting to a smoking hot guy. It took her only a moment to realize who he was. Daisy Ann's husband, Mason. Amber had met him before, of course, at Jake's funeral, but she'd barely paid attention that weekend with everything else going on. He must be at least six four, with wavy black hair, and smoldering green eyes. She wouldn't kick him out of bed, that's for sure. Too bad she had little chance of that, considering she was about to take his wife down. She pretended to be scrutinizing the bracelets as she moved closer to hear what the two were talking about.

"Such a nice turnout, don't you think so, son?" the older woman said.

"Yes, ma'am. Looks like things are finally starting to turn around for her. She looks so happy tonight."

Not for long, Amber thought as she rolled her eyes.

The woman waved to someone across the room and moved away. Amber walked over to Mason. She wondered if he'd remember her. She sidled up next to him and put a hand on his arm. He turned to look at her. "Has anyone ever told you that you look so much like Henry Cavill?"

"Um, no." He stared at her for a long moment. "Do I know you?"

Amber laughed. "If you mean in the biblical sense, unfortunately no. Trust me, you'd have remembered."

Before he could put two and two together, she walked away then glanced at her watch. Seven thirty. Wade had said Daisy Ann would be giving her welcome speech at seven forty-five. She didn't want to be seen until just the right moment. She relished thinking about what was about to happen. Moseying over to the earrings collection, she pretended to examine some of the pieces while eavesdropping on the two women a few feet away. Both were dressed to the nines, in high heels, formfitting jumpsuits, and enough jewelry to start their own business. Hadn't these women heard of understated? Amber's ears perked up when she heard one of them mention Daisy Ann.

"I don't know how she does it all. You know she was president of the Women's Club last year while running her business and takin' care of her little ones. She's a dynamo, that Daisy Ann. And all the while looking hot enough to scald a lizard."

"Well, who wouldn't be with all her help. Come on now, her daddy practically owned the state. Talk about being born with a silver spoon. I'd be a dynamo too with a full-time staff at my disposal. And she gets to sleep with that yummy Mason. I bet he gives it to her good."

The other woman chuckled and slapped her friend's arm good-naturedly. "Simone, you're awful."

They both were, Amber thought, as she moved away. Her heart began to beat faster when she looked across the room and saw Daisy Ann move to the front, holding a microphone. Amber grudgingly admitted that she looked gorgeous. Her blond hair was blown out to perfection just past her shoulders, and she wore a burnt orange silk coatdress and high-heeled gold strappy sandals. She was decked out in all her own jewelry and looked as though she'd stepped off the pages of a fashion magazine. Daisy Ann addressed the crowd.

"Thank y'all for coming tonight. It means so much to see so many familiar faces and some new ones as well who I'm sure will become good friends. I hope you love our new collection as much as we do. We'll also be taking some custom orders. In the meantime, I hope you'll enjoy the delicious appetizers provided by the amazing chefs. Now let's shoot the lights out!"

It was now Amber's moment.

"Excuse me," she said to the tall man in front of her who'd been blocking her from Daisy Ann's view.

"Well, howdy, Daisy Ann."

Daisy Ann's eyes narrowed. She handed the mic to a woman next to her and strode toward Amber.

"What are you doing here?" she whispered through clenched teeth. Her eyes moved to Amber's neck. "Where the hell did you get that?" She pointed at Amber's necklace. Amber looked around and was gratified to see that all eyes were on both of them.

Amber raised her voice so that everyone could hear. "Now, is that any way to treat your new partner?"

"What are you talking about?"

Amber smiled. "I am Delancey-Flynn. Hugo Bennett? Just a front. And, sorry, but the royals aren't lining up to wear your designs."

"What . . . I don't understand . . . how—"

Amber pulled out copies of her stock certificates. "You've been had, my dear. Oh, and just so you know. I not only own the twenty-five percent you sold to my LLC, but I bought Wade Ashford's shares as well. You see, your old partner is as crooked as a barrel of fishhooks." She laughed. "Did I get that expression right?"

Daisy Ann looked around the room frantically, her mouth open, eyes wide.

"If you're looking for Wade, he slipped out right when I got here. But here's a copy of my other certificates. I'm now the majority owner of White Orchid Designs. Would you like to introduce me to my clients?"

39

DAPHNE

Our session with Hannah is almost over and I can see she's just as fooled by Jackson as I originally thought. Now that he's made it clear that the accusations I made in our first session were completely false, she is free to believe he's the wonderful father and husband he pretends to be. I, on the other hand, have been painted as a woman battling mental illness, hearing voices, and making up wild stories. At first, I refused to come here, but then Jackson alerted DCF about my failed escape and they mandated it. Hannah has notes from my therapist, Dr. Marshall, as well as a copy of the letter sent to DCF on my behalf, but it doesn't seem to make any difference. She points out that mental health can change, and the only true barometer is how I'm doing now. And since Jackson has made it appear that I'm having paranoid delusions again, which were the reason behind my runaway attempt, my behavior is considered unstable. It's maddening.

"I'm so glad that you both agreed to come back," Hannah says, smiling at Jackson then turning to me with a sympathetic look. "And I'm so sorry for what you're going through, Daphne. But I promise, the medication is going to help." She can't prescribe anything as she's not an MD, but she's in practice with a psychiatrist who's already evaluated me.

She goes on. "I agree that Seroquel is a good start. I know you've managed your bipolar with diet and exercise, but clearly, you're in a crisis right now. Sometimes these depressive episodes can cause psychosis. You're lucky your husband is so understanding."

"My *ex*-husband," I remind her, my face hot, but then I stop before I say anything else to jeopardize my position. I don't have bipolar disorder and this woman—I won't call her a therapist—is a total moron if she can't see through Jackson's facade. She has my notes from my referring therapist, but all it took was Jackson telling her that I'd hidden my condition from my therapist to make Hannah believe his lies.

"We'll make sure to get the prescription today," Jackson says, patting me on the leg and smiling at Hannah.

Hannah looks at her notes, then back at me. "I know this may seem intrusive, Daphne, but DCF is requiring you to be tested weekly to make sure you're taking your meds. I'll be monitoring you, so when you come for your sessions, you'll need to give me a urine sample."

"Why would you think that's intrusive?" I say, glaring at her.

She stands. "Yes, well. I'll see you both next week."

I don't say anything on the way to the car, still seething. Jackson walks around to open my door for me, but I beat him to it. I don't want his faux chivalry any more than his phony concern. I slide into the car and take a deep breath. He pulls out of the parking lot then gives me a quick glance.

"This could have all been avoided if you hadn't pulled that crap at the play."

"So now you're going to have me take heavy-duty medication that I don't need. Doesn't that make you feel like less of a man, having to drug a woman to stay with you?"

He cocks an eyebrow. "Darling, I'm only doing what's best for you. You're not in any danger, yet you concocted that crazy escape plan. Made my daughters believe I was going to hurt you all. I can only conclude that you are indeed delusional. So, no, I'm not feeling like less of a man. I think it's admirable that I'm committed to our family despite your mental health issues."

I laugh bitterly. "You can really talk some shit, Jackson."

He makes a face. "Really, Daphne. Such vulgar language doesn't suit you."

I turn and look out the window, not bothering to answer. I've got to do something and soon. We're both quiet the rest of the ride home and my mind is going in a million different directions as we walk into the house. Edgar greets us.

"There's a prescription that needs picking up at the drugstore. Please have someone see to it," Jackson tells him.

"Yes, sir."

The house is quiet. The girls are at camp, not due home for another two hours, and Jax must be napping.

"Why don't you go and let the cook know we'll have dinner at eight. She can feed the girls when they're home from camp. But I'd like some quality time with you tonight."

I nod. "I think I'll take one of the kayaks out for a bit, if that's okay with you."

"Fine. I don't worry about you going anywhere without the girls. I have some business to conduct anyhow."

"So nice of you to not keep me locked up in a tower."

"Now, Daphne, I'm not a monster. How many times do I have to tell you that this is all for the good of our family? You have your freedom. After that stunt you pulled with Meredith, did I take your phone? No, I didn't. I believe you can learn from your mistakes. Once we are fully reconciled, you'll be able to resume your normal life here. It's just going to take some time."

Later that evening the girls are in the media room watching a movie, Jax is down for the night, and Jackson and I are dining alfresco on the deck. It's a gorgeous evening, just a slight breeze, and the air redolent with the smell of the sea. There are candles, wine in crystal glasses, and a beautiful table set. Anyone looking on would be envious. I'm still thinking about the phone conversation I had before coming down to dinner, and it fills me with hope. After the botched attempt to get away, I had given up the idea of imposing upon Meredith again. Jackson threatened her, warning that if she helped me again, he'd have her charged with aiding and abetting a kidnapping. But I've found that women are willing to take all kinds of risks when it comes to helping another woman. So now I have a new plan in place, one that I feel sure will succeed. I need to give it a few days, lulling Jackson into a false sense of security and making him believe that I'm starting to come around to his way of thinking.

"I have to admit, you've gone all out tonight," I say.

"You're worth all the trouble in the world." Even though the staff did everything, he has no problem taking all the credit.

"Cheers," I say as I lift my glass to his.

"To many more beautiful evenings," he replies.

I take a small sip. I can't afford to have my senses dulled around him, although after tomorrow when I have to start taking the medication, I'm not sure how much in control I'll be. "How did your business calls go today?"

"Fine."

"Tell me, what's your next venture? Now that Parrish Industries is gone, are you planning a new company?" I've been wondering how he's affording to keep up his lifestyle. The FBI took most of his assets, but if I know Jackson, he has money hidden somewhere.

"I've got some deals going. Looking more into passive income these days. I don't need to go into the office every day. Get back into that rat race. I'm ready for a nice home life with you and the kids."

"That does sound nice. I guess maybe you've changed. The old Jackson loved the rat race. Being out there conquering the world."

He takes a bite of his lobster, gazing at me for a few moments. "That's what I keep telling you. I *have* changed. I had a lot of time to think while I was in prison. And I realized I was cruel to you at times."

At times? Talk about revisionist history. He was nice to me at times would be more accurate. "Go on."

"I know I was a control freak. I thought if I made sure everything was a certain way then nothing bad would happen. It was wrong. I promise, Daphne. This time will be different. We'll be the golden couple that everyone's envious of."

"I want to believe you, but you have to understand I still need some time. There's a lot of water under this bridge. You scared me, and you humiliated me. How do I know you won't do that again?"

His cheeks color slightly, and I can see his temper right under the surface. He tries to hide it with a smile and a gentle tone. "I guess I'll have to earn your trust back. Prove it to you. But you have to give me a chance."

"How do you suggest I do that?"

"For starters, a little affection? I'm not asking you to move back into our bedroom yet, but I thought we were headed in the right direction. I can still feel your lips on mine from that night on the porch. That's why I was so hurt that you tried to leave."

I feel really bad about what I'm about to say, but Meredith will understand. "It wasn't my idea. I *was* starting to have feelings for you again and when I confided that to Meredith, she convinced me that you could never change. She encouraged me to try to get away."

His eyes light up, and I know he believes me. "Oh, Daphne. You don't know how happy that makes me. She's just jealous! Always has been. You have to promise me to cut her off. She's trying to poison our relationship."

I nod. "I already have. I don't want anything to get in the way of my family."

He reaches across the table and takes my hand in his, his thumb caressing the top of mine. "It's going to be so wonderful. I'll give you time, but I hope it won't take you long."

I squeeze his hand. "You can't put a timetable on trust. I need to go at my own pace. That's the first step in earning my trust back. Letting me."

I've hit the bull's-eye with that remark, and he knows it. He can't push me without risking everything. But I know, despite that, I'm still on borrowed time.

- 40 -

DAISY ANN

The sun was just rising when Daisy Ann punched in the key code and walked into the offices of White Orchid Designs. She flipped on the lights and walked through the design rooms, scanning the drawings sitting out on drafting tables, then into the shop where workbenches were covered with metals, gemstones, and creations in various stages of completion. Sighing, she ran her hand over a long necklace of silver and turquoise and then walked to the end of the hall to her office, passing empty cubicles along the way. The thought of Amber stepping foot into this place Daisy Ann revered made her stomach turn.

Her office door was open, and she stepped inside. It was a stark room, with minimal decoration, just clean white walls with black-and-white photographs of their most iconic designs from the last ten years. She found this sterile environment, with no distractions, conducive to artistic creativity. Everywhere, the emphasis was on the jewelry. Her mother would be so proud. But last night's performance by Amber would have infuriated her. It had taken a lot to make Marylou Crawford lose her temper, but when she did, the intensity of her anger matched her flaming red hair. Daisy Ann smiled as she thought about her, thoughts that were always tinged with sadness and wistfulness, but also with gratitude for the wonderful mother she'd been. There was no way in hell Daisy Ann would allow this legacy of her mother's to be stolen.

She sat thinking about what she wanted to say to her employees until she heard the first sounds of footsteps. Rising from her desk, she walked down the hall to see that Rory, her silversmith, had arrived. He looked like he hadn't slept, lines of worry etched around his eyes.

"You look awful. Did you sleep at all last night?" she asked.

"Not much. What about you?"

"No, not much either. I've been worried about you. About everyone. I'll talk to them once everyone's here. In the meantime, come sit with me."

They sat together in her office, and she began. "Last night looked really bad for us, but I want you to know that there's no way I'm going to let that vile woman anywhere near this company. So please, don't worry about her and her crazy antics and just concentrate on your work. As always."

He shook his head. "It sounded pretty dire, Daisy Ann. I mean, if she has majority ownership, how are you going to stop her?"

"You let me worry about that. Have I ever let you down?"

Rory gave a defeated shrug, pressing his lips together, but said nothing.

"Rory, listen to me. I'm going to take care of this. You have to trust me. We can't let the others see us worried and afraid. Do you understand?" The most important thing right now was to keep morale up.

"I guess. If you say so. I can put on a front for the time being. But—"

"No buts," she interrupted, looking away from him when she heard the sounds of people coming into the offices. "Now, let's go talk to our employees and give them our assurances that nothing is going to change."

When Daisy Ann left her offices, things were buzzing again, although the atmosphere was a trifle subdued despite what she thought had been a good talk with the entire staff. At least they weren't showing signs of doom and gloom, so she considered that a win. She slid into the driver's seat of the Porsche 911 Speedster. She'd thought it ridiculous when Mason bought the sports car five years ago and had ridden in it only a few times with him, flying along dusty country roads like a bat out of hell. She'd never driven it herself, but today it was just the vehicle she needed, because after her talk with Wade Ashford, she knew she'd need to be able to open up that little sports car and drive the hell out of her fury and hatred. She drove slowly, eased into the parking lot of his building, and sat in the car a few minutes, drumming her thumb against the steering wheel. When she felt calm enough, she got out of the car and walked up the five flights of stairs from the garage to Wade's office.

"I'm here to see Wade," she said to the receptionist.

"Hi, Mrs. Briscoe. Let me buzz him for you."

Daisy Ann waited until the girl looked back up at her. "Uh, he's in a meeting. He asked if you could come back at three. He said he'd be free then."

Daisy Ann turned away before the girl finished talking and strode toward Wade's office. She threw the door open and marched in.

Wade vaulted from his seat, his face turning scarlet. There was no one else in the room.

"Who are you meeting with, the ghost of Christmas past?" Daisy Ann slammed the door behind her.

"You can't just come barging in like this. I'm a busy man," he sputtered.

"Yeah, real busy. Busy skulking around like a sneaky backstabbing rat behind my back."

"Now hold on. Just what are you accusing me of?"

Daisy Ann laughed at his audacity. "Just the little matter of selling all your shares of White Orchid. If you wanted to sell, you should have come to me."

"And what would you have said, huh? Valene Mart came to you, and you turned them down flat. They offered you a lot of money plus a continued interest in the company. You and I, we could have made a lot of money on that deal, but you said no. That was stupid, Daisy Ann. Even your daddy would have told you that."

"My daddy had more integrity in his little finger than you have in your entire body. You don't even know the meaning of integrity, Wade Ashford. What I think Daddy would have told me is to never get in bed with you in White Orchid in the first place. That's what I think."

"Jake Crawford never did like to get his hands dirty. Thought he was above the fray, better than everybody else. Mr. Honest Abe. But don't kid yourself. He was a shrewd businessman. He would never have let such an opportunity pass him by. You shoulda taken that offer, Daisy Ann. When you refused, well, that's when I knew I wanted out, and when that Bennett woman came to me, I thought, why the hell not. Sure as hell ain't gonna make any money holding on to this stock." He sat down at his desk.

"You're wrong, Wade. But you're too foolish to understand why. That's the difference between you and my daddy. He was a wise and honorable man. You? You're a sleazy parasite. All you care about is Wade Ashford and what's good for him. That's the mark of a true good for nothing."

Wade looked at her with contempt. "I think we're finished here, Mrs. Briscoe."

"Oh, Wade, you have no idea how very true that is." She gave him a contemptuous smile and swept out of the room.

41

DAPHNE

When I go downstairs for breakfast, I'm surprised to see only Jackson at the table. It's just a few minutes after seven.

"Where is everyone?"

He doesn't answer right away, just glares at me; then he clears his throat. "I had Chloe take them to breakfast before camp. I wanted to speak with you in private."

"Why? What's wrong?"

He lifts his hand from the table, and it's then that I see it. My cell phone. What is he doing with it?

"You're seeing someone."

Dread fills me. "Why do you have my phone?" I ask, stalling.

"It was in Bella's room. She was playing Candy Crush on it this morning."

I groan. Bella has a habit of "borrowing" my phone. I should have been more careful. She knows my password, so I know what's coming next.

"Your texts make very interesting reading. Who's Sebastian?"

I blow out a breath. "He's just a friend."

Jackson raises his eyebrow. "Really?" He begins to read out loud. *Can't wait until you're back again and we can take that trip to Carmel. Our first weekend away together. I want to fall asleep with you in my arms and wake up to your beautiful face.* You answered that you can't wait either." He shakes his head. "Shall I continue?"

"No. I, you know, I-I . . ." I stumble over my words, scrambling to figure out the best approach. "I know what it might look like, but to be fair, I didn't know you and I were going to get back together."

Jackson gives me a scorching look. "Have you fucked him?"

I recoil. "No. Of course not. It's new. Like I said, he's just a friend."

His face is red, a tornado brewing behind his eyes. "He sounds like way more than a friend. Waking up together? I can't believe a word out of your filthy lying mouth. Here I am, trying to put our family back together, and you're messaging with some man behind my back. What kind of a slut have you turned into?"

"Jackson, please. Stop. I swear, I'll end it with him. It's nothing."

He stands up. "Trust me on this. I am never giving these children up. I had hoped that the four of us could be a family again. But if it has to be a family of three, I guess I'll settle for that." He hands me my phone, leaning over as he presses his hands onto my shoulders and brings his face so close to mine that we're almost touching. "End it. Now," he hisses.

Jackson's been gone all day, which in one way is a relief but in another way is worrying because I wonder what he's up to. I've been too anxious and troubled to do much more than ramble around the empty house or sit and stew. My stomach is in such knots that I'm sure I'd vomit if I ate anything, even though I'm hungry. Finally at a little after five, all of them walk in—Jackson, the girls, Jax, and Chloe. Jackson holds a large bunch of white roses, and I try without success to remember what the white rose symbolizes. He hands the flowers to me, the smile on his face almost a sneer. "For you."

"Thank you; they're lovely. I'll go put them in water." I start to move, but Jackson stops me and turns to Chloe.

"Chloe, would you be kind enough to put these in water for Daphne? Tallulah, Bella, why don't you go help pick a vase and take

Jax with you?" Once they've left the room, he gives me a frigid stare. "I asked for black ones, but the florist didn't have any, so white it had to be."

I want to scream at him to go fuck himself and stop all these stupid games, but I know that will get me exactly nowhere, so I say nothing.

He walks to the cart and picks up a glass and a bottle of Macallan scotch. "I've planned a special occasion for us tonight," he says, his back to me as he pours himself a drink.

I close my eyes and take a deep breath. What now?

He pivots around to me. "I thought we'd take a romantic moonlight boat ride tonight. Just the two of us. You know, maybe help get your mind off your sad breakup this afternoon."

"I told you we were just friends. There was nothing to break up."

"You're lying, Daphne." He lifts the glass to his lips and drinks until it's empty. "But I'm going to give you one more chance." He slams the glass down on the cart and walks toward me. "Let's go, my dear," he says, taking my hand and leading me to the front door.

"Wait. What are you doing? I'm not dressed for a boat ride. And what about the kids?"

"All taken care of. Boat's gassed up, there are clothes for you, and Chloe knows it's an important date night for us. She'll be with the children. Come on," he says and pulls me along.

I try to talk him out of this boat ride the whole way over in the car, but Jackson won't be moved, and the fear inside me builds with each mile we travel. The sun is setting and the air thick with humidity when we arrive and walk along the pier to the boat. The gold letters on the transom that spell out the name, *Bellatada,* seem to mock me. Jackson boards first and extends a hand to me.

Once on board, I see that he's made preparations. A bottle of Veuve Clicquot sits in a bucket of ice next to two crystal flutes. A silver tray holds caviar along with toast points, lemon wedges, and crème fraîche. My stomach roils at the sight of it all.

Jackson says nothing as he starts the engine. We glide slowly from the slip and motor for almost an hour, until we are so far out onto open water that the lights on the shore are barely visible. The sickening realization that I am completely helpless in the middle of nowhere with a madman keeps playing over and over in my head. We've still not said a word to each other when Jackson turns off the engine and lowers the anchor. He leaves his seat in front of the wheel and comes over to where I'm sitting, pours two glasses of champagne, and hands one of them to me. "Drink up," he says and sits close to me.

The glass shakes in my hand as I bring it to my mouth and take a slight sip, hoping to keep it down.

"You're shaking," he says. "Are you cold?"

"Maybe a little."

"Or maybe you're nervous?"

I press my lips together to keep myself from crying out in frustration. How am I here?

"Listen, Daphne," he says, and suddenly his hand is moving up and down along my back. "I would like tonight to be the beginning of something good between us. We had it once, didn't we? Those long nights of lovemaking when my mouth explored every part of your body and brought you to the boil." With this, his lips are on my neck and his tongue flicks along its side and up to my ear. I want to vomit. He stops and sits back to look at me. "Remember those nights, Daphne? No one will ever love you the way I did. We can have all that again." He pours himself another glass of champagne and downs it in one gulp, then leans in and kisses me, thrusting his tongue into my mouth. "Let's go below," he says, his voice husky. "Let me show you how much I want you." He grabs my wrist and wrenches me from the cushion.

"Jackson, no, it's too soon. We need to wait."

But he's not taking no for an answer and continues to drag me behind him, pulling me as I stumble down the steps to the salon. He spins around and takes me into his arms, kissing me, his hands rubbing my breasts and pulling at the buttons on my blouse. "I need you, Daphne. Can't you feel how much I need you?" he whispers into my ear and shoves his groin more forcefully against me.

"Jackson, stop," I scream at the top of my lungs.

And in that instant, he releases me.

I'm shaking, and Jackson freezes. He looks like he's in shock. I need to lower the temperature, to try and reason with him. "I told you, Jackson, you must give me time. We've talked about this already."

His face is a dark mask. "You're right, we have. In fact, we've talked too much about it, don't you agree?"

I don't like where this conversation is going. "I don't know. But it's hot down here. I need some air."

"Of course, whatever your little heart desires. We wouldn't want you to be uncomfortable, now, would we?" His voice is contemptuously solicitous.

I say nothing and go to the stairs, where I feel his body close behind mine as we ascend. Once we're topside Jackson refills the glasses.

"Come," he says and stands at the railing, holding the glass out to me.

I hesitate a moment and then go to him. We stand next to each other looking out over the deep inky water. Night has fallen, and there's a slight chill in the air. The haze from the day has not lifted, cloaking the moon and stars and leaving the sky dark. The only sound is the lapping of the water against the hull.

"Have you ever wondered, Daphne, how many people have drowned in Long Island Sound?" Jackson doesn't look at me but continues to stare out across the water. "Did you know that the Sound is a combination of salt and fresh water? Quite an amazing estuary. The salt water lies under the fresh water. A body sinks faster in fresh water. Did you know that?"

Alarm bells are clanging in my head, but something tells me to stand my ground and show him he can't intimidate me. "I didn't know that. Be careful that you don't slip and fall in, Jackson."

He turns to me and smiles. "That's my Daphne. I like it when you show courage. But here's the thing, Daph. You're either with me or with no one. Do you understand what I'm saying? Tonight is decision night. You dump that piece-of-shit chump in California and you come back to me and your family. I'm hoping you're telling the truth and he hasn't touched you. I can't abide the thought of another man's hands on you."

"Jackson, I told you—"

"Enough excuses, Daphne." His lips curl with disgust. "The choice is yours. A family again or not. But one thing you will never be is with another man. You are with me or no one." He looks out over the water again. "Understand?" His hand is on my back, a slight pressure forward, and my breath catches.

It's as if a fist has clamped its fingers so tightly around my heart that every breath brings crippling pain. His dead eyes tell me everything I need to know. What I say next will determine whether I live or die.

42

DAISY ANN

aisy Ann dove into the pool, the initial shock of cold salt water quickly dissipating as she rose to the surface and swam a few laps before the kids finished their snow cones and barreled back in, splashing and hooting. She swam to the deep end and leaned against the side, spreading her arms along the coping and kicking her feet out in front of her. They spent every Sunday at Birdie and Chandler's, all thirteen of them, soon to be fourteen since Rose and Royce were expecting their fifth child in December. Daisy Ann made a face as she imagined what "R" names Rose might be dreaming up to go with the other four kids—Ryder, Rayne, Royall, and Rebel. She thought about suggesting Ridley, short for Ridiculous. Submerging once more to cool off, she swam to the steps and climbed out of the water. Birdie walked over to her, handing her a towel.

"How are you doing?" Birdie asked as they sat side by side on two lounges shielded by a large umbrella. Her mother-in-law, in white linen shorts and top, made sure that only her legs were in the sun. "You look tired. Like you've been chewed up and stepped on, as my Chandler would say." Birdie chuckled, but Daisy Ann knew she was in no joking mood and prepared herself for what was to come.

"You shouldn't worry about me. I'm fine. Really."

"You're not fine when you stop going to church on Sundays and go to work instead. You've been understandably shaken by what happened at the showcase. But still, honey, you can't let this consume you."

Daisy Ann started to speak, but Birdie cut her off. "You have a duty to your family. I've always respected your decision to work outside the home, but there are limits. Adding to that your running around to Colorado and Idaho . . ."

"Missouri," Daisy Ann corrected her. "You saw how she acted at the showcase. I'm not going to let her get away with it."

"What are you intending to do?"

"For the moment there's not much I can do but wait. But I'll tell you one thing, there's no way in hell she's getting her hands on Mama's designs. I'll make sure that doesn't happen if it's the last thing I do. I'd rather see the company burned to the ground than be controlled by Amber. She's a liar and a cheat. If I had one wish, it would be for her to be punished for all she's done."

"I still don't understand why you don't just turn her in for what you found she did in Missouri. Let them deal with her."

Daisy Ann blew out a breath. "She killed Daddy! I'm going to prove it. I don't care if I have to travel to the ends of the earth to prove it."

Birdie waved her hand. "Let the authorities deal with it. Your place is here. The boys need their mother."

Daisy Ann felt like she could scream. "I'm so tired of that old refrain making women feel guilty for having a life outside of their family. I love my boys, and I'm there for them. And your son here works twelve-hour days. But I don't see you lecturing him about his familial duties!"

Birdie raised her brows. "Maybe you think I'm old-fashioned, but you can always work. Tucker and Greyson won't be little forever. It goes by fast, Daisy Ann. You're missing it all."

Daisy Ann was too furious to speak.

Birdie gave her a long look and nodded once. "Okay. I told Mason I'd try to talk some sense into you, but I see your mind is made up. I won't bring it up again."

"Thank you," Daisy Ann said, and she meant it. Birdie could be forceful and authoritarian, but she knew when to gracefully back down and not hold a grudge. Things were always clean with her.

Birdie stood. "Well, honey, at least do your best to put it out of your mind for today. Try to enjoy the family."

"That's just what I intend to do." Daisy Ann pulled her wet hair up into a ponytail.

"I think it will be good for you to get away for a while. No work, no hassles. Just time to be with the family and enjoy some well-deserved downtime," Birdie said.

"Right." Daisy Ann leaned back and closed her eyes. On Friday they were due to leave for the annual monthlong summer stay at the Briscoes' Jackson Hole compound. It was something Daisy Ann looked forward to with mixed feelings. Wyoming was beautiful and an amazing place to explore, and the retreat itself was a cornucopia of things to do, but a month with extended family was a long time. It was also a long time to be away from the office, especially with all that was going on, but perhaps it was a good thing. Dallas was only a two-and-a-half-hour flight from Jackson Hole if she needed to get back fast.

She got up from the lounge and walked to the backyard where Chandler and Royce were already at the grill, each holding a beer and Chandler poking at the spareribs with grill tongs. Mason grabbed a cold bottle of Lone Star and went over to join them. The smell of barbecued ribs and mesquite wafted over from the grill, and helpers from the kitchen were carrying serving trays and dishes of baked beans, corn on the cob, and potato salad. The last serving bowls to be set out contained grilled asparagus, a green salad, and a luscious-looking peach salsa. Daisy Ann knew that her mother-in-law's plate would contain almost wholly the greens and salsa.

Birdie had bowed to the "no glass" rule around the pool, but that didn't mean her table wouldn't be set in her own refined and tasteful style, even if it was just for a picnic or outdoor barbecue. She owned several sets of Mario Luca Giusti acrylic dinnerware in

different colors and designs. Today's dishes were a stunning turquoise and were accompanied by light blue synthetic crystal glasses,
which, if dropped, would merely crack and not shatter. A gorgeous
cluster of white dahlias sat in the center of the table.

"Okay, everyone. Come and get it," Chandler called. The kids
ran to the grill, and their grandfather began piling ribs and brisket
onto their plates. Just as they all sat down to dinner, Daisy Ann's
phone rang again. She looked down to see a Colorado number. "Excuse me," she said, pushing her chair back and standing.

"Hello?" she said, taking a few steps away from the table.

"Mrs. Briscoe?" a deep male voice said.

"Yes. Who's calling?"

"This is Sheriff Frank Campbell, from Gunnison County. Mrs.
Briscoe, we're in possession of some new evidence that might shed
more light on the death of your father."

Daisy Ann gasped. "What evidence?"

"Would it be possible for you to come to Gunnison so we can
discuss this in person?"

"Of course. I'll come as soon as I can." She stood there trem-
bling, unable to move.

"What is it?" Mason was instantly standing next to her, looking
at her with concern.

She blinked a few times, still staring at the phone in her hand.
"That was the sheriff from Gunnison. They have new evidence
about Daddy's death." She looked up and saw that they were all
watching her. "I have to go to Gunnison right away."

"What kind of evidence?" Mason asked.

She shook her head. "I don't know. He wants to talk to me in
person."

"Of course, you must go right away," Birdie said.

"I'll call and see if we can get a flight plan filed. We could be
there in a few hours or at the very latest tomorrow morning," Mason
said.

"Yes. Good. I need to go home and pack." Daisy Ann felt dazed. "I'm sorry to leave so abruptly." She scanned the faces at the table.

"You go. We understand," Chandler said, getting up from the table. "You leave the boys with us while you and Mason make arrangements."

"Yes, thank you," she said. As Mason took her hand and led her away, she heard Rose say, "I guess she'll use this as an excuse for not coming to Jackson Hole."

In other circumstances Daisy Ann would have turned around and told Rose off, but the only thing on her mind was that her father's murderer would finally be brought to justice and that evil bitch would pay for what she'd done.

43

DAPHNE

"Let's have a baby." The words had seemed to leap from my mouth as we stood on the deck last night, the words I now believe had saved my life. The shock on Jackson's face mirrored my own surprise at what I'd uttered, but I pushed on. "It's my fault you left me for Amber. You wanted a son, but I was too selfish. I was worried about gaining weight. That's why I hid the fact that I was using an IUD. But when she got pregnant, it about killed me."

His hand slid from my back and both hands reached for my shoulders, turning me toward him.

"If this is a trick . . ."

I shook my head. "It's not. Look, I'm sorry about that text. I promise, we haven't been intimate. The truth is I haven't been attracted to anyone since we've split." That much was mostly true, but not for the reasons Jackson would believe. "I'm ready to take my share of the blame for the disintegration of our marriage. I want to rebuild the trust."

I could tell he was still wary, could see it in his eyes. "Do you swear you haven't had sex with him?"

"Yes," I answered immediately. My mind raced, trying to figure out how to make him believe I wanted a child with him and keep him out of my bed at the same time. What the hell had I done?

"A baby. A new start for us." He nodded. "We can start tonight. Here, on the boat."

"But the meds. That could be bad for a baby and I have to take them or else when Hannah tests me, I'll get in trouble. We have to wait until I'm able to stop the meds. Maybe you can talk to Hannah, get her to wean me off? Say I'm doing better."

I'd been taking Seroquel for two weeks. It's wreaked havoc on my stomach and shrouded my mind and senses in a fog. By early afternoons, I'm so tired that I have to take a nap. We see Hannah on Thursdays and that's when she checks my medication levels. Otherwise, I'd do whatever I could to not take it. At first, Jackson insisted I take the pills in front of him, but now that he sees the accuracy of the tests, he trusts me to take it on my own. As for DCF, the OTC hearing appeal was postponed due to some clerical error.

He put his arms around me and pulled me closer to him. "There's no reason we can't enjoy each other in the meantime. We can use protection."

I prayed he'd heed my next words. "I want it to be perfect. I haven't showered or, you know, prepared. Let's go home. We'll plan our reunion for this coming weekend."

"When?"

"Saturday night. Let me spend the day thinking about you. Let's have a romantic dinner. Send the kids to spend the night with Meredith. I want to be able to be free with you."

"Meredith? You're not friends with her anymore, right?"

I reached up and stroked his face, mustering up all my acting skills. "She's apologized. She realizes that I'm happy now and she promised to be supportive. Besides, the girls love her, and it would give us our privacy. She's even offered to take Jax. I remember the things you liked. We could even go get some new toys to use." As the words left my lips, the feeling in my stomach grew sicker.

He gave me a salacious smile. "Daphne, you little minx. I like the sound of that."

.   .   .

Tonight's the night, and I haven't taken the Seroquel for three days—I took my last dose on Wednesday so I'd test fine at our appointment. Meredith picked up the girls and Jax an hour ago, so it's just the two of us, and the kitchen staff who will leave once they've served dinner. Everything is ready. Under my bed is a bag. A car rented in another name waits for me at the Bishops Harbor train station. He'll think I took Metro-North to New York and from there took a train to D.C., since I've booked three tickets to Washington on my credit card to throw him off. Meredith will have prepped the kids on everything, telling them the truth so that they'll understand the necessity of going on the run. This is my last chance, and I cannot fail.

I look at the items we picked up earlier and shake my head. Jackson's gotten kinkier, but it will work to my advantage. I put on the black leather bustier and attach the sheer hose to the garters, then slip the red silk dress over my head and choose the highest pair of Louboutin's from the closet. Taking a deep breath, I walk out of the room and downstairs where Jackson awaits out on the deck.

He smiles as I approach and hands me a glass of red wine.

"I'm not sure I should drink on the medicine," I say.

"A teeny bit won't hurt."

I accept the glass and take a small sip. "How soon can we eat and get rid of everyone?" I lift my dress up to reveal what's underneath.

"I'll go check."

As soon as he's gone, I pour the crushed pills into his drink and mix it up with the stirrer I've hidden in my cleavage. The white residue doesn't look like it's dissolving all the way, and I stir harder. This has to work. I hear footsteps, and put the glass down, glancing again, and seeing it appears to all be dissolved.

"About twenty minutes till dinner. Come sit down, I have something for you."

We sit on the love seat, and he puts his wine down on the table next to it. He hands me a small package.

"What's this?"

"Open it."

I tear the gold foil. It's a black box and as soon as I see the HW logo, I know what I'm about to find. I open it and see a gleaming cushion-cut ruby ring.

"I-I don't know what to say," I stammer.

He takes the ring from the box and slides it on my finger. "I thought the red was perfect. Symbolizes our passion for each other. A new start with a new ring."

Drink your wine, I want to shout. "Let's toast."

I lift my glass and watch as he takes a sip of his. He makes a face. "This wine is off."

My stomach tightens in dread. What am I going to do now? What if he realizes I tried to dose him, that the acrid taste is because of the pills? I counted on him drinking the wine. Those pills would have knocked him out for hours. My mind is racing, and I desperately try to regroup. We sit down at the table that is set for dinner, and I'm numb with anxiety as the branzino is placed on my plate.

I try to manage an even voice. "Really? I thought it tasted fine."

He takes another long swallow then makes a face. "Let's have our dinner and we'll get a new bottle." He calls to Edgar. "Open a bottle of the Screaming Eagle." He turns back to me. "It's a special occasion after all."

Edgar returns and opens the bottle in front of Jackson, hands him the cork, then pours a small amount into a new wineglass. Jackson sips, nods. "Perfect." Edgar pours a glass for me, then fills Jackson's glass and leaves us.

"Cheers," he says, lifting his glass.

"Cheers," I respond, and we touch glasses. I take another small sip, wishing I could down the whole glass to calm my nerves, but knowing better. We make small talk, and I try keep my mind from wandering.

After the staff withdraws, I swallow my food without tasting it, scrambling to come up with a plan B. An idea comes to me, one that's as much of a long shot as it is distasteful, but I have no other choice.

"I should have brought a sweater out with me, it's chillier than I thought."

Jackson jumps up, the epitome of chivalry. "I'll go grab one for you."

As soon as he goes into the house, I unhook my Apple watch from the back of my garter, scroll to the voice memo app and hit record, then place it on my lap with my napkin loosely on top of it. The sun has gone down and the lighting is low out here, so I'm confident he won't notice.

"Here you go, my dear," Jackson says as he places a sweater around my shoulders.

"Thanks."

We make idle small talk for a few moments. I look over at him. "I need to say something."

"What is it?"

"I know I've fought you on all this, but I realize now that if you hadn't forced my hand we'd have never reconciled."

He smiles. "I'm glad you're finally seeing that."

"I'm surprised, though, that you were able to get Amber to go along. Isn't she jealous that we're getting back together?"

He rolls his eyes. "The only thing Amber cares about is Amber. She was only too eager to make a deal if it meant I would help her get what she wants."

I don't waste time asking what that might be. I appeal to his ego instead. "Well, she's always been brilliant. That's one thing I can't take away from her. She came up with a great plan."

He scoffs. "It wasn't her plan. It was mine."

"So you were the one who figured out how to make it look as though I was neglecting the children? I realize now that you must have drugged the lemonade. But what I don't get is how did you know I'd drink that particular drink?"

He taps his temple. "Think, Daphne. I drugged them all. I put the Klonopin in each drink, with a little vodka in the lemonade, and Bailey's Irish cream in the coffee."

"It was very smart. But what if DCF doesn't clear me? Now that you've drummed up a false case against me, it could backfire. They might tell you that you can't have permanent custody if I'm living here."

"Nonsense. I already have the judge in my pocket. He'll do whatever I ask. You forget that I still have a lot of power in this town."

We finish dinner, and I dawdle over my coffee, silently urging the staff to clean up and get the hell out of here. Finally, Edgar steps outside.

"If you won't be needing anything else this evening, sir?"

"It's fine. Everyone can go."

I take the opportunity to stop the recording while he's distracted talking to Edgar. When I hear the last of the cars drive away, I stand. "I've been waiting all night to get my hands on you," I say.

He gets up and comes toward me, pulling me into an embrace. We kiss and he forces his tongue into my mouth. I close my eyes and remind myself that everything is on the line here. We head back into the house, and I grab his hand.

"Let's go to our old bedroom. I want to reclaim it as my own."

We walk up the stairs and my skin feels clammy, my heart beating furiously. I stop by the bedroom I've been using and scoop up the things we bought earlier that day. When we reach Jackson's bedroom, I stop a moment to take it in. Amber has redone it, of course, and it's just as tasteful as when I lived here, but her decorator used bolder colors. A wave of dizziness overcomes me as all the bad memories of this room come rushing back. I push them aside and tell myself to buck up, I can't lose it now.

I pull the dress up over my shoulders and toss it on the floor. Jackson looks at my leather-clad body with desire. It's now or never. I throw my shoulders back and make my voice strong.

"Strip. Now."

He looks at me in surprise. I pick up the leather whip and crack it a few times. "Did you hear me, slave? Do it." I raise my hand menacingly.

"Yes, mistress," he says, throwing off his shirt and stepping out of his slacks.

I have to be very careful about my next moves. I stare at him, then walk toward him until I'm inches away. "You may undo my garters."

He smiles and reaches for my leg, and I smack his hand with the whip.

"I didn't say when. You must ask first."

"Please, may I undo your garters?" His pupils are hugely dilated, and he gapes at me hungrily.

"Yes."

He does and my stockings fall to my ankles. I step out of my heels. I run a hand over his chest and down his stomach, stopping before his groin. "What do you want me to do?"

"Touch me." His voice is thick with yearning.

"What's the magic word?"

"Please."

I move my hand down and fight my revulsion and caress his hardness, squeezing for a moment. "On the bed," I command.

He walks over to the bed and lies down on his back. I straddle him and he reaches his arms to pull me down.

I smack him again. "Who's the boss?"

"You are," he says with a smirk.

"You're a bad boy. Just for that, I'm going to have to restrain you." I get up and come back with the handcuffs and he yields his wrists to me. I secure them to the bedpost and pull on each hand to make sure they're secure.

He moans in anticipation.

I slide down until I'm straddling him again and he tries to move his body to meet mine. Then I scoot off the bed and grab my dress and shoes.

"What are you doing?"

I should just leave without any explanation but the pent-up fury that's built over the past weeks explodes.

"You narcissistic sociopath. I'm leaving, that's what. You're never going to see me or the girls again. I can't believe you actually thought I'd ever love you again. You make my skin crawl, and if it's the last thing I do, I'm going to prove what a lying, amoral scumbag you truly are."

His face turns crimson, and his eyes are hate-filled. He tries to sit up, furiously jerking against the restraints hindering him. "You treacherous bitch. I'll make you pay for this. You're the one who's never going to see those kids again. I'll make sure you spend the next twenty years in prison for kidnapping. You will—"

I put my hand up. "Shut up. I'm through listening to you."

The last thing I do is to get my iPhone and take some pictures of him. They may come in handy.

- 44 -

DAPHNE

run to the guest room and grab the bag I've already packed from under the bed, throw on jeans and a sweater, doing my best to ignore the obscenities Jackson is yelling from the bedroom. Fortunately, there's no one to hear him, and the size of the house and grounds are large enough to ensure there are no close neighbors to investigate. I fly down the stairs, rush into his study, and grab the keys to his Mercedes. I lock the front door, jump in the car, and roar out of the driveaway. Once I'm off the street, I pull over and call Meredith.

"I'm on my way. Meet me at the train station." After I end the call, I text her the recording I took at dinner with Jackson's confession. I mentally prepare for my conversation with the girls. Tallulah is old enough to understand, but I'm very concerned about Bella having to hear the harsh truth. Meredith will have prepared them somewhat, but it will be up to me to give them the whole story, or at least as much of it as I think they can handle while still conveying the necessity of this rash action.

It's close to eleven when I pull into the mostly deserted parking lot. Meredith is waiting for me, the kids are still in her car. I park, put the keys under the mat, and shut the door.

"I've been a nervous wreck," she says, pulling me into a hug.

"How are the girls?"

"Upset. As you can imagine. I told them that Jackson and Amber were responsible for what happened at the beach, but that's all."

I nod.

She hands me a set of keys. "Here you go. It's the blue Honda Civic right there." She points. "Untraceable to you and there's a map with stops along the way. Also, some clothes, baseball caps, toiletries. Try to stay out of sight as much as possible. Airbnbs have been booked and the codes for each are all in the folder in the car. Burner phones and cash too."

"Thank you. Jackson's going to be furious with you, you know. I don't know what he might do when he comes to pick up Jax. Once the staff shows up tomorrow and finds him . . ."

"Don't worry about me. Just be safe. I'll take the recording to the lawyers."

"I hope it's enough," I say.

"Just stay hidden until you get my message. I'll save it as a draft in the Gmail account. The burner is already logged into the account. Just don't send anything from it. Remember to save any message as an email in the draft folder," Meredith says.

I shake my head. "I feel like I'm in an espionage movie. How do you know all this?"

"I had help."

She returns to her car and the girls come out. Bella runs to me and hugs me; Tallulah just stares.

"Come on," I say. They follow me to the car, and we get in. Bella, used to being relegated to the back, automatically gets in behind the driver's side. I'm surprised when Tallulah gets in next to her, but I say nothing.

"Buckle up."

We pull out of the parking lot, and I blow out a pent-up breath.

"I'm so sorry for all this," I start.

"Aunt Meredith said that Dad drugged your drink and lied to the police," Bella says. "Why did he do that?"

"It's a very long story and one that I had hoped not to tell either of you for a long time. Your father is a sick man. I should have never brought you back here, but—"

"I made you," Tallulah says, her voice strained. "It's all my fault. If I had listened to you, none of this would have happened but I believed her." She's crying now.

"It's not your fault, honey. Believed who?"

"Amber. When I got in touch last year so I could call Dad in prison, she told me that you were angry at him for leaving you and that you'd made him out to be a bad person. She said that you and Dad had been unhappy for a long time but that you still couldn't forgive him for leaving you, so you took us away. I'm sorry, Mom. I should never have listened to her."

I bite back my anger at Amber and focus on my daughter. "I want you to listen to me, Tallulah. None of this is your fault. Amber is a good liar, she's as sick as your father, and trust me, she fools most people. For a while, she fooled me too. It's only natural that you would want a relationship with your father, and you had no way of knowing the truth about him because I protected you from that. The important thing is that we're getting away from him, and I'm going to prove what he did."

"You tried to tell me. But I wouldn't listen."

"Sweetie, please. I know you think you're all grown up, but you're still a child. It's not your fault. Please believe that."

"What if they take us away from you and we have to live with him?" Bella asks.

My hand tightens on the steering wheel. "I will never let that happen. We have to get far away from here now, and people are working to help us. You have to trust me. We'll be driving all night. No one will be looking for us until tomorrow so we'll get a good lead, but then there will be a lot of people with our pictures searching for us."

"I'm scared," Bella says.

"I know, baby, I know. But it's going to be okay. I promise."

"Mom?"

"Yes?"

Tallulah's voice is small. "Did he abuse you?"

I sigh. "He was abusive, yes. He didn't beat me up, but he was abusive in other ways."

"Why did you marry him?" she asks.

"I didn't know until it was too late. I thought he was wonderful at first. He swept me off my feet. He charmed my family, made me feel like the most special person in the world. By the time he showed his true colors, I couldn't get away." I think about how to frame the rest of it. Tallulah already feels responsible for our situation; if I tell her that the reason I came back was to protect her, it will destroy her. I need to give them a version of the truth that helps them understand why I couldn't leave but doesn't place any burden on them. "Girls, listen. I still think this is too much for you to hear right now. It's enough that you understand that I did what I had to do until I was finally able to get away from him. We can talk more about everything together with Dr. Marshall once we're back home. All you need to know is that I love you with every fiber of my being and I promise I will do everything in my power to make sure you are both safe and out of his reach forever." I only hope it's a promise I can keep.

45

AMBER

A mber had barely slept all night, and this morning her excitement was so high she thought she might burst. Everything was coming together. Amber now had 55 percent of the shares of White Orchid in her possession. She'd paid four and a half million dollars for Daisy Ann's 25 percent and six million for Wade's shares, but today Valene Mart would buy them all from her for eighteen million. A profit of seven and a half million dollars. Not bad for a day's work. Unfortunately, she'd have to split some of that with Jackson. But with the five million she still had in the offshore account and the cash in the safe-deposit box, she'd wind up with almost ten million all to herself. If Jackson thought he was going to get any of the money she had put in those bank accounts, he was sadly mistaken. Plus, she still had three of those precious little pink gems stashed at the house in case of emergency.

Still lying in bed, she hugged herself with glee, picturing the sun-drenched skies and cerulean seas of the Maldives that she'd seen in a travel magazine. Paris would have to wait. She was in some serious need of some relaxing days on a beach. What a glorious place to take a luxurious time-out and decide what she wanted to do with the rest of her life. She would be finally and fully free. No encumbrances, nothing to keep her from seeing the world and enjoying all the finer things in life. It's what she wanted and what she deserved. She was smart and she'd turn that money into much more, until she was rich, rich, rich. And then she would do something that would make her famous and adored. She could probably find a way to use her money to get the charges back home dropped and then she would no longer have to hide from the world. She'd cruise the Nile, explore India from the Taj Mahal to its Mughal splendor, spend weeks at the Hermitage in St. Petersburg, the Uffizi in Florence, and the Rijksmuseum in Amsterdam, read Rousseau and Voltaire and Zola in the original French. And then, she would hold court with the literati and wealthy who would all vie to spend time with the brilliant and beautiful American at her fabulous Paris abode. Throwing the covers back, she slipped out of bed to shower and dress.

Her appointment with Vivienne Wallace at Valene Mart was scheduled for tomorrow afternoon. Amber had insisted that the meeting be with Vivienne alone, woman to woman. No pompous buffoon Roddy the Third and no mind-numbing sex toy Todd. She didn't have to put up with asinine men anymore. Today was all about celebrating. She went downstairs where Bobby was waiting for her.

"We're off to the races, Bobby," she said as she got into the car and gave him the address of the jeweler she wished to visit.

Amber could have walked the short distance, not even a mile away, but only a masochist would walk a mile on a summer day in Dallas. In a few minutes Bobby pulled the car up to the Hotel Crescent Court and let her out.

"I won't be long." Amber had called ahead to let them know she'd be coming in to pick up the ring she'd chosen a few days ago, a Sylva & Cie gold and diamond Ten Table Ring, part of the brand's Ten Table Collection, apparently named thus because pieces so stunning could be seen from ten tables away.

"Ah, Mrs. Parrish. Your ring is ready. Would you like to try it on once more?"

"Yes, thank you." Amber took the ring from its box and slipped it onto her finger, holding her hand out to admire it. It was positively eye-popping, with sixteen beautifully cut baguettes set in gold. "I love it," she said, returning it to the box and handing him a credit card.

"It looks beautiful on your finger. Wear it in good health," he said.

As soon as Amber got back into the car, she took the diamond wedding ring from her left hand and moved it to her right hand, then slid the long rectangular Ten Table ring onto her left index finger. The diamond wedding ring Jackson had given her when they married was a four carat Graff diamond worth over $500,000, and her new ring had cost a mere $22,500. But from now on, every time she looked at her left hand to see the ring that she had bought for herself, Amber would be reminded that the only person she could really love, trust, and count on was herself.

When they got back to the hotel and Amber was back in her suite, she undressed, put on the hotel robe, and poured two fingers of whiskey into a crystal glass. Opening up her laptop, she navigated to the Secretary of State website and typed in White Orchid Designs LLC. Delancey-Flynn had been added to the names of owners, but she frowned when she saw the percentage. Only thirty. Wade's transfer had been recorded, but not the 25 percent from Daisy Ann.

She downed her drink in one gulp, then poured another and sank into one of the cushioned chairs to call Jackson.

"Amber. I've been waiting for your call."

"The deal isn't done. Only one transfer has been recorded. I'm royally pissed. We're supposed to meet tomorrow morning to settle everything with Valene Mart."

There was a short silence on the other end of the phone and then laughter.

"What the hell is wrong with you, Jackson? Did you hear me?"

"Sleep in tomorrow, Amber. Relax. You may as well cancel your meeting with Valene Mart."

"What are you talking about?" Amber tapped her foot on the floor, growing more anxious by the minute.

"You see, I formed a little partnership with Daisy Ann. Your stock certificates are phony. She played you. *We* played you. And the four and a half million you shelled out for her stock? All gone. All mine." He laughed again.

"You and Daisy Ann? You're bullshitting me. This isn't funny."

"You're right. It's deadly serious." His voice had taken on a hard edge. "Daisy Ann has known what you were up to from the very beginning. I told her. Of course, we all know she hates you for killing her dear daddy, so she was more than happy to work with me against you. The stock certificates she sold you? Well, you can wipe your ass with them. That's about all they're good for."

"You son of a bitch. How dare you steal my money."

"No, Amber," he roared. "*My* money. Those diamonds were mine, you ungrateful thieving bitch. And when I find the account number, you'll be back in the gutter where you belong."

Good luck with that, she thought. Unless he could get inside her head, he'd never find the account number. "We had a deal. I helped you get Daphne back. This isn't fair." She almost spit out that he could kiss his son goodbye, now, but decided not to give him any warning.

"Fair? Daphne's in the wind. She thinks she won, but I'll make her pay for trying to screw me over. Just like I've made you pay for stealing from me. Have a nice day." He disconnected.

Amber threw the phone across the room and screamed at the top of her lungs. How could she have been so foolish as to trust that bastard? She pictured Daisy Ann laughing with Jackson at her expense and was so filled with rage that another scream erupted from her throat. She picked up the glass of whiskey and threw it against the wall. She wanted to kill someone. She flashed back to the night of Daisy Ann's party. That bitch must have known then and her reaction was all an act. She'd made a fool of her once again. The

humiliation was almost too much to bear, and Amber paced, screaming and shaking her head in fury. "Enough, calm down," she said
out loud to herself. She still legally owned 30 percent of White Orchid from her purchase of Wade's stock. Surely, she could figure out
a way to use that to make Daisy Ann's life miserable. And she had
the other diamonds too. She'd retreat for now, but she'd be back
with a plan that would take Daisy Ann down. And Jackson was
going to regret screwing her. Next time she would count only on
herself. For now, she had to book the next flight to Bishops Harbor,
grab her son, and get the hell out of Dodge.

46

DAPHNE

The girls fell asleep an hour into the trip, and I'd drunk copious amounts of coffee to keep myself awake over the past thirteen hours. The quiet drive in the dark of night gave me plenty of time to think. I'm still astounded Jackson allowed himself to be handcuffed to the bed. And almost as astounded at myself for the acting job I was able to execute. Still, when he suggested we engage in some bondage play when we were shopping for lingerie earlier that day, I was terrified he would insist I be the one to wear them. I had counted on him drinking the drug-laced wine and passing out long before that became a possibility.

I don't know how I was able to play the role of dominatrix so convincingly, and I had little confidence it would work. But I saw it in his eyes the moment I gave him the first command. He loved it. I've read that many powerful men crave domination in the bedroom. It's the one time they can relinquish control. But given our situation, I wasn't sure Jackson would allow me to exert any control over him. The only explanation I can come up with is that his ego is bigger than his brain. I can't wrap my head around the fact that he actually believed I was grateful to him for bringing us together. Now so much makes sense. For years I wondered if the times he was kind and loving were an act, but now I see that for Jackson, cruelty and kindness grow in the same garden. He is a master of self-deception, believing in his own twisted rhetoric. A man who could believe that any means justifies the ends is capable of anything. I wonder once again how he ended up this way. Did someone damage him or was he simply born that way? But I can't muster any empathy or sympathy for him. He's taken too much from me for that.

Close to noon, I pull up to the house, a small rancher on a quiet street, and I leave the girls asleep in the car while I try the lockbox with the code Meredith left for me. My legs are practically numb from the long drive, my back is screaming, and my eyes feel dry and itchy. I breathe a sigh of relief when it opens, and I unload our meager possessions from the car. Tallulah yawns and opens her eyes.

"We're here," I say.

She rouses her sister and the two of them follow me into the house, still half asleep.

"Where are we?" Bella asks.

"Tennessee. We'll stay here overnight. I need to get back on a regular schedule so I'm going to push through and stay awake today and then hopefully I'll sleep tonight."

"Are we driving all the way to California?" Bella asks.

I shake my head. "No, sweetie. We're just going to get some distance from Connecticut until my lawyers can straighten everything out. We can't go home again until that happens. Are you guys hungry?"

"Yeah," they answer in unison. Meredith had packed us a bag of protein bars and waters, but the girls need real food. The staff will have arrived at Jackson's four hours ago, and by the time they find him and release him, he'll need some time to get himself together. Plus he has no idea where we are, and he still needs to pick up Jax from Meredith's. He'll be there for a while, interrogating her, I'm sure. I think it's safe to go out to lunch. The girls use the bathroom, and we all freshen up and are back out the door in fifteen minutes.

"How long do we have to do this?" Tallulah asks. "Aunt Meredith took our iPads and my phone. I can't talk to any of my friends or see what's going on. It's not fair."

I'm gratified to see her acting like a kid again and that last night's self-recrimination seems to have fallen away. "I know it's hard, honey. But Dad could track us with your phone. We have to be really careful. It will be over soon. I promise." In reality, I don't know how long it will be or if I'll be arrested. But at least my mother will be back from South America next week, so at the very least, the girls could be released into her custody while this all gets sorted out. Now that I have recorded proof that Jackson set everything up, his statement about her dementia won't hold water. I'm confident Jackson won't have a leg to stand on when that recording is shared with the authorities.

"I noticed a pancake house not too far from here. Sound good?"

"Yeah!" Bella answers enthusiastically.

"Fine" is all I get from Tallulah.

It's a weekday and the restaurant is only half full. We take a seat in a booth by the window. The waitress brings waters and coffee, and we all order pancakes. I involuntarily flash back to the first time I defied Jackson and instead of eating fruit like he suggested, piled my plate with pancakes slathered in maple syrup. On that occasion, I was still reeling from earlier that morning when he'd presented me with a blank journal in which to keep track of my food intake and calories and record my daily weight. I was postpartum and not yet back to my prepregnancy weight. My little act of rebellion had cost me a visit from my mother and was the start of his cycle of abuse.

"Mom?" Bella's voice is tinged with annoyance.

"Yes?"

"You're not answering me."

"Sorry, what were you saying?"

"Can I get a milkshake to go with the pancakes?"

I nod. "Yes. You can get whatever you like."

Our food arrives and we all dig in. It's been almost six weeks since I've been alone with the girls and away from Jackson's watchful eye. It feels great, like I can get a full breath again. But then reality comes crashing back and I remember how tenuous our freedom is. I glance at my watch and start to get nervous. I flag the waitress over to get our bill, my stomach suddenly churning. No one is paying us any attention, but I can't help feeling paranoid. Finally, she returns with the bill, and I pull out some cash and leave it on the table.

"Let's go."

"I'm not finished with my milkshake," Bella complains.

"Okay, hurry, please."

My phone buzzes and I jump. No one should have this number and Meredith knows better than to call me on it. I pull it from my pocket and freeze. It's an Amber Alert. Tallulah's and Bella's photos pop from the screen with their names and pertinent information. I'm filled with dread as I read the narrative:

THIS AMBER ALERT HAS BEEN ACTIVATED BY THE CONNECTICUT STATE POLICE DEPARTMENT. TALLULAH AND BELLA PARRISH LAST SEEN WITH THEIR MOTHER, DAPHNE PARRISH. DAPHNE PARRISH SHOULD BE CONSIDERED MENTALLY UNSTABLE AND DANGEROUS. IF SEEN CALL 9-1-1.

I lower my voice. "Girls, look at me."

They look up, wide-eyed.

"We have to leave now. There's an Amber Alert on you both. Don't run, just follow me casually out the door."

I slide from the booth, my head light and my heart pounding. The girls follow silently, and we make our way out the door and into the car. I'm about to shut the door when the waitress comes running out.

"Excuse me, ma'am."

I freeze, suddenly unable to move a muscle.

47

DAISY ANN

A s Daisy Ann's plane began its descent into Gunnison, the sun was rising over a sea of wildflowers blanketing the mountains in vibrant shades of orange, yellow, blue, and purple. It was a glorious sight and one that filled her with nostalgia. She and her parents had never missed the annual wildflower festival held in July, and Daisy Ann had collected the official posters of every one of them. She turned from the window to face Mason seated next to her.

"I told myself I'd never come back here. I'm glad you're with me. Thank you for coming," she said.

He put his hand over hers and gently squeezed. "Of course. I wouldn't have let you come alone."

The plane touched down with a bump and eased along the runway to a stop. When she and Mason disembarked, Brian came walking toward them.

"Hi, Daisy Ann, Mason," he said, shaking Mason's hand. "Can I get your bags?"

"No bags. Just a small carry-on. I've got it," Mason said.

They walked to the waiting Jeep, and Daisy Ann looked at her watch. "We're meeting with the sheriff in half an hour, so maybe we should go right into town and grab a coffee there."

"You don't want to go to the house first? Brenda's keeping some homemade cinnamon muffins warm for you," Brian said.

"Maybe later." Already filled with disquiet about what she was about to discover, Daisy Ann couldn't face walking into that house right now. She was of a mind to get right back on the plane to Dallas after their meeting with the sheriff. "Let's just go to the Coffee Company drive-through. We can park in front of the building and drink our coffees in the car till it's time to go in."

When Brian parked in front of the Public Safety Center where the Gunnison County Sheriff's Office was housed, they still had twenty minutes to wait.

"How're things?" Mason asked Brian as they sat in the car.

"Good, good," he said, and proceeded to fill the time with small talk about the goings-on.

Daisy Ann half listened, too distracted to pay much attention to what the two men were saying. She was spending the time looking from her watch to the building and back again.

"It's time," she said, placing the half-full coffee cup in the holder and getting out of the car.

"You don't have to wait, Brian. We'll call you when we're done," Mason said.

"Nah, I'll wait. It's no problem."

Mason nodded at Brian and followed Daisy Ann into the building.

"Mrs. Briscoe?" A thickset man with a balding head came toward them and extended his hand. "I'm Sheriff Campbell."

"Hello." They shook, and she put a hand on Mason's back. "This is my husband, Mason Briscoe."

"Nice to meet you both. Why don't we go into my office." He led them down the hall.

Once they were seated, he began. "First, let me say again how sorry we all were about what happened to your father. Jake Crawford was a fine man, and people here were saddened by such a tragic accident." He stopped and opened a file on his desk. "Some evidence has come into our possession, however, that casts doubt on whether his death was accidental."

Daisy Ann's heart was beating so hard it felt like a hammer was thudding against her chest. "What kind of evidence?" she asked, leaning forward in her chair in an attempt to see what was in the folder.

"A young man has come forward with an SDXC card he found among his late father's belongings. The card is from a game cam that was on your father's property. It was recording on the day of the shooting."

"I don't understand." Daisy Ann knew that all her father's game cameras for tracking animal movement had been collected and searched by investigators at the time. None of the cameras had been turned on to record that day. "Are you saying the investigators missed one of my father's cameras?"

"It wasn't your father's. It was the camera of a poacher, Levi Jones. Either the camera was very well hidden, or Levi removed it before the Bureau of Investigation came and took your father's cameras. I believe he retrieved the camera after he heard about the shooting because he didn't want us to find it. We don't take kindly to poachers or them setting up game cams on other people's property. That's probably why he never turned the card over to us. Anyway, his son came across the card when he was sorting through his father's things. He was curious to see what was on it, and after he viewed the video, he brought it to us."

"What's on it? There must be something on it or you wouldn't be talking to me. I want to see it," she said.

He put his hand up. "It's very disturbing, but—"

Daisy Ann interrupted him. "I want to see it."

"Are you sure?" Mason said to her.

"Yes. Show me."

The sheriff plugged the card reader into his computer and turned it so that all three of them could view the screen, then pressed play.

Daisy Ann sat transfixed, her eyes filling as the video showed her father coming into view. Amber was walking next to him. The two of them stopped and Amber said something to Jake. He nodded and began walking alone. The time stamp at this point was 6:45:03. Amber walked to a clump of sage and stopped, watching Jake as he walked away from her. At 6:46:11 she picked up the muzzle loader and brought it to her shoulder. The gun bucked and a cloud of smoke erupted from the end of the barrel. At 6:46:14 Jake's body dropped to the ground.

Daisy Ann's chest constricted, her body shaking as she watched her father fall. "Stop the tape," she sobbed.

Mason put his arm around her, and she rested her head on his shoulder, weeping.

"I'm sorry, Mrs. Briscoe. I know this is extremely difficult to see. I'll tell you the rest."

She raised her head and looked at him, wiping her eyes. "No. I need to see it to the end."

"Are you sure?"

"Yes."

He started the video again and they watched Amber lower the gun and stand still for a long five minutes, then walk slowly to Jake's body. She looked down at him, then rolled his body over onto its back, continuing to stand next to him. She took a cell phone from her pocket but put it right back, making no attempt to place a call. Then turning, she began to slowly walk away until she was out of the frame, and the video, detecting no movement, ended. At this point the time stamp read 7:01:34.

The sheriff closed his computer. "There is a fifteen-minute interval between the time of the shot and her leaving the scene. The call to the police came in at 7:40 A.M., almost an hour later. She took her sweet old time getting to the house to call for help. If this tape isn't proof enough that she shot him on purpose, the fact that she waited an hour to call it in should convince any jury of her guilt."

"I knew it," Daisy Ann said. "I knew that bitch killed him, and this proves it."

"We've issued a warrant for her arrest. Any jury looking at that video is going to hand back a verdict of first-degree murder."

"She's in Dallas. Staying at Rosewood Mansion." Daisy Ann stood. "Thank you, Sheriff, for seeing that justice will be served."

"You'll let us know if there's anything we can do to help," Mason said, extending his hand.

"I sure will. We've already alerted the FBI since she's no longer in Colorado."

Mason and Daisy Ann walked hand in hand from the building. Before they reached the car she said, "I think I'd like to go straight back to the airport."

"I understand," Mason said.

It was just a five-minute drive and when they got there, Daisy Ann asked Brian to apologize to Brenda for her. "Please tell her I'll call her when I get home." She didn't have the energy right now to divulge all that they'd learned.

An hour later they were in the air on their way back to Dallas. Daisy Ann put her seat back and closed her eyes, replaying the video in her head. Her father must have been so lonely, so longing for someone to love him. She'd assumed that it was enough that he had her and his grandsons, and after all, he was sixty-five and past the romance stage. How foolish she'd been to believe that the desire for someone to love and love you back ended at a certain age. It made her sad to think that her father wanted that so badly that he'd been taken in by a woman like Amber, a woman who'd lied to him and used him. How many lonely people did that happen to, she wondered, good people who just wanted to be loved. There was a special place in hell for the ones, like Amber, who took advantage of them. And Daisy Ann was going to make sure that Amber ended up in that very special place. But right now, her tears were for a good man who didn't deserve to die the way he did.

48

DAPHNE

wait for the waitress to continue, the car in reverse, ready to bolt if necessary.

"You forgot your wallet."

I exhale, put it in park, and get out of the car. "Thank you so much." I take it from her and return to the car. It takes everything I have not to tear out of the parking lot. I take deep breaths and drive away, wondering if my heartbeat is ever going to return to normal.

When we get back to the house, I look around to make sure no one is outside before we exit the car and go in. After locking the door and pulling down the shades, I sit the girls down.

"We have to stay inside until we leave. I know I said we'd leave in the morning, but now it's too risky to drive during the day. I'm going to sleep now and we're going to get back on the road as soon as night falls. We've got another thirteen-hour drive ahead of us, and we can only stop for gas and bathroom breaks."

"Are we going to get arrested?" Bella's eyes are huge, and she looks at me with raised brows.

I pull her to me. "No, sweetheart. You didn't do anything wrong. We just need to get to our next stop and wait there until Meredith tells me it's safe to stop hiding."

Tallulah clenches her fists. "I hate him! I wish you'd never married him."

I release Bella and take Tallulah's hand. "I don't."

Her face is red, and she narrows her eyes. "Why not?"

"Because then I wouldn't have the two of you. No matter what your father has done, I can never regret marrying him because he gave me the two most precious gifts in the world."

Tallulah scoffs. "That's such a load of bullshit!"

I recoil in surprise.

"Don't talk to Mom that way," Bella says.

"If you'd married someone else, you'd love those kids just as much and they wouldn't have a psycho for a father." She shakes her head. "And now we're on the run like criminals while he gets to act like the good guy."

"I understand you're angry. But I stand by my statement. I don't believe anyone is born by accident. And yes, my judgment was wrong when it came to him, but there's no point in regretting something that can't be changed. Regret is a wasted emotion."

Tears spring to Tallulah's eyes and she throws herself into my arms. "I'm so stressed out."

I hug her tight to me, rubbing her back. "I know, I know. We're going to get through this. Just hold on a little longer."

After a few minutes she pulls away. "Come on, let's go watch TV and let Mom rest."

I go into the bedroom and lie on the bed, but sleep eludes me, my mind racing. Grabbing the burner phone, I navigate to the Gmail account and open it. There's a message in the draft folder.

He just left with Jax. I told him nothing, of course, despite his attempt at browbeating me, even threatening to have me arrested for aiding and abetting. That's when Randolph came downstairs and told him to leave. Randolph's mere presence was enough. Jackson knows the pull my husband has in this town. I'm seeing Howard this afternoon and I'll let you know what he says about the recording. I'll write more when I know more. Be careful, Daph, and put a message in the drafts to let me know you're still safe.

I start a new message. *I'm halfway there. Amber Alert out now so I'm going to drive through the night instead of waiting until tomorrow. Plan to arrive around noon tomorrow.*

I put the phone down and close my eyes. I need to sleep if I'm going to drive straight through. I think back to when I was younger and had a hard time falling asleep. My sister, Julie, used to lie next to me and count backward from one hundred. I'd be out by the time she got to fifty. I picture her now, pretending she's with me, and listen to her voice as I slowly drift off.

We leave the house at seven thirty, just as the sun sets. I hand Tallulah and Bella baseball caps.

"You need to wear these when we stop for gas and bathroom breaks. Don't look at anyone, try to keep your head down."

Tallulah grabs it from me and rolls her eyes. Bella takes hers and puts it on. The girls are restless; they're not used to having to sit in the car for hours with no tech to distract them. Meredith packed books for them, but it's getting dark, and I can't keep the interior light on in the car. I turn the radio on and find a station with music I hope they'll like and brace myself for another marathon session in the car. I was able to sleep for a good five hours, but I'm still exhausted. The only thing fueling me is adrenaline and caffeine, but I keep telling myself I can do this.

"Wanna play I spy?" Bella asks her sister.

"No. It's a stupid game. Besides it's getting dark."

"It's not stupid. You're stupid."

"Shut up!"

"Girls, please."

Tallulah sighs. "This sucks."

They continue to bicker, and I do my best to tune them out. Hopefully Meredith will have good news for me after she meets with Howard and shares all the information. The girls finally settle down, and to my surprise both fall asleep again. I suppose it's the stress, but I'm grateful for the quiet. I have to keep myself from speeding, because the last thing I need is to get pulled over, but it's torture, and the temptation to go faster on the quiet roads is strong. *Slow and steady*, I tell myself. *Slow and steady*. My thoughts shift and I wonder what all this is doing to Tallulah and Bella. There's no question that this trauma will leave its mark. Is therapy going to be enough to heal them? All I've ever wanted was a family. To be a good mother and wife, and to raise strong, kind children. And yet I ended up marrying a sociopath and spending over ten years in an abusive relationship. What does the future hold for my girls? How will this nightmare manifest in their choices? The possibilities are terrifying. Such are the tormenting thoughts that keep me company the entire journey.

Two bathroom and gas stops and fourteen hours later we finally arrive. I pull down the long driveway and park the car. There's a truck in the driveway and I assume it belongs to her—the woman who's provided the car, the houses, and the instructions.

"Now where are we?" Tallulah asks as she and Bella follow me to the side door.

"Texas."

"Why—"

The door opens and a blond woman I've never seen before, dressed casually in jeans and a blouse, smiles at me.

"Daisy Ann?" I say.

"Welcome. I've been waiting for y'all."

We follow her into the house and I'm about to thank her for her help when there's a pounding on the door. I look at her in alarm. She turns and opens the door.

"Well, it's about time you arrived."

She opens the door and in walks a smiling Jackson.

49

AMBER

A mber scrambled to get her things together and check out of the hotel. She'd booked a nonstop flight to New York, and she needed to be at the airport within the hour for her five o'clock flight. When she landed, the car she'd ordered would be waiting to take her to Bishops Harbor, an hour's drive from JFK.

"Bobby, you need to drive like lightning. I have to be at the airport pronto."

"Bad time of day for traffic, ma'am, but I'll do my darndest."

The drive seemed interminable between the beginnings of rush hour and red lights along the way, but miraculously they made it with time to spare. Since she still had forty-five minutes before boarding, Amber settled herself in the first-class lounge and waited. It would be sometime around eleven, maybe even close to midnight before she finally arrived at the house. Jackson had no idea she was coming. He really didn't understand who he was dealing with. No, he'd always underestimated her, thought he was smarter than she was. He'd screwed her over, but he'd forgotten that she had all the goods to get even, the dummy.

He would never see his precious son again. Jackson had pined for years for a son. It was the reason she'd been able to steal him from Daphne—she'd purposely gotten pregnant and, as luck would have it, was carrying a boy. She could still remember the look of pure joy on Jackson's face when she'd given him a copy of the sonogram of his son. It would kill him to lose Jax. His little man. She would take

Jax far away and Jackson would live the rest of his life having no idea where he was. Maybe she'd even send him a postcard occasionally just to taunt him. By the time Jax was an adult, she would have brainwashed him to the point he'd never want a relationship with his father. Jackson wanted to play dirty, and this was the kind of arena where Amber fought best.

It was a full flight, and sitting next to Amber in first class was an old man who fell asleep minutes after takeoff. She was thankful that she didn't have a chatty Cathy beside her, but when she noticed drool trickling from his open mouth, she almost threw up. She shuddered, reflexively moving away from him even though the large seats provided ample separation. He continued to snore and grunt throughout the flight, and she almost cheered when they finally landed. How disgusting it was to be old. She really needed to fly private in the future.

It was only adrenaline keeping Amber awake on the drive to Bishops Harbor. She was dead tired, and her eyes burned with fatigue, but sleep was light-years away. She sat up and put the window down when the driver pulled through the gates. The house was dark, only the outside architectural and landscape lighting illuminating the night. The car came to a stop and the driver got out and went to the trunk.

"You can just leave the bags on the porch. I'll get help to take them in," she directed, handing him a wad of cash.

The house was still when she entered and slipped off her shoes. She wondered if Jackson was asleep already. Should she surprise him? Putting her ear against the bedroom door, she stood very still and listened. There was no sound, but breathing wouldn't necessarily be heard from where she stood. With her heart racing, she turned the knob as slowly as she dared and opened the door a slight crack. Moonlight filtered into the room through the sheer curtains, and as her eyes adjusted to the light, she saw that the bed was empty. What the hell was going on? Suddenly the sound of heavy footsteps startled her, and she let out a shriek as she turned around.

"Amber. You frightened me. I thought you were a burglar." Chloe was holding a broom in one hand and a flashlight in the other.

Amber began laughing hysterically in both relief and at the sight of the broom as a defense weapon. "Where is Jackson?"

"After Daphne ran away with the girls two nights ago, I thought Mr. Parrish was going to have a stroke. He was furious, screaming and yelling, stomping around like a madman. He left this afternoon for Dallas."

"Dallas? Why did he go to Dallas?"

"He said he had business there and then he was going to find Daphne and the girls. He has the police and the FBI looking for them. Put out an Amber Alert and everything. But so far, nothing."

"Where's Jax?"

"He's in bed."

"Okay. Why don't you go back to sleep? I need to get some sleep too. We can talk more in the morning. And put the broom away."

Chloe laughed. "Good night, Amber. See you in the morning."

All at once the tension of the last thirty-six hours swept over Amber in what felt like a tidal wave of exhaustion. She set the alarm for five A.M. and then fell into bed. She was asleep within five minutes.

When Amber awoke at five, the house was still quiet. Jax usually slept until seven or seven thirty, so she had time. Daphne was on the run and Jackson was in Dallas. What did that mean for Amber? It seemed to her that nothing good would come from her hanging around. She needed to get out of this house and out of Bishops Harbor. In fact, the smart thing for her to do was to get the hell out of the country. After making herself a strong cup of coffee, she retrieved her and Jax's passports, stuffing them into her handbag.

Taking their son would be a delicious kick in the balls for Jackson. Next, she packed a carry-on with only necessities. She'd add just a few of Jax's things as soon as he woke up. There'd be time and money to buy whatever they needed or wanted at the other end.

After a second cup of coffee, Amber booked two first-class tickets to the Maldives on Qatar Airways for nine thirty tonight. It was a twenty-five-hour trip with one stop in Doha, and then she'd plan her new life. She'd change her name to something like Juliette de Vere or Emmeline Percy or something equally fitting. With the right amount of cash, it would be no problem to obtain counterfeit credentials. From there she would decide on the location of her new home. Perhaps Geneva or maybe Florence. Amber's imagination was already weaving the threads of her new persona into her head. She would be the beautiful young American widow, grieving the loss of her husband and caring for her dear little son. She could picture it all, like a classic scene from a great movie, with Amber the star.

There was just one more thing to do before she and Jax left. The three pink diamonds Jackson didn't know she'd kept. Opening the box of tampons, she pulled the cotton out by the string and dumped them onto the palm of her hand. A feeling of satisfaction surged through her. Despite Jackson screwing her out of the money she'd invested in Daisy Ann's company, she still had these. When the time was right, she'd sell them, three of the most precious of the stash, and then she'd never, ever have to worry about money again.

50

DAPHNE

look at Daisy Ann in shock. I thought she was helping me. "What did you do?" I say, my voice shaking. She doesn't answer me as Jackson strides into the house.

The girls stand behind me; I square my shoulders up.

He sneers at me. "Did you really think you'd get away with it?" He shakes his head and lowers his voice, leaning in to whisper in my ear. "You are going to pay for what you did back at the house."

I glance over at Daisy Ann and see she's texting something on her phone.

"Dad, that's enough!" Tallulah comes to my side, her eyes blazing. "We know what you did to Mom. How could you? What kind of a person are you?"

Jackson's face turns crimson, and he narrows his eyes. "How dare you lie to my children about me." He tries to take Tallulah's hand, but she snatches it back.

"Lu, I promise I didn't do anything. I told you Mom has problems she—"

"Stop it. I know you're lying. I'm not a baby, and I don't believe anything you say."

I take a step toward him, putting myself between Tallulah and him. "I have a recording where you admitted what you did. My lawyers are straightening everything out. You're the one who's going to pay for what you did."

He pokes a finger at my shoulder. "You're going to prison for kidnapping. The FBI agents are on their way. Right, Daisy Ann?"

"I'm afraid so."

As if on cue, there's a knock at the door. Daisy Ann opens it, and four federal agents barge in and flash their badges.

"FBI. We're here from the fugitive task force."

"Come in," she says.

Jackson smiles at me. "Say bye-bye, Daphne."

The taller of the two walks up to me. "Daphne Parrish?"

"Yes,"

"I'm Agent Preston; your ex-husband is accusing you of parental kidnapping."

"Leave my mom alone," Bella cries and rushes in front of me.

Preston nods toward the two men still standing at the door. One of them walks over to Jackson.

"Jackson Parrish?"

"Yes, and let's get this over with. Arrest her so I can take my children home."

"Sir, you're the one who's under arrest."

"What are you talking about?"

"We have a warrant here for you."

"What the hell do you mean?" He points to me. "She's the one who took the kids."

"Sir, you're under arrest for perjury, assault, and public corruption, parental interference, the list goes on." He looks at the paper in his hands. "Says here you bribed a judge."

"This is ridiculous."

Daisy Ann walks over and puts an arm around me. "Everything's going to be okay now."

Jackson turns to look at Daisy Ann. "You tricked me? We had a deal."

Daisy Ann laughs. "I don't make deals with men who abuse their wives."

I look at her in amazement. "You did this? How?"

Before she can answer, the agent with the warrant speaks again. "You can have your lawyer call this number." He hands Jackson a card. "We're going to the federal courthouse for a venue hearing and then you'll be taken back to Connecticut."

"Can I at least take a piss first?"

"Make it quick."

Jackson looks at Daisy Ann. "Where's the bathroom?"

She points and the agent follows him.

"Am I under arrest?" I ask Agent Preston.

"No, ma'am. The federal prosecutor has dropped those charges in light of the evidence your lawyers presented. But we do need to get you back to Connecticut safely to get all the paperwork taken care of there."

"Daisy Ann, I don't know how I can ever repay you."

While I was Jackson's prisoner at the house, I took every opportunity whenever possible to surreptitiously listen to his phone conversations. That's when I overheard him talking to Amber about their plan to take over Daisy Ann's company. I snuck into his office on a day he'd gone out and discovered the papers of his bogus LLC and Daisy Ann's contact info. I asked Meredith to get in touch with her, and the two of them worked together to hatch the escape plan for me and the girls.

"I was happy to help. When Meredith told me about the doctor you saw all those years ago, I had my detective track him down. The man is dying, and a dying man has the need to die with a clear conscience. He signed an affidavit admitting that he falsified your medical records at Jackson's behest to have you committed. Your ex is almost as despicable as Amber. They belong together. As we speak, agents are going to her hotel to arrest her."

"You called them about the Missouri warrant?"

She shakes her head. "Murder. I have proof."

My attention is pulled to the agent standing outside the bathroom door, now pounding. "Mr. Parrish, open up. You've been in there long enough."

There's no answer from the other side. One of the other agents yells across the room before the three of them sprint out the door. "He's getting in his car."

We all run to the door and watch as Jackson races toward his rental car.

Daisy Ann throws her hands up, yelling after him. "Did it not occur to y'all that he'd go out the window? Come on!"

I watch as Jackson is thrown to the ground and handcuffed. My heart feels like it's beating out of its chest. The other agent puts him in the car and two of them get in and drive away. The third agent returns and stands next to Agent Preston. Preston shoots him a look, but says nothing. After an awkward silence, I speak.

"When do we go back to Connecticut."

"We'll fly back with you this afternoon. We'll wait outside and let you have some privacy."

"Let's go in the kitchen. I've got some chili warming up. I imagine you all are starving," Daisy Ann says.

We follow her and sit around a rectangular table. Daisy Ann pours drinks and fills bowls. The girls eat greedily, and I take a sip of coffee and lean back in the chair.

"You scared the hell out of me. I thought maybe Jackson had you tricked, and you'd turned on me."

She shook her head. "No chance of that. But I didn't want to tip you off. I had to make sure he had no idea and stayed here. I wasn't sure how long it would be before they arrived to arrest him. I know a snake when I see one. Like, something just didn't sit right with me when he got in touch and told me Amber's plan. Of course, I knew she couldn't be trusted, but I found it hard to believe he was this innocent man he claimed to be. And then when your friend Meredith called me and told me all about your history, well, I knew I had to help."

"Jackson told you that Amber framed him and got him put in prison, right?"

"Yeah. I looked everything up. Years of tax evasion going back before she knew him. Things have a way of working out for the godly. Or at least that's what Mama used to say. Clean living and all that." Daisy Ann laughs.

"So now there's a conundrum," she continues.

"What's going on?"

"Jackson transferred four and a half million dollars into my account for that fake stock. He said it was money Amber stole from him. So I was supposed to give it back to him, but that doesn't really seem right now, does it?" Daisy Ann said.

"What are you suggesting?"

She shrugs. "After what I read about his initial arrest, he wasn't supposed to have many assets left. The government took everything but the house and some other assets. So I'm guessing that money was come by illegally. We could turn it over to the authorities, or . . ."

"Or?"

"Donate it to a women's shelter."

I think a moment. "You said that Amber's going to be arrested for your father's murder, and now Jackson will likely go to jail for his new crimes. That leaves Jax with no parents. What about putting half in a trust for him and donating the other half?"

Daisy Ann nods. "Yes, I didn't even know they had a son."

"Yes, he's innocent in all this. Only two years old. Such a shame." I take a spoonful of chili. It tastes especially good in this moment. "This is heavenly."

We spend the next hour chatting and getting to know each other while the girls take showers and change into the clothes Daisy Ann brought for them. Her thoughtfulness knows no bounds. Despite not being arrested, I'm still nervous about returning to Bishops Harbor. Who knows if DCF is going to understand why I ran with them. They could decide that I'm unfit. After everything I've been through, I can't lose my children.

51

DAISY ANN

After Daphne and the girls left with the marshals, Daisy Ann drove straight to Rosewood, eager to be a witness to the FBI parading Amber out of the hotel in handcuffs. Mason had several friends in the FBI field office and was told they would be there at five o'clock. There was no guarantee that Amber wasn't out shopping or doing whatever frivolous things Amber did, but eventually she'd have to come back, and Daisy Ann was prepared to wait there all night if necessary.

Daphne and the girls were headed back to Connecticut to get things straightened out with DCF before finally going back to California. They'd both promised to keep in touch. Daisy Ann felt an immediate kinship with Daphne from the first time she'd spoken to her. She thought back to that initial phone call from Jackson Parrish. Daisy Ann had been surprised to hear from him—her research into Amber had made her familiar with who he was. She had to admit, he was a smooth operator and if Daisy Ann didn't have better instincts, she may have fallen for his story. It was a little over a month ago when the call came.

"Daisy Ann Briscoe?" the smooth deep voice came over the line.

"Yes, who's this?"

"You don't know me, ma'am. I'm Jackson Parrish and I believe we have a common enemy."

She'd sat up straighter. "I know who you are. What do you want?"

"I want to help you, and I need you to help me."

"You're married to that con artist, and I don't want anything to do with you." She had been about to hang up, but his next words stopped her.

"I can help you prove she killed your father."

"Go on."

"She admitted it to me. I'll testify but first you have to help me."

"What did she tell you about my father?"

"That she shot him on purpose."

The old fury overtook her again. "Hold on." She'd put the phone down and gone into the next room and screamed. After a moment she returned to the call. "I need you to meet me in Colorado and tell the sheriff everything you know. Right away."

"Just a minute, Daisy Ann. Before I betray my wife in such a shameful manner, I need something from you."

That's when he told her the whole scenario. "Amber's stolen millions from me. She's the reason I went to prison and while I was there, she found a way to transfer everything into an offshore account. And it may interest you to know that she's trying to take over your company. Wade Ashford has already agreed to sell her his shares."

"Why would Wade do that?"

"She has something on him. A patent he stole. Point is, he's going to sell his shares and then before you find out, he'll try to convince you to sell your shares to a man named Hugo Bennett of Delancey-Flynn, who will take your designs to Europe. But Hugo Bennett and Delancey-Flynn are a front. When the deal is done, Amber will be the one who owns the majority voting stock, and then she'll turn around and sell all the shares to Valene Mart who will then have controlling interest in the company. They'll be able to do whatever they want with the designs."

It was a brilliant plan, and one that might have worked. "So what do you want?"

"Pretend to sell to Bennett. Delancey-Flynn is the LLC she and I set up together. I'll transfer the four and a half million to your company, and you'll issue fake certificates to us. Afterward, you'll return the money to me, and we'll both stick it to Amber. Then I'll testify."

When she'd pressed him further about her father's shooting, the details didn't add up. The time of day was wrong, the weapon, everything. That's when she'd known he was using her to get his money back from Amber.

"Give me a day to think about it."

When Meredith had called and told Daisy Ann all about Jackson Parrish and his history of abuse, her instincts where proven correct. She'd been appalled to learn how he had committed Daphne to a sanatorium against her will years ago and held the threat of taking her children away to keep her from leaving. So together she and Meredith had hatched their own plan. Daisy Ann pretended to work with Jackson because the idea of helping Daphne was irresistible. An added bonus was getting back at Amber. And that's when Daisy Ann decided both Amber and Jackson could kiss those millions goodbye.

She pulled up to the hotel and parked. Once inside she headed to the bar and took a seat at the table closest to the entrance and on the cushioned seat. After ordering a scotch, she leaned back and took a deep breath. Amber was finally going to pay. Daisy Ann had been carrying this burden for so long she didn't know how to lay it down. But this would be the start of the healing. With the evidence they had now, she was certain Amber would be convicted. There would be the wait for the trial and the emotional journey of walking through everything again, but Daisy Ann would be there in that courtroom every day until Amber was put away for good. She finished her drink and pulled out her phone. A text from Mason. She went cold as she read it.

Just heard from my friend. Amber checked out yesterday. They're checking the airlines. No update yet.

Daisy Ann threw a twenty on the table and left.

- 52 -

AMBER

Jax was still asleep when Amber tiptoed to his crib. In the short time she'd been gone he looked so much bigger to her. Watching him sleep, she pondered the wisdom of taking him on this journey. There was no question that he would make everything more difficult, not to mention that Amber would be solely and completely responsible for him. At least until she settled somewhere permanently and hired a new nanny. The romantic visions of her as the doting mother were beginning to fade. On the other hand, leaving him here would make Jackson think he'd won. Just the thought of how crushed he would be to lose his precious son gave her strength.

"Mommy," Jax said, sitting up and smiling.

"Hi, monkey. Did you miss me?" she said, picking him up.

As she changed his diaper, Chloe came into the bedroom.

"Oh, you're both up. Shall I get him dressed and fed for you?" she asked.

"Yes, that would be great. I still have some things to finish up, and then I'll be down."

As soon as they left the room, Amber began to gather clothes and supplies to pack for Jax. There was a creepy sense of apprehension settling over her, and the more she thought about Jackson, the more she worried he'd set a trap for her. Why would he have gone to Dallas? It didn't make sense. He would be here in Bishops Harbor waiting for word about Daphne's whereabouts. Maybe Daphne hadn't

really run away at all. Maybe she and Jackson were conspiring together to get Amber. To try and get their hands on her offshore account. Chloe could have lied for him. After all, she'd never really
liked Amber. Her gut was telling her to leave right away, and her
gut was usually right. She quickly took Jax's things and carried
them into the guest room where she'd slept, packing them with
hers.

The clock on the nightstand read eight o'clock. They didn't have
to leave for the airport until six tonight, but it wasn't safe to stay
here until then. She sat down, thinking what to do, and then picked
up her phone.

"Remi," Amber said before she even heard hello.

"Amber. *Ça va?* You are back?"

"I am, but listen, Remi, I need to leave. I'm scared. I have to get
away from Jackson. He's dangerous. I don't have time to tell you
everything right now, but I need a place to stay. Just till tonight.
Can I use your apartment in New York?"

"Of course. But tell me, is there some way I can help you? Is he
there with you? Threatening you?"

"No, but he might come at any minute. That's why I need to get
out of here now."

"I will call the doorman and he will let you in. You must call me
when you get there and let me know you are all right. Should I call
the police, Amber?"

"No, don't do that. I'm going to leave very shortly. I'll be okay.
And don't worry. I'll call you when I get to the apartment."

"Make sure you do. And be careful."

"I will. And, Remi . . . don't let anyone know I'm there."

Amber ended the call, then went to settings, turned off location
services, and powered off her phone. Now Jackson wouldn't be able
to track her using Find My iPhone. Next, she emptied the suitcase
and put almost all of it back in the drawers. She'd take her large
Prada tote bag, which would hold enough to get them through the
day, and buy whatever else they needed once she got to New York.

Chloe had to believe that Amber was taking Jax out for the day and not suspect anything more, since Chloe could not be trusted either. She would tell Chloe they were going to the park, that way it wouldn't seem unusual for her to take the stroller and diaper bag. First, she'd get the cash from the safe-deposit box, then she'd leave the car a few blocks from the train station and take Metro-North into Grand Central. From there she'd get a cab to Remi's and hang awhile, maybe do a little shopping, and then head to the airport.

Jax was enchanted by the train ride and greeted every passenger that passed by with a cheery hi and a big smile. Maybe traveling with him wasn't going to be as difficult as she'd imagined. Grand Central was a noisy and crowded maze of people as usual, and Amber was thankful she'd brought the stroller. The cab ride to Remi's took just ten minutes, and although it was only eleven, the adventure had been tiring for Jax. Amber put him on the king-size bed and settled next to him, first using the bedside phone to let Remi know she was safe. Remi had offered Amber the use of her Avenue Montaigne apartment, but to Amber's vexation, that would be the first place Jackson would look, and so she'd had to refuse. Soon, she was dozing on and off, mostly off, wondering where Jackson was and if he was following her.

Jax was sleeping soundly when she got out of bed to see if there was any food in the place. When she opened the fridge, she was glad to see a carton of eggs, several cheeses, and a large container of yogurt. A bowl of apples sat on the counter. She didn't want to leave the building if she didn't have to, just in case. She asked the doorman to get her a cab for six o'clock.

The minutes seemed to drag by like hours, but eventually Jax awoke, they ate something, Amber played with him, and finally it reached the time to leave. Amber had found the waiting some of the most nerve-racking hours she'd ever endured. The taxi was waiting for them when she and Jax exited the building. Amber looked nervously around before getting in, relieved to see no sign of Jackson or Daphne. Maybe she really had run away and maybe he'd really gone to Dallas. When they got out of the cab at the airport and there was still no Jackson anywhere in sight, Amber began to relax. She was being overly cautious, she decided, which wasn't a bad thing, but clearly it was unnecessary now. Her shoulders relaxed as her apprehension eased and some of the tension left her body. She and Jax were anonymous travelers in a sea of travelers. No one was even looking at them.

They were fast-tracked through security and sitting in the lounge by 7:15, with less than two hours until boarding. She was amazed at how good Jax was being and what an attention-getter he was. It seemed people couldn't resist talking to him, and he was enjoying every minute of it. He was just possibly going to be an asset rather than a liability. He was occupied with a play telephone she'd bought in one of the airport shops. She'd also done some shopping to augment the few belongings she'd brought from the house, along with a small suitcase in which to pack them.

As she sat watching almost everyone around her glued to their phones, she was sorely tempted to turn hers back on, but she resisted. Once she was on the plane, she'd do that. And have a very stiff drink as well.

Finally, the announcement came that their flight would be boarding shortly. Amber slung the tote over her shoulder and pushed the stroller with one hand and the small case with the other. Now that she was so close to leaving, she allowed herself to get excited about the adventures that lay ahead. With a first-class boarding pass and a child in tow, Amber and Jax would be two of the first passengers to board. As soon as boarding was announced, she rolled the stroller to the kiosk and handed the agent their passports and boarding documents. The woman looked at her boarding pass and then raised her eyes to Amber.

"One moment, ma'am," the agent said and, looking past Amber, nodded her head once.

Amber turned around, alarmed to see two large men in dark jackets rushing toward her. She tightened her arms around Jax, looking around and frantically searching for a place to run, but all she saw was a sea of bodies clustered around the gate and penning her in. From the corner of her eye, she could see the men moving closer until finally they were standing in front of her.

"Amber Parrish?" one of them said as he thrust a piece of paper toward her.

"Who wants to know?" Her tone was belligerent, but she was shaking inside.

He flashed a badge. "Federal marshal. We have a warrant for your arrest. You have the right to remain silent."

There was an increasing hush at the gate and people were staring at her.

"For what? I haven't done anything," she interrupted him.

"The charge is murder, ma'am." He finished reading her her rights. The other officer took Jax from her arms, and he began to cry.

"Now turn around and put your hands behind your back." Her mortification ramped up as he slapped a pair of handcuffs on her wrists.

Amber interrupted him, trying to buy time. "No, wait. What about my baby? Do you expect me to leave him here? What kind of monsters are you, anyway? This is a mistake, I didn't kill anyone!"

"Someone from Child Protective Services is waiting at arrivals. Your child will be taken care of. You can call your lawyer when we reach the federal courthouse."

They moved away from the gate, Amber holding back tears of humiliation. People were staring at her, and she looked down at the ground as she was jostled down the long hallway and to the escalator. Finally, they reached the exit and walked through the double doors. She looked up and gasped. Standing there, a smug smile on her face, stood Daisy Ann.

"You're finally going to pay, you lowlife." Daisy Ann's eyes were slits as she spit the words at Amber.

"You did this!" She turned to the agent next to her. "She's lying. She's out to get me."

Daisy Ann shook her head. "Save it. They have you dead to rights. Plenty of evidence to prove what you did. You're not talking your way out of this one. Take a deep breath, Amber, or should I say, Lana. This is the last time you're going to be outside for a very long time." She turned and got into a limousine, putting down the window. "Oh, Amber, I hope your claustrophobia doesn't act up when you're in that tiny jail cell." The car pulled away leaving Amber standing there, fuming.

"Let's go, ma'am." The agent moved her toward the waiting car. Daisy Ann was bluffing. But how did she know Amber's real name? Her heart began to beat faster. Was it possible that they really did have evidence? No. More likely, Daisy Ann had used her connections and her money to bribe someone. There was no way she could have real proof. But this was still a disaster. Once Amber was in the system and they fingerprinted her, they'd find out her real name. She'd have to answer for what she did back in Missouri even when the murder charges were dropped, which of course, they would be. It wasn't fair. These rich assholes always getting the better of her just because they'd been born with a silver spoon in their mouth. But she was rich now too. She'd figure out a way to get herself out of this. It was what she did best.

- 53 -

DAPHNE

The girls and I are headed back to California next week. It took a couple of weeks, but the DCF investigation is closed, all the charges unsubstantiated. We're just waiting for the final paperwork before we return to California. I've never been so eager to leave a place in my life. My phone rings and I walk over to the nightstand to answer. I glance at the screen; it's Jackson. I thought he was in federal custody.

"What do you want?" I say, my voice cracking.

"Just thought you'd like to know that the charges against me have been dropped."

This must be a joke, a trick on his part. "What are you talking about?"

He laughs. "They had to drop the perjury charges. The doctor who was going to testify about your little trip to the sanatorium all those years ago died. A pity. And that recording you made of me. Inadmissible. My lawyers made mincemeat of the charges. So you see, I'm a free man. And I fully intend to pursue full custody. I don't care how long it takes, I will prove that those kids belong with me."

"You will never get those children. Do you hear me? They hate you. They know what you did to me. How can you think they'd ever want to be with you again?"

He laughs again. "I'm sure I can convince them that you lied. You continue to underestimate me, my dear. We could have had it all, but you just had to screw me over. Now you're going to lose everything. Have a safe flight. Enjoy them while you can. I think we both know who's better at winning."

My hands are shaking and I stare at the phone, dumbfounded. A surge of energy flows through me. "It's over, Jackson. You can't control me any longer. You've already lost." And I disconnect.

JACKSON

Voices, muffled voices, surround him and he tries to move, to open his eyes. Where is he? Words here and there penetrate the fog. He thinks he hears Daphne's voice but he can't be sure. Why can't he make out what they're saying? What the hell is going on? He tries to open his eyes but nothing happens. All around him he can hear beeping noises and the hiss of machines. Throbbing. His head is going to explode. What is happening?

"Daphne," he tries to say, but his mouth remains closed, and no sound comes from his throat. His throat burns. He raises his hand to feel, but nothing happens. Why can't he lift his hand? Is this a dream? "Daphne!" He tries again. Nothing.

Think, think. Slowly it comes back to him. Swimming. A night swim. Jax was asleep as was his nanny, Chloe. It was close to midnight and all was quiet. It was his favorite time to do laps. Daphne had gotten the girls back and all the charges against her cleared. The girls, his girls, angry and yelling at him. Swearing to never speak to him again. At least he still had Jax. And Daphne, he'd figure out a way to get her back. He would never let her go. With each stroke he felt more confident, more assured. He'd finished, pushed himself up and out of the pool, then grabbed the towel and began to dry his hair.

"Mr. Parrish. We meet again. So nice of you to save us the trouble of breaking in."

Jackson froze, his insides turning to ice. It couldn't be. Slowly, he turned around and faced the man he'd hoped to never see again. The man was dressed flawlessly in a black Kiton suit tailored perfectly to his form, his silver hair sleek and slicked back. He wore his signature black-framed glasses with the unusual red-tinted lenses. Jackson knew the man suffered from achromatopsia, the inability to see any color with the exception of black, gray, and white and that was the reason for the special lenses. On either side of him stood two hulking men, their legs splayed, their arms crossed in front of their groin, each one gripping a black automatic pistol with a long silencer attached.

"What do you want?" Jackson asked, trying to sound braver than he felt. He had known this day was inevitable when he'd found that Amber had sold the diamonds. He would never have taken them to New York where they could so easily be traced back to him. Jackson's plan had been to hold on to them for a few more years and then sell them to his contact in Europe who would have made sure he stayed anonymous. The man in front of him was not someone to be double-crossed. He could be generous—fair, even—but he had a strict moral code that had no tolerance for betrayal. Jackson scrambled to think of something to say to help himself.

The man laughed, a mirthless chuckle. "What do you think? I want my diamonds, but sadly, you've sold them. So I'll have to settle for the money."

Jackson shivered, the cool night air against his wet skin and the sight of the two guns making the hair on his arms stand up. "I, uh, I don't have it," Jackson said, taking a slight step back.

The man shook his head. "Do you think I'm stupid? I've been informed that you've set up an account offshore." He inclined his head toward the table where Jackson's phone sat. "You're going to transfer those funds now."

Jackson hesitated, looking around, trying to figure a way out of the situation. "I don't have the number. My wife set it up. The rest of the money was used for an investment and I lost it."

The man moved closer until he was inches from Jackson's face, close enough that Jackson could smell the tobacco residue that clung to his clothes. "Don't fucking bullshit me."

He moved toward the table, picking up Jackson's phone and throwing it at him. "The account number. Now."

Jackson caught the phone with both hands but continued to stand, mute.

The man tilted his head toward one of his goons. The tall redhead strode forward and grabbed Jackson's hand, bending the thumb until there was an audible crack. Jackson fell to his knees, howling in pain.

"I don't know where the money is," he panted, rising on wobbly legs.

The man shook his head. "No one steals from me. You might have gotten away with it. You hid your betrayal well. But surely you must have known that to sell them so carelessly would be your demise."

"It wasn't me. My wife . . . my stupid . . ."

The man came closer. "Your wife is guilty only of getting you caught. You were the one who stole from me." His expression hardened and he spat on the ground. "Where are the three pink diamonds that were never sold?"

Jackson shook his head. "That's what I'm trying to tell you. I don't know. Amber must have them."

"No doubt they will surface in time. But for now, this concludes our business together."

He moved away and nodded to his men.

"You don't have to kill me. I'll find a way to get the money. Give me a chance. Don't kill me," Jackson said, his voice shaking.

The man turned and smiled at him. "You're out of chances. By the time these two are finished with you, you'll be begging to die."

Jackson turned and tried to run. One man grabbed him and held him while the other began to rain punches on him. He was pushed to the ground, his head ricocheting off the hard cement. He tried to cover his face with his hands, but one man held both his arms down while the other smashed his fist into Jackson's nose. Red hot pain exploded through him.

"Stop, please," he begged. The man's hands were tight around his throat, choking him, and he sputtered for breath, desperate for air. Just when he thought he would pass out, the man let go. Jackson's relief was short-lived. The guy reached for something behind him, and he realized with horror it was a tire iron. The swing connected hard with Jackson's neck. Suddenly the area was bathed in lights and Jackson heard the sound of sirens. That was the last thing he remembered.

He hears a door close, and the sound of Daphne's voice pulls him back into the present. It *is* her. He can hear her as clear as day. Why can't he talk?

"Do you have the test results yet?"

A throat clears. "Yes, it doesn't look good."

"Tell me."

"It's been three days since we evacuated the subdermal hematoma. We were able to wean him off the breathing tube and reduce the sedation, but . . ."

"But what?"

"He should have woken up, but he remains unresponsive. Further testing reveals that there's been a vertebral dissection, likely as a result of the neck trauma."

"What does that mean?"

"It's a tear in the inner lining of the artery. It caused a blood clot, which shot off into the basilar artery—that's the main artery to the brain stem—and caused a brain stem stroke. As a result, MRI imaging shows major damage to his brain stem. He's lucky he's able to breathe on his own."

"I don't understand. Can you fix it?"

"No, the damage is permanent. To simplify, the brain stem is what executes actions for us. Talking, moving, and so on."

"So he's brain dead?"

No! I can hear you, he screams, but no sound comes out. He has to let them know. How is this happening? Unable to move. Them talking about him like he isn't even there. The doctor speaks again.

"No, not brain dead. There doesn't appear to be any damage to his cortex. That means it's possible he can think, hear, and even see. But he can't move."

What is this idiot doctor saying? What the fuck? They can't give up on him. If he can hear them and think, he has to be okay. They need to do something! His eyes fly open. The two of them are still talking, acting like he isn't there. *Look at me. I'm awake!*

The doctor approaches the bed. "His eyes are open."

No shit! I told you!

"Jackson, can you follow the light?" The doctor holds a flashlight and moves it from side to side. Jackson tracks it with his eyes.

The doctor turns back to Daphne. "We're almost certain your ex-husband has locked-in syndrome. He can't move or speak but is likely cognitively aware."

"Are you saying that his mind is working, but he's trapped in a body that can't move or communicate?"

"I'm sorry to say, but yes. I'm afraid he'll require a feeding tube and twenty-four-hour care."

Jackson can't believe his ears. He is going to be like this forever? That can't be right. It was unthinkable. *Ask again. Daphne, get clarity! Look at me.* He moves his eyes back and forth hoping to get their attention, but neither look his way.

"So what's going to happen to him?" Daphne asks.

"Once his acute injuries are healed, he'll need to be moved to a long-term care facility." The doctor puts his hand on Daphne's arm. "A social worker will be in to speak to you and help you navigate the decisions to be made."

"Is there any chance he can recover?" she asks.

"I never say never, but it's extremely unlikely."

Jackson closes his eyes, terror and despair washing over him. This is all Amber's fault. She ruined his life. He'd still be married to

Daphne if it wasn't for her. The FBI would never have found out about his tax evasion and he would never have gone to prison. And then her greed and stupidity in selling the diamonds. One stupid mistake on his part had caused his entire life to fall apart. Why had he ever allowed himself to be seduced by that Medusa? The only good thing to come from her was Jax, but now Jackson would be denied even the pleasure of his son's company. This was to be his life? No way to communicate, forever at the mercy of strangers for every little thing. It was unbearable. They should have killed him. It would have been better.

55

DAISY ANN

aisy Ann stood in front of the large tombstone that bore the image of her father. She ran a hand over the cool stone and took in the words. *Beloved husband and father. Loving grandfather.* She inhaled deeply and wiped the tears from her cheeks.

"We got her, Daddy. Justice is being served. You'd get a kick out of this. It was a poacher's camera that sunk her." She shook her head. "It doesn't bring you back, though. I like to think you're with Mama. The two of you dancing together in heaven." Daisy Ann placed the two sets of flowers on the graves next to each other. White orchids for her mother, and yellow roses for her father—the flowers he always gave Daisy Ann on birthdays. "I'm sorry, Daddy. I should have been there. I would've stopped her."

It wasn't your job, she heard him say in her mind, and she realized it wasn't. Her father had been a brilliant man, but easily ruled by his heart. Because he was a man of his word, genuine to his core, he always believed the best in others. Amber was a master manipulator, expert at homing in on others' vulnerabilities and using them to her advantage. If Daisy Ann had tried to intervene, no doubt Amber would have found a way to damage her relationship with her father. She realized now that she'd been carrying around a burden of guilt that didn't belong to her. Her father would have made his own choice whether or not Daisy Ann had been around to try to talk him out of it. How many times had he reminded her that the world would turn without her help? It was a hard lesson to learn, but it was time she stopped trying to shoulder everyone else's load. She supposed it wasn't the worst trait—trying to control things, to make things safe and good for those you loved. But it rarely worked, and she had to accept once and for all that she wasn't all-powerful.

What she could now rest in was the fact that she'd left no stone unturned in proving Amber's guilt. No matter what the outcome of the trial, Daisy Ann now knew beyond a shadow of a doubt that she'd been right and that all the energy and time she'd put into her pursuit had been worthwhile. The toll it had taken on her and her family was not for nothing. That was a comfort in and of itself.

She felt a hand on her shoulder and turned to see Mason behind her. He opened his arms and she fell into them, weeping, letting all her sorrow and regret flow until there were no more tears.

"How'd you know I'd be here?" she asked her husband.

"After all these years, I know you pretty well, babe. And I know your daddy is proud of you. He can rest in peace now. We can all have some peace now."

She took his hand and they walked together to his truck and got in. As they drove away, she looked up at the sky, imagining her parents smiling down at her. No matter what happened now, she would look ahead. She was finished letting Amber contaminate her happiness. She wouldn't attend the trial—she'd leave it to the prosecutors to do their job. Daisy Ann had done all she could do. She'd found the truth. Her part was over. And one way or the other, she knew in her heart that justice would prevail. She wouldn't waste one more precious moment of her life thinking about Amber.

She heaved another sigh and smiled at Mason. "I hope Birdie's making a big roast for Sunday dinner. I'm starving."

56

DAPHNE

Our return to California was put on hold by a few weeks due to Jackson's condition. I've been cleared of all charges, and the lawyers have assured me that based on the evidence that came to light against Jackson, he has no chance of ever regaining custody, even though the criminal charges were dropped. It's all moot now anyway. He can't even take care of himself. If Chloe hadn't awakened and called the police, Jackson would likely be dead. The police have no leads or any idea what the motive was. Taking care of all the paperwork and finding a long-term care facility for Jackson has been all-consuming but everything is settled now, so I can finally leave. There's just one more piece of business awaiting my attention.

I enter the living room, and I smile when I see Jax. He's sitting on Tallulah's lap and they're building a tower with blocks. The woman standing there looks nervous; she's twisting the strap of her handbag in her hands and looking at the floor.

I walk over to her. "Mrs. Crump?"

She looks up. "Florence, please. Thank you for seeing me. After everything that's happened, I was afraid you wouldn't."

"None of this is your fault. Can I get you some coffee or tea?"

She shakes her head. "No, I'm fine, thank you."

"Why don't we go out on the deck and talk." I turn to Bella. "You and your sister keep an eye on Jax, please." Since Jackson is incapacitated and Amber charged with murder, temporary custody has been awarded to his maternal grandmother, Amber's mother. And if Amber, by some miracle, is able to beat the charges against her, she'd still have to go back to Missouri and face prison time there for those charges.

We sit across from each other, and I wait for her to begin.

"I hope you know we don't approve of the things Amber's done. We did our best with her ..." She sighs. "I never could have imagined she would kill someone. It's just unbelievable. That poor man and his family. I didn't even know she was married ... twice. I should have looked harder for her. Tried to stop her. Maybe so much of this could have been avoided."

I can't imagine what she's going through. To have your daughter disappear and then just a few years later discover the trail of horrors her actions left behind ... it's beyond comprehension.

"Florence, you can't blame yourself. She's an adult. No matter how hard we try to shape our children, sometimes they are who they are from the moment they're born. I won't pretend to understand what you're going through, but I don't believe anything you could have said or done would have changed a thing."

She nods. "Thank you. The reason I'm here. It's about Jax. He has a brother back in Missouri. Did you know that?"

"Yes, I did know."

"We don't get to see little Matty as much as we'd like, but we're happy to raise Jax and it'll be good for the boys to have each other. We don't have much in the way of material things, don't need much anyway, but I do want Jax to have everything he can. Has his father made any provision for him? I understand he's in a bad way from the assault."

"Um, well, I do know that there is a significant amount of money in a trust for little Jax. I'll have the lawyers get in touch with you." I don't mention that it's the money Jackson tried to hide from Amber that Daisy Ann has returned to me.

"Thank you. That's wonderful. And a relief. Clark and I aren't getting any younger, and I do want to make sure Jax is always taken care of."

"Of course. Florence, I have something I want to ask you."

"Yes?"

"As you said, it's important for Jax and his brother to have a relationship. My girls and I have become very fond of him. Would you consider letting him spend summers with us in California? I'd really love for them to grow up together."

Tears spring to her eyes. "You mean you don't hate him?"

I'm taken aback.

"He's *her* child and all. And didn't she break up your marriage on account of being pregnant?"

It's then I remember she knows nothing about the real Jackson or the truth of my marriage. But even if her assumption were true, how could I hate a child? "Of course I don't hate him. None of this is Jax's fault. He's my children's brother and that makes him family. Besides, I fell in love with him the minute I laid eyes on him."

She beams. "I think that your summer offer would be just marvelous."

On the flight home, Tallulah is sleeping, and Bella reads a book. I simply sit and stare, decompressing from the events of the past weeks. Would I have returned to Bishops Harbor if I'd known what lay ahead? I nearly lost my girls. The fact that we are together and finally on our way home fills me with gratitude.

I can't wait to see my mother and hear about her trip. I'm grateful that she was away and spared the agony and worry she would have felt had she been aware of what was happening to me. A part of me wishes that I'd listened to her and never come back. But if I hadn't, would that have damaged my relationship with Tallulah beyond repair? As horrific as it was, maybe the only way for my girls to ever have peace about the absence of their father in their lives was to learn the truth. That wasn't something I was prepared to share for a long time. It's tragic, really. If only Jackson had truly changed in prison, the outcome would have been so different. I could have learned to forgive him for the past and he could have had a relationship with his daughters. There's no way I'd ever have gone back to him, but we could have co-parented and given the girls what they need. Now none of us will ever get that chance.

I took the girls to the hospital to say goodbye to Jackson. Walking into the room and seeing him lying there so vulnerable and helpless felt like an out-of-body experience. A rush of memories flooded over me, both good and bad, almost as though I was seeing our whole life together flash before my eyes. I wept, more tears than I thought I had, and I don't know who I was crying for more, the children, me, or even, yes, him. Because no matter what, there was a time I loved him. A time when I thought he was everything I ever wanted and needed and so I cried for the death of all of it.

Surprisingly, the house was never put into Amber's name, and Jackson's will leaves it and all its contents to be equally divided among Tallulah, Bella, and Jax and put in a trust administered by me. I guess he really believed I was coming back to him. The trust named me as power of attorney in the case of his incapacitation. The house is on the market now for twenty-five million dollars. The artwork is being appraised as is the furniture. The money will be used for Jackson's care, and whatever is left over will go to the children when Jackson dies.

As for Tallulah and Bella, at first they were so angry at Jackson for what he'd done that it didn't seem there was any room for their grief. But when they saw him, they both broke down. They're going to be heartbroken for a long time, but I'll be there to pick up the pieces. I'm no Pollyanna, but I try to find something good that has come out of this summer. There's Jax, of course. If we hadn't come back, they wouldn't have met their brother. I'm glad for their sake as well as his. He'll be raised by people who love him and want the best for him. No doubt he'll have his own demons to battle. A father unable to care for him or even speak to him and a mother who will either be in prison or, if not, sweep in and out of his life when it suits her. I know in my heart not only that Amber murdered Jake Crawford but also what Amber is capable of. She is a master of escape and reinvention, like a Svengali and Houdini wrapped in one Machiavellian package. If she somehow manages to go free, it would not surprise me in the least. For everyone's sake, I hope I'm wrong. But at least Jax will have his grandparents, a brother, and the two best big sisters in the world. And I will love him like he's my own and make sure he gets all the support he needs. Jackson wanted us to be a family again and I suppose in a way we are. No matter what he's done, he will always be the father of my children and so I'll oversee his care and make sure he's looked after.

After we land and disembark, I breathe deeply, so happy to be back home again. As we exit the airport I lift my face to the sky, and the California sun envelops me in what feels like a welcome home hug. After a few minutes, an SUV pulls up and my mother parks and jumps out of the car.

"My girls!" she says, pulling us all to her in a group hug. "Thank God you're home!"

We pile into the vehicle, the girls chattering a mile a minute, seeming almost like their old selves as we pull onto the highway and head for home.

"Mr. Bandit has been pacing around all day. I think he knows you're coming home," my mother says, referring to our yellow lab.

"Guess what, Grandmom?" Bella says.

"What?"

"When we were in Texas, we made new friends and they have two yellow labs. And guess what their names are?"

"Hmm?"

Bella giggles. "Buck and Shot."

My mother gives me a curious look.

I laugh. "She's telling the truth. They're Daisy Ann's dogs, the woman I told you about who helped us. In fact, we're all invited to go out to their ranch next summer."

My mother gives me a long look. "Well, that's a summer trip I can give my blessing to."

AMBER

A mber's journey to the Gunnison County Jail, where she was now housed awaiting bail, had been fraught with indignity. They'd confiscated all her cash, and after her hearing before a judge in New York, the FBI had turned her over to two police officers from Colorado who had slapped handcuffs on her as they escorted her back on a commercial flight in full view of everyone. Her attorney was working on finding her the best criminal attorney in Colorado, but in the meantime, he had sent some shmuck who looked like he'd just graduated from law school. She'd kicked him out after ten minutes, when it became clear he was a moron.

She sat up in bed, if you could call the hard cot in her cell a bed, and stretched. The prison uniform itched, and it galled her that she wasn't allowed to take it off even to sleep. She'd already gotten in trouble for that. Why the hell she couldn't sleep in her undies she had no idea. It's not like there was another person in her cell. But there were rules for everything in this godforsaken place. She had the seventeen-page inmate handbook to prove it. Last night she'd brought a bag of chips from dinner to her cell. She didn't know that if she didn't eat it before lockdown, the guards would take it. It was almost like they got a kick out of making arbitrary rules just to screw with you. Her hair felt like straw from the cheap off-brand shampoo they gave her, and the soap left her skin dry and itchy. This was hell and she'd only been here for a few days. And this was a small-town jail. She didn't allow herself to imagine what it would be like if she got sent to prison.

She could play the good girl, though. She had to bide her time only until she could post bail.

"Lana. You can use the phone now." Amber flinched at the use of her given name. She wasn't Lana Crump anymore, but according to the system she was. Eddie, the day guard, opened her cell. She gave him her most charming smile. "Thank you, Eddie. How was your night? Did you watch that movie I recommended?"

He smiled at her. "Yeah. It was cool. Had no idea how Jordans got so popular. Thanks."

When she'd noticed he had a sneaker fetish, she'd recommended the movie *Air*. She was nothing if not adept at spotting a person's hot buttons and using them to her advantage. He escorted her to the pay phone and she called Scott Hamon, the attorney who'd represented Jackson. Once she was put through, she wasted no time on pleasantries.

"What's up with my bail?"

"As you know, your husband is in the hospital and unable to post your bail. I have the name of a bail bondsman out there. You'll need fifteen percent of the two million dollars bail and he'll guarantee the rest. So, three hundred thousand dollars."

She rolled her eyes. He'd told her about Jackson's assault a few days ago. She should have felt sorry for him, but she didn't. Whoever beat the shit out of him must have had their reasons. Jackson wasn't short on enemies. He wouldn't have paid her bail anyway. She could just imagine how much he would love to see her sitting in jail. There was no one else. Remi was her only friend in town, and she was in Paris. She thought a moment. "I've given you my power of attorney. Take a loan out on the house. It's worth almost a hundred times my bail."

"Well, that's the thing. The house isn't in your name. I already tried that."

"What do you mean it's not in my name? After we were married, Jackson had me sign paperwork to put me on the deed." She thought back, trying to visualize it in her mind's eye. Had he faked her out? "Are you sure?"

"Quite. The house is held entirely by him, and Daphne has his power of attorney."

She could feel her face burning up as anger coursed through her body. That idiot had really believed Daphne was coming back to him. How stupid could he be? She shook her head. "Doesn't matter. I have the money. I'd transfer it but they took my phone." Shit. She had to think. "Okay, okay. Look, I have plenty in an offshore account. I can transfer or wire the money, but I need my phone. You have to arrange to pick my things up from the holding area here." She thought of something else. She had a debit card for the account. Maybe that could be used to transfer the money instead of her having to get the guards to allow her to handle her phone. "There's a debit card hidden at the house. It's in a waterproof bag in the kayak in the boathouse. You should have no trouble getting it."

"Okay, I'll go there now."

"Do whatever you have to do. Get the money to the new firm or whatever but get me the hell out of here. I can hardly breathe in here. I'm going crazy."

"You didn't like the first guy we sent, even though he came highly recommended. You want the best, you need to give me a chance to get a better referral. Just sit tight. Someone will be there soon, I promise."

"I certainly hope so."

Eddie approached. "Time's up. Lana."

She hung up and went back to her cell, still fuming, and lay down on the cot. She had to get her hands on that damn money and get the hell out of this town where there were only bad memories. The last time she'd left Gunnison, Jake was dead and she was newly widowed and rich. Or so she'd thought, until she'd learned after his funeral that his will had left her nothing. This time when she left it would be different. She really *would* be rich, and she'd never look back. She'd always known this day was possible. Oh, not that she'd be arrested for murder, but that her misdeeds in Missouri would catch up to her. That's why she'd spent thousands of dollars preparing a contingency plan. The idea came to her after Jackson went to prison and she had free rein over the finances. For enough money, anything could be had. She'd paid to have a new passport, license, and birth certificate in a different name. Once her bail was posted and she got out of here, she'd get her new credentials from the safe-deposit box and abscond. She'd be strolling along a European cobblestone street before they even realized she was gone. Amber would never come back to the United States, it was too risky, and this country was on the decline anyway. She could even affect a new accent, French perhaps. Her future was in Europe. She fell asleep dreaming about all the fabulous clothes she'd buy in Paris.

"Lana, wake up."

She turned over and squinted at the figure standing at her cell door. Eddie. "What?" she said, sitting up and rubbing her eyes.

"You made bail, Lana. You're free to go."

"What do you mean?"

"Like I said, you made bail. It's paid. He's here for you," Eddie said, unlocking the cell door.

She smiled. So Jackson's lawyer had finally got his ass in gear. With what he was charging, it was a good thing. Elation filled her as she pictured her new life. Her only regret was that she wouldn't be there to see the look on Daisy Ann's face when she realized Amber had finally beat her.

After paperwork and processing, Amber, holding a bag with her possessions, was escorted to the man responsible for posting bail. She'd been informed that while she couldn't leave the country, she didn't have to stay in Colorado until the trial. How stupid did they think she was? Not only would she be leaving Colorado, but she'd be leaving the United States as well.

"It's about time someone did their job," she said to the man waiting for her. The man merely raised an eyebrow.

"The car is right outside."

"Great, you can drop me off at the airport. I can't wait to get out of this Podunk town."

Together they walked outside into the bright sunshine where a black sedan sat waiting. She took a deep breath, inhaling the fresh air of freedom and grinning. This was the first step in the beginning of her exciting new life.

The man accompanying her opened the trunk and reached out to take her bag. She clutched it to her chest—the three pink diamonds were mixed in with her jewelry in the little pouch she'd packed.

He gave her a strange look. "Your bag will be safe in the trunk."

Reluctantly she handed it to him, realizing she was being silly.

He opened the door of the car and she slid into the back seat. She heard the click of a lock as the car pulled away. There was a man in the front passenger seat but Amber couldn't get a good look at him. He didn't turn around when he spoke.

"So nice to finally meet you, Mrs. Parrish."

Something was wrong. The energy in the car felt charged. Amber leaned forward, trying to get a better look at him. "Are you my new attorney?"

"No. I'm actually an associate of your husband's."

Confusion clouded her face. "An associate ... what does that mean?"

"My business with your husband was sadly interrupted. But he did inform me that you have something of mine." He turned to look at her, and Amber saw her face reflected in the red lenses of the glasses he wore.

Acknowledgments

When we finished *The Last Mrs. Parrish*, we had no idea that the characters' stories would continue. We have you, our remarkable readers, to thank for keeping Bishops Harbor alive and ensuring that Daphne and Amber would go on to new journeys and adventures. Thank you for your loyalty and support—you mean the world to us. Tremendous appreciation and thanks to the librarians, booksellers, and book bloggers for all you do to help us reach readers.

Deepest appreciation to the entire Bantam team. Heartfelt thanks to Jennifer Hershey for your continuing support. To our fabulous editor, Jenny Chen, your insightful notes and editorial guidance were invaluable in sweeping us to the finish line. Your brilliance, encouragement, and faith in us made all the difference. We're so fortunate to work with you. We owe a debt of gratitude to Mae Martinez for the myriad and critical things you do to keep everything moving toward publication. To marketing wizards Quinne Rogers, Allison Schuster, and Emma Thomasch, whose creativity is unmatched. A special thanks to Allison for all your help with our newsletter. To our fantastic publicist, Sarah Breivogel, who tirelessly promotes us and our work and, with Katie Horn, keeps us on schedule, endless appreciation. To Elena Giavaldi who designed the most gorgeous cover imaginable, thank you. Many thanks to Kara Welsh, Kara Cesare, Kim Hovey, Mark Maguire, Steve Messina, Pam Alders, Jo Anne Metsch, Fritz Metsch, Cindy Berman, and Paul Gilbert.

Huge thanks to our wonderful agent and friend, Jenny Bent, whose wisdom and guidance assure us every day that we are in the very best hands. We are so lucky to have you in our corner! Gratitude to Nissa Cullen and Victoria Cappello for your hard work on our behalf.

To our film agent, Dana Spector, we so appreciate your tireless efforts and expert counsel in bringing our work to the screen.

One of the most interesting and rewarding parts of writing a story is learning from experts in their field. We have many to thank for generously giving us their time and expertise. To Tim Hall, MD, and Lori Cretella, MD, for their medical advice, Robin Pendino and Fred Brown for sharing their vast knowledge of the New York Diamond District and all things diamond. And to Marina Lillie and Evan Krometis for the introductions. Thanks to Matthew Rees for sharing his financial and banking expertise. To proud Texan Lesal Kilcrease, a huge thanks for your critical eye and for all the hours we spent learning more about Texas. To Drew Murdza for answering any and all hunting and Colorado questions. To our brothers, Stanley and Michael, and to Jim Lillie, for help with financial and stock matters. To Wendy Walker for advice on family law and for always being there to listen and encourage. To Special Agent Chris Munger for help with all of our law-enforcement questions. And last to Christopher Ackers, for a listening ear and excellent advice.

To Lynne's husband, Rick, who cheerfully reads every finished draft, acts as a sounding board when she's stuck on a plot point, comes to all her author events, and has encouraged and supported her way before she became Liv, a heartfelt thank-you for all that you do.

And, finally, to Valerie's husband, Colin, who brings her tea and reminds her to sit up straight while she's working—she could never say a big enough thank-you for all the years of love and support. The dedication from *The Last Mrs. Parrish* bears repeating: "You make it all possible."

About the Author

LIV CONSTANTINE is the pen name of sisters Lynne Constantine and Valerie Constantine. Lynne and Valerie are national and international bestselling authors with over one and a half million copies sold worldwide. Their books have been translated into twenty-nine languages, published in thirty-four countries, optioned for development for both television and film, and praised by *The Washington Post, USA Today, The Sunday Times, People,* and *Good Morning America,* among many other publications. Their debut novel, *The Last Mrs. Parrish,* was a Reese's Book Club selection.

livconstantine.com
Instagram: @livconstantine2

About the Type

This book was set in Walbaum, a typeface designed in 1810 by German punch cutter J. E. (Justus Erich) Walbaum (1768–1839). Walbaum's type is more French than German in appearance. Like Bodoni, it is a classical typeface, yet its openness and slight irregularities give it a human, romantic quality.